WHERE
THE
LOST
WANDER

D0062873

ALSO BY AMY HARMON

Young Adult and Paranormal Romance

Slow Dance in Purgatory

Prom Night in Purgatory

Inspirational Romance

A Different Blue

Running Barefoot

Making Faces

Infinity + One

The Law of Moses

The Song of David

The Smallest Part

Historical Fiction

From Sand and Ash

What the Wind Knows

Romantic Fantasy

The Bird and the Sword

The Queen and the Cure

The First Girl Child

WHERE
THE
LOST
WANDER

AMY HARMON

LAKE UNION
PUBLISHING

Published by Lake Union Publishing, Seattle

www.apub.com

Amazon, the Amazon logo, and Lake Union Publishing are trademarks of Amazon.com, Inc., or its affiliates.

ISBN-13: 9781542017961
ISBN-10: 1542017963

Cover design by Faceout Studio, Lindy Martin

Printed in the United States of America

For my husband, a direct descendant of the real John Lowry,
and for Chief Washakie, who predicted people would write books about him

PROLOGUE

NAOMI

The wheel is in pieces. It's not the first time one of the wagons has lost an axle or broken a rim since our journey began in May, but it's a long, dry stretch with no grazing, and it's not a good place to stop. We didn't have much choice. Pa and my brother Warren have been working on the wheel for hours, and Mr. Bingham is helping them. Will and Webb are supposed to be keeping watch for Wyatt and John, but the day is bright and still—warm too, and they're playing among the black rocks and bristly sage, hiding and seeking and chasing each other, and I let them be, too weary to scold or find something better for them to do. Will has the bow John gave him. As I watch, Will rises and takes aim at an unknown foe, his arrow winging through the air and disappearing into the ravine below us. He lets a few more fly, straight and true, before ducking down behind another outcropping, Webb scrambling after him like a faithful pup, eager for his turn. Sunshine is something we've had plenty of the last few weeks. I wouldn't mind a cool breeze or a handful of snowflakes on my tongue, though winter and wagon trains don't mix.

Babies and wagons don't mix either, and Homer Bingham's wife, Elsie, is trying to deliver her baby in the Bingham wagon while the men fix the wheel on ours. The rest of the train has gone on, promising us they will wait at the springs they claim are only a day's travel ahead if we just "follow the wheel ruts." We're a good mile away from the main ruts now. We veered off the road to find water and grass last night. That's when Pa busted his wheel and Elsie Bingham said she couldn't go another step.

She'll have to. Not today. But certainly tomorrow. There will be another ridge to climb and another river to cross. When Ma gave birth to little Wolfe, she was walking again the next day.

I had prayed for a sister. I'd prayed hard. Ma already had four sons, and I wouldn't be living in her house forever. I'm twenty years old, married and widowed once already, and I have my own plans once we reach California. Ma needed another daughter—one that lived longer than a day—to help her when I couldn't. My prayers fell on deaf ears because the Lord gave Ma another son, and He gave me another brother. But my disappointment didn't last long. I took one look at baby Wolfe, wriggling and wailing, fighting for life and breath, and I knew him. He was mine. Ours. He belonged.

"He looks just like you did, Naomi," Ma cried. "Why, he looks like he could be *your* son."

He felt like my son, right from the start, but with so many brothers to take care of and no husband, I haven't thought much about my own babies. But Ma says she's seen my children in her dreams for years.

Ma has vivid dreams.

Pa says her visions are like Joseph's from the Bible, Joseph with the coat of many colors who was sold into Egypt. Pa even bought Ma a coat like Joseph's—the sheep's wool was dyed into varying shades and woven together—to wear out West. She reprimanded him, but she was pleased.

It's been hot, but Ma is still wearing that coat. She can't ever seem to get warm, and baby Wolfe is always hungry. Ma said her body was too old and tired for another baby, and she didn't have enough milk. God thought different. God and Pa. I told Pa he needed to leave Ma be for good. I hadn't meant to say it, but sometimes words just come out of my mouth when I think them. Pa hasn't forgiven me yet, and Ma scolded me something fierce.

"Naomi May, if I want that man to let me be, I can surely speak for myself."

"I know, Ma. You always speak your mind. That's where I get it."

She laughed at that.

I can hear Ma telling poor Elsie Bingham to get up on her knees, and I tuck my leather book and a lead pencil into my satchel and take Wolfe to find Gert, our goat, who is grazing with the unyoked oxen. Ma told me to take him and go. His cries were upsetting Elsie, and there's not much room in the wagon. The grass is sparse along this stretch, and the little there is has been eaten down. A sluggish spring between a circle of rocks has provided us with a little water, and the animals are crowded around it.

I tweak Gert's teats, and she doesn't even raise her head from the shallow pool. I catch the stream of warm milk in my palm and wash her teat with it before moving Wolfie's hungry cupid mouth beneath it. If I crouch down with him lying in my lap, I can milk her and feed him at the same time. I've gotten better at it, and Gert's grown accustomed enough that she doesn't bolt. She's sweet tempered for a goat, unlike every other goat I've ever known, who bleat like the Israelites did when Moses destroyed their golden calf.

Gert whines, and her cry confuses me for a minute. I freeze, and the cry comes again. It isn't Gert.

"Elsie's had her baby," I say to little Wolfe, who gazes up at me with eyes that Ma says will someday be as green as my own. "Praise the Lord," I breathe, and Mr. Bingham repeats my sentiments.

"Praise the Lord," he bellows, and the wheel is forgotten and the men stand. Pa pounds Mr. Bingham on the back, whooping, clearly relieved for him, relieved for poor Elsie. Someone else whoops, and I am not alarmed, rapt as I am in the wriggling babe in my lap and thoughts of the babe just come into the world. I assume it's Webb or Will celebrating too. As quickly as my thoughts provide an explanation, my eyes swing, discarding it. My brothers don't sound like that. The land rolls and the rocks jut, creating a thousand places to hide, and from the nearest rise, horses and Indians, speared and feathered, spill down upon us. One is clutching an arrow buried in his belly, his hands crimson with blood, and I wonder in dazed disbelief if Will accidentally shot him.

Gert pulls away, and I note the way her teat streams, watering the dry earth as she flees. The oxen bolt too, and I am frozen, watching the Indians fall upon Pa, Warren, and Mr. Bingham, who stare at them in rumpled confusion, their sleeves rolled and their faces slicked with sweat and grime. Pa falls without even crying out, and Warren staggers back, his arms outstretched in protest. Mr. Bingham swings his arms but doesn't succeed in shielding his head. The club against his face makes an odd plunk, and his knees buckle, tipping him face-first into the brush.

I clutch Wolfe to my chest, frozen and gaping, and I am confronted by a warrior, his hair streaming, his torso bare, and a club in his hand. I want to close my eyes and cover my ears, but the cold in my limbs and lids prevents it. I can only stare at him. He shrieks and raises his club, and I hear my mother scream my name. *Naomi. NAY OH ME.* But the final syllable is cut short.

I am ice, but my ears are fire, and every scream of pain and triumph finds the soft drums in my head, echoing over and over. The warrior tries to take Wolfe from my arms, and it is not my strength but my horror that locks my grip. I cannot look away from him. He says something to me, but the sounds are gibberish, and my gaze does not fall. He swings his club at my head, and I turn my face into Wolfe's curls as the blow connects, a dull, painless thud that stuns and blinds.

Time rushes and slows. I hear my breath in my ears and feel Wolfe against my chest, but I am floating above myself, seeing the slaughter below. Pa and Warren. Mr. Bingham. The Indian with the arrow in his belly is dead too. The colorful bits of feather wave at the placid blue sky. It is Will's arrow. I am sure of it now, but I do not see Will or Webb.

The dead Indian is hoisted onto his horse, and his companions' faces are grim and streaked with outrage at the loss. They do not take anything from the wagons. No flour or sugar or bacon. They don't take the oxen, who are as docile in war as they were in peace. But they take the rest of the animals. And they take me. They take me and baby Wolfe.

And they burn the wagons.

I will myself higher, far away, up to the heaven that awaits me with Ma and Pa and Warren, and for a time I am blessedly unaware, wrapped in gauzy delirium.

But I am not dead; I am walking, and Wolfe is still in my arms. A tugging, distant and weak, narrows the distance between the me who floats and the me who walks. The pull grows stronger, and I register the rope around my neck that tightens and releases as I stumble and straighten, my wooden legs marching along behind a paint pony, the spots on his rump like the blood that seeped through the cover on the Binghams' wagon. There was so much blood. And screaming. Screaming, screaming, and then nothing.

It is silent now, and I have no idea how long I have been walking, wrapped in odd unconsciousness, seeing but not seeing, knowing but not knowing. I am suddenly sick, and the violence of my stomach's upending catches me unaware. I fall to my knees, and the mush I ate for breakfast hours ago splashes over the clumps of grass, the longest strands tickling my cheeks as I bow above them, retching. Wolfe wails, and the rope at my throat tightens, and my vision swims. There's a hand on my braid, and I am jerked up from my knees. The Indians are arguing among themselves, blades wielded, and Wolfe screams and screams.

5

I turn his face into my chest to muffle his cries and tuck my spattered cheek against his, my lips at his tiny ear.

"Be still, Wolfe," I say, and my voice is a shock to both of us.

I don't know why I am still alive. I don't know why Wolfe is still alive, and my skin is suddenly raw and ready, prickled with the expectation of a blade against my brow. It doesn't come, and I lift my eyes to the Indian nearest me, and he hisses and touches the tip of his blade below my right eye. I feel a pinch, and blood wells and trickles down my cheek, heavy and slow. His companions hoot, and Wolfe's cries are drowned by their hollering. I leap to my feet and try to run, but the rope around my neck yanks me back, and I fall into my own vomit.

The man who cut me climbs back on his horse. And we move again. Now it is only my fear that floats above me, watching, and I'm left blessedly numb. No thoughts, no pain, my brother in my arms, and my life wafting up into the sky behind me with the smoke from our wagons.

MAY 1853

1

ST. JOSEPH, MISSOURI

JOHN

She is perched on a barrel in the middle of the wide street, a yellow-frocked flower in a white bonnet, studying the crush of people moving past. Everyone is in a hurry, covered in dust and dissatisfaction, but she sits primly, her back straight and her hands still, watching it all as if she has nowhere to go. Perhaps she's been assigned to guard the contents of the barrel; though come to think of it, the barrel was in the street yesterday and the day before, and I'm certain it's empty.

I have a new hat on my head and a new pair of boots on my feet, and I'm carrying a stack of cloth shirts and trousers to shove in my saddlebags along with the coffee, tobacco, and beads that will come in handy on the journey to Fort Kearny. Maybe it's the cheerful color of her dress or her womanly form; maybe it's simply the fact that she is so still while everyone else is in motion, but I halt, intrigued, shifting my package from one arm to the other as I look at her.

After a moment, her eyes settle on me, and I don't look away. It isn't insolence or arrogance that makes me stare, though my father always bristles at my flat gaze. I stare because self-preservation is easiest if you know exactly who and what you are dealing with.

She appears surprised when I hold her gaze. And she smiles. I look away, disconcerted by her pretty mouth and welcoming grin. I cringe when I realize what I've done. I've let her unnerve me and cause me to shy like Kettle, my big Mammoth Jack. I immediately look back, my neck hot and my chest tight. She pushes away from the barrel and strides toward me. I watch her approach, liking the way she moves and the set of her chin, knowing it's wasted admiration. I expect her to walk by, perhaps swishing her skirts and fluttering her eyelashes, intentional yet dismissive in the way of most beautiful women. Instead she stops directly in front of me and sticks out her hand, her mouth still curved and her eyes still steady. She isn't skittish at all.

"Hello. I'm Naomi May. My father bought a team from your father, Mr. John Lowry. Or are you both called John Lowry? I think my father said something about that."

Her palm is smudged, and the tips of her fingers are black, her nails as short as my own. Her dirty hand is at odds with her tidy appearance and pale skin. She sees me eyeing her fingers and winces slightly. She bites her lower lip as though she's not happy I've noticed but keeps her hand outstretched.

I don't take it. I don't answer her questions either. Instead, I tip my hat with my free hand, acknowledging her without touching her. "Ma'am."

Her smile doesn't falter, but she lowers her arm. Her eyes are a startling shade of green, and brown freckles dot her cheeks and dust her nose. It is a fine nose, straight and well shaped. Every part of her is well shaped. I want to slide a finger along the bridge of my own nose, along the bump that makes it rise a little higher between my eyes, and feel foolish for comparing myself, in any way, to a slender white woman.

We study each other silently, and I realize I don't remember what she asked or what she said. I'm not sure I even remember who I am.

"You *are* Mr. Lowry, aren't you?" she says softly, hesitant, as if she can hear my thoughts. I realize she is simply repeating her question.

"Uh, yes, ma'am."

I tip my hat again and step past her, excusing myself. Then I walk away.

I curse, the soft word a burr on my lips, but manage to swallow the sharp edges and keep moving. I am a man, and I notice pretty women. It is nothing to be ashamed of or think twice about. But she isn't just pretty. She's interesting. And I want to look back at her.

St. Joseph is bustling today. It's spring, and the emigrant trains are readying for the journey west. My father has sold more teams in the last two weeks than he sold all last spring. People want Lowry mules, but we've sold everything we have, and the ones we're selling now—mules we've traded for but never worked with—we don't guarantee. My father is quick to tell people they aren't Lowry mules, and he sells them for less. I wonder if my father sold her father a Lowry team or a couple of the green mules he took off someone's hands. She knows who I am, but I've never seen her before. I would remember her.

I look back at her. I can't stop myself. She is watching me, her bonnet-covered head tipped slightly to the side, her hands clasped in front of her, settled against the skirt of her faded yellow dress. She smiles again, seemingly unoffended by my dismissal. Why should she be? I am obviously interested. I feel like a fool.

She has not moved out of the street, and the people hurry around her, wagons and horses and men hoisting bags of flour and women herding children. She knows my name, and it bothers me, though I've been called John Lowry since I was a child. I am named after my father—John Lowry—though he is ashamed of me. Or maybe he is ashamed of himself. I can't be sure. His wife, Jennie, calls me John Lowry—John Lowry, not John, not Johnny—to remind us both exactly who I am at all times. My mother's people called me Two Feet. One white foot, one Pawnee foot, but I am not split down the middle, straddling two worlds. I am simply a stranger in both.

My mother pulls at the hair on my head, frantic, angry, and her sharp hands surprise me. I cry out, and she falls to her knees, her head bowed, the neat line between her braids pointing toward the floor. I touch it, that line, to remind her I am still here, and she begins to keen as though my touch pains her.

"John Lowry," my mother says, her palms smacking the wooden slats for emphasis.

The white woman grasps her apron, and the man is silent in front of the fire.

"John Lowry. Son. John Lowry," my mother insists, and I don't know what it is she is trying to convey. I know some of the white man's language. My mother takes me with her when she works in their homes and on their farms.

"Son live here," my mother demands, firm.

"Mary," the white woman gasps, reaching for my mother. I've heard others call my mother Mary.

My mother moans her Pawnee name, shaking her head. She stands again, reaching for me. She pulls at my hair again, the way the children in the village do. My hair curls, and it does not look Pawnee. I hate it, but my mother has never hurt me this way before.

"White boy," my mother says. "John Lowry son." She points at my father. "Son."

I shake the memory away and open the door to my father's store without looking back to see if the woman is still there. My father sells tack in the front—anything you need to yoke your team to a wagon— and mules in back. We have corrals that stretch behind the shop and stables beyond that. Jennie's two-story clapboard house sits on the street behind. He's done well, my father, since coming to St. Joe with nothing but a jack donkey, two mares, three children, and a wife who had no wish to be there.

Jennie could have turned me away. She could have turned my mother away. But she didn't. I was not wanted. Not by my mother's people. Not by my father's people. But in Jennie's home I wasn't hated, I wasn't harmed, and I was never hungry for long. Jennie took good care of us. Of him. She still does. The household is well run, and supper is always on the table, and I suppose my father looks after her too, providing food and shelter and a steady hand. He takes care of the mules and the mares in the same way, though, and I daresay he likes them more. My father wasn't ever violent, and he has never raised his hand to me or to his family, but he is cold and quiet, and I used to fear him. When he was present, I would watch him so I could maintain plenty of space around him.

My father is alone in the shop—a rare occurrence. He would rather be out back with the animals. Leroy Perkins sells the riggings, and my father and I work the mules. He will need to hire another hand while I am gone. I will miss the shop. The corrals smell like chaos—sweat and horseflesh wrapped in dust and dung—and the shop smells like order, leather and oil and iron, and I breathe in the clean sterility and hold it in my chest. My question bubbles out on my exhale.

"Did you sell a team to a man named May?" I ask.

My father looks up at me, eyes blank. I know the look. He is thinking. He is blue eyed and ruddy cheeked, and when I was a child, he seemed enormous, though now I am as big as he. My body looks like his; I am tall, broad through my shoulders and narrow through my hips, with long legs, big feet, and strong hands. I don't have his icy stare or his straw-colored—now white—hair, but I move the way he does. I walk the way he does. I even stand the way he does. I have learned his ways, or maybe they were always my ways too. I do not fear him now. I am simply weary of his shadow.

"He may have had his daughter with him?" I add and keep my face as devoid of expression as I am able. I don't think my father is fooled.

My father's face relaxes with memory. "William May. He had his whole family with him. Bunch of kids, some grown, some not, and his wife looking like she is expecting another."

I say nothing, my thoughts on Naomi May, her yellow dress, her green eyes, and the spray of color across her fine nose.

"Why?" my father asks, the word clipped as though he expects to hear bad news.

"Was it a good team?" I press.

"It wasn't one of ours. But well matched. Steady. Accustomed to people and wagons. The man has oxen to pull his wagons. He wanted the mules as a backup. Most of the time they'll be ridden or they'll be packing."

I nod once, satisfied.

"I remember the daughter now. Bright eyed. Lots of questions." He raises his eyes to mine again. "Pretty."

I grunt, emotionless. My father and I do not discuss women or make small talk. We talk mules, and that is all. His willing commentary surprises me.

"They signed on with Abbott's company, so you'll be able to keep an eye on their . . . mules . . . if you're concerned," he adds.

I nod, stifling my reaction. Grant Abbott is Jennie's brother—a man who fancies himself a mountain man, though he's never spent much time trapping. He went all the way to California in '49 and didn't have much luck striking it rich. He's been back and forth three times to the Oregon Territory and has finally decided the emigrant boom pays better than furs or panning for gold. Plus, the man just can't keep still. He's convinced me to travel with him as far as Fort Kearny; I've driven mules to Fort Kearny, just below the Platte, half a dozen times. Every time I make the trek, I think about continuing west, and every time, I return to St. Joe and my father's house.

If I go with a train, I don't need to hire a hand to help me with the mules, and Grant Abbott will pay me to carry a gun and assist where necessary; having a few mules at his disposal doesn't hurt either. The numbers in the company provide safety and support, even though it'll slow me down considerably. I've never had any trouble. I'm good with the animals; I keep to myself; I work hard. I'm just a mule skinner, and if I look a little different, no one has ever made a big issue of it. I was called a "filthy Injun" once by a man who never washed, but he died from cholera two days later, too lazy to walk upstream for clean water.

"You ready?" my father asks. He knows that I am. The mules Captain Dempsey requested have been corralled separately so they aren't sold, and they've been fitted and fed, their packs—including my gear—readied for the journey.

I raise the packages in my arms. "I just have to stow these. Shirts and trousers. Good for trade."

"Cloth's a whole lot more comfortable than buckskin," my father says. He is talkative today. I hardly know what to think. "Jennie wanted me to remind you to go home for a haircut," he adds.

"I'll go right now," I say, agreeable. Jennie worries about things like that. When my hair grows long, I look more like a Pawnee than a Lowry, and I make people nervous. I keep it tamed and cut short. It hasn't been long since I was a child. When I first came to live with my father, Jennie did her best to untangle my hair but ended up cutting it instead. The curls never came back. For a long time, I was convinced they followed my mother when I could not.

Jennie has asked me to call her Mother, but I can't. I know it is not Jennie's pride that seeks the title or even her shame. It is simply easier on us all for people to think I am hers because I am *his*. Jennie is fair, but her hair is a deep brown and her eyes too. People in St. Joe just assume I favor her instead of my father, though I am considerably darker than she is. That, or they don't ask. The girls—my half sisters—have my father's blue eyes, and their hair is several shades lighter than Jennie's. I call Jennie by her name when no one is around. When others are near, I simply call her ma'am or nothing at all. To call her Mother would be to deny the Pawnee girl with the heavy hair and the crooked smile.

My mother turns and begins to walk away, telling me to stay.

I hurry after her. She pushes me back, her thin arms firm and her face set, jaw jutting out in warning. Her eyes are fierce. I've seen that look before, many times, and I know she will not yield, but I don't care. I remain beside her. My mother walks back to the man who has followed us from the house, her hand tangled in the mess of my hair. She points at him. She points at me. She tries to walk away again, and when I trail after her, she sits, folding her legs, her hands on her knees, eyes forward. I sit beside her. We sit this way all night, my mother pretending I am not beside her. She is ill. Her breathing rattles like the medicine man's shaker, and her skin burns when I touch it, but she doesn't complain, and the white man brings us blankets when she refuses to move or follow him back inside, though he beckons us both. In the morning we are both stretched out beneath the sky, but my mother's eyes are fixed and her body is cold.

The white man takes my mother away, and his woman takes me inside the little house. I am empty. My belly, my mind, my eyes. I do not cry because I am empty. I am convinced I am dreaming. Two little girls, their hair woven into skinny braids that touch their shoulders, stare at me. They are small, smaller than me, and their eyes are blue like those of the white man who took my mother. The white woman is dark eyed and dark haired, like me, though her skin is like the moon, and her cheeks are pink. I look at her instead of the blue-eyed children and hope she will feed me before I wake. I am empty.

"Is he an Indian, Mama?" one girl asks the white woman.

"He is a boy without a family, Sarah."

"Are we going to be his family?" The littlest girl is missing two teeth, and she makes a hissing sound when she speaks, but I understand her well enough. I've spent plenty of time around white children.

"What is his name?" the toothless one asks.

"His name is John Lowry, Hattie," the white woman says.

"That's not an Indian name." Sarah wrinkles her nose. "That's Papa's name."

"Yes. Well. He's Papa's son," the white woman answers, her voice soft. I begin to cry, a keening that makes the woman's daughters cover their ears. The little one begins to cry with me, and I am not empty anymore. I am full of terror and water. It streams from my eyes and my mouth.

"Will you come back this time, John?" my father asks. His eyes are on the ledger in front of him, but his hand is still, the pencil cocked, and I don't understand.

"I'll only be gone an hour. Where's Leroy? Do you need me out back?"

"No. Not now. Not that. Will you come back . . . to St. Joe?"

I stiffen at the words, as if he is telling me he doesn't want me to return, but when he raises his pale eyes to mine, I see his strain, glittering like sun on the water. His face is expressionless, his words flat, but his eyes are so bright with emotion I am taken aback.

"Why wouldn't I come back?" I say.

He nods once as if that is answer enough, and I am convinced the odd conversation is over. I turn again to go, but he speaks again.

"I would understand . . . if you didn't. There's a whole big world out there." He raises his hand slightly, indicating everything west of the wide Missouri River that runs past St. Joseph. "I hear there's a Pawnee village near Fort Kearny."

"You want me to go live with the Pawnee?" My voice is so dry it doesn't indicate the layer of wet that runs beneath. "Is that where you think I belong?"

His shoulders fall slightly. "No. I don't want that."

I laugh. Incredulous. I don't think I am bitter. I have not suffered greatly. I have no reason to lash out or try to wound him. But I am surprised, and in my surprise I discover there is also pain.

After my mother died, I would sometimes steal away to the Pawnee village and visit my grandmother, but the Pawnee did not like me, and they wanted me to bring them things. They were hungry, and I was not. I took all of Jennie's flour and sugar once so they would welcome me. I knew my father would get more, and the Pawnee had so little. Jennie beat my backside with a switch, tears streaming down her cheeks, Hattie and Sarah watching from the window. Jennie said if she didn't punish me, I would do it again.

I *did* do it again, despite the licking. My father always got more, though it took him a while and there was no bread on the table for weeks.

Not long after that, we moved to St. Joseph, and my father sold everything to buy a good-quality jack donkey for breeding. Independence, Missouri, farther south, already had plenty of breeders and muleteers. St. Joseph was smaller but still perfectly situated to become a jumping-off point for the Oregon Territory, and he told Jennie that with the new hunger to go west, mules were a sure thing, and he wasn't ever going to be a good farmer. Jennie was convinced we would all starve, though feeding the Pawnee village couldn't have been much easier on our situation. But my father was right. He was a mule man. Not only did he manage to breed good stock; he understood the mules and they him. Within five years he was supplying the army at Fort Leavenworth and Camp Kearny along the Missouri with all the pack mules they needed. When Camp Kearny moved from Table Creek to the wilds of Nebraska, just below the Platte, I accompanied an army supply train, driving a dozen Lowry mules across two hundred miles of prairie. I've done that every spring for the last five years, and tomorrow I will start again.

"I loved her," my father says, in a voice that does not sound like his own, and I am pulled back from thoughts of seeking acceptance with bags of flour and our exodus to St. Joe.

"What?"

"I loved her," my father repeats. He's set the pencil down, and his hands are splayed on the ledger, like a startled cat trying to find his balance. I think he might be ill . . . or drunk, though he doesn't really appear to be either.

"Who?" I ask, though I suddenly know exactly who. I reach for the door.

His eyes spark, and his mouth hardens. He thinks I am mocking him, but I am too discomfited for scorn.

"Mary," he answers.

"Is that what you tell yourself?" I blurt, and again my feelings shock me. I sound angry. Uncertain. My father has never talked about my Indian mother. Not even once. I don't know what has inspired him to do so now.

"It is what I know," he responds. "I know you think I'm a son of a bitch. And I am. But I'm not . . . guilty of everything you imagine I am guilty of."

"Why are you telling me this?" I hiss. I don't believe him, and I don't want to leave St. Joe with this conversation between us.

"Mary did not like her life with me. When she wanted to leave, I let her go. And I will let you go too. But you need to know I did not force her. Ever. Not at any time. And I would have cared for her all the days of her life had she let me. I did not know about you until she brought you to me—and Jennie—eight years later."

I don't know what to say. My mind is empty, but my heart weighs a thousand pounds.

"Every time you leave, I wish I'd told you. I promised myself I wouldn't let you go again without making it clear," he says.

"Are you sick?" I ask. My mother began acting strange when she knew she was going to die.

"I'm not sick."

We are silent, standing among the harnesses and yokes, the reins and the riggings, my hands on my hips, his curled into big white-knuckled fists on the counter of the establishment he raised from the ground. I watched him do it. I admired that. I admire him, much of the time. But the rest of my feelings are knotted and frayed like an old rope, and I won't be unraveling them here and now, with him looking on. Not even with this new revelation. Especially not with this new revelation.

With a ragged inhale and a curt nod, I open the door and walk out, shutting it quietly behind me.

∞

I don't go home to Jennie right away. My innards are twisted and my chest is hot. My father has a way of slicing me open and making me study my own inner workings, as if repeated examination will help me better understand him. I do not believe he loved my mother—I am not sure he is capable of the emotion—but that he even spoke the words is beyond comprehension. I am convinced once more that he is ill, terminally so, and stands at the edge of a gangplank, a sword at his back, like Shakespeare's Pericles, which Jennie read aloud. The heat in my chest scurries down my arms and tickles my palms. I stop abruptly, hating that he has made me care.

I have halted directly in the path of a small child, and he stops, befuddled.

"Pardon me, mister."

The boy steps back, peering up at me, eyes narrowed against the afternoon sun. His hat falls off his head as he cranes his neck to meet my gaze. He has a shock of reddish-brown hair that stands up in all directions. A boy behind him stoops to pick up the rumpled felt hat, setting it atop the smaller boy's woolly head. The hat is too large, and his unkempt hair reminds me of my task. I turn back toward my father's store, toward Jennie and her shears, but the boy's mother is not far behind him, and she stops in front of me, a third son bringing up the rear.

"Mr. Lowry." The woman sticks her hand toward mine, her other palm resting on the swell of her impossibly large abdomen. Her bonnet shades green eyes, and I shake her small, rough hand, distracted by their color. It is the second time today I have been greeted by name by a green-eyed female I do not know. But this woman's eyes are faded. Everything about her is faded—her dress, her bonnet, her skin, her smile—and her weariness is palpable. The boys cluster around her, and they all look too much alike, too much like the woman, not to be her children. The smallest boy with the reddish mop and the too-big hat begins to chatter excitedly.

"We're the Mays. We're traveling west with Mr. Abbott. Shoving off tomorrow. We bought mules from your pa, Mr. Lowry. Ma said I could name them. Mr. Lowry said I should name them something easy and sharp, like a command. So I figure I'd name 'em Trick and Tumble, 'cause the one is naughty and the other is clumsy. Pa said you're a mule skinner. I'm gonna be a mule skinner one day too. I'm gonna have corrals full of 'em. Webb May Mules is what I'll call my breeding farm, but don't worry, Mr. Lowry. I won't put you and your pa outa business, 'cause I'm not stayin' in St. Joe. I'm going to California."

I nod once, but I have not hidden my surprise, and the woman smiles wearily.

"You were in the back paddock yesterday when we purchased the mules. We saw you, but you did not see us. Your father told us you would be traveling with our wagon train. Forgive us for the poor introduction."

The tallest boy, probably fifteen or sixteen years old, sticks out his hand. "I'm Wyatt May, Mr. Lowry." He seems earnest, and the timbre of his voice is that of a man, though he still looks like a boy. The voice changes first. It did for me. One day I woke to a toad in my throat that mimicked my father every time I opened my mouth.

"I'm Will," the middle-size boy says. I will never remember their names, but I nod in greeting.

"I met . . . Naomi," I offer. I remember her name well enough. As soon as I speak, I wish I hadn't. To call her by her first name is too familiar, but her family doesn't seem to notice or care.

"She's always wanderin' off," the littlest boy says. What was his name? Wyatt? No. Webb. *Webb May Mules.* "She's probably drawin' somethin' somewhere. She wouldn't make a good mule skinner. She's as stubborn as the mules, Pa says. But a mule man's gotta be patient, right, Mr. Lowry?"

"You don't know where Naomi is now, do you?" Mrs. May asks.

"No, ma'am. It was nigh on an hour ago." The crush of people is almost stifling, and the disquietude from the conversation with my father becomes fear for the missing Naomi. "But when you find her . . . you should tell her not to go off on her own. St. Joseph is full of rough men and strangers."

"She's probably buyin' paper, Ma. Paper and pencils," the oldest boy chimes in.

"There's a general store beside the post where one can buy such things," I say.

"Rough men and strangers," Mrs. May repeats, and her eyes rove the crowds. "We feel fortunate to have you traveling with the company, Mr. Lowry. Someone so experienced on the trail will be greatly appreciated."

"I'm only going as far as Fort Kearny, ma'am."

She studies me soberly for a moment. "I think you'll find that's not far enough, Mr. Lowry."

It is an odd thing to say, especially considering how difficult those first two hundred miles are on most families. Wet, windy, endless. I feel bad for the woman, for what she is about to endure.

"Pa says it's two thousand miles to California," Wyatt, says, somber.

I nod. The family stares at me, chins tipped up, eyes wide, waiting for me to say more. They are a strange bunch. I amend the word immediately. Not strange. Frank. Forthright. They don't lower their eyes or shift away like they aren't certain whether they want to be seen with me.

"We meet again, Mr. Lowry," a cheerful voice calls out. Naomi May, a brown paper parcel in her arms, skips over the rutted street, sidestepping man and beast as she approaches. I look away when she stops at my side as though we are old friends. She doesn't loop her hand through my arm or brush against me as some women do, wearing innocence on their faces and conniving in their hearts.

"Miss May," I say, suddenly winded.

"Her name is Mrs. Caldwell, Mr. Lowry," Webb informs me. "But we just call her Naomi."

I ignore the sinking sensation in my belly and step back, my gaze swinging back to the elder Mrs. May.

"When do you cross?" I ask, keeping my gaze on the older woman.

"The line is so long . . . but I think Mr. May has secured us a ride across on a scow." The groove between Mrs. May's eyes deepens.

"I saw a boat capsize yesterday, Mr. Lowry! The wagon and the people all went into the water," Webb crows like he enjoyed the show.

"Don't try to cross on the scows. If you don't have anyone who knows the river, don't swim your animals across. Go to Decker's Ferry. It's a bit of a battle to get to it through the trees, but there'll be a pasture and a place for you on the other side to wait until your company has arrived—Whitehead's Trading Post too, in case there are things you need once you've crossed," I say.

"I'll tell my husband. Thank you, Mr. Lowry."

"Will you be crossing on Decker's Ferry as well, Mr. Lowry?" Naomi chimes in.

"I'll swim my mules across here. But I'll be at Whitehead's Trading Post on the other side tomorrow to assist Mr. Abbott where I can." I still do not look at her, and I take a few steps back, not wanting to tarry any longer. I am unsettled, and she is unsettling.

"Then we will see you there, Mr. Lowry," Mrs. May says, inclining her head, and I tip my hat in return. They all watch me go.

∽

Jennie is dozing in front of the broad window, the rays of the setting sun softened by the fluttering white curtains she keeps drawn across the wide panes. Her Bible is in her lap, open, and her palms rest on the pages as if she is not napping but receiving revelation, communing with the written word. The bright light blurs the fine lines on her skin, and for a moment she looks younger than her forty-five years. My father is fifteen years older than she is, but it's easy to forget the age difference when I've never known them independent of one another. She hears me, and her eyes snap open. Closing her Bible, she rises and sets it aside.

"John Lowry," she says, greeting me.

"Jennie." I've removed my hat as I've been taught, and her eyes move to my uncovered head.

"Your hair needs trimming," she says, as though she's just noticing and didn't send my father after me. "I'll get my shears."

"I'm leaving tonight," I blurt, a warning that I'll not linger long.

"What?"

"I'm going to swim the animals across tonight. I'll make camp on the other side. If I swim them across in the morning, I'll waste daylight getting dry." I have not planned any of this, but the words spill out smoothly, as though I have thought it all through.

"You're leaving tonight? But your sisters will want to say goodbye."

"I'll be gone for four weeks—five at the most. I don't need to say goodbye." The last thing I want is a big send-off.

She leads the way through her immaculate kitchen to the back porch that overlooks the pasture behind my father's stables. The mares are grazing with their little ones. We've had ten foals born in the last few weeks, ten Lowry mules that will be ready to sell next spring. But it is the mares I stop to admire. Some muleteers make the mistake of breeding their best jack donkeys with inferior horses. My father says, "It's all in the mare. The best mules come from superior mothers. The jack's important, but the mare is everything."

So far he's been right.

I sit down on the stool we always use. It sets me low so Jennie can reach, and my knees jut up awkwardly at my sides. I feel like a child every time I relent to a cropping, but it is our ritual. Jennie is not affectionate or warm. When she cuts my hair, it is the only time she touches me. When I was thirteen, I ran away from St. Joe, all the way back to my mother's village. It took me three days to get there on horseback, but the village was gone, and I returned to my father's house after a week, filthy and bereft, expecting a switch and a severe scolding. Instead, Jennie sat me down and cut my hair. She didn't ask me where I'd been or why I'd come back. Her gentle hands made me weep, and I cried as she snipped. She cried too. When she was finished, she made me wash until my skin was raw. Then she fed me and sent me to bed. My father told me, in no uncertain terms, that the next time I left without word, I would not be welcomed back. *You wanna go? Go. But be man enough to tell us you're leaving.*

"You have a fine head of hair, John Lowry." It is what she always says, yet she always wants to cut it off. She begins her work, snipping and clipping, until she sets down her shears, brushes off her apron, and lifts the cloth from my shoulders, shaking it out briskly into the yard.

"Is my father unwell?" I ask suddenly. I can see I have startled her, and her surprise reassures me. Little gets past Jennie.

"You live here, John Lowry. You work with him every day. You know he is not."

She brushes the clippings from my neck.

"He is not himself today," I grunt.

"He suffers when you go," she says softly.

"That's not true."

25

"It is. It is the suffering of love. Every parent feels it. It is the suffering of being unable to shield or save. It is not love if it doesn't hurt."

I know she's right. She knows she's right too, and we fall silent again. I put my hat back on my head, covering Jennie's handiwork, and I stand, towering over her. I realize, like a boy who has hit a growth spurt overnight, that Jennie is very small. I have never thought of her that way, and I stare down at her plain little face like I am seeing it for the first time. I want to embrace her, but I don't. She reaches out and clasps my hand instead.

"Goodbye, John Lowry."

"Goodbye, Jennie."

She follows me through the house and out onto the front porch, watching as I descend the steps and move out into the street.

"John?" she calls, and the plaintive sound of my first name, alone without the Lowry tacked on, makes me stop.

I turn.

"It's worth it, you know."

"What is, Jennie?"

"The pain. It's worth it. The more you love, the more it hurts. But it's worth it. It's the only thing that is."

2

THE CROSSING

NAOMI

After supper, Wyatt, Will, Webb, and I leave the sprawling encampment of waiting wagons and impatient travelers and climb a bluff overlooking the city and the banks of the churning river. The water of the Missouri swirls like Webb's hair when he wakes, bending in all directions. I asked the man at the tack shop—the man named Lowry who has a reputation for selling the best mules—why they call it the Big Muddy.

"The bottom of the lake is sand, and it's always shifting and reset-tling, creating new channels and swales beneath the surface. It bubbles and churns, kicking up the mud. If you fall in, you'll have a hard time coming out."

This place is not what I expected. We came from Springfield, Illinois, and Illinois didn't seem like it would be all that different from Missouri, but there is no quiet in St. Joseph. No stillness. No space.

Music spills from the gambling houses, and men seem to be drunk at all hours of the day. Crowds gather everywhere—the outfitters, the landing areas, the auctions. There's even a crowd outside the post office, where people push and shove, wanting to get their letters sent before they head out into the unknown. When I closed my eyes and thought of the journey west, I always pictured distance, endlessness. Wide open spaces. I guess that will come, but not in St. Joe.

Everywhere I look there are wagons and animals and people—all kinds of people. Some dirty and some dandified, and in every manner of dress and dishabille. White men and dark men and minstrel girls and preacher's wives, thumping their Bibles from wagon beds. Some folks are selling and some are buying, but they all seem to want the same thing. Money . . . or a way to make it. Yesterday, outside of Lowry's Outfitters, a group of Indians—there had to be more than two hundred of them—walked right down the center of the street, their feathers and colors on full display, and the crowds parted for them like the waters of the Red Sea. They hurried down the banks to board the ferries, along with everyone else, but no one made them wait in line. I learned later they were Potawatomi, and I stared until Wyatt grabbed my arm and hurried me onward.

"You're staring, Naomi. Maybe they don't like that," he warned.

"I'm not staring. I'm memorizing," I said.

Memorizing. It is what I am doing now. Noting the details and committing them all to memory so I can recreate them later.

The line of clustered wagons waiting to cross the Missouri stretches from the landing docks to the bluffs that rim St. Joseph. There is a great fervor to be among the first to cross. Better grazing, less dust, better camping, less disease. We thought about crossing the river farther north, in Council Bluffs, and staying on the north-side route all the way to the Oregon Territory. But Council Bluffs is nothing more than a campground with everyone fighting to cross the river first and no safe way to do it. In Council Bluffs there are too many Mormons, and Mr.

Caldwell doesn't want to travel with them. Mr. Caldwell doesn't like the Mormons, though I don't think he's ever met one and probably wouldn't know if he had. Mr. Caldwell doesn't like anyone he doesn't understand, which to my way of thinking includes women, Indians, children, Mormons, Catholics, Irishmen, Mexicans, Scandinavians, and anyone who is different from him, which—again—includes most people.

The rumors of no steamboats in Council Bluffs and disastrous crossings on scows that could only hold two wagons convinced us that jumping off farther south would be safer, even if it extended our initial journey. Plus, we heard tell that St. Joseph was a real city with shops and streets. St. Joe had outfitters and steamboats and mules—good *Missouri* mules.

The younger John Lowry flits through my thoughts, and I push his image away. I've been pushing it away all day. The knowledge that he is traveling with us has filled me with a strange anticipation, and I haven't yet sorted myself out. I plan to think about him before I sleep, when my brothers aren't chatting in my ears and there isn't so much to see.

We wanted to be in the first wagon train on the trail out of St. Joseph, but that was what everyone wanted, and everyone couldn't be first. At this rate, we might be last. The moment the grass covered the prairie, the wagon trains began leaving the jumping-off points along the river, pushing westward. Pa has been saying for weeks, "Leave too early, and there's no grass for the animals. Leave too late, and the grass will be gone, consumed by earlier trains." He's also said, more times than I can count, "Leave too early, and you'll freeze and starve on the plains; leave too late, and you'll freeze and starve in the mountains."

Early or late, I'm just ready to go. I'm as hungry for this journey as I've been for anything in my life. I don't know why, exactly. Going west was never my dream. It was Daniel who wanted to go west. It was Daniel who convinced our families to sell their farms in Illinois and strike out for California. It was Daniel who persuaded us all and Daniel who would never see it. Three months after we were married and a few days shy of my nineteenth birthday, he took sick and was gone in a week. When he died, I suspected I was pregnant, but heavy cramping and bleeding a few days after Daniel's death removed that fear. I was heartbroken and . . . relieved. I didn't want to be a widow *and* a mother. It was not an emotion I could easily explain without sounding vile, even to myself, so I didn't try. I'm convinced everyone is a little vile, if they are honest about it. Vile and scared and human.

I missed him terribly in the weeks after. I tried not to. It didn't do me any good. The pain was useless, and I was never one to wallow. I got angry instead. I got busy. I worked from sunup to sundown. It was planting season, and there was plenty to do. So I did it. I worked all my anger into the ground where Daniel slept, but I didn't water his grave with my tears. It wasn't until I sat down on a Sunday afternoon, when the harvest was over and the cold was setting in, that I found myself drawing his face. And then I couldn't stop. I drew picture after picture—Daniel in all the stages of his life. Daniel as a boy pulling my hair and scaring the chickens. Daniel as a brother. Daniel as a son. Daniel as a husband, and Daniel in the grave.

I cried then. I cried and drew until my fingers were bent like claws. But I only kept one. I gave another to his mother—an unsmiling portrait of the man I married—and buried the rest in the dirt beside him.

I haven't cried the same way since. It still hurts, but it's been more than a year, and I am resigned to it. The Caldwells say that I am one of them now, that I am part of their family, but I still feel like a May, and without Daniel, I feel no permanent obligation to them. When I informed them that I would be traveling west with my parents in their wagon, Mr. Caldwell protested vehemently, and Elmeda, Daniel's mother, looked at me with Daniel's wounded eyes.

"My mother needs me," I said simply. It was true, but mostly I couldn't abide being anywhere near Mr. Lawrence Caldwell. Had Daniel lived, I would have been driven crazy by the end of our journey.

Their daughter, Lucy, and their new son-in-law, Adam Hines, will be traveling with them, along with their sixteen-year-old son, Jeb. They'll make do just fine without me. And being called Mrs. Caldwell makes my hackles rise. Mr. Caldwell has taken to calling me Widow Caldwell, as if I have entered old age without having ever lived the intervening years. I think Mr. Caldwell likes drawing attention to Daniel's death. It makes folks behave more kindly to him, and it's his way of laying claim to me. Ma and my brothers are the only ones who just call me Naomi. I suppose widowhood at such a young age gives me a certain freedom some girls don't yet enjoy, if freedom means being allowed a bit of leeway in speech and conduct. People who hear my story shake their heads and cluck their tongues, sometimes in judgment but generally in sympathy, and I am mostly left alone, which suits me fine.

Webb tugs at my skirt and points to the river, his words tumbling over themselves trying to be first. "There's Mr. Lowry! He's got his mules. Look at his donkeys! Those are Mammoth Jacks. For breeding with the mares." Webb knows too much about breeding for an eight-year-old, but I'm sure he's right. He goes right on babbling about stallions and jennies and their offspring, called hinnies, which supposedly aren't nearly as desirable as mules.

John Lowry is one of a swarm, and it takes me a moment to pick him out. John Lowry Sr., his shock of white hair easily identifiable, follows behind, waving his hat and driving the animals forward. Twelve mules are strung together in two long lines behind the younger John Lowry's horse, the two donkeys Webb is so excited about bringing up the rear. Fine animals, the lot of them. The donkeys are black and lanky, with long ears, thin noses, and oversize eyes. They look almost comical, like childish drawings that trotted off the page and grew with every step. Despite their spindly legs and narrow hips, they are the biggest donkeys I've ever seen, their backs as tall as the powerful string of Lowry mules being led to the water's edge.

With no hesitation, the younger John Lowry urges his horse, a tawny bay with powerful haunches and a thick neck, into the muddy waters. The mules and the jack donkeys follow him with only a little urging and immediately begin swimming hard toward the opposite shore. A skiff, loaded with packs and paddled by a huge Negro, sets off about the same time, keeping an easy distance from John Lowry and his animals. I'm guessing the man's been hired to get Lowry's supplies across so they don't get wet in the swim.

"Look at 'em go!" Webb crows, jumping up and down and waving his arms, cheering them on.

"He makes it look easy, doesn't he?" Wyatt says, less exuberant but every bit as transfixed. "Everyone else fighting and pushing for a place in line, and he just goes into the water, easy as you please, and starts swimming."

"Mr. Lowry didn't even say goodbye to his pa," Will says, his mouth turned down, his eyes fixed on John Lowry Sr., who watches his son's progress across the river. The elder John Lowry doesn't wave, and he doesn't shout goodbyes. He stands silently, observing, unmoving, until his son and the skiff reach the opposite shore. Then he turns, puts his hat back on his head, and climbs the bank, back toward the main thoroughfare. I cannot see his expression from this distance, but his stride is slow and his back slightly bowed, and I am overcome with sudden sadness, though I'm not sure why.

"Why are you crying, Naomi?" Will asks, concern lacing his voice, and I realize with a start that I am. At twelve, Will is more sensitive than all the other May boys combined, and he notices things the others don't. Maybe it's being a middle son of many, but he's the designated peacekeeper in the family and takes every rift and row personally.

"I'm not sure, Will. I just feel a little melancholy, I guess."

"Do you miss Daniel?" Will asks, and I feel a flash of guilt that my tears are not for my dead husband but for a stranger I know nothing about.

"Are you scared of crossing the river?" Webb's interjection saves me from answering Will, whose eyes are narrowed on my face, and I swipe at my cheeks and smile.

"No. Not scared. I just don't like goodbyes," I say.

"Pa says once we head out, we ain't never comin' back. So I been sayin' goodbye to everything I see. But I sure am glad I'll get to see Mr. Lowry's mules and those jack donkeys a bit more," Webb chortles.

"Do you want to go back to the camp, Naomi?" Will asks, his brow furrowed.

"No. I'd like to draw for a bit. Would you sit here with me?"

Will nods agreeably, and Wyatt and Webb are more than willing to linger as well. A barge is being filled with livestock that won't stay put. One mule is herded aboard only to have another bail over the side into the drink, much to the delight of my brothers, who laugh so hard Webb almost wets his pants, and Wyatt has to take him to find a bush where he can relieve himself.

The landing dock is full of people to watch and adventures waiting to happen, but my mind is too full, and my eyes rest on my page while my hand recreates the myriad faces I've seen in St. Joe over the past three days, faces I don't want to forget. I draw until the sun begins to sink, turning the sea of white-topped wagons a rosy pink, and my brothers and I make our way down the hill, back to our family, eager for the morrow.

∞

We wake before dawn and are readied and clopping along toward Duncan's Ferry before the sun begins to change the color of the sky. Pa has a wagon; my oldest brother, Warren, and his wife, Abigail, have one too. Pa thought about getting a third, there being so many of us, but he didn't think Wyatt could handle a team every day on his own. Abigail and Warren don't have any little ones yet, and we decided that between the two wagons, we would make do. The Caldwells have two wagons as well, along with a dozen head of cattle. I imagine there will never be a moment's silence on the trail with all the bleating and bellowing.

It takes us a little more than an hour to reach the cutoff and the sign for Duncan's Ferry that points us through a boggy forest so thick and deep we are cast in shadows almost as dark as the predawn. Pa stews and makes a comment about Mr. Lowry's character and good sense. Mr. Caldwell almost turns back to St. Joe, and his son, Jeb, and my brothers have a dickens of a time keeping the livestock together as we navigate the trees and do our best to avoid the mud.

"We might never come outa these woods, Winifred," Pa grumbles to Ma. "Perhaps they send unsuspecting travelers into these parts to get them lost and rob them blind."

Ma doesn't respond but walks calmly, her arms wrapped around her bulging belly; she was the one to tell Pa about Mr. Lowry's advice to use the upper ferry, and if she is worried, she doesn't let on. But within an hour we indeed find ourselves, if a little more weary and wary than when we set out, at Duncan's Ferry with nary a wagon in front of us. We are able to board both wagons, eight oxen, two mules, two cows, and eight people in a single trip. The Caldwells cross immediately after us with all their cattle and wagons as well. Both crossings are uneventful, much to Webb's disappointment, and Pa has to take back some of the things he said, though he mutters that he'd rather wait in line for a week than ford that path again. Ma just pats his hand, but we are the first wagons in our company to arrive at the designated clearing at the head of the trail.

We missed the window the previous spring. Daniel's death took the wind out of all our sails. So we waited and planned. Then Ma got pregnant, and it seemed as if maybe the journey would have to be postponed once more. We hoped the baby would come before the trek began, but it hasn't, and the wagon company won't wait. The baby could come anytime—Ma thinks she still has a week or two—but Ma insists we stick to the plan. And Pa always listens to Ma.

We wait all day for the wagons in our company to assemble. John Lowry is at the meeting site, along with our wagon master, Mr. Grant Abbott, a man who has been back and forth across the prairie "more times than he can remember," though I suspect he could recall exactly how many if he wanted to. He worked for the Hudson's Bay Company in the Rocky Mountains for a season but says he prefers people to the fur trade, and he comes highly recommended as a guide. Forty families have signed on with him for this journey, paying him to see them through to California as painlessly as possible, and he seems very proud of that fact. He is amiable enough, with a woolly gray mustache and hair that skims his shoulders. His tunic and leggings are fringed like those of a mountain man, and he wears beaded moccasins on his feet and a rifle slung across his back. He seems to know John Lowry well and introduces him as his nephew.

"John's mother, Jennie, is my little sister. John will be with us until we reach Fort Kearny on the Platte," Mr. Abbott says. "He speaks Injun too, in case we have any trouble with the Pawnee. The area along the Platte is Pawnee country. It's Kanzas country too, though we'll see more Kanzas in the Blue River valley. I don't suspect we'll have any trouble with any of 'em. They usually just want to trade . . . or beg. They like tobacco and cloth and anything shiny."

It doesn't make much sense to me, John Lowry's mother being Grant Abbott's sister. Grant Abbott may wear buckskin, but he's as white and ruddy as Pa. I've seen John Lowry Sr. He's white too, but the resemblance between them is there. Still, a resemblance doesn't account for the way John Lowry looks. He's tall like his father, with rangy shoulders and a long gait, but his skin is sun colored, and his hair is the color of black coffee. He keeps it mostly hidden beneath the brim of his gray felt hat, but I can see the inky edges that hug his neck and touch the tops of his ears. His features are cut from stone, hard lips and an uneven nose, sharp cheekbones and a squared-off chin, granite eyes and the straightest black brows I've ever seen. I can't tell how old he is. He has a worn look around his eyes, but it's not time, I don't think. He's a few years—or a decade—older than I am. Impossible to know. But I like looking at him. He has a face I'm going to draw.

Webb trots after him, asking to be introduced to his mules and the jack donkeys, and Will and Wyatt are quick to follow. He doesn't seem to mind the company and answers all their questions and listens to their commentary. I want to join them, but there is work to do, and Ma is trying to do it, ignoring Pa when he insists she rest while she can.

Wagons start to arrive at the staging area near the trading post. Some folks have painted their names, slogans, or the places from which they hail on their canvas covers. *Oregon or Bust; California Bound; Born in Boston, Bound for Oregon. The Weavers; The Farleys; The Clarkes; The Hughes.* Pa decides we should paint our name too, and he writes *May* in dripping red letters along the sides. Ma isn't happy with his handiwork.

"Good heavens, William. It looks like we've marked our wagons so the angel of death will pass us over."

Every wagon is packed to the brim with supplies—beans and bacon and flour and lard. Barrels are strapped to the sides, and false bottoms are built into the main body of the wagon—the wagon box—to stow tools and possessions not needed during everyday travel. Pa has extra wheels and enough rope and chains to stretch cross country, along with saws and iron pulleys and a dozen other things I can't name and don't know how to use. Ma has her china stowed below, packed in straw and prayed over. We eat on tin—cups, plates, saucers—with iron spoons because they don't break.

One woman has a table and chairs and a chest of drawers in the back of her wagon. She claims the furniture has been in her family for generations, and it made it across oceans, so why not across the plains? Some people have far more than they can use, far more than they need, and some don't have nearly enough; some don't even have shoes. It's a motley assortment of fortune hunters and families, young and old. Like St. Joe, except most everyone is white. Everyone but John Lowry, but I'm not exactly sure what he is.

Mr. Lorenzo Hastings wears a three-piece suit with a watch chain and a neatly knotted tie. His wife, Priscilla, has a lace parasol and sits primly in a buggy pulled by a pair of white horses. They also have a huge Conestoga wagon pulled by eight mules and driven by two hired men. Wyatt got a look inside, and he claims it has a feather bed in the back. Mrs. Hastings has two middle-aged sisters serving as her "companions"; they are traveling to California to join their brother. The sisters introduce themselves to me and Ma as Miss Betsy Kline and Miss Margaret Kline, but we don't visit long. Mrs. Hastings keeps them running for this and that, scrambling to make camp. I overhear Mr. Abbott telling Pa that the Hastingses won't last a week, and it'll be better for everyone if they don't. Every train has its share of "go-backs," he says. I hope for the two sisters' sake that they don't.

Regardless of their possessions or their position, it seems everyone has the same dream. They all want something different than what they have now. Land. Luck. Life. Even love. Everyone chatters about what we're going to find when we get there. I'm no different, I suppose, though I'm more worried about what we're going to find along the way. Some people have so many belongings wedged into their wagons it's a wonder their teams can pull them, but pull them they do, and the next morning, following a breakfast of mush and bacon, the long train rolls out, everyone jostling for position.

They call it a road, and I suppose it is, the ruts and the wear of thousands of travelers creating a path that stretches for two thousand miles over plains and creeks and hills and hollows from a dozen points along the Missouri to the verdant valleys of places most of us have never been.

With so many wagons in the train, the travelers are either stretched out across the trail, following the ruts of the wagons that have gone before, or lined up like waddling white ducks, one wagon behind the other, bumping over the terrain. Mr. Caldwell insists on being at the front near Mr. Abbott, and he manages to spur his family and his animals to lead the pack. We happily fall back to the end of the line, which looks more like a sloppy triangle formation than a tidy row. Ma needs a slower pace, and it's a great deal more pleasant to walk without another wagon nipping at one's heels. The distance from the Caldwells is good. I won't see Elmeda Caldwell's mournful glances or be put to work looking after Daniel's family. I will barely be able to keep up with my own.

The constant jostling of the wagon bouncing along the ruts and rolling plain makes us sick when we try to ride in back; I imagine it's like being tossed on the waves of the sea, and most of us choose to walk. Even Ma walks, though her great belly protrudes out in front of her, drawing the eyes of other travelers. She says little about her discomfort, but I see it in her face, and I am alarmed by it. Pa sees it too and begs her to ride.

"If I sit on that gyrating schooner, this baby will fall out, and I'd prefer it stay in a week or two more," she says. Pa isn't the only one who listens to Ma. The baby listens as well, and it stays put.

∞

There is little to see—not because it isn't beautiful but because we move so slowly that the eye consumes everything in one fell swoop, growing accustomed to the sights within the first hours of morning. Spring wildflowers dot the swales, and streams and creeks bisect the trail. Every mile or so, a wagon sinks to the hubs in mud, and ropes and muscle are employed to pull it out just in time for the next wagon to fall prey to the same thing.

The slow monotony makes us drowsy, especially in the afternoons, and more than once someone in the train has tumbled from their wagon, lulled to sleep by the endless motion. The oxen don't have reins or drivers like the wagons pulled by mule teams. They are simply yoked in, two by two, with someone walking alongside them, prodding at them with a stick and a quirt when they need a little encouragement to move along. Pa and Warren and Wyatt take turns, rotating between the two wagons, and within a couple of days, Will has the hang of it too.

The clatter wears on me. Not the walking, not the work, not the vastness or the mud. It is the noise. The jangle and bump of the wagon, the endless cacophony of screeching wheels, harnesses, and cowbells. Everything squeaks and rumbles and lurches and groans. The motion is good for something, though; we put cow milk in the churn and set it in the wagon in the morning. By the time the day is done, we have butter, with no effort whatsoever. Making bread takes a little more doing. When the train stops in the evening, we are too hungry to wait for the dough to rise and the loaves to cook, and the fires aren't the right mix of coals and ash.

The first day out, I tried to make it in the morning, but there wasn't sufficient time for the bread to cook and the dutch oven to cool, and Will and I ended up carrying the heavy pot with a broomstick shoved through the handle until it cooled down enough to tuck it away without burning a hole in the wagon. With so much to do and Ma needing her rest, I decide that making it once a week, even if I'm baking bread all night, is the most I can manage.

We end up eating stew made of bacon and beans for supper three nights in a row. Pa promises there will be fresh meat when we can kill it, but the trail from St. Joe is remarkably devoid of big game—mosquitoes, butterflies, and all manner of birds and crawling things, but no herds. Webb looks for signs of the buffalo each day through the spyglass, but Mr. Abbott says the buffalo herds are greatly diminished, and we're more likely to see them when we reach the Platte.

The mornings and evenings are the hardest part of the day, with the constant loading and unloading, reorganizing and reconfiguring, but I dread mornings the most. Maybe it's because the day stretches ahead, long and arduous, and leaving is always more work than arriving.

Setting camp, breaking camp—it's all a mad scramble to move when sitting still would be so sweet. After breakfast, coffee and mush and a bit of bacon, we take down the tents and fold the blankets, packing the kettle and the pots and pans, washing the breakfast dishes the way we washed them after supper the night before, rinsing the remains with water that leaves behind a bit of silt we always have to wipe free when we use them again.

In some ways, life is simpler. All our duties and chores have been narrowed to the path before us, the steps we take each day, the rumble of wagons, and the plodding of weary travelers with nothing to do but move forward. Sometimes, when I'm not walking with Ma, I ride Trick, one of the mules Pa bought from Mr. Lowry, my sketchbook propped against the saddle horn while I draw. Pa is keeping a diary on our journey, but I've always been better at pictures than words. Ma says I made pictures in the mud before I could even say my own name. Drawing is the only time I have to myself. Every other waking moment is spent walking or working.

We all have responsibilities. Pa and Warren see to the animals and pitch the tents; Webb, Will, and Wyatt are kept busy gathering wood for the fire, hauling water, and unloading the wagon; and Ma and I do most everything else. Warren's wife, Abigail, tries to help me and Ma, but she is weak and pale, and the smells of camp make her retch and feel faint. I suspect she's in a family way too, though not far along. Warren seems to think so as well and tries to make life as easy as possible for his wife, but there is no easy to be found. Ma and Abigail aren't the only pregnant women in the train. A young couple by the name of Bingham pulls their wagon just ahead of ours the first few days. Elsie Bingham isn't as big as Ma, but her swollen abdomen is well defined beneath her dress. She seems cheerful enough, her husband too, and isn't bothered by the bumping and bouncing of riding in the wagon like the rest of us.

Cleanliness is impossible, and the boys don't seem to mind so much, but I can't abide the filth. I see folks getting their water from the banks and the shallow pools created after a hard rain, even when there's a dead animal carcass abandoned nearby. John Lowry insists the boys haul it from the waters upstream of camp each night, and he often helps them, but even then, I worry. It seems to me if everyone tried a little harder to keep clean, fewer people would be sick. Rumors of cholera on the trail are already starting to spread.

The fourth day out, we start seeing graves by the roadside, most of them marked only with a bit of wood with a lettered inscription burned in. I remark on it the first few times, my arm linked through Ma's as we walk past, but Ma refuses to acknowledge any of them after we see the fresh grave of a two-month-old baby girl.

"I don't have to see death to know it exists, Naomi," Ma says. "I gotta keep my mind right. I don't have any strength for fear or sadness right now, so I'm just gonna walk on by, and I'd appreciate it if you don't tell me what you see."

I tighten my arm in hers, and she pats my hand.

"Are you afraid, Ma?" My voice is low, and what I'm really telling her is that I'm afraid. Ma might be keeping her mind right, but my mind is full of awful scenarios.

"Not for myself. I know what to do. But I don't want to lose another child, and I don't want to think of that poor mother who had to bury her baby back there."

Ma has given birth to five healthy children, but she's lost a few too—babies that didn't make it more than a day or two and a baby girl that was born as still as a china doll. I can't help but think she might be better off without a newborn to care for on the trail, but I know better than to say as much.

"You're scowling, Naomi."

"It's what I'm best at. Scowling and drawing. My two greatest gifts."

Ma laughs, just like I knew she would, but my anger billows like the dust that moves with the cluster of wagons, mingling with the muggy skies that continually threaten rain.

"You're not very good at hiding your feelings," Ma says.

"No. Scowling and drawing. That's all I'm good for. Remember?"

Ma doesn't laugh this time. "Tell me why you're upset."

"I hate being a woman."

"You do?" Her voice squeaks in astonishment.

"I hate how hard it is."

"Would you rather be a man?" she challenges, as if I have lost my wits completely.

I think about that for a moment. I am not so blind as to think being a man would be much better. Easier, maybe. Or not. I'm not sure. Every path is likely just a different version of hard. But I'm still angry.

"I'm mad at Pa. At Daniel. At Mr. Caldwell. At Warren. I'm mad at Mr. John Lowry too, if you want to know the truth. I'm just angry today."

"Anger feels a whole lot better than fear," Ma concedes.

I nod, and she squeezes my arm again.

"But anger is useless," she insists. "Useless and futile."

"I don't know about that." It isn't useless if it keeps the fear away.

"Are you angry with the bird because he can fly, or angry with the horse for her beauty, or angry with the bear because he has fearsome teeth and claws? Because he's bigger than you are? Stronger too? Destroying all the things you hate won't change any of that. You still won't be a bear or a bird or a horse. Hating men won't make you a man. Hating your womb or your breasts or your own weakness won't make those things go away. You'll still be a woman. Hating never fixed anything. It seems simple, but most things are. We just complicate them. We spend our lives complicating what we would do better to accept. Because in acceptance, we put our energies into transcendence."

"Transcendence?"

"That's right."

"You'll have to explain that one to me, Ma. I don't know what *transcendence* means."

"That's where your mind goes when your hands are drawing," Ma explains. "It's a world, a place, beyond this one. It's what could be."

I nod. That much I understand. When I draw, it *does* feel like I go somewhere else. I escape. It's the reason I'll never stop, even when it seems like a waste of precious time.

"Put your energy into rising above the things you can't change, Naomi. Keep your mind right. And everything will work out for the best."

"Even if there's a lot of pain along the way?"

"Especially if there's pain along the way," Mama says firmly.

We walk for a moment, side by side, lost in thoughts of a better place.

"Why are you mad at John Lowry? I like him," Ma asks suddenly. She doesn't ask why I'm mad at Pa or Warren or Mr. Caldwell, as if my anger toward them is justified. I throw back my head and laugh before I confess.

"I like him too, Ma. That's why I'm mad."

3

THE BIG BLUE

JOHN

I am worried about Winifred May. I don't understand her husband.
I would not have taken a woman on the brink of childbirth onto the
plains. She does not ride in the wagon but trundles along beside it, her
daughter's arm linked through hers. I cannot blame her. The jostling
wagon will break her waters. She is better off walking.

They are a handsome pair, Winifred and Naomi, though the
mother is worn and softly wrinkled, her chestnut hair threaded with
gray. Naomi is vibrant and slim beside her mother, but they share the
same stubborn chins and smiling mouths, the same green eyes and
freckled noses.

The May boys, especially Webb, have attached themselves to me like
cockleburs, and though I keep gently picking them off, they latch on
again before too long. Webb has memorized the names of my animals

and rattles them off in a long greeting each time he sees them, like the apostles from the Bible that Jennie made me read.

"Hey, Boomer, Budro, Samson, Delilah, Tug, Gus, Jasper, Judy, Lasso, Lucky, Coal, and Pepper," Webb cries, but he always lowers his voice reverently when he greets the two jacks, Pott and Kettle, who seem to like the boy. My horse, Dame, likes him too, and Webb doesn't forget to greet the mare with the same enthusiasm.

"Hey there, pretty Dame," he says, and he doesn't shut up until I send him off or someone comes to fetch him.

I want to ask the boy questions I have no right asking. I'm curious about his sister, about her missing husband and the leather satchel she always carries, but I don't. She introduced herself as Naomi May, and that is how I think of her, but Webb said she is Mrs. Caldwell, and the Caldwells in the train are clearly connected. I do ask Webb how his mother fares, and the little boy wrinkles his nose as if it never occurred to him that his mother might not be well.

"She's just fine, Mr. Lowry. She says you're welcome to come to supper round our campfire if you want to, since you don't have anyone to look after you," he says.

"I look after myself, Webb. Grown men do."

"My pa doesn't. Warren doesn't. They let Ma and Abigail and Naomi take care of them."

"Your pa works hard. Warren too."

"Not as hard as Ma."

"No. I reckon nobody is working as hard as your ma right now," I murmur.

"Come to supper, Mr. Lowry. Naomi's cooking, and she's not as good as Ma, but it fills the empty places, and Pa says that's all that matters."

Webb invites me every day, but I don't ever accept. After several refusals, he delivers a loaf of bread with his visit. "From Naomi," he says, and I am awash in pleasure. I don't know if it is a thank-you for putting up with her brothers or an invitation for something more, but I savor the bread because she made it. I am too aware of her, and I keep my distance even as I keep an eye out, falling back in the train and bringing up the rear, telling myself it is to keep Webb from straying too far from his own. Abbott approves of my playing caboose. It allows him to remain at the front without worrying about the stragglers.

Each night, the wagons are circled, the oxen are unyoked and taken to graze, and the men watch in shifts to keep the animals together and see that they don't wander too far after better grass. When the animals begin to settle and doze, they are hobbled or picketed or driven back to the circle of the wagons, which are chained together to form a corral, and put up for the night. Those with bigger herds have a more difficult time of it and often bed down among their animals outside the circle. Most nights it is what I do, pitching my tent where my mules are grazing or simply throwing down my saddle for a pillow and sleeping underneath the sky.

On the fifth day, I awake to rolling thunder and black clouds so thick the sunrise barely lights the sky. We've been plagued by drizzle and light showers since leaving St. Joe, but the storm gathering is something new. Instead of preparing to move out at dawn, we keep the wagons circled, and Abbott sounds a warning to drive the picket pins and the tent stakes deep, to chain the wagon wheels and tie everything down. All the animals are moved into the center, the oxen, cattle, horses, and mules all crowded together beneath the writhing skies. I hobble my mules along with Dame and the jacks near Abbott's wagon and roll beneath it for cover as the heavens break and begin to pummel the prairie.

The rain doesn't fall in drops but in sheets, slicing the air and splashing against the sod with enough force to churn the soil. We hunker down beneath it, cowering in tents and wagons that blunt the impact but are useless against the wet that finds the cracks and seeps through the corners. Beneath Abbott's wagon, the puddles grow and spread until even the high ground is turned to mud beneath us. Abbott doesn't complain overmuch. I like that about him. He's like Jennie in that way, though he has plenty to say and always has a story to tell. I let him yammer, lulled by the torrent and the forced inaction. It is wet but not windy, and there is nothing to do but wait it out. I am half-asleep when Abbott pauses in his tale of a brush with the Blackfeet in the Oregon Territory, a tale I have heard before.

"What is she doing?" Abbott asks, but I'm tired, and I don't care to know. I don't even open my eyes. It's wet, but I'm short on sleep, and with my animals discouraged by the rain, I'm not worried about them getting spooked or stolen. They are clustered together, their hinds turned out, heads in, and I don't even lift my hat to see what Abbott is muttering about.

"Well, I'll be. I thought I'd seen it all," Abbott mumbles.

I wish he'd keep his musings to himself. I know he's trying to draw me in.

"That infernal woman is doing her wash in the rain."

My eyes snap open. I don't know how I know it's Naomi, but I do. I push back my brim and peer out into the onslaught. The May wagons are lashed beside Abbott's; they were the last to bring their wagons into the fold the night before, closing the gap between the head and tail of the train.

Naomi May has two buckets and a washboard and is scrubbing away in the downpour, a brick of soap in her right hand. She's soaked to the skin beneath a thin wrap, and she's wearing Webb's hat instead of her bonnet, but she's making short work of the family's laundry. She doesn't bother to rinse the soap or grime away but tosses each garment over the ox chain stretched between the wagons and lets the heavy rain do it for her.

"*Aka'a*," I huff beneath my breath and crawl out into the deluge. I am immediately drenched, and I stomp toward her, holding the streaming brim of my hat. I tell myself it could be worse. There is no wind in the rain, only the weight of heavy water, but it isn't pleasant.

"You're going to catch your death," I bark, ducking close to Naomi, spreading the sides of my sodden coat to provide some cover over her head.

"I never get sick," she shouts and continues scrubbing away.

"Don't say that. The man who says *never* is quickly made a liar." It is something Jennie always says, but Naomi May just shakes her head.

"I never get sick," she insists.

I watch her for a moment, wanting to make her stop, wanting to demand she take cover, and wondering why I never thought to wash my clothes in the rain. They're getting a good scouring now. All I need is a little soap.

"Where are your brothers?" I will be giving Webb and Will and Wyatt a talking-to.

"I took their clothes. They're all in their underthings, shivering beneath their blankets in the wagons." She snickers.

"That's where you should be," I say.

"I can sit in the wagon and be miserable, or I can do the wash and be miserable. At least this way, the clothes are getting clean."

"If the wind picks up, those lines won't hold, and your laundry will be in the mud."

"Then I'd best hurry," she says without rancor.

"Âka'a," I grunt again. I cannot leave her, so I might as well help.

The rain is beating down so hard that wringing the clothes is futile, but I do it anyway, twisting and shaking the suds and soil from the wash as she scrubs away beneath the deluge. When the last shirt is lathered and wrung, I upend the barrel of dirty water, and she piles the clothing inside of it, the garments sopping but remarkably clean.

"I'll hang them to dry when the skies clear," she says as I push her back toward her father's wagon. She thanks me with a wide smile, makes me promise I will come to supper the next time she invites me, and finally takes cover.

"You sweet on the pretty widow, Junior?" Abbott asks as I roll back beneath the wagon and begin to strip off my sodden clothes. For a moment I still, the word *widow* clanging in my head. I am no longer cold.

"I got some dirty clothes if you got a hankerin' to do the wash," Abbott chortles. I ignore him, pulling dry trousers and a shirt from my saddlebags. Both are immediately damp, but I wriggle into them, tugging my woolen poncho over my head and toeing off my waterlogged boots.

"You shoulda stayed here. She didn't ask for your help, and you can bet everyone was watchin' you two carrying on out there. You just called all sorts of attention to yourself. Mr. Caldwell isn't a man you want to make an enemy of. She was married to his son, and he still considers her his property."

"Then why wasn't he out helping her?" I grumble.

Abbott snorts, but he shakes his finger at me. "Stay away, son. She ain't for you."

I bristle, but I don't respond. After wringing out my hat, I shove it on my head, pulling the brim over my eyes the way it was before I was so rudely interrupted. I sink back against my saddle and prepare to wait out the storm with my eyes closed.

"Doin' laundry in the rain. Damn fool thing to do," Abbott mutters. "If you get sick, don't expect me to be your nursemaid."

"I never get sick," I say, parroting Naomi May, and stiffen when Abbott laughs.

"You already are. Lovesick. I can see it all over your face."

∞

The storms have turned the Big Blue, usually only a few feet deep, into a raging torrent. Wagons are gathered on the banks in both directions, and from the clouds churning overhead and threatening rain, I know the river is only going to get worse if we wait to cross. Abbott agrees, and he's quick to instruct the company to start unloading their wagons so the supplies can be ferried across. The men waste an hour haggling over the best place to cross and the wisest way to attempt it. Even with the elevated water levels, the wagons have to be lowered down the banks with ropes, one by one, to avoid them crashing into the river below.

A half dozen Kanzas Indians, stripped down to a bit of fabric looped between their legs and moccasins to protect their feet from the rocks, have constructed crude rafts to ferry people and supplies across and are charging four dollars per wagon and a dollar per person. The animals can swim across for no charge, but they want a cloth shirt for every load of supplies. The people hesitate at the prices and try to bargain with the Kanzas, but the moment a wagon tips over, spilling a family and all their worldly goods into the river, the emigrants decide it's money well spent.

My mules halt at the edge of the water, but I give them plenty of slack, wading out until the water laps at my chest, my arms extended, showing them it's safe. When I give a little tug, Dame follows me without protest. She begins to swim, her long lead rope stretching to the suspicious mules watching her from the banks. Pott and Kettle, my jacks, take a few steps and enter the river, kicking their way toward me, their heads high, their ears perked. The mules, strung in a long line, take to the water immediately after, as if shamed by the donkeys and my mare.

I leave the wagons and supplies to the Kanzas and the company and instead spend two hours swimming animals across—oxen and horses, sheep and cattle—and the men of the company leave me to it. Everyone except Mr. Caldwell, who, just as Abbott predicted, has not stopped glowering at me since I helped Naomi do the wash. Mr. Caldwell is convinced he knows best and bellows and beats at his animals, which he has kept harnessed to his wagon. His mules balk despite his whip, and I reach for the first one, murmuring softly.

Mr. Caldwell's whip slashes down and catches the brim of my hat and snaps across my face. I can feel a welt rising on my cheeks, but I don't release the reins. Instead, I snag the end of the whip and yank it from Mr. Caldwell's hands.

"They won't be goaded, Mr. Caldwell. They're bigger than you and stronger than you, and if you whip them, you'll have trouble at every stream and creek you cross for the next two thousand miles. You want to convince them there's nothing to fear from you or the water. I'll swim them across. You don't even have to unhitch them."

"Damn grifters. I can get my own team across," Mr. Caldwell yells.

"Mr. Caldwell, let the man help. He's good with the mules," Naomi insists as she picks her way down the bank toward us. I thought she had crossed hours ago. I'd walked Webb across on my back, and Will and Wyatt had waded over on Trick and Tumble around the same time.

"I am not paying this half breed or any of the others to do what I can damn well do myself," Mr. Caldwell argues. Mrs. Elmeda Caldwell is sitting beside him on the seat, and her face is as white as the canvas cover that frames them both.

"Come, Elmeda," Naomi says primly, moving to Caldwell's wagon. "Come down from there. Ma and I are walking across. If Mr. Caldwell wants to upend your wagon in the river, I'd just as soon not have you in it."

Mr. Caldwell sputters and glares at her. "Elmeda will be just fine, Widow Caldwell," he barks, and his eyes shift back to me. He yanks at his reins once more.

"I don't want your money, Mr. Caldwell," I say. I don't either. I just don't like him waling on his mules. "I'll swim your team across. Let go of the reins and hold on to the box. Mrs. Caldwell will be just fine there beside you."

Naomi shoots me a look I cannot decipher, a look both curious and cautious, as if she isn't sure where and how I fit. It is a look she's worn before. I reach for the harnesses on Caldwell's mules once more, and this time he doesn't argue but watches me with his lips tight and his hands a bit looser on the reins.

I coax Mr. Caldwell's mules into the river without a quirt or a quibble, showing them exactly what I want and what I expect, and before long I have the wagon, the mules, and the Caldwells on the opposite bank. Mr. Caldwell does not thank me, but Elmeda allows me to help her from the seat and clings to my arm for a moment as she steadies her legs.

Fifty wagons and two hundred–odd folks cross the Big Blue without mishap, though we are all wet and weary when we set up camp on the other side. We are not the only ones camped along the river, and we won't be the last. By nightfall, campfires dot the darkness, hot pokers in an inky dusk, each company making its own circle and establishing a watch over its animals, though there have already been squabbles over meandering cattle and claims of ownership when the herds mix. The Kanzas Indians who were running their ferry stroll into our camp and demand to be fed, and the emigrants are quick to oblige them. They've been told stories of Indian attacks and degradations. It makes them amenable to sharing their supplies. The Kanzas eye me with suspicion. They don't know what to make of me.

"You aren't like them." Naomi May hands me a bowl of something that smells like salt pork and pignuts, and I wonder if I have spoken out loud. I am so startled I take her offering, though I have already eaten. I've drawn early watch, but the grass is abundant, and the animals graze within a stone's throw of the nearest wagon.

"Who?" I grunt.

"Every Indian I've ever seen." She shrugs.

"How many have you seen?"

She doesn't lower her gaze, though I am trying to make her uncomfortable. It is only fair. She makes me uncomfortable.

"Some."

"Well . . . there are many tribes." I take a huge bite of the stew. It isn't bad, and I take another, wanting to finish quickly so she will take her bowl and her spoon and go.

"Which tribe do you belong to?" she asks softly, and I sigh.

"I wasn't raised in a tribe," I snap.

"You aren't like the white men I know either."

"No?"

"No. You're very neat and tidy."

I snort, half laughing. "I was raised by a very fastidious white woman. Everything had its place. Even me."

She eyes my freshly scrubbed face and my rolled-up sleeves. My clothes are clean—as clean as they can be—and my hair too. I know how to darn a hole and mend a tear, and there are neither in any of my garments. Naomi smooths her skirt as if she is suddenly self-conscious about her own appearance. She needn't be. She has three dresses—pink, blue, and yellow, all homespun and unadorned, but she looks good in all of them.

"Where is your place, Mr. Lowry?" she asks, and the breathlessness in her voice makes my chest tight.

"Ma'am?" I ask, a little slow to follow.

"You said everything has its place."

"Right now, my place is with the mules, Mrs. Caldwell." I tip my hat and move past her, handing her my empty bowl. She follows me.

"I would prefer you call me Miss May if you won't call me Naomi."

"Where's Mr. Caldwell?"

"Which one?"

"The one who made you a missus, ma'am." I sound pained, and it embarrasses me. I know she is a widow, but I don't know the circumstances that made her one. How long has it been? How long was she wed? I want to know, but I'm afraid to ask. And I don't want to draw attention to myself or to her or to the fact that we're together. Again.

I quicken my step. When she quickens hers in response, I duck behind a cottonwood where I've picketed Dame, hoping to shake her off. She's as persistent as Webb.

"Daniel Caldwell made me a missus. But he died. And I wasn't a Caldwell for very long. I never really got used to being one. I forget sometimes and say the . . . wrong . . . name," she explains. "If you call me Mrs. Caldwell, I'll think you're talking to Elmeda." She stops beside me and reaches out to Dame, who greets her with a bump of her nose and a quiet chuff.

"Âka'a," I chide softly.

"You say that a lot. What does it mean?" Naomi asks.

"It doesn't really mean anything."

"You say it when you sigh."

"It's that kind of word." Most of the time I don't even realize I'm saying it. It is a word from my earliest memories, something my mother would whisper when she was weary or wondering, an exclamation of nothing and everything.

"I like it."

"You're going to get me in trouble, ma'am," I say under my breath.

"I am?"

"Go back to your wagon. I'm on watch. And I don't want someone finding you with me."

"We're within shouting distance of a dozen campfires, Mr. Lowry. There is nothing indecent about conversation."

I take several steps back, widening the space between us, remembering what Abbott said. *She is not for you, son.*

"Everything has its place," I say, and my tone is firm.

"I've offended you."

"You haven't."

"I did not mean to insult you when I said you were not like other Indians. I only wanted to understand you."

"Why?"

"You act like a white man. You speak like a white man—most of the time—and yet you are not."

"I am." I am as white as I am Pawnee.

"You are?" Naomi sounds surprised. "You said you were raised by a white woman. Was she your mother?"

"Yes," I say. Jennie was a mother in every sense of the word, and I don't want to explain myself. Yet when Naomi raises luminous eyes to mine, tilting her head to the side in patient observation, I find myself doing just that.

"I was raised by my father and his wife, Jennie. Jennie is Mr. Abbott's sister. She did not give birth to me, but she still . . . raised me."

"Who gave birth to you?" she asks, and my temper flashes. Naomi May is the nosiest woman I've ever met.

"A Pawnee woman. And you are not like the rest of them either," I snap.

"The rest of who?" she asks, mystified.

I point at the companies, the camps, indicating the people huddled over fires and tin bowls, scooping beans and bacon into their mouths. "The other women. You are not like them."

"How many women do you know?" Her voice is wry, and I recognize my own words turned back on me. She is not cowed by me. She is nosy . . . but I like her. And I do not want to like her.

"And how am I different?" she demands.

"You are here, talking to me." She cannot argue with that, as everyone else—except her brothers—gives me plenty of space. I know it is more my fault than theirs. I am not friendly, and I cannot be Naomi's friend. Time to run her off.

"You don't seem to care what anyone thinks. Either you are stupid or you are arrogant, but I can't afford to be either one," I say.

She flinches like I have slapped her. It is exactly what I intended. Harsh words are not easily forgotten, and I need her to hear me.

Women are trouble. They have always been trouble; they always will be trouble, a truth I learned early. When I was still a boy, dangling my feet over the lake of manhood, a woman in St. Joseph, a friend of Jennie's—Mrs. Conway—cornered me once in Jennie's parlor and stuck her hand down my pants and her tongue down my throat. When I froze in stunned terror, she grew impatient and slapped me. A few weeks later she tried again, and I kissed her back, curious and conflicted, not knowing where to put my hands or my mouth. She showed me, and I enjoyed myself, though when Jennie caught us, the woman screamed and bolted, claiming I'd forced myself on her. I learned then that women couldn't be trusted and I would not be believed; the woman's husband came looking for me, and my father gave him his best mule colt from the spring stock to soften his ire.

I didn't go to school with my sisters because the girls at school were afraid of me—the teacher too—and the boys always wanted to fight, though I usually started it. Fighting made me feel better, and I was good at it. The teacher asked my father to keep me away until I could behave. My father turned me over to Otaktay, a half-breed Sioux who worked for him for a while. Otaktay was good with knives, he knew how to grapple, and his rage was almost as big as mine. He wore me out and worked me over while Jennie taught me to read and write and do my figures. Language and numbers were never hard for me, and I had a good mind beneath my fine head of hair.

I "knew" some women at Fort Kearny—some Pawnee, one Blackfoot, and a handful of whores from Illinois—who set up in a row of lodges at the rear of the fort. Everyone knew who they were, and no one said a word. They just paid their visits and took their turns, and the women made their living. Captain Dempsey had a wife somewhere, but Dawn, the Blackfoot woman, was his personal favorite, and he didn't like to share. When she smiled at me and touched my chest, it almost cost me my father's spring contract. Captain Dempsey ordered me to take my attentions elsewhere, and I obliged him by heading back home. Women were trouble.

"You don't think much of me, do you, John Lowry?" Naomi asks, pulling me out of my reverie.

"I don't think about you at all, Mrs. Caldwell," I lie, emphasizing her name for both our sakes. I don't like it when she calls me John Lowry in that Jennie-like tone, and I am angry with her, though I have no real reason to be. "I've found that women can't be trusted," I say.

"And I've found that men are just frightened boys. God gave you stronger bodies to make up for your weaker spines."

"I'm not afraid of you," I lie again.

"You are terrified of me, John Lowry."

"Go away, little girl. I will not be your fool."

"I am many things. But I'm not a little girl, and I've never befriended a fool."

I think of the woman who wanted me to kiss her and then screamed when I acquiesced. I wonder if Naomi will scream and make a scene if I kiss her too.

"What's your game, Mrs. Caldwell?" I sigh.

She gazes at me steadily, blinking once, twice, the long sweep of her lashes drawing me in. Her wrist is narrow, and my fingers touch as I wrap my hand around her arm and pull her toward me. She lifts her chin, her nostrils flaring like a mare sensing danger, but she comes willingly. Her breath tickles my face, and when my mouth nears hers, it is all I can do not to crush the small bones beneath my fingers.

I decide I will be rough. Harsh. Then she will run off crying and leave me alone. Or her father will come with his big rifle and insist I go. Fine with me. I am weary of the slow pace of the wagon train and can make it to Fort Kearny by myself. I'll get there in half the time. Better to be done with the train and teach Naomi Caldwell a lesson she should have learned long ago.

But at the last minute I cannot do it. I can't be harsh, and I can't kiss her.

I avoid her mouth altogether, even though she's lifted it to me. Instead of passion and punishment, the peck I lay on her forehead is soft and sweet, a child's kiss on a mother's brow.

She pulls away and looks up at me expectantly.

"That is not the way I want to be kissed," she says.

"No?"

"No," she answers solemnly. She takes a deep breath, and her words bubble out in a nervous rush. "I want you to kiss me like you've been thinking about it from the moment we met."

I laugh at her pretty words so that I don't feel them. I see her swallow, her throat working in discomfort. I have embarrassed her. Her fingers curl in her skirt, gathering it as if she is about to flee. Good. That is what is best for her.

Yet I reach for her again.

This time I am not gentle or timid, and her lips flatten beneath my mouth, but she does not pull back or push me away. She slides her fingers into my hair—my hat has fallen—and tugs so hard my teeth snap and my back bends. Her ribs are slim and dainty beneath my palms, and I encircle her, lifting her up and into me. For a moment I kiss her blindly, boldly, invading her mouth and suckling her lips, teaching us both a lesson.

But she is softer than I anticipated—softer lips and skin, softer swells and softer sighs. And she is sweet.

It stuns me, and I shove her away, ashamed of myself. She staggers and reaches for my arm, but I have stepped back, and she crumples, falling to her knees, catching herself with the palms of her hands.

I curse, long and low, a word Jennie would slap me for saying. My father says it all the time, but even he knows better than to say it in front of a woman. I step forward to help Naomi up, but she ignores my proffered hand and rises nimbly without my assistance. Fine. It is better that I don't touch her again. My hands are shaking and my legs aren't steady, and I wipe the kiss from my mouth with the back of my hand.

She brushes off her palms and shakes out her skirt. Even in the shadows her lips are crimson. I have kissed her too hard, and I desperately want to do it again. She avoids my gaze, and I am certain I have accomplished my aim; she is angry with me. That is good. That is best. But my heart is pounding with the need to redeem myself.

"I know why you are being unkind." Her voice is gentle, stunning me all over again.

"Why?" I gasp.

"You don't think we're the same."

"Good night, Mrs. Caldwell," I say, dismissing her. I need her to go. To stay. To forgive me. To forsake me.

"The Andersons are from Norway. The McNeelys are Irish. Johann Gruber is from Germany. You're part Indian, and I'm a widow." She shrugs. "We all need each other. We can all live side by side peaceably, can't we? We don't all have to be exactly the same."

"Some cultures do not mix. It is like having fins but trying to live on land," I whisper.

She says something beneath her breath, and I duck my head trying to catch it.

"What?" I ask.

"So be a turtle," she repeats, enunciating each word. She grins suddenly, her teeth flashing in her pretty face, and I laugh out loud. I *laugh*, disarmed in the face of her honesty, my discomfort and defensiveness melting into the moonlight.

"Good night, John," she says, turning away. She walks from the clearing, leaving me smiling like a fool in the copse of cottonwoods, my horse the only witness to my undoing.

She is so different.

Most everyone I know is afraid. Including me.

But Naomi May—Naomi Caldwell, I correct myself—is not afraid.

4

CHOLERA

NAOMI

"Ma?" I ask. I don't know if she's still awake. Ma and I are bedded down in the wagon. The camp has been quiet for half an hour, yet my mind won't settle, and my heart hasn't slowed since I made John kiss me. I knew exactly what I was doing. I suspect he knew it too.

"Did you say something, Naomi?" Ma's voice is wan, and I almost say *never mind*, but I need to talk.

"From the moment I saw John Lowry on the street in St. Joseph, I wanted him," I confess in a whispered rush. "I don't even know why."

"I know," Ma murmurs, and my heart finds its rhythm. Ma always has that effect on me.

"Is that the way it was with you and Pa?" I ask. "You just knew, right then and there?"

"No." Typical Ma, no lies and no careful tread. "Me and Pa were more like you and Daniel."

"Friends?"

"Yes. Friends. I liked him, though. And he really liked me. That's always nice, when someone really likes you. And your pa, he let me know that he liked me."

"I've let John know I like him."

"I know you have."

She is trying to tease, but I feel shame well up in my breast. I don't want to chase John Lowry. I don't especially like the way I want him so much. But I can't help it.

"What if he's a bad man . . . and he decides to let me catch him?" I worry.

"I've had dreams about Mr. Lowry. He's not a bad man. But even so . . . I'm not sure he'll let you catch him. He's full of distrust and denial. It's going to take patience, Naomi, patience and understanding. And I don't know if he's going to be around long enough for you to show him either of those things."

I don't know what to pounce on first, the dreams or the disappointing truth that I might be left wanting forever.

"Tell me about the dreams."

She is silent for too long, and I sit up, bending my back with the curvature of the wagon top. I can't see her expression in the darkness, but her eyes gleam, and I know that she is not sleeping but thinking.

"Have you ever seen a great bird come off the water?"

"Ma," I groan, thinking her thoughts have wandered, but she continues, her voice sleepy.

"In my dreams, a big white bird lifts off the water in a great flapping of wings. As the bird rises, he sprouts the body of a man, and his wings are a feathered headdress. Like the one that Potawatomi chief was wearing in St. Joe that day. In my dream, the bird turned man walks on the water . . . like Jesus in the Bible . . . until he reaches the shore.

The man has John Lowry's face. I'm not sure what that means, Naomi, but I've been having that dream long before I ever met John Lowry."

"How do you feel . . . in the dream?" I know that for Ma, the way the dream makes her feel is the most important part.

"Sad. I am so . . . sad, Naomi, but I am grateful too," she whispers. "It's like he has come to help us. I'm beginning to sink, like Peter, and he reaches out his hand and lifts me up." When Ma references the Good Book, no one argues.

"Like Jesus, walking on water?" I speak so softly I can hardly hear myself, but she repeats my words.

"Like Jesus, son of Mary, walking on water."

JOHN

Once we cross the Big Blue River, we are able to follow the Little Blue River north toward the Platte and Fort Kearny, where my journey with the company will end. The terrain is familiar—I have traveled this road before, but Naomi has not. After the noonday meal, her mother relents to riding beside Mr. May, and Naomi rides Trick, who has turned out to be a remarkably sound mule, just as my father promised. Naomi is writing in her book again; it is propped up by her satchel, which rests against the saddle horn, and her body sways with the gait as her hand moves across the page. I kissed her so she would run away, yet I am the one who seeks her out, sidling Dame up beside her to see, once and for all, what she is doing.

"You're always writing in that book," I say, my voice accusing. "You are going to fall."

I try to keep my eyes forward, as if my presence beside her is happenstance.

"I'm not writing."

When she doesn't say more, I am forced to look at her.

She shakes her head at me, wrinkling her nose a little as she grins. Her bonnet has fallen back on her head, and the afternoon sun turns strands of her brown hair red. She's going to have a hundred more freckles if she doesn't fix it, but I say nothing. "I have no interest in words," she says.

"No?" I ask.

"Not the kind you put on paper."

"What other kind are there?"

"The kind you speak. I'm interested in those words."

I grunt, not really understanding.

"I like a good conversation. At least with interesting people. You are an interesting person. I would like to talk to you more often." Her brow furrows, and she frowns. "Pa says if I don't learn to hold my tongue, I'm going to get myself in trouble. Do you think I'm trouble, John Lowry?"

"You know I do."

She laughs.

"And don't call me John Lowry," I grumble. When she says John Lowry like that, it makes me think of Jennie, and I don't want Naomi to remind me of Jennie.

"How about I call you John and you call me Naomi?"

I nod once, but I don't think I'll be calling her anything other than Mrs. Caldwell. Not out loud. "If you aren't writing words, what are you doing?" I press.

"Drawing. If the pictures are good enough, you don't need words."

"Can I see?" I ask.

She thinks about it for a minute, her eyes on mine, like she's trying to unpeel me. I look away. I find I can't look at her very long. I forget myself, and my mules always know when I'm not paying attention.

"All right. But promise me one thing," she says.

"What's that?"

"Don't be afraid of me."

I jerk, surprised, but I don't think she's teasing. She hands me the leather book and swiftly turns her head, looking forward. I don't think she wants to watch me look through her pages. Her embarrassment, something she seemed impervious to, makes the moment more intimate, and I am suddenly reluctant to open the small clasp that keeps the pages together.

"You promised you wouldn't be afraid," she scolds.

I didn't promise, but I suppose my looking means I accept her terms. I wrap Dame's reins and the lead ropes around the horn on my saddle so my hands are both free. I open Naomi's book, wanting to see inside more than I've ever wanted to see anything, yet feeling like I'm about to bed her, inclined to rush yet not wanting to cause pain.

I expect landscapes—the river, the hills, the sky, with the plains stretching out on both sides—and there are some of those, all immediately recognizable. The creeks in Kansas and the lightning-forked skies and rain-soaked swales, the dead carcasses and the littered trail of belongings strewed across the ruts. A little grave, and then another, sitting beside an abandoned chest filled with delicate bone china. She's labeled the picture *Bones in Boxes*.

But it is the faces that move me.

Faces fill the pages. I recognize Naomi's mother—a weary smile beneath knowing eyes—and her father, who the boys favor, worn and hopeful. Pictures of her brothers, Abbott, the women who walk and the children who never seem to tire. She's even drawn the little boy, Billy Jensen, who fell off the tongue of his father's wagon three days out of St. Joe and was crushed by the wheels before the oxen could be halted.

She notes that I have paused and glances over to see what picture I am studying.

"I wanted to give that one of Billy to his mama. But I thought it might hurt too much just yet."

I nod and turn the page. There are many pictures of me. Left side, right side, straight on, and from behind, and I like my face the way she sees it. I am stunned by her skill. Green-eyed women with pink mouths and freckled noses who talk too much and can't take no for an answer don't draw like that. I don't know anyone, man or woman, who draws like that.

"I wanted to draw you the first time I saw you. I couldn't stop staring," Naomi says. "I sent you running off, but I couldn't help it. You have a . . . a beautiful . . ." She stops midsentence and changes words. "You have an unforgettable face."

I am hot and cold, pleased and puzzled. When I say nothing, she continues as though she desperately wants me to understand. "I would rather draw faces than anything else. Pa says the landscapes would have a better chance of selling to the newspapers or maybe in a printed book someday, but most of the time, the world just can't compete with the people in it."

I don't know what to say as I stare down at my eyes and my mouth and the set of my chin. I see my father. My mother. I even see Jennie, and I wonder how that can be.

"It's the emotion, I think," Naomi says, still trying to explain herself amid my silence. "The expressions. The wind can blow and the rains beat down, and a landscape can be transformed eventually, but a face is *always* changing. I can't draw fast enough to keep up. And every face is different. Yours is the most different of all."

I shove the book back toward her, and she takes it uncertainly.

"John?"

"You're very skilled, Mrs. Caldwell," I say, so wooden and stiff I could toss myself into the Little Blue and float down it like a raft. I spur Dame forward, leaving Naomi and her many faces behind.

∾

I do more than my fair share of night watch, considering there are sixty-five men and twenty-five grown boys in the company, but I won't sleep well until the mules are delivered. I worry about my animals. The men are sloppy and weary, and there are too many cattle to watch and horses to picket. I keep my animals as close as I can, but more often than not, I pitch my tent where they graze and sleep with my ears wide open. Catching a nap most nights after dinner has saved me from exhaustion. Two nights after we cross the Big Blue, Webb May is waiting for me in my tent at the end of my shift, curled up on my bedroll with his head on my saddle and my blanket over his shoulders. I shake him awake.

"Webb. It's the middle of the night. You have to go back to your wagon, boy. Your folks will worry."

He sits up in alarm, clearly upset that he fell asleep at all.

"Ma's havin' her baby. She's crying. It hurts real bad to have a baby, Mr. Lowry. We didn't want to hear her cry, so I came here."

"Let's go. Come on," I say, my chest tight with worry.

We aren't far from the wagons when a cry splits the air, like a wolf on the wind.

"Do you hear that, Mr. Lowry?" Webb crows, and his drowsy face blooms in wonder.

The babe fills its lungs with breath and lets out another howl, and though it's nigh on two in the morning, the camp stirs and shifts in audible relief.

I wait with the boys, huddled by the campfire Wyatt has kept stoked, and when William May climbs from his wagon, tears streaming down his cheeks, announcing that all is well and he has another son, I bid the boys good night.

When I round the wagons, I see Naomi, washing from a bucket brought up from the creek, her sleeves pushed up and the buttons at her neck opened to expose the pale column of her throat. Her dress is smeared with dark blotches, and her hair has come unbound. It reaches past her narrow waist and dances in the moonlight.

"The baby is well? Your mother too?" I ask.

"Yes. They're doing just fine." Her voice is flat, lifeless, and I draw up short. She shakes her hands dry, turns the bucket over, and sinks down on it, using it for a stool.

"It's another boy. A beautiful . . . little . . . boy."

"You wanted a sister?"

"I did. Not for me . . . for Ma. But he's . . . he's . . ." She doesn't finish her sentence, like she isn't even sure how she feels. She tries again. "Ma wants me to name him. I can't think of any names that begin with W. We've used them all up." She looks up at me, her eyes weary and her mouth sad, and I don't know what to say.

"Your name . . . is Naomi. Surely you . . . can pick a different letter."

"They were going to name me Wilma, but Ma had a dream before I was born about Naomi from the Bible. She said it was a sign, so I'm the only one with a name that doesn't start with W."

"I like Naomi better than Wilma," I confess softly.

"So do I. Thank you, Lord, for sending my ma a vision. Maybe you could send me one too? So I know what to do?" She doesn't really sound like she's praying, though she's looking at the sky. She sounds exhausted, and I search for the words to give her comfort and come up empty.

"Why are you here, John? It's the middle of the night," she asks.

"I found Webb asleep in my tent. He didn't want to hear your mother cry."

Naomi's chin wobbles, and her lips begin to tremble, and I curse my fool self. She looks down at her soiled dress and takes a deep, steadying breath before she speaks again.

"She didn't cry but for a minute, when the pain got real bad. And she cried quietly. She is the strongest person I know. She hardly even needed me. She knew what to do, every step of the way. I was too young to help when Webb was born—twelve years old—but Ma had a bed and midwife. I thought Mrs. Caldwell would come assist, but she's down with the sickness. So many are laid low."

"Joe Duggan, one of Mr. Hastings's hired men, died tonight. Did you hear?" I ask, reluctant to share the news. The man succumbed to the disease quickly. He'd been fine at noonday.

"How many deaths does that make?"

"Five."

"Good Lord."

"Abbott says we'll move out tomorrow, away from the cholera, if that's what it is."

"Oh no," she moans. "I wanted Ma to have a day of rest."

"It's best we continue on to better water. People are getting their water in the puddles and along the banks."

"It's hard to get down to the creek. The mud is like a bog, and it sucks you deep. Will lost a boot trying to fill the buckets this evening."

"I know."

"Can we run from it? If people are sick, can we really run from it?"

"Running is all we can do," I say. Naomi nods. She does not look like she could outrun a turtle at the moment. The word *turtle* makes me smile, despite myself.

"Is someone with your mother and the baby now?" I ask, hoping I can persuade her to retire. Dawn is not far off, and she needs to rest.

"Abigail is with her. The baby suckled, just the way he should, and he and Ma are sleeping. He is a sweet, precious little thing. He's gonna be easy to love. In fact . . . I already do." She presses a hand to her mouth like she's holding back tears but doesn't break down. She stiffens her back instead.

"You should sleep too; you try to do too much."

"I don't want to sleep. Not yet. I need to think of a name for my brother. He needs a name. He deserves a name. But I think best when I'm moving, so I'm going to walk a bit. Will you walk with me?"

I groan. We walk all day, yet she wants to walk.

"I won't ask you to kiss me again," she says, rueful. "I promise."

I extend my hand to help her rise. "Five minutes. We will walk for five minutes. You are weary. I am weary."

She sighs but nods her head in agreement.

"Do you have another name, John Lowry?" she asks.

I am silent a moment, considering. *Is she asking for my Pawnee name?*

"Just John Lowry? No middle name?" she presses, and maybe it is the darkness and her plaintive tone, but I find myself telling her something I have never told a soul.

"My mother called me Pĩtku ásu'."

"Say it again," she whispers, and I do. She tries to copy the sounds and does a fair job of it. "What does it mean?"

"Two Feet."

"And how do you say *turtle*?" she says, teasing.

"*Ícas.*"

"I like it. But it doesn't start with a *W*," she says.

I smile, and she wilts, the steel in her spine bowing under her fatigue.

"He sounds like a wolf pup. It is the first thing I thought of when I heard his cry," I offer.

She raises her eyes, studying me in the darkness. "My great-grandmother's name was Wolfe. Jane Wolfe."

"Wolfe May," I say, testing it.

"Wolfe May," she murmurs, nodding. "I like it. Lord knows he's gonna need a strong name."

"And it starts with *W*," I add. She laughs softly, and my heart quickens at the glad sound.

"You should sleep now, Naomi." Her name is sweet on my tongue, and I know I have revealed something I did not want her to see.

"I think I will, John. Thank you for helping me. Someday my brother will want to know how he got his name. I'll tell him about you and about this journey." She sighs and smiles faintly. "Wolfe May. Little wolf. It's a good name." She sounds at peace, and my heart swells at her words. I fold my arms so I'm not tempted to touch her, to comfort her further.

I do not say good night this time, but it is all I can do to walk away. I want to be near her. I duck inside the tent, where I found Webb only an hour earlier, but I do not stay there. Instead, I strip off my shirt and use a bit of soap and a bucket of water from Abbott's barrel, scrubbing at my skin, trying to wash Naomi May from my thoughts. When we reach Fort Kearny, I will go back to Missouri, and she will continue to California. I will never see her again, and the knowledge sits like hunger in my belly, churning away at me the remainder of the night.

NAOMI

Ma resumes walking in the morning, baby Wolfe wrapped in a cloth bunting and secured to her chest. She and Pa don't balk at the name I have chosen. In fact, they nod approvingly, recalling Grandma Wolfe, as I knew they would. I don't tell them that it was John's suggestion; it is a secret between the two of us. I do my best to absorb Ma's duties for the first few days, allowing her to rest as soon as the train stops, preparing food, washing clothing, and looking after the family.

The sickness along the trail is making everyone jumpy. One family in the company loses their father and mother within hours of each other, leaving their four children, all under the age of ten, orphaned. An uncle takes them all in, only to lose his own wife the following day. The whole family—two wagons, eight children, one man, three sheep, and two teams of oxen—turns back for Missouri, a boy of fourteen at the helm of one team, and we all watch them go, stunned at the sudden wrath of death. If we were under any illusions about the difficulty and suffering we would all endure, those illusions have vanished, though I'm convinced the mind whispers little lies to us all. *You'll be fine. You're stronger. You're smarter. You're better. You'll be spared.*

Daniel's death has taught me that death is fickle and final, and it doesn't spare anyone. It doesn't spare us. Abigail starts the day walking beside the wagon with Ma, but by lunch she is doubled over with terrible cramps, and her bowels are so loose she removes her bloomers so she will not soil them. She insists it's the baby she's carrying, but she is so ill by nightfall she does not respond when we try to make her drink. Warren holds her hand and begs her not to go, but she does not wake again, and my brother becomes a surviving spouse, just like me.

We make a coffin out of the extra box seat, burying her in a shallow ravine beside a single line of trees not far from the Little Blue. John Lowry helps Pa and Wyatt dig the hole, and we mark the spot with a cross fashioned from the slats of Ma's rocking chair. After the endless bump and sway of travel, none of us may ever want to rock again.

Ma sings a song—*To the land I am bound, where there's no more storms arising*—and the Methodist deacon in the train, a man named Elias Clarke, says a few words about God's eternal rest. But there is no rest. We are moving again as soon as the crude coffin is in the ground.

"She didn't even want to come. She wanted to stay in Illinois close to her ma," Warren cries. "I didn't think there was anything for us in Illinois. I didn't listen. Now she's gone. Now I have to leave her in the middle of nowhere, all alone."

We can't console him, and by nightfall he is so ill with the same thing that brought Abigail low we fear he will follow in her footsteps. Wyatt drives his oxen, and Warren lies in the back of his wagon, inconsolable, racked by pain in his limbs and his bowels, mourning a wife who was darning the hole in his socks only yesterday. I ride with him, trying to ease his pain with remedies that don't seem to help at all. Ma wants to tend to him, but I won't let her. She is weak, and if Ma gets sick, Wolfe will die too. We may all die if Ma dies.

Pa asks us if we want to turn back. We are barely two weeks out of St. Joe, and life is no longer recognizable. We are walking sideways in an upside-down world. The talk of land and possibility in Oregon and

California has been silenced by glum reality. Pa says we can follow John Lowry when he returns to Missouri and pay him to help us get back home. My heart leaps at that, but Ma just looks at me in that knowing way and shakes her head, though she addresses us all.

"There is nothing behind us, William," Ma says. "We have nothing to go back to. If we turn around . . . Abigail will still be gone. Our future is out there. Our sons are going to make it to California. They are going to have a better life than the one we left. You'll see."

Somehow Warren holds on, but it takes us eight days to travel from the banks of the Big Blue River to the Platte. The wagon train is slowed by the death that dogs our heels, and Fort Kearny, sitting south of the shallow stretch of river, has no walls or fortifications. It's an unimpressive, dusty encampment with corrals and barracks and cannons to keep the Indians away, though not too far away. A few lodges dot the landscape beside the main building, and I overhear talk of a Pawnee village within riding distance. The night we arrive, a group of Pawnee women, children, and old men stagger into the camp, crying and wailing. Someone says a band of Sioux attacked the village, took their animals, and burned some of the lodges. We saw the same thing along the Missouri River when we traveled from Council Bluffs to St. Joe. A band of Omaha Indians had been run from their village. Pa gave them what he could, and they continued on, mourning and moaning as though the Sioux were still behind them. I was relieved to reach St. Joseph, but the images of the bedraggled and bloody Omaha remained fixed in my memory. I sketched some of their faces in my book, trying to shake them loose. It brought them to life again, and I wished I had simply let the images fade. I'd captured anguish on paper and had no idea what to do with it.

The wind blows like nothing I've ever seen or heard. We circle the wagons, stake the wheels, and put the animals inside so they don't scatter in the gale, and the circle seems to give the wagons a bit of protection, but I expect to be swept up at any moment. The boys are beneath the wagon, and Mama, Wolfie, and I are inside. I can't hear Ma moaning in her sleep when the wind howls like this, and for that I'm grateful. She isn't doing well. She talks in her sleep, and she's pale and weak. I am worried she will get the dreaded cholera, but she just smiles and tells me not to worry.

"I never get sick; you know that, Naomi," she says. And I realize I have learned all my bravado from her.

Ma moans and baby Wolfe wails, and it is hours before the winds calm and they settle, but I don't sleep. Just before dawn, I pull on my boots and climb from the wagon. I can't wait a moment longer to relieve myself, wind or no wind, and I don't want to wake Ma to come with me. The stillness is eerie, the camp deep in relieved slumber, and I listen for the rattle of Pa's snore, a sound to orient me in the dark. I don't go as far as I'd like, but habit and the need for privacy force me farther than is probably prudent. I bunch my skirts and sling them over my shoulder, crouching so I won't wet my shoes or my drawers, and empty my bladder into the prairie dirt.

The wind has blown away the clouds, revealing inky darkness prickled with stars, and I don't want to return to the wagon. I'm tired, and the weariness will find my limbs and weight my lids when the day drags on, but the solitude invigorates me. I loosen my hair and comb it with my fingers before rebraiding it and washing in the water Pa brought up from the river last night. I try not to think about the wide brown expanse of the Platte. The spring rains have flooded the banks, pulling debris into the current. The water tastes terrible, but boiled and flavored with coffee, it's bearable. Abbott says to sprinkle oats in a bucket of water and let them sink to the bottom, taking the silt with them. It works, but it wastes too. I comfort myself with the knowledge that it doesn't seem to be the dirt that makes us sick.

I get a fire started and make some coffee, hoping it won't encourage anyone out of sleep too soon. I'm not ready for the day or the sun or the company, and as I sit with my cup in silence, I breathe slowly, willing time to follow my rhythm. With the animals inside the circle, I have built the fire beyond the perimeter of the wagon train, far enough to avoid a disturbance and close enough to welcome my family when they rise.

A soft tread lifts my chin and scatters my morose thoughts, and John Lowry, his sleeves rolled and his clipped hair dripping, separates from the darkness that stretches toward the Platte. My fire makes him look like a mirage, and I stand, awkward, like I've been waiting for him. Maybe I have. Maybe I've summoned him with my desperate thoughts. It's been only a week since he kissed me, since I asked him to kiss me again, to kiss me better, but it feels like it's been a thousand years.

"Would you like coffee?" I ask and immediately wish I hadn't given him any choice. I don't wait for his answer but rush to refill my cup and hand it to him while I search for another.

"Sit. I'm harmless," I insist.

He bites his lip like he wants to disagree, but he sinks to his haunches obediently, cradling the tin cup between his big palms. I want to set the cup aside and crawl into his arms. Abigail's death and Wolfe's birth have turned me into a hollow-eyed ghoul; I've been putting one foot in front of the other, all my strength dedicated to keeping my family from falling into the hole of despair sucking at our plodding feet. I've had no time for thoughts of John, but my heart has kept the fire burning, and I want to beg him not to leave the train.

"You're up before you need to be," he says, his tone hushed, saving me from blurting out in anguished pleading.

"You are too," I reply, but my voice sounds like I'm being strangled.

"The wind forced me beneath Abbott's wagon, and Abbott forced me back out again. He was louder than the gale."

At that moment, Pa's snore reaches a crescendo, and baby Wolfie wails, the sound tired and cantankerous. We both laugh, but the ache in my throat intensifies.

"We move on tomorrow. What's next for you, Mr. Lowry?"

"Abbott wants me to remain with the train. He's offered me a job."

I nod, trying not to reveal my pounding heart.

"Are you going to take it?" I whisper.

He sips his coffee and studies the fire as though he's not made up his mind. Light and shadows writhe on the bridge of his nose, the swell of his cheek, and the jut of his chin.

"Yes. And I'm going to run half my mules to Fort Bridger. I'm going to keep Kettle and Dame . . . maybe start my own breeding farm in California." He says the words with a finality that makes me believe the decision has just settled on him with a sudden, considerable weight. My heart skips, and my next question sounds a little breathless.

"Where's Fort Bridger?"

"About a thousand miles . . . that way." He points downstream, his arm parallel to the Platte.

"Why mules?" I press, trying to keep him with me a moment more.

"It's what I know. They're strong. And smart. And stubborn. The best parts of a horse and a donkey rolled into one."

"Horses are prettier. Better to draw too."

"Horses are like big dogs. Men and dogs belong together. Men and horses too. But mules . . . they just put up with us. They aren't eager to please."

"And you like that?"

"I understand it."

"Do you have a girl, Mr. Lowry?" I blurt out. I am not eager to please, but I *am* eager. I don't know what it is about him, but he makes me want to stake my claim on him, hard and fast. My boldness is not new, but my interest is. Widow or not, I have not felt like this before.

"Are you looking for another husband, Mrs. Caldwell?" John Lowry counters around the rim of his coffee cup.

"I wasn't. But then I met you." I meet his gaze, steady. No games. No giggles. "But I think you're probably like the mules, Mr. Lowry, and I'm going to have to work for your attention."

Surprise leaps among the light and shadow. His eyes cling to mine for a startled second, and he makes a sound like a laugh—just a puff of breath—but it doesn't turn up his lips or wrinkle his eyes.

"You've got my attention, Mrs. Caldwell. But I'm not sure that's what you really want." He sets his coffee down and begins to rise.

"I know my own mind, Mr. Lowry. I always have. My own heart too."

"But you don't know the terrain."

"I'm counting on you to guide me through it, John, all the way to California."

"I've never been," he murmurs. "I don't know how to do this . . . any of it."

"So we go steady and slow," I say.

"Like ícas."

It takes me a minute to remember the word and realize what he's said.

Like the turtle.

I stand as well, my weariness forgotten, my eyes searching his.

"Yes. Just like that," I say.

5

THE PLATTE

JOHN

I herd all my mules and my two jacks into the rear paddock behind the fort and leave Dame in the care of a Pawnee boy in an army cap, a faded uniform, and a pair of moccasins that makes me think he's not an official recruit.

When I thank him in his native language, telling him I am there to see Captain Dempsey, he rattles off a stream of Pawnee, commenting on the quality of the mules and the size of the jack and asking if he can help me when I'm working with the mares. I am recognized from years past, it seems. When I tell him I won't be at Fort Kearny long, his shoulders sink, but he points me toward the main building of the fort and Captain Dempsey's quarters and tells me he'll keep an eye on the animals until I return.

Inside, I am greeted suspiciously by a Corporal Perkins, whose fastidious mustache, slicked-down hair, and ironed tunic and trousers make me feel every dusty mile between St. Joseph and the Platte. When I tell him the purpose of my visit, he nods, instructs me to wait, and raps on Captain Dempsey's office door. After a few muted words, I hear a squeaking of floorboards and steady footfalls. Captain Dempsey appears in the doorway, his smile wide behind a graying beard. His black belt is cinched beneath a rounded belly swathed in army blue and bisected by gold buttons. He's a big man, hearty, and I like him.

"John Lowry. You're here. I want to see those animals. Do you mind if we take a look right now? Pleasantries later?"

I nod. Pleasantries be damned. I've never especially liked tea. It makes me feel clumsy and constricted. I would rather eat and eat heartily than sip from a little cup and wonder how many cookies is polite. And I would rather be done with the conversation ahead. I am not going to hold up my end of the bargain, and I am nervous but resolute. The captain asks me about the trail and travel from St. Joe as we retrace the path from the corrals I took only moments before.

"Charlie's been excited for you to arrive. He's been watching every emigrant train, searching for you and your mules."

"Charlie?"

Captain Dempsey points across the corral at the Pawnee boy, who has already unsaddled Dame and is brushing her down. Dame stands perfectly still, her eyes closed, her head bowed like she is afraid any movement will make him stop. Pott is sniffing at the boy's shoulder, and Charlie reaches out and pats his nose, spreading the love around.

"Damnation, that is a fine animal." Captain Dempsey whistles. "The biggest jack I've ever seen. I guess that makes your job easier, eh, Lowry?"

I nod. "He's the finest. But I'm willing to sell him." The jacks themselves have never been part of any contract we've ever had, and the captain's eyebrows disappear beneath the wide brim of his gray hat.

"The contract is for ten Lowry mules," Dempsey stammers. "But what did you have in mind?"

"I'll give you five mules and that jack . . . the darker one."

"The jack? Why?" His eyes narrow, and he strokes his beard, considering me. A quality jack donkey with the proven record and size of Pott and Kettle could be sold for more than three thousand dollars. I'd heard of one selling for five.

"I've decided to continue on with the wagon train to California, and I need the other mules. Take the jack. It's a good deal."

The captain circles Pott, who scampers toward Kettle, perhaps sensing a parting.

"It's a good deal if you know a thing about mule breeding, which I don't. I'm a cavalry man, Lowry. The army needs good Missouri mules, not donkeys." He is bartering already, I can hear it in his voice, and I curse myself for starting the bidding with my final offer. Captain Dempsey knows horseflesh and livestock. I have no doubt he knows the value of the jack, but I am the one who is altering the agreement. I say nothing, letting my offer stand.

He scratches his beard like he's considering something deep, and I brace myself for a proposal I can't accept. "I tell you what. Maybe you can make up the difference some other way. A band of Sioux attacked the Pawnee village last night. Burned lodges. Stole horses. And now we're caught in the middle of an Indian war."

Charlie has gone still, the brush motionless against Dame's flanks. She chuffs and butts him softly, and Charlie resumes his ministrations slowly, but he is listening to our conversation.

"The army has offered incentives to the elders if they will move north of the Platte—just abandon the village altogether—but they don't want to go," the captain continues.

"Moving north of the river will put them farther into Sioux territory," I say.

"Yeah. But the fort won't be caught between them."

"I don't want any part of that."

Captain Dempsey sighs wearily and nods but scrunches his face like he's trying to remember something.

"I believe our contract says that the army has purchased ten Lowry mules and stud services to be supplied to Fort Kearny no later than June fifteenth, 1853. I have it on my desk."

"Ordered. Not purchased. You fulfill payment upon delivery. You are aware of those terms, Captain," I say. It isn't the first time the captain has done business with my father, but I know where he's going.

He sighs again. "I can agree to the five mules and that jack. But I'm not getting the Lowry stud service outlined in the contract. You have some language skills I need, and it will only take you an afternoon. An afternoon, John. You'll be ready to ride out with the emigrant train tomorrow, as planned. Consider it good business. I just need you to be my representative."

I have kept my heritage to myself, but the captain knows my father, and he's well informed. I'm sure he knows the habits and aptitudes of the men in his command as well as their stories and situations. He knows mine, though we've never discussed it. Considering I was supposed to spend a week coaxing my jacks to cover every mare in estrus in Fort Kearny's paddocks, his demand for one afternoon in his service is not unreasonable, and I nod slowly, agreeing to his terms.

"I won't be anyone's representative. I will relay your words. I will listen. And I will tell you what is said."

"I'll send a load of flour and corn behind you. Charlie here will show you the way. Remind them there will be more if they go north."

"Will there be?"

Captain Dempsey sighs, but he nods. "There will as long as I'm in charge."

Without being told, Charlie heaves Dame's saddle back in place, tightening the cinch and patting her nose. He looks at me expectantly, and I step forward to take the reins.

"You can leave the rest of your animals here," Dempsey says. "We'll keep an eye on them. Report back, Lowry. Tonight. I'll send the wagon with the corn and flour within the hour."

Charlie opens the gate to let me out, and after swinging it closed and dropping the bolt back in place, he starts to run, obviously expecting me to follow. I do, digging my heels into Dame's sides and trailing after the fleet-footed boy in surprise. I call after him, asking him in Pawnee if he is going to run all the way. He laughs, picking up speed, and for a while I simply keep pace beside him, letting Dame canter.

"Do you run to the fort every day?" I ask.

He nods, his eyes ahead, his stride long and easy. He continues this way for a couple of miles, the river to our right, an endless rolling prairie to our left. He takes me across the tufted swales, up one low rise and down another, until I can't stand it any longer and pull up short. Charlie slows to a stop too, his hands on his hips, his gaze quizzical.

"Your turn," I say. He is hardly winded, but his eyes widen at my command.

"Oh, no. No, Mr. Lowry." He shakes his head, adamant. "We don't have much farther to go."

"Good. You ride. I will run."

"You will run?" he squeaks. His teeth flash in his brown face, and I grin back.

"I used to run just like you, all the way back to my mother's village. You think I can't?"

"You are wearing boots. You will be slow."

I slide off Dame and hand him the reins, but he is still reluctant.

"This way, your village will know that I am a friend," I insist.

He doesn't look convinced, but his desire to ride my horse is too great, and he scrambles up on her back. He flaps his legs and yips like he has spotted a buffalo herd. Dame bolts, and Charlie whoops, leaving me behind without a backward glance. I break into a dead run that isn't nearly as easy or fast as the one I relieved him from. It has been a while since I used my own two legs to travel any sort of distance, and my limbs protest, stiff from days in the saddle and nights stretched out on the hard ground. I pray Dame doesn't step in a hole and break her leg. The homes of the prairie dogs dot the expanse, and I keep my eyes on the ground so I don't step in one myself. I continue to cover the ground as fast as I dare, trusting that Charlie will return, hoping the village is not as far as I fear.

Minutes later, Charlie comes back, still kicking up dust. He circles me in celebration, his arms raised, his face wreathed in triumph. He is a fine horseman for a man with no horse. He points at a suggestion of lodges in the distance, and for the final stretch, he trots along beside me, enjoying his ride.

I expect flurry and interest when we enter the village, but no one seems to notice we've arrived. A sheep bleats, and a few children chase it, stopping briefly to stare at me before resuming their game. The village feels empty, occupied only by the dogs, the sheep, and the handful of children. The corrals are empty too, not a single Indian pony anywhere, and I wonder if Charlie runs every day because there is literally nothing for him to ride. Several brush huts are burned to the ground, the blackened grass around them the only indication of where they stood. The earthen lodges have fared better, and they circle a big center lodge, where I know the men gather, talk, and pass the pipe. It is something I've never done.

"Where is everyone?" I ask Charlie.

"Many are still at the fort. The warriors are gone. They've gone to fight the Sioux and recover our horses and cattle." His voice is glum, like he doesn't believe it will happen. Or maybe he fears they won't return.

"Then why am I here?" I mutter. "Who will I talk to?"

"The brothers are here. You can talk to them," Charlie reassures me.

"The brothers?"

"They do not run anymore. They don't even ride. They sleep, and they eat, and they pass the pipe. When the Sioux came, they did not even leave their lodge. They say they are ready to die. But for some reason they never do." He shrugs.

"How many brothers?"

"Three. They are the oldest men in our village—maybe the oldest of all the Pawnee. So old they have outlived their sons and their daughters. My uncle, Chief Dog Tooth, is the grandson of one of the brothers."

"Is he a good chief?"

"I don't know," Charlie says slowly. "What is a good chief?"

I'm not sure I know the answer either and remain silent, following Charlie toward the big lodge. He ducks through the door, telling me to wait, and I can hear the murmur of voices, though I can't make out the conversation. After a moment, two women scurry out, their eyes darting from me to the ground, and I am ushered inside. It is dark inside and warm, and though it is only midday, a fire burns, the smoke rising up toward the hole above the center pit.

The three old men sit beside it in their buffalo robes, sleepily peering at the coals. They don't have shaved pates or bristled forelocks in the old Pawnee way. Their hair is long and white, their hoary heads almost identical—their faces too—and I can see why they are simply called *the brothers*, with no distinction between them.

I sink down across from them, waiting silently for them to acknowledge me. Charlie sits beside me, his thin legs folded, his hands loose at his sides, but I am not fooled. This is a first for him too. After an interminable silence, I state my purpose, eager to be gone.

"Captain Dempsey wants you to move north of the Platte." There. I have done my duty.

The old men mutter, puffing away with bowed backs and bent heads. I don't think they have heard me. I don't really care. I begin to rise, but the brothers lift their heads in affront.

"And how long before they ask us to move again? Does Dempsey speak for all the whites? Does he speak for the Sioux or the Cheyenne?" one asks, his trembling Pawnee words pricking my conscience.

"*Káki*," I answer. *No.*

"Do you think we should move? Did your people move?" the same brother asks.

I think of my mother's village. Missouri is no longer the land of Pawnee. I'm not sure it ever was, though my Pawnee grandmother told me the Pawnee nation spread from sea to sea when her great-grandfather hunted the buffalo. I don't know if that is true or if it was simply the wistful myth of a dying people. But Missouri is no longer the home of the Shawnee or the Potawatomi either. It belongs to others now and is dotted with homes made of brick and stone. The Pawnee don't migrate like the Sioux. The Pawnee grow corn and build lodges from the earth.

"There are not many Pawnee in Missouri," I say.

"Soon there will not be many Pawnee anywhere," another brother replies. "Dempsey wants us to leave so he does not have to deal with us. We are a nuisance to him. But if we move, we will never stop moving, and we were here first."

I have no doubt that what he says is true, and I have no response.

"Who are your people?" the last brother asks me.

It is a question I have never been able to answer, and it is the question everyone eventually asks. "My father is a Lowry. My mother was Pawnee. I am . . . both. Pítku ásu'." I shrug, turning my palms up.

"Pítku ásu'," the brothers murmur, nodding their heads as if it makes complete sense, and they fall silent again. I think they have fallen asleep, and Charlie wriggles beside me.

"What should I tell Captain Dempsey?" I ask. "I will tell him whatever you wish me to say."

They all begin speaking at once, mumbling over the top of one another, and I don't know who says what.

"Tell him the Kanzas are below us. The Sioux above. Cheyenne too."

"They steal from us. We steal from them. We understand each other. But we don't understand the whites."

"They trample on the sacred burial grounds of our ancestors. The wagons go through—we see the tracks of their wheels."

"One man makes a promise, we sign a treaty, and another man breaks it."

Their anger is palpable, and they glower at me as if I am to blame. I am grateful I am speaking to old men. I suspect Dog Tooth and his war chiefs would run me out. Or run me through.

"You tell him we will stay right here," a brother says.

"Let him fight the Sioux with his cannon. We do not want to fight them," another adds.

"I will tell him," I say, but I know it will do no good. Someone will visit the village again, asking the brothers to go, and they won't take no for an answer. I tell them that a wagonload of corn and flour will arrive in their village, a gift from Captain Dempsey, but this time when I rise, they don't look up at me, and Charlie follows me out. When I step from the big lodge, my eyes adjusting to the light, I see that the village has repopulated itself as though the old men and the smoke from their fire have called their people home. The corn has been delivered from Fort Kearny, the flour too, and the women are unloading it; they glance up at me in suspicion and pause in their work.

In Pawnee, I ask them what else they need. Their eyes widen with surprise, the typical response when I speak the language. But they scoff.

"Are you going to get it for us, half man?" one woman says.

Half man. It is a new twist on the more common *half breed.* I was run out of my mother's village enough to know that I am no more welcome among the Indians than I am among people like Lawrence Caldwell. It was a stupid thing to say. I do not have the power to grant them anything or give them what they need.

Charlie tugs on my arm. "Can you find your way back to the fort, Mr. Lowry? Or would you like me to run with you?"

"I can get back, Charlie."

He claps my shoulder, his eyes sober. "Thank you for letting me ride your horse. It was a good day. I hope I will see you again."

I nod. "I would like that."

"And I hope you find your way," Charlie adds.

It is not until the village is behind me, the prairie and the Platte stretched before me, that I wonder if perhaps Charlie wasn't talking about returning to the fort.

∞

I report back to Captain Dempsey, who doesn't seem surprised by the response but sighs and makes a notation in his ledger, like he is keeping a record of his attempts at peaceful removal. Then I write a letter to my father and another to Jennie and post them with a trapper who says he'll take them to St. Joe. I don't know why I write two—I assume they will share them—but with my father I can never be sure, and I do not speak to them in the same way. To my father I report the condition of the mules and Captain Dempsey's reaction to their quality, size, and overall demeanor. I also tell him Captain Dempsey says good, amenable breeding jacks are in great demand and that I will be able to sell stud services at every fort and trading post from here to California. Pott and Kettle are mine, though the contract for the mules was my father's. I don't tell him the particulars of the deal, only that the full contract payment will be made to his account in St. Joe. Then I tell him I'm not coming home.

I do not tell him about Naomi May or the pictures she draws. To speak of her would be to admit that she is the reason I cannot make myself return, and so I simply tell him I will send word at Fort Laramie, at Fort Bridger, and again when I arrive at my journey's end. I reassure him that I have plenty of money; I never travel far without it. It is the fear of being caught unprepared, at the mercy of fate and a friendless world. It is the fear of finding myself completely alone. At the bottom of the letter, I sign my name.

To Jennie I report on Abbott's well-being and his desire to keep me on the train all the way to California. I tell her the government is giving away land in Oregon. They're giving it away to lure emigrants across the country to settle it—320 acres to a single man, 640 acres if he's married. I'm not sure they'll give it to an Indian; maybe they'll only give me half. Maybe I'll go to Oregon.

I don't know if Jennie or my father will be fooled by my talk of land. It's never been land that interests me, or farming, or even space, though I think I'd like it well enough. They know I am happiest with a handful of mules, a dozen good mares, and a few jack donkeys that don't turn their noses up at a horse's hindquarters. Breeding mules is what I know, and I've always felt a sort of kinship with the beasts. They can't reproduce; a mule will never pass down a pedigree. No posterity, no bloodlines, one of a kind, every time. Created by a mother and a father that don't belong together, mules are bred for strength and labor, and that is all. I don't need to belong, despite what my father thinks. I'd take a mule over a man any day.

I don't tell Jennie about the deaths or the hard days either. I do not mention the cholera or the color of Naomi's eyes. I don't tell her about the Pawnee camp and the hardship there. I do not tell her how hopeless it made me feel. I simply tell her I am well, and I end my letter with the last thing she said to me, that love is the only thing worth the suffering, and if I know Jennie, she'll read between the lines. She'll know I've met someone that I can't part with.

I do not know if I love Naomi . . . not yet. It seems to me people make the admission too lightly and tumble head over feet down the hills to chase it. I am not ready for that, but I *am* falling. She is like a speck in the distance—something so far away and unknown that I can't quit staring, trying to identify what I'm seeing.

I'd take a mule over a man any day . . . but Naomi May is another proposition altogether.

NAOMI

"We need to cross over to the north side of the Platte," Mr. Abbott informs us as the day begins. "Captain Dempsey says there's less sickness on the other side, although word is it's bad all the way to Fort Laramie. Worst they've ever seen. We're going to have to cross eventually. I say we do it now."

The Platte is a mile wide, if not more, and on an average day, it isn't more than hip high at the deepest parts. But it lures you in with all its shallow innocence. Mr. Abbott says he's seen men and mules wade out across and suddenly be slammed by a rush of water barreling toward them from rains and runoff from mountains a thousand miles away. He says sometimes you can see the water a few minutes before it swells, but even then, the river is so wide that once you're out in it, you can't get out of the way. And the bottom is quicksand. If you stop or your animals balk, the wheels of the wagons promptly sink to the axles. Mr. Abbott says the Platte swallows oxen whole. It is grueling to cross no matter where or when you attempt it, but most of us think Abbott is right. It must be crossed eventually, and when Captain Dempsey says the cholera is worse on the south side, it's reason enough to ford it now.

Though there is a great deal of grumbling, discontent, and genuine fear about crossing a river so wide, when Mr. Abbott makes the decision, the company rushes to prepare their wagons. The company has been carved down to forty wagons and fifty fewer people by death and desertion. The Hastingses, with their big wagon and their funny horse-drawn carriage, have not abandoned the trail, despite Mr. Abbott's prediction. They've complained bitterly, along with a few other families (including the Caldwells, who have fared better than most), but they have not turned back. Mr. Caldwell got wind that John is continuing on with the train. He's been whispering in Pa's ear and stirring up trouble, and he's already pulled me aside to warn me about being "dragged off by the half breed." I told him John doesn't want to drag me off, but if he did, I'd go willingly. It wasn't the wisest thing to say, I suppose, but I am too weary to abide him or his opinions.

We cross about ten miles west of Fort Kearny, where the river is narrowest and the sandbars sit like miniature islands in the coffee-colored sludge. I overhear John telling Webb that the Platte is worse than the Missouri because it must be forded and not swum, and each step threatens to suck you under.

John doesn't waste any time and puts Webb and Will on Trick and Tumble, attaching their leads to Dame and his string of mules. He leads them the way he did on the Missouri, showing them what he expects before he returns to the banks to coax them into the water.

"Keep going, boys. Hang tight, and don't panic," he says, and Webb and Will obey, murmuring softly, "Go, mules, go," as Trick and Tumble rush through the waters, the silty bottom sucking at their hooves.

"Attaboy, Trick," Webb encourages, like it's all just a grand adventure. Will is a little more cautious, but Tumble trots through the water behind John and Dame, and they make it across without mishap, then wait for us on the far side.

We raise the beds of the wagons as high as they will go and tie down all the supplies as best we can. Little Wolfe is swaddled and secured in his basket, tied down amid the sundry supplies. It is the safest place for him, but Ma sits beside him, clinging to his basket with stark fear stamped all over her face. Pa drives one team, walking alongside the oxen with his Moses stick; Warren is still too weak to walk through a mile of turbulent water beside the oxen, so Wyatt drives the other. I climb up on the front seat, and Warren lies in back, promising to keep the supplies from tumbling out. Pa hems and haws, and Ma's lips have gone white with terror. She prays loudly for the waters to be calm and the wagons to have wings.

With a crack of the whip and a "Giddyap," we lurch forward into the Platte, the water lapping at the sides of the wagons, the oxen groaning, and the far shore so distant it's like a mirage. Suddenly John is back, splashing toward us, shouting directions and then circling around, bringing up the rear. We are more than halfway across, gaining confidence with every rod, when Pa's wagon begins to list to the side and Ma begins to holler. The supplies bump and slide as wheels sink deep. The water sloshes into the wagon bed, and Ma's prayers become a scolding.

"Keep those oxen moving, William," John yells to Pa, threading his rope through the front wheel and wrapping it around his saddle horn. He spurs Dame, and the wagon jolts forward with a sudden sucking sound. The oxen bellow, stumbling as the weight of the wagon surges against the yoke.

Just as quickly as Pa is freed, Wyatt begins to panic, pulling back on the team instead of pushing the pace. I don't think twice but swing down from the box into the river to help Wyatt. The water isn't deep, but it pulls at my skirts, and I wade ahead, determined to keep the wagon from getting stuck. I trip and go under, but only briefly, before I get my hands around the tug on the harness of the lead ox and pull as hard as I can. Everyone's yelling as I'm yanking, but the wagon rights itself, and the team surges forward, crisis averted.

John leans down and, with a grunt and a hiss, hauls me up into the saddle in front of him, my skirts streaming and threatening to pull me right back down into the water.

"Please don't do that again, Mrs. Caldwell," he barks, his mouth at my ear, and I wipe the muddy tendrils of hair from my cheeks, inordinately pleased with myself. I am wet, filthy, and so close to John Lowry I can feel his heartbeat thudding against my back. Crossing the Platte is not as bad as I anticipated.

6

ELM CREEK

JOHN

It takes an hour to cross a single wagon, two to cross another, and by the time the entire train is assembled on the north side of the Platte, some with supplies that have been ruined by the water or lost in the finicky flow, there is little will to continue on. We stagger a few miles to finish the day and set up camp at a place called Elm Creek, about eight miles west of where we crossed.

That night we suffer a storm the likes of which I've never seen. The wagon wheels are staked and the animals corralled, but every tent is blown over, and the Hastingses' buggy topples end over end, having survived the Platte only to be dashed to pieces by the storm. It is not the weight of the rain but the strength of the gale that accompanies it, and we spend the next day drying out at Elm Creek, though we desperately need to make up for lost time. And I am ill.

I say nothing to anyone, hiding my misery as I see to my animals, but I am in trouble, and I am scared. I tell myself it is simply the chill from the hours I spent moving wagons across the Platte and the storm that deprived me of rest and a chance to get dry, but by midnight my bones ache and my bowels are on fire, and I fall into my damp blankets after my watch, praying that Webb will stay away, wishing I'd seen my sisters like Jennie wanted me to, wishing I'd told my father goodbye when he'd stood on the banks of the Missouri and watched me go.

There is little privacy but distance, and I lurch from my tent to relieve myself beyond earshot of the wagons and the eyes of the second watch. I dare not go back to my tent only to have to rise again to empty my bowels. I don't have the strength to do anything but huddle in a swampy ravine, disgusted by my own filth and unable to do anything about it. I've put a bit of peppermint and laudanum into my canteen—I consider pouring it out, not certain if the water I carry is the water that made me sick, but then consider that no water might be worse in my condition than tainted water. The peppermint eases the cramping, and the laudanum muffles the clanging in my head, though it feels like I am drifting away. The ache in my throat and the screaming in my limbs let me know I am still alive.

More than pain, I am riddled with deep regret. I have not told Naomi May how I feel about her. I have not told her that I want to watch her grow old. I have not told her so many things. And I desperately want to.

It is that desire, even amid the agony, that has me dousing myself in the creek to clean the waste from my limbs and my clothes and staggering back to my tent so that no one will spend time looking for me when morning breaks.

If I had known I was going to die, I would have urged the Mays to go back. The journey is only going to get worse, and they need me. I would have given Kettle to Webb and Dame to Naomi. When her face looms above my own, I am sure I am dreaming.

"Mr. Lowry. John?"

Oh God, she is in my tent.

"Go away, Naomi."

I like her name on my lips and grit my teeth against another surge of fear. I want to say her name tomorrow and the day after that, but I know I'm going to die.

"John, you're sick. I'm here to help you."

"I don't want you here." I want my dignity, and there is none in the sickness that sweeps through the emigrant trains. Loose bowels and heaving sides—no one can keep the medicine down, though the medicine simply gives the fretting something to do. I'm not sure it helps all that much.

"I'm going to help you sit up," she says. "You need medicine. It'll make you feel better. I mixed it myself."

"Please . . . go away. I can look after myself," I moan.

"Drink," she demands, scooping her arm beneath my neck. My head lolls against her breast, and I press my lips together to hold back the bile that rises against my will. I heave myself to the side before retching into a bucket she has placed by my head. I fall back, pushing her away with a weak shove.

"I won't keep the medicine down," I say.

"Then just sip it slowly. The best time to drink is when you've just been sick," she says, confident, calm, like she's certain I'm going to be just fine. I believe her for a moment, and then my stomach rebels again.

I push her away once more.

"If you don't let me help you, someone else will try, and I know you like me," she says.

"That's why I want you to go away," I groan.

"I know. And that's why I won't. Now drink."

Hours pass. I am hardly aware of anything beyond my own agony, yet the shadows change and the temperature too, and when I am at last delivered, the pain becoming an echo instead of a roar, Naomi is still beside me.

"I was afraid you were going to die," she says.

She looks as ragged as I feel. Her lips are dry, her eyes are ringed, and her hair is a curling mess around her wan face.

"You're beautiful," I say. And I mean it. She smiles, a radiant beam of relief and surprise, and I say it again, dazzled. Her very presence is beautiful.

"And you're delirious," she argues.

"No." I try to shake my head and am overcome by dizziness. I wait for the nausea, for the pain to sweep through me, but I am simply weak, simply tired, and I open my eyes when the spinning slows, finding her face above mine. I don't think she is breathing.

"John?"

"Cikstit tatku," I whisper. *I am well.* "The pain is gone. I'm just tired."

"Do you promise not to leave?" she asks. I know she isn't talking about the trail or the journey west. She's talking about dying.

"I promise."

"Then I will let you sleep. But drink a little first." She helps me lift my head and holds the tin cup to my lips. It is brackish, and I take little sips, willing my stomach to hold steady.

"You should sleep too," I say. Her head is bobbing with fatigue. I reach for her hand and pull it to my chest, laying it across my heart. I must look a sight and smell even worse, but she curls at my side, her head in the crook of my arm, our hands clasped across my body, and we sleep, lost in the weightlessness of the newly pardoned.

∽

When I wake again, I feel almost restored, though a weakness remains in my limbs, and my thirst is overwhelming. Naomi is gone, though a strand of her hair clings to my shirt.

Webb sits in the opening, the two sides of the tent making a vee above his head.

"Naomi says I'm to tell her when you wake. Are you awake, John?" he asks.

"I'm awake, Webb."

"You're not going to die like Abigail, are you, John? I liked Abigail. But I like you more. Don't tell Warren. Or Pa. Pa doesn't like you, I don't think. He says you've got your eye on Naomi. Do you have your eye on Naomi, John? Naomi had a husband once. His name was Daniel. But he died too. You're not going to die, are you, John?"

My thoughts are slow and my neck is stiff, but I manage to follow the stream of questions Webb hurls at me, shaking my head in response to the question he started and ended with. "Not right now, no."

"That's good."

"Webb?"

"Yes?"

"Have you been looking after my animals?"

"Yep. I been watchin' 'em. I picketed Kettle and the mules just like you showed me. Dame too. There's plenty of grass just over the rise."

"Good boy."

"Everyone else is getting ready to move on. We're to catch up as best we can. Mr. Abbott doesn't want to leave you, but seeing as how the cholera is following us, he said he had to."

"Are you all waiting on me?"

"Nah. There's a few people sick. Lucy died. Just like Abigail, and Ma said Mrs. Caldwell is laid real low. Mr. Bingham is sick too, though he's better than he was. Pa says we gotta move on, but Naomi says not without you. Do you think you're well enough to ride in the wagon, John?"

"I need a drink, and I want to wash . . . without Naomi. How about we wait to tell her I'm awake, okay?"

Webb fetches a bar of soap and digs through my saddlebags for clean clothes. He keeps watch for me as I wash in the creek, stripping off my soiled things until I'm naked as the day I was born and almost as helpless. By the time I've washed and wrung out my clothes and dressed myself in the dry ones, I'm shivering and unsteady, but Webb slings his arm around my waist and pulls my arm over his shoulders, providing a crutch as we make our way back to the camp.

NAOMI

John often sleeps in a little tent that he breaks down and packs up each day, but when it storms or the wind blows, he finds shelter beneath Mr. Abbott's wagon. He is among the first to wake and is usually packed and ready before the rest of us, often helping others gather their stock and yoke their teams.

I know all his habits and patterns; I have been shameless in my interest. So when I see his tent, still pitched and standing off to the side, though the camp has been stirring for hours, I know something is wrong. I stand abruptly, my duties forgotten, and stride toward it, trying not to run, to draw unwanted attention.

Crossing the distance between where I was and the little opening of his tent feels like walking another mile in the Platte, my feet on shifting silt, my legs heavy and bogged down by fear, and when I call his name, it is a shrill bleat that hurts my throat. He doesn't answer, and I do not hesitate, parting the canvas sides and crawling inside.

It is just as I feared, and he is already vomiting, the final stages for Abigail. She didn't last an hour after she began retching. But John has enough strength to insist I leave, enough fire to push me away, and I take heart in that.

I spend the remainder of the day at his side, leaving only to gather medicine and tell my family they will have to leave me behind until

John is improved. Ma understands, Pa too, though he grouses about the impropriety of my care.

"Surely Mr. Abbott can see to his needs. After all, they are family," he protests, but Grant Abbott keeps his distance, worried that he too will find himself ailing, and Pa says nothing more. Arguments about indecency ring hollow when death comes to call.

It ends up that the entire wagon train remains at Elm Creek, only eight miles from where we crossed the Platte two days earlier. John is not the only one stricken down by cholera. Several others, including Lucy Caldwell Hines, Daniel's sister, have succumbed to the deadly plague. Lucy dies just before sunset.

Ma sends Webb to tell me—for some reason the children have more resistance to the disease—and I leave John's side to stand beside a hole in the earth, watching as my sister-in-law is put in the ground by poor Adam Hines, who has the same stunned expression that Warren still wears about his eyes. She is clothed in her wedding dress, blue silk with lace collar and cuffs, and rolled in a rug instead of a winding cloth. The rug once graced Elmeda's parlor, but there is nothing else, unless we want to start tearing apart their wagons.

Lucy said she would wear the dress again when we reached California and attended Sunday meetings. It is Sunday today, and I suppose a funeral is a sort of worship. Deacon Clarke, who is not well himself, says something akin to the words he said for Abigail, and everyone hitches out a wobbly rendition of "Nearer, My God, to Thee." Ma's the only one who knows every word. *Though like the wanderer, the sun gone down, darkness be over me, my rest a stone, yet in my dreams I'd be nearer, my God, to thee.*

I don't sing. My voice has all the beauty of a honking goose, and the words of the hymn weaken my control. I don't cry either; I can't. I cared for Lucy, cared for Abigail, but grief is draining. I am hoarding my strength and my stamina for life, and I will not spend it on death. *Gotta get your mind right, Naomi May.* If all I have is my will, then I must use it well. For Ma. For Wolfe. For my brothers. And for John Lowry, who is still very much alive.

And so I turn away from the shallow grave when the words are spoken and the song is sung, my teeth clenched and my spine straight.

"How can you be so cold, Naomi?" Elmeda Caldwell wails at my back. "You tend to a man who isn't family when my Lucy lay dying?"

I say nothing. I do not defend myself because it is the truth. But Lucy had her mother. Lucy had her husband. And John has no one but me. I know whose death will break my spirit, and it isn't Lucy Caldwell's. But I turn back to embrace Elmeda, preparing myself for her clinging sadness, girding myself against her need. I am tired. I washed my hands and face, straightened my hair, and changed my apron before joining the others by the grave, but I know I look as depleted as I feel. Elmeda pushes me away, her hands on my shoulders like gnarled claws, and I immediately step back, oddly relieved by her rebuff. Anger is good. Anger is better than fear; anger is better than grief. I let Ma console her. Mr. Caldwell sputters his condemnation at my back, but I return to John and to the hope that still lingers.

∞

I wake to darkness but sense the dawn. The camp will soon wake too, and we have to move on, whether or not death has further winnowed our numbers. I have slept three hours, maybe four, but it is all I can afford. John is breathing deeply beside me, his hand still wrapped around mine. I want to weep with relief. With joy. His condition is much improved. He is going to be okay.

I ease myself up, careful to not disturb him. His skin is cool, his limbs relaxed. I whisper a grateful prayer to the God of my mother, to the power she swears is present in all things, and I leave John's side, convinced that I have done what I can do, and he will not slip away.

He won't leave me. He promised he wouldn't, and John Lowry strikes me as a man who keeps his promises.

When breakfast is done and the sun is pressing us onward, I send Webb to keep watch over him with firm instructions to tell me when he wakes. The entire camp is in a state of weary dishabille, children crying, animals braying, entire families brought low by disease and discomfort. Abbott is making the rounds, assessing who can move on and who cannot and putting out the word that the train will move out by noon, regardless. Homer Bingham needs someone to drive his team, another family has decided to return to Fort Kearny and wait for another group, and Lawrence Caldwell is demanding we leave immediately or we'll all be stricken down. Elmeda has not left her bed in the back of their wagon, but she is not racked with cholera; she has simply given up.

When I check on her, she doesn't speak to me but lies with her eyes closed and her hands folded. She won't respond to anyone, though her eyes flutter beneath her lids, and occasionally tears slide down her cheeks. Her son, Jeb, has retreated to the comfort of caring for their animals, and Mr. Caldwell has taken his frustration out on anyone unfortunate enough to cross him. He is throwing gear into the wagons, muttering to himself, rumpled and raging.

"It's your fault she's sick, Widow Caldwell," he snaps at me as I climb down from his wagon.

"How so?" I say, my voice level.

"Have you forgotten Daniel so easily?"

"Daniel's gone, and I can't bring him back, Mr. Caldwell."

He wags his finger at me, jutting out his chin. "You're glad. You've already hitched your wagon to Lowry like we never even mattered."

Lawrence Caldwell is grieving, but there isn't a soul in camp who isn't. He leaves me hollow with his trembling chin, his shaking jowls, and his judgments. Elmeda too. If she dies, it will be because she is desperate to escape him. It is an uncharitable thought, and I bite my tongue so it doesn't get loose. I turn away, feeling his eyes on my back as

I make my way back to our wagons. I can hear Wolfe crying and know I've left Ma to fend alone for long enough.

I rush to gather blankets and dishes, scrubbing and folding and packing as quickly as I can, my eyes constantly straying to John Lowry's tent. Sleep, especially now that the worst has passed, is the best thing for him, but I've just about decided to check on him again when he and Webb make their way from a cluster of willow trees rising up from the banks of the shallow creek.

John is pale, his eyes hollow, the angles of his face sharper, but he is upright, he is dressed in fresh clothes, and he is walking toward me, his arm slung around Webb.

"Here he is, Naomi," Webb crows. "He's wobbly as baby Wolfe, but he says he's not sick no more. He even took a bath."

I rush to them, my eyes searching John's face, and he smiles a little, though it is more a grimace than a grin.

"Do you think you can travel?" I ask. "Mr. Abbott says we have to move out. We've lost so much time. Ma says we can make you a bed in Warren's wagon. He's well enough to walk along beside the oxen. Wyatt and Will can drive your mules, especially now that you've got less than you did."

"I can ride."

"No. You can't." I shake my head. "Not yet. Riding in the wagon may not feel like rest, but it's the best we can do. One day. Maybe two. Please, John."

He wants to argue, I can see it in the strain around his lips and the furrow on his brow, but he doesn't. I doubt he has the energy to take me on. He can barely stand.

"I need to gather my animals. I think I can string them to the wagon, now that there are fewer. Will can ride Dame . . . at least for today."

"I can round 'em up for you, John," Webb says. "I'll get Will to help me."

"I'll do it, Webb. But you can come too. Walk beside me, like you're doing now. Keep me steady," John says. "We'll bring them in together."

"John, let the boys go. You need to sit," I insist.

"Naomi." John's voice is low, his eyes soft. "They spook easy, and I need to attend to them. They've been neglected for two days."

I watch the two of them pick their way slowly across the circle and beyond to the line of willow trees that obscures the view. Five minutes later, Webb is back, and John isn't with him.

"Pa!" Webb hollers. "Pa! Mr. Lowry's mules are gone. Kettle and Dame too. They're all gone. We found their picket pins. All of 'em. They got pulled out, like someone went to gather them and the animals got spooked or something." His little nose is running, and tears stream down his dirty cheeks. "We looked all around. John whistled for Dame, and she didn't come."

"Where is John now?" I gasp.

"He doesn't want to quit looking, but he's awful weak. He told me to come back and tell Mr. Abbott."

My brothers, Pa, and Abbott fan out, searching in an ever-widening circle, but within fifteen minutes they all return to camp without the animals in tow. John is with them, but he is gray faced and bent over, and Mr. Abbott insists he sit before he collapses. It is a testament to his condition that he obeys, and I run to him, trying not to cry.

Mr. Abbott blows his little horn, calling everyone together, explaining what has occurred. There is genuine empathy and alarm, and most of the men—those in good health—volunteer to conduct another brief search.

But every man returns empty handed.

I pack John's tent and gather his things, insisting he conserve his strength, but when Abbott tries to convince him that there is nothing to be done, John just shakes his head.

"We gotta keep going, John," Mr. Abbott insists. "We've been laid up here for two days waiting on you and the others. We've got a stretch of country ahead that's dry and long, and with the number of trains goin' through, what grass there is will be gone."

John is frozen in stooped shock, his eyes on Abbott's face, his hands clasped between his knees. He stands slowly, his expression bleak. He doesn't argue, but he turns to Pa.

"I need to borrow a mule, Mr. May," John says.

Abbott hisses in protest, but I beat him to it.

"You can't go, John. You can barely stand. You're still sick," I argue, terrified.

"I have to go. If I don't find my animals, I can't continue." He doesn't say my name or address me directly, but when his eyes find mine, I hear what he's telling me. If we're going to have a future together, he has to have something to build it on.

"Then I'm going too," I say.

"Naomi!" Pa barks. His face is grim, his jaw set. "That's enough."

"Someone has to go with him!" I shout.

"I'll go," Webb cries. "I'll go find 'em." He is upset, tears streaming down his cheeks like he believes he has failed John. Someone has failed John, but it isn't Webb. Lawrence Caldwell didn't help search when Abbott put out the call, and now he waits, sitting on the box seat in his wagon, his mules harnessed, ready to pull out, Jeb and Adam in the wagon behind him. Webb says Kettle, Dame, and the mules were still there before breakfast, and no one is pointing the finger of blame at anyone else, but I have no doubt Mr. Caldwell set them loose.

"John can't go alone," I say, looking from Pa to Mr. Abbott. "You know he can't."

"I'll go with him, Naomi," Will says, slipping his hand into mine. "I'll look after him."

"Wyatt should go with Mr. Lowry, William," Ma says quietly. "It's only right."

"We need Wyatt to drive the second team," Pa protests.

"I can walk beside the oxen, Pa." Warren speaks up, his cheeks gaunt but his chin firm. "I've been laid up long enough."

"No one is going. Not Wyatt, not Will. Not Naomi. No one," Pa insists, shaking his head. "I'm sorry, John. But your mules aren't as important as my boys."

"Pa!" I shout.

"Pa . . . Mr. Lowry has helped us plenty. We have to help him," Warren argues.

"William," Ma chides.

"Damnation," Pa moans. "Damn it all to hell."

"Go get the mules, Wyatt," Ma says, and Wyatt rushes to obey, Webb at his heels chattering about gathering the canteens and lariats and lead ropes.

∞

When they ride away, Wyatt is tall and wiry in the saddle, his slim shoulders set with purpose, but John is hunched like he's lived a hundred years, and I want to run after them, begging them to come back. I remain standing with my back to the wagons, watching my brother and John Lowry sink into the prairie, lost from my eyes. I don't know that I've ever felt more discouraged, and the weight of hopelessness has left me brittle. A statue made of sticks, a shelter made of straw. It is Ma who finally approaches me, Wolfe in her arms. She stops at my side, but she does not touch me; she must know it would be my undoing.

One by one, the wagons begin to pull out, Mr. Abbott leading the way. I am so angry with him that for a moment I entertain thoughts of vengeance; I consider turning his animals loose, walking among them with my pots and pans and howling like the Omaha Indians on the banks of the Missouri when they thought all was lost.

"If they were Mr. Abbott's animals, you can be damn sure we wouldn't be pulling out," I tell Ma. She doesn't protest my language, but she does defend him.

"Don't judge him too harshly, Naomi. Someone has to make the hard decisions. That's what we've all hired him to do."

"And what about Mr. Caldwell? How should I judge him, Ma? If I had a dollar to my name, I'd bet he's the one that spooked John's mules."

"Lawrence Caldwell will reap whatever he has sown," Ma says, her voice mild, but her eyes are bleak and hard. She closes them briefly, takes a deep breath, and then looks at me.

"They'll be all right, Naomi." But I can see her mind isn't right either. She's aged ten years in the last month, or maybe it's just me. Maybe I am the old one.

A torrent rises inside me, and if I speak, the clouds will break, so I nod, pretending I believe her. Pa beckons to us, and we turn back to the wagons and the west, the last to leave Elm Creek.

7

THE NORTH SIDE

JOHN

"Which way should we go?" Wyatt asks.

The prairie undulates, and I am not certain what is reality and what is mirage. My thoughts are muddy, my reason impaired, and I know only that if I cannot retrieve my animals, I am done for. I tie myself to Tumble's saddle horn, looping the rope around my waist to give me a little support. I don't think it'll hold me if I topple, and I might very well bring the mule down on top of me if I do, but I won't stay in the saddle without it.

"Wouldn't they come back toward the water? Even if they were crazed enough to run for miles, they would come back toward the water, don't you think?" Wyatt asks.

I nod in agreement. "The train's going west, so we'll go east, back the way we came." I just hope that if my mules have gone the way of the train and someone spots them, they will go after them.

"Will and Warren and Webb are all on the lookout. Naomi too. You know that they'll be searching, Mr. Lowry," Wyatt says, answering my worried thoughts.

I trust they will, but I don't trust Lawrence Caldwell. I have no doubt he pulled the pins and scattered my animals. Someone did. It wasn't random, and no one else in the train was missing a single cow. Caldwell loosed them and then drove them out with a slap and a whistle, maybe rattling something or making his whip writhe in the grass to make them bolt. Whatever he did, they're gone. Rustling among travelers in the same train isn't much of a problem because there is nowhere to hide the stolen livestock. But there is no surer way to doom a man than to scatter his animals.

Every so often I whistle, a shrill gull-like shriek that dissipates in the guileless skies, but the action exhausts me, and I abandon even that. All my strength is centered on staying in the saddle. I trust Wyatt to scan the swales and search the banks, and I close my eyes against the pulsing expanse.

I hold on for an hour, then another, clinging to my saddle as we reach the place where we crossed the Platte two days before. The Pawnee village is across the river, the fort too, though it is a good ten miles farther east. There are no trains crossing today. The silence is a sharp contrast to the bellows and brays of our passage, the shrieks and squeals of wheels and women. I scooped Naomi up from the water and into my saddle with no difficulty at all. Now I can barely lift my own head. I consider fording the river again, returning to Fort Kearny and sending Wyatt back to his family with Trick and Tumble. I have no doubt I can find work there; Captain Dempsey will be glad to have my mule-breeding expertise for a week or two. I'll make enough to get a horse to make the journey back to St. Joe.

"There's the Hastingses' dining room table," Wyatt says, pointing. "You'd think they woulda put it to use." I know what he means. Coffins have been constructed from sideboards and wagon beds, from crates and boxes and anything else people had. The Hastingses' table could have provided proper burial for three grown men, including the hired man who died of cholera driving their wagon.

The Hastingses hauled the damn thing across the Platte in their huge Conestoga, only to decide they weren't hauling it a step farther. Their hired man—the one still living—shoved it out onto the prairie, bidding it good riddance as he tossed out six tufted chairs to keep it company. Someone thought it amusing to set the table upright and tuck the chairs in around it. Buzzards circle overhead as though waiting for dinner to be served. It is the only good shade for miles, and buzzards or not, I can't continue.

"I gotta stop, Wyatt. Just for a bit," I whisper, but he hears me and has slid from his saddle before I can untie the rope around my waist. I am much bigger than the boy, and he teeters beneath my weight but manages to half drag, half carry me to the abandoned table, pulling out a chair so I can climb beneath it. He shoves something beneath my head, lays my rifle beside me, and forces some water down my throat. I am asleep before I can thank him.

I dream of Charlie and the Pawnee village, of Kettle being bred to Indian ponies and throwing foals with human faces.

"What are you going to do, half man?" an Indian woman asks in my mother's voice.

I don't know what I'm going to do. I don't know. She pats my cheeks, her hands insistent.

"Pïtku ásu'." *Two Feet. Put one foot in front of the other, Two Feet.*

"Mr. Lowry. Mr. Lowry, wake up." Wyatt is trying to rouse me. Memory floods back, and the Indian woman is gone, along with my mother's voice.

"Cikstit karasku?" Wyatt asks. *Are you well?* I peer up at him, disoriented and dry mouthed. Wyatt doesn't speak Pawnee.

"What?" I moan.

"What happened to you, Mr. Lowry? Why are you here?"

It isn't Wyatt. It's Charlie. They are Charlie's hands, and it is Charlie's voice. I reach for my canteen, not sure if it's real, not certain Charlie is real, or if I am still caught in the dream space. Charlie helps me drink, holding my head the way Wyatt did, and the warm slosh of liquid down my throat convinces me I'm awake.

"Where is Wyatt?" I croak. I do not ask in Pawnee, but Charlie seems to understand.

"There is no one here but me and you, Mr. Lowry. Me, you, Dame, and your jack."

Relief washes through me, and I peer beyond him. Kettle is partially hidden behind Dame, but I can see his spindly legs and the tips of his big ears. Dame chuffs and extends her long nose toward me in greeting.

"They came back to the fort, back to their friends," Charlie continues in Pawnee. "Captain Dempsey said something must have happened to you, and he said I should bring them back across the Platte, just in case you were looking for them. When I saw you, I thought you were dead. This is a strange lodge." He pats the table with a cheeky grin.

"And my mules? Any sign of my mules?"

"No." Charlie shakes his head. "What has happened to you?" he asks again. "Where is your train?"

"Help me stand," I plead, and Charlie shoves the table out of the way so he can get above me. He wraps his arms around my chest and hoists me up, grunting a little at our mismatched size. He is probably the age of Wyatt but several inches shorter and much leaner.

"Is that your . . . Wyatt?" Charlie asks, pointing to a rider racing toward us, ringed in dust and leading a mule. For a moment I think I am seeing double, then treble, and beyond him the cloud grows as if he leads an army.

"How many men do you see?" I ask Charlie. He begins to whoop and dance, waving his arms, and I cling to the table, trying to make sense of what I'm seeing.

"I see many, many men, Mr. Lowry. The warriors have returned!" Charlie yells, and my breaths turn to fire.

"Where the hell is Wyatt?" I mutter.

And then I realize I'm looking at him.

From a distance it almost appears as if he leads the charge, but upon closer inspection, it becomes obvious that he is fleeing from the Pawnee, riding Trick and leading Tumble, who are running full out toward the water, more terrified by the presence behind them than by the long stretch of river laid out in front of them. I straighten, drawing my rifle up beside me, resting it on the table so it can be seen.

"Charlie! Take my horse. Ride out to meet them. Tell them I am a friend."

Charlie doesn't argue but fists his hands in Dame's mane, swings himself onto her back, and races toward the riders barreling toward us. Poor Wyatt must think he is being cut off. He shouts my name, and I wave my rifle, trying to reassure him.

Kettle brays in terror.

"Whoa, Kettle," I demand. "It's Trick and Tumble. We know Trick and Tumble." But it is not just Trick and Tumble, and Kettle brays and kicks up his heels. I beg him to go easy. If he decides to bolt, I don't have the strength to stop him.

For a moment, I fear for Charlie, running toward his people on a borrowed horse and wearing a cavalry cap, but he is yipping with the confidence of family, and the band of Pawnee braves begins to pull up, abandoning their hard pursuit of Wyatt, though they do not stop completely.

Wyatt reaches me, sliding from Trick without coming to a complete stop. He's lost his hat, but somehow he's kept his seat and control of Trick and Tumble, who are shuddering to escape the band of Pawnee coming over the rise.

"They've got your mules, John," Wyatt pants. "And I don't think they're inclined to give them back." I am proud of the boy. He hasn't lost his wits or his tongue, though his face is slicked with sweat and his eyes are wide with fear. Together, we watch them approach, not speaking, not plotting, just waiting for whatever is to come.

The Pawnee are bloodied, and their ponies are coated in dust. Across the backs of three of the ponies are slung the bodies of their dead. Charlie is no longer celebrating, no longer smiling. He calls out to me in his language, and the warriors around him frown in confusion. They do not know what to make of me. No one ever does.

"John Lowry, this is Chief Dog Tooth. My uncle. He has found your mules," Charlie calls, and the man called Dog Tooth grunts and scowls at me. I don't think he agrees with Charlie's statement of ownership. His head is shaved but for a protrusion of matted black hair that bursts forth from a single patch on the top of his head. His eyes rove to and fro, taking me in, assessing my strength. He sniffs at me and puffs out his chest.

"Kirikî râsakitâ?" Dog Tooth asks. *What is your tribe?*

"Pawnee *tat*," I answer. "But I have no village. No people. No squaw. Only those mules." I point at the seven mules, ticking them off in my head. Boomer, Budro, Samson, Delilah, Gus, Jasper, and Judy. I sold Tug, Lasso, Lucky, Coal, and Pepper to Captain Dempsey.

"We found them," Dog Tooth says.

"I know. But they are mine. The boy will tell you." I do not call him Charlie. I don't know if it is simply the name Captain Dempsey has given him, and I don't want to insult him with a white man's name in front of his chief.

Charlie slides off my horse and leads her to me, but he does not attempt to gather my mules.

"My nephew tells me you trade with the Dempsey," Dog Tooth says. He pronounces the name *Dempsey* with the emphasis on the second syllable, like the captain is a great body of water, the Demp Sea, and not just a barrel-bellied man running a fort in the middle of nowhere.

"Yes. For many years. But I am going west now. With my mules."

"They are our mules now, John Loudee," argues a brave with the same protrusion of hair as his chief and a fresh scalp hanging from his spear. Someone calls him Skunk, and it is fitting. The *r* of my name becomes a soft *d* on his Pawnee tongue, but Wyatt recognizes that I have been challenged, and I see him inching toward the gun on his saddle.

I touch Wyatt's arm and shake my head. I will not let this descend into a shootout. Wyatt is not going to die today. No one is going to die today.

"They carry my mark," I say. The Lowry brand is small and obscure, a chicken track on the left flank, a simple *JL*, the *J* hanging on the back of the larger *L*. But I point it out on Dame and Kettle and then, using my rifle to support me, walk among my mules, touching my brand on each of them. They bow in shamed welcome. They ran away and now want rescue, but I will be lucky to leave with my life, not to mention my mules.

"Dempsey knows these are my mules. The boy knows they are my mules." I point at Charlie. "If you take them, Dempsey will know you took them from me. That will not be good for your people."

"We left many Sioux dead in the grass. We are not afraid of the Sioux, and we aren't afraid of Demp Sea," Dog Tooth says, but his braves are silent around him, and I wonder if they are simply bone weary or they know he lies. They do not look like victors, and I am fearful that they will consider my mules the only spoils of war available to them.

"You are weak," Dog Tooth says to me, noting my pallor and my ginger movements.

"I am sick. While I was sick, my mules were scattered."

"So maybe you will die anyway," Skunk yells, and the men around him grunt and snicker.

"Maybe I will. But I'm not going to die today. And those are my mules," I say.

"We have just gone to battle with our enemies, the Sioux. We don't want to go to battle with Demp Sea," Charlie says, anxious, and the braves grow quiet again. I hope the boy has not drawn the ire of his chief.

"I will give you one mule. You choose," I say to the chief. "My gift to you for finding my animals."

"What about those mules?" Dog Tooth points at Trick and Tumble. "They are not your mules. They do not bear your mark."

"They are his mules." I nod toward Wyatt.

"If we take his mules, Dempsey will not care," Skunk says. Dog Tooth raises his hand to silence the brave. Then he holds up his pinky and his ring finger, sign talk for two.

"You give me one . . . and he gives me one. Two mules. One from each of you. And you will not die today." The chief looks at Wyatt, who has not understood a word of the negotiation.

"I cannot give you another man's mules," I say.

Dog Tooth is defiant, shaking his head so his thatch of hair dances above him.

Two. He enunciates the word with his fingers once more. Charlie is still standing next to Dame, and I ask him to lead her back to his chief.

"Do you like my horse?" I ask Dog Tooth.

He grunts. "I like the horse." His expression is stony, but Charlie gasps.

"I will give you the horse." The words pain me, and I can hardly look at Dame. Skunk crows, his enthusiasm for the trade apparent. Dame is a beautiful horse, and the mules, for all their worth, do not inspire the same enthusiasm.

"I will take the horse . . . and one mule," the chief insists, showing me two fingers like I am slow.

I run my hands down Dame's sides and across her belly, feeling my way, making a great presentation of my movements. I tell Charlie to run his hands down her flanks and up her sides too, though he won't be able to feel anything. It is for show.

"After the snows, she will foal. And you will have your mule," I tell Dog Tooth, raising two fingers. "One horse. One mule."

"You lie," Dog Tooth says.

"I don't. The donkey is the sire." I nod at Kettle. "I've bred them before. I traded the foal to Captain Dempsey last year." He was a beauty too, tawny and strong, with dark legs and a dark face. I bred Kettle to Dame in late March, when her season began, in hopes of another. It will be months before I know for sure if it was successful. But the indications are there. Dame refused another go-round before I left St. Joe—a sure sign—and she hasn't shown signs of estrus ever since.

It will be better to leave her behind. I know that. The rigors of the next three months would be hard on her and the unborn foal. But I could not bear to part with her. Now I must.

I make the sign of a good trade, keeping my eyes averted from my horse.

Dog Tooth nods and returns the sign. He tells Charlie to mount Dame, and Charlie obeys, his eyes clinging to my face. Without another word, the Pawnee chief spurs his pony forward toward the Platte, and his men follow, leaving me, Wyatt, and our mules behind.

NAOMI

Webb rides at the front of the train with Mr. Abbott, sitting up beside him in his wagon to be on the lookout for John's mules. We remain at the back, doing the same. Ruts stretch across the plain. One has only to follow them to know where to go and where we've been, but I leave pictures behind, a trail of them, skewering them into the ground with sticks. It is foolish, but I can see the bits of white as I look back. The wind will take them away. The rain too, when it storms again. But I want John and Wyatt to know which ruts are ours.

We follow the road for four miles until we reach a place called Buffalo Creek and then continue alongside the water for about three miles before we camp. Mr. Abbott blows his horn, indicating quitting time, and the wagons begin to circle around a spot of green that hasn't been thoroughly trampled and eaten down by earlier herds and trains. My eyes ache from searching the horizon all afternoon. We've seen no sign of John's animals, and my anger hasn't abated.

There are no trees, but we pull a little driftwood from the water, collecting it for future use. It'll do us no good tonight, but the willow bushes provide enough fuel to make a fire. I boil some water for coffee and begin to make stew from salt pork and potatoes, hoping the light will guide Wyatt and John to us. I prepare dinner with my back to the rest of the train, my eyes to the east, watching; I cannot bear to look upon anything else.

If I squint, the long grass to the north shivers and sways like waves on the sea. Pa still talks about Massachusetts and living near the ocean. I imagine it's one of the reasons he wants to go to California. He was born in Massachusetts, but his family moved to New York when he was ten and then to Pennsylvania when he was thirteen, trying to find work on lands that had to be cleared and farms that didn't produce enough to make a good living. When Pa was eighteen, his father moved the family to Illinois, where Pa met Ma. Pa says in Massachusetts there are great lighthouses that sit in the bays, signaling to the ships on the water.

There are no lighthouses on the prairie and no ships in sight. No Wyatt, no John, no loose mules or horses either.

"Make enough stew for the Caldwells too, Naomi," Ma says, moving up behind me. Her voice is soft, but I hear her strain. She's been watching the waves too.

"What happened to Lawrence Caldwell reaping what he sows?" I mutter.

"Only God decides when and how the reaping comes. That has nothing to do with us. We worry about what *we're* sowing."

"I can live with that . . . just as long as the reaping is slow and painful and I get to watch," I say.

"Naomi," Ma scolds, but I don't apologize. Ma is a better woman than I am. Or maybe she doesn't want to invite God's wrath with her thoughts of vengeance while Wyatt is in need of His blessing.

"Jeb and Adam and Elmeda could use some looking after," Ma adds softly, "whether you think Lawrence is deserving or not."

"I'll make enough, Ma," I relent, but when she moves away, I whisper, "Are you watching, Lord? I'm doing a good deed, so I'd like one in return."

Adam and Jeb are grateful for the stew and thank me kindly, eating with fervor, their eyes on their bowls and their hands filled with bread. I know Mr. Caldwell is hungry too, but he turns his back to me and folds his arms, as if I am invisible to him. I don't bother to make myself seen. I simply climb in the back of his wagon to check on Elmeda, prepared to spoon the supper into her mouth if I have to. Her eyes are open this time, but her hands are folded in the same position, and she won't take the spoon I offer. Her hair is matted and in need of a wash, and she hasn't changed her dress since Lucy's burial.

"You're going to eat, Elmeda," I say, folding myself beside her on Lucy's little wooden chest. It is filled with all her favorite things.

"I don't want to eat," Elmeda whispers, and I am encouraged that she is talking at all.

"I know you don't. But Jeb wants you to eat. He's lost his brother and his sister, and now his mama is carrying on. So you can do it for him if you don't want to do it for me."

Mention of Jeb makes tears rise in her eyes. Elmeda loves her children, all of them, but she still won't raise her gaze to mine.

"I'll help you. And then I'm going to brush your hair. You'll feel better when I'm done." I prop her up, pulling the pillows beneath her head so I can feed her without choking her. She lolls against me like a rag doll, but I hear her stomach gurgle and know she is hungry.

"I'm not asking you to talk. I'm not asking you to look at me. I'm asking you to eat."

She still doesn't look at me, but she opens her mouth when I hold the spoon to her lips, letting me shovel little bites onto her tongue. When the bowl is empty, I help her drink a little water, and then I brush her hair and rebraid it, talking to her softly as I do, telling her what a beautiful evening it is and how full the moon is going to be. When I'm done, Elmeda rolls over, turning her back to me.

"I brought you something, Elmeda. I thought you could put it in Lucy's chest with her things. When we get to California, you can put it in a frame and hang it on the wall of your new house. That way Lucy can be there with you . . . and you can look at her every day."

Elmeda doesn't respond or roll back toward me. I set the drawing of Lucy, the one I made on her wedding day, on the blanket she has pulled over herself.

I leave her like that, hiding beneath the covers from a world she's not ready to face, but as I climb down from the wagon, I hear the crinkling of the page and know she's just been waiting for me to go. I've only taken a few steps beyond the Caldwells' wagon when the crying starts. Great gulping sobs rip from Elmeda's throat, and I press my hand to my heart, willing my compassion to leave me be. I have no strength for it. Adam and Jeb stare at me, and Jeb rises, handing me their empty bowls. Either they wiped every last taste with their tongues or they've rinsed them clean. Ma was right. They were hungry and needed supper.

"Thank you, Naomi," Jeb says. I nod, distracting myself with the dishes and swooping up the empty stewpot that someone has finished off.

"Crying is better than silence," Jeb says. "Don't worry. I'll look after her."

I nod again, and without a word for Mr. Caldwell, I hurry back to my own fire, as far from Elmeda Caldwell's sobs as I can get. And I continue to watch for John and Wyatt.

With the moon so huge and high, the prairie is lit up well enough to travel. Some members of the train want to resume walking after supper to make up for lost days, but Abbott appeals to the men—who have gathered in council without us womenfolk—to hold up one more night to let the ill rest, as well as those who've been tending to them. He doesn't mention Wyatt and John, but he's added another guard to the rotation to make sure no one else's animals turn up missing. I hear Pa telling Ma everything that was discussed, the way he always does.

I pitch John's tent in case he comes back in the middle of the night, but when dawn comes, I have to take it down again.

Breakfast is cleared, and the oxen are yoked in when Webb begins to shout. "I see 'em. I see Wyatt and Mr. Lowry and the mules!"

I begin to run, following Webb's voice, shading my eyes against the glare of the rising sun. I hear Webb clambering down from the wagon box behind me, where he's been on lookout since dawn, but I am the first to reach them.

John is listing in the saddle, Wyatt too, and for a minute I can't tell who is who. They are both riding mules, and Wyatt is wearing John's black felt hat, though beneath it his cheeks are scarlet. His jaw is clenched, and his hands are fisted tight in Trick's wiry mane. He's exhausted, fighting for control of his emotions. John lifts his head enough to greet us, but he can't dismount by himself. I reach for him, not caring who's watching, but Wyatt is suddenly there beside me, his arms upraised, and together we pull John down, supporting him between us.

"Where's Dame, John? Didn't ya find Dame?" Webb asks, incredulous, looking over the mules. Will and Pa and Warren have come running. Ma too, and Warren and Will start herding the animals toward the water.

"We found her," Wyatt says, and his voice cracks with emotion. "But I lost my hat. John made me wear his."

"Where is she, John?" Webb presses, his chin starting to wobble.

John doesn't answer, and I'm not sure he's completely conscious of anything but his feet and the next step. Wyatt speaks for him.

"Some Pawnee braves found the mules. They wanted two of them. One of mine, one of John's. But John wouldn't let 'em go. He gave 'em Dame instead."

"Dame's livin' with the Indians now?" Webb cried.

"Shh, Webb. It's all right," John mutters. "It's better this way."

"What took you so long? I thought you was never comin' back!" Webb howled, giving voice to everyone's feelings. It has been a long twenty-four hours.

"We had to go slow, almost as slow as the oxen do, 'cause John could hardly stay in the saddle," Wyatt says. "But he did. He did, and we made it. And we got the mules."

"That's right. You're here now," Ma says, patting Wyatt's sunburned cheeks.

"You did good, Wyatt," John murmurs. "I'm proud of you." And Wyatt can only nod, his tears creating dirty stripes across the red.

"You're all grown up, Wyatt. All grown up," Ma whispers. "And you're a fine man."

∞

John rides in the back of Warren's wagon for two days, too weak to do much but sleep and eat the little bit of mush I force upon him. Pa says if I am going to spend so much time alone with him, he's going to ask the deacon to marry us.

I tell Pa, "Fine with me," and that shuts Pa right up. I sit with John as much as I can, trying to draw as we lurch along.

"We found one of your pictures, me and Wyatt," John says softly, and I raise my eyes from the page.

"I left five or six. Maybe more."

"Why?"

"I was leaving you a trail," I say. "Silly, I know. But it felt wrong to just go on without you. People leave signs and mile markers. I left pictures." I shrug.

"I wish I'd found them all."

"They weren't my best. I had no trouble parting with them."

We are quiet for a moment, me drawing, John's eyes closed.

"Do you know the problem with your pictures?" he says after a while.

"What?" I think he's going to criticize the many I have drawn of him.

"None of them are of you," he answers.

John does not flirt. He doesn't say pretty, empty things. He listens, soaking everything in. John's a doer. An observer. And his thoughts, when he shares them, are like little shoots of green grass on a dry prairie. The flowers on the prickly pears that grow among the rocks.

"I've never tried to draw myself," I muse. "I'm not sure I could. It's hard for me to summon my own face to my mind's eye."

"I would like a picture of you," he says, and I am touched by the soft sincerity in his voice. "I would like many pictures of you," he adds.

"You can look at me whenever you like." I realize I sound coquettish and cover my mouth, wishing I could take the words back. "You know what I mean," I amend.

"Not anytime I want."

"You can look at me now." I stick out my tongue and pull out my ears, trying to make myself look as homely as I can. John just raises his eyebrows, but the silliness eases the tension that always starts to build inside of me when I'm with him. I sigh, letting it out in a whoosh.

"If I were to draw a picture of myself . . . for you . . . would you want a portrait . . . or a place? Would you want a picture on the trail or perched on Trick? Or bouncing around in this awful wagon?" I ask.

"All of those would be just fine."

I shake my head and laugh.

"I want a picture of you sitting on a barrel in a yellow dress and a white bonnet in the middle of a crowded street," he says, looking up at me.

It takes me a minute to remember. When I do, my nose smarts and my eyes sting, but I smile down at him.

"I'm gonna sleep now," he says, closing his eyes.

I spend the next hour sketching the day we met, imagining myself the way he described me, but when I'm done, the arrested expression on my face reflects the way I felt when I saw him standing there beneath the eaves of the haberdashery, his arms full of packages, his stance wide, and his eyes unflinching, watching me. One long gaze, one meeting of our eyes, and I was caught. I haven't been able to look away since.

Just like I did with Elmeda, I leave the drawing on his blanket for him to find.

8

THE SANDY BLUFFS

NAOMI

The bluffs are soft with sand, and the travel is slow, but we have no trouble finding water, though we veer north one day to avoid a swamp, hugging the low bluffs that extend for miles, only to swing south again when the bluffs push us back toward the Platte. In some spots there is ample timber, which we need for our fires, but no water for our teams. In other spots there is good water but nothing but sage or willow bushes to burn.

We hoard kindling and branches when we can; I threw a felled branch into Warren's wagon at Elm Creek when Mr. Abbott warned us about the difficulty of finding timber on the road ahead, but the branch was infested with tiny insects. By the time we stopped for the night, the bugs had burrowed into the bedrolls and blankets. The branch made a great fire, but I had to beat the bugs out of the bedding with the broom, and even then we all had bites for days after.

Maybe it was the bugs in the bedding, but John returned to riding, his mules strung out behind him, after only a couple of days in the wagon. By the time we reach the junction where the Platte forks into two, North and South, he shows no sign of having been laid low.

Elmeda Caldwell decides to rejoin the living as well and slinks into our camp, lonely without her Lucy. It's not pleasant to be a lone woman among men, and Ma and I welcome her after supper one night. Elmeda holds baby Wolfe for the first time, swaying to soothe him as Ma mends a hole and I sketch the dense grove across the river. Some say it's Ash Hollow, marked on the emigrant guide we bought in St. Joe, though none of us can tell what kind of trees they are from this distance. On the north side, where we are making our way, there is only a single solitary cedar, its branches thinned by earlier trains desperate for wood. It is the saddest-looking tree I've ever seen, standing all alone, with nothing but plains and sky and a lazy river winding beside it. There are initials scratched in the trunk, man's unending need to mark our presence. *I was here. I AM here. This is proof.*

I'm surprised the tree has survived so long. Standing alone has made it a target, and eventually, all the attention will destroy it.

"Mr. Abbott tells us we won't see another tree for two hundred miles," Elmeda says, her eyes on my sketch.

"I've never seen such a lonely place," I say, making conversation.

"It is that. It makes a soul feel lost," Ma says on a long sigh.

"You and Adam are both alone, Naomi," Elmeda says softly. "Maybe you could . . . help . . . each other. Marriages have been built on less."

My hand stills, but I don't raise my head.

"Adam might need a little time, Elmeda," Ma says, leaving me out of it.

"But . . . time is the one thing we don't have," Elmeda says. "Lucy and Abigail proved that. Gone in the twinkling of an eye." She swallows, trying to control her emotion.

"Well then, we best spend it with people of our choosing," Ma replies. I say nothing, but I don't need to. Elmeda knows full well that Adam is not my choice.

"He's got his eye on the deacon's daughter anyway," Elmeda says, defensive at my silence. "Lydia Clarke."

Lydia Clarke came sniffing around Warren too, but Warren was ill. He wouldn't have noticed anyway. Warren's body is on the mend, but his spirit keeps tripping back to the Big Blue, where Abigail lies.

"She's as brazen as you are with Mr. Lowry, Naomi." Elmeda sniffs. "Lucy wasn't even in the ground one day when Lydia started offering to mend Adam's socks and wash his clothes."

"Mr. Lowry washes my clothes as well," I say, my eyes on my page, drawing a coiled snake beneath the trees wearing Elmeda's bonnet. "In fact, he washed all our clothes, didn't he, Ma?"

Ma begins to laugh, the sound pealing like bells on the wind, and after a moment Elmeda laughs too, the resentment falling from her grief-lined face. I grin up at them both, squinting against the setting sun.

"Brazen," Elmeda says again, but the judgment is gone, and I turn the snake into a rose.

We say nothing for a time, but when Elmeda lays a sleeping Wolfe into Ma's arms and turns to go, she looks at me with a sad finality.

"I have been mourning you, Naomi. When Daniel died, we lost you too, and now Lucy is gone."

I abandon my sketch to embrace her, not knowing what else to do, and she cries on my shoulder, her graying hair tickling my nose and brushing my cheeks.

"Thank you, Naomi," she whispers, her chin wobbling as she finally pulls away.

"Come be with us whenever you need to, Elmeda," Ma says, and Elmeda promises she will. She brings Adam and Jeb with her too, eating supper at our fire, but Mr. Caldwell keeps his distance. He watches John with suspicion, as if John is the one to fear.

One day, we noon at a creek called Raw Hide, named for a white man who was skinned alive after he killed a squaw with a babe in her arms.

Elmeda gasps as Abbott tells the tale, and Mr. Caldwell shakes his head. "Savages," he says. "All of 'em." And he looks at John.

"Who is the bigger savage?" Abbott asks. "The man who kills a young mother or the man who makes him suffer for it? Seems to me he got what he deserved. Justice is a little swifter out here, Mr. Caldwell. We might not skin folks alive, but plenty of trains have happily hung men in their companies accused of killing."

"What about stealing? Or setting another man's stock loose?" Wyatt asks, but Pa sends him off to fill the water barrels, and his question goes unanswered. My brothers are almost as defensive of John as I am, and they all believe Lawrence Caldwell got away with a crime. They also blame him for the loss of Dame.

Wyatt told us the story of the trade as best he could without knowing all that was said, telling us about the bloodied warriors and the hostility he felt, the certainty that he and John were going to be stripped of their animals or their lives.

John does not talk about it at all, but it bothers me greatly.

"I'm going to get you another horse," I promise him one night, bringing him a bowl of beans and a loaf of bread, then lingering by his fire while he eats it.

"You are?" he asks, smiling a little. "Are you going to draw me one?"

"No. I don't know when, and I don't know how, but I'm going to get you another horse, just as good as Dame."

"That might be hard to do. She was a good horse," he says softly, his eyes searching the stars too. "It was Caldwell who ran my animals off. Abbott warned me about him. He doesn't want me here."

"I know. And that's my fault. So I'm going to find a way to replace her."

"How was it your fault?" John asks.

"He was trying to hurt me by getting rid of you."

"Mr. Caldwell?" he asks.

"Yes."

"Getting rid of me . . . that would hurt you?" he asks.

"It would hurt me."

He is silent for several heartbeats, thinking that over, finishing off his supper.

"You are like Jennie," he says, his voice odd.

"I am?" I gasp. "The white woman who raised you?"

"Yes."

"How am I like Jennie?" I'm not sure the comparison pleases me.

"You are very stubborn."

"Says the man who loves mules." I shrug.

He laughs, startled. I seem to startle him a lot. "I do love mules."

"Do you love Jennie?" I ask. I don't want to remind him of someone he dislikes.

"Yes. But I don't understand her."

"What is it you don't understand?"

"She loves my father."

"Your father didn't seem all that hard to love."

"He is cold. I am afraid I am like him." John sounds as if he is warning me away. "Why would Mr. Caldwell want to hurt you?" he asks, changing the subject. His eyes cling to the darkness beyond the wagons as though he is not intent on my answer, but I am not fooled.

"I haven't grieved enough," I say, my voice flat.

His eyes swing back and hold mine for several breaths.

"Was he like his father?" he asks, and it takes me a moment to catch up.

"Who?"

125

"Your husband. Daniel. Was he like his father?" He is not looking at me again.

"I would say no . . . but I'm not sure if that is true. Maybe he would have become like his father. I don't think we knew each other very well. Not deep down. We were children together, but we weren't . . . grown . . . together. Then he was gone, and the growing and learning ended."

"It's hard to truly know someone," John whispers.

"Yes. It is." I nod. I feel like I hardly even know myself.

"But still . . . you married Daniel."

"We were friends. We were fond of each other. And there was no one else. It was a very . . . obvious thing to do." I want to defend myself further, but I stop. John knows what kind of world we live in. Women and men marry. It is survival. It is life. I have no doubt Warren will marry again. Adam Hines too. It is simply the way of things.

"You do not know me either, Naomi," he says, challenging me, using my words against me. "Not deep down."

"But I *want* to," I say, enunciating each word. "I want to know you. Deep down. How many people do you truly want to know?"

"I can't think of any," he admits, reluctant to concede the point. And I can't help but laugh.

"I can't either," I say. "It's too hard. I'd rather draw faces than know what's going on behind them. But I don't feel that way about you. I want to know you."

He begins to nod, and I'm encouraged to ask, "Do you want to know me, John?"

"Yes, Naomi," he murmurs. "I want to know you."

And that is enough for me.

∽

We settle into a weary acceptance of life on the trail; I call it the daze of endless days, but death has fallen behind us, perhaps wearied by our plodding steps, and we pass two merciful weeks without digging a grave or counting a loss.

I am happy.

It is a peculiar thing, being happy when life is so hard and dirty and tiresome that every day feels like a war and every night I sleep on a bed so hard my skin is as bruised as my face is freckled. I have never known such utter and complete exhaustion, and yet . . . I am happy. Ma gave Wolfe life, but he is mine in a way that I can't put into words. Maybe it is all the time I spend caring for him or the responsibility I feel for him. Maybe it's a continuation of the love I have for Ma, who is too weak and tired to mother him alone, but he is mine, and my arms feel empty when he's not in them.

The boys mother him too; it's like he's always been ours, waiting eagerly on the other side of transcendence for his turn to be a May, and now that he's here, none of us can remember life without him. He smiles—Ma says I was a smiler early on, just like him—and he's so aware and bright eyed, kicking his legs and moving his mouth when we talk to him, like he's trying to talk back. Webb hovers only inches above his face and has long one-sided conversations with him, telling him about the mules and the horses and California, and Wolfe just seems to soak it all in.

Still, as sweet as he is, as good as he is, he doesn't want to settle at night. Maybe it's the constant rocking of the wagon that lulls him to sleep during the day, but at bedtime, Ma and I take turns walking him so he doesn't keep the whole company awake.

Some nights I walk to where John keeps watch—he always takes the first shift—and sit beside him, letting Wolfe fuss where no one can hear him, and we talk of stars and simple things. He's taught me some Pawnee words. He doesn't call Wolfie by his name, even though he chose it. He calls him *Skee dee*—the Pawnee word for *wolf*. And there are plenty of them. We've seen signs of the buffalo, their chips and skulls bleached white in the sandy swales, but our most frequent guests are the wolves. They lurk on the ridges and follow the trail, and Ma has dreams that they'll drag Wolfie away.

One night, so weary I cannot stay awake, I fall asleep in the grass with Wolfe in my arms and wake without him. For a moment I don't know where I am or how long I have slept. I can't remember if it was I who held him last. I jump to my feet, noting John's blanket around my shoulders, and I see his silhouette against the blue-tinged darkness. I almost cry out, caught in Ma's nightmare. Then I see the smooth line of Wolfe's head bobbing against John's shoulder, an occasional hiccup blending with the lowing of the cattle and the whisper of night sounds all around. He walks with him, talking softly in a language I can't understand, pointing at the sky and the cows, the moon and the mules, and I am overcome with grateful awe.

John is careful. He says little and rests even less. Maybe his quietude is simply the wear of long days and short sleeps, and I don't know if he shares the same comfort in my presence that I feel in his, but I think he does. I feel more than comfort. I feel fascination and fondness and a desire to follow wherever he goes. I want to hear his thoughts. I want to look at him.

He does not touch me. He does not take my hand or sit as close as I'd like him to. Not since the day in his tent when he told me I was beautiful has he indicated how he feels, and I can only guess that his words of admiration were delirium, caused by his illness. But when I seek his company, he does not ask me to go, and when the night is deep and the camp is quiet, he talks to me. And though we do not speak of love or a life together, I am happy. I know it's wrong to be so when Warren and Elmeda are so lonely and Ma is so worn. But John makes me happy, little Wolfe makes me happy, and my happiness makes me strong.

"How old are you, John?" I ask him one night.

"I don't know. I think I am probably twenty-five or twenty-six."

"You think? You don't know when you were born?"

"No."

"Not even the season? Your mother didn't tell you anything?"

"I think it must have been winter. There was snow on the ground. She said when she rose from her bed after my birth, there was a single set of footprints around the lodge. The tracks were odd, like a man wearing two different shoes, and they weren't deep even though the snow came to her knees. She followed them a ways, and they just suddenly stopped." He is silent for a moment, contemplating.

"Who was it?" I press.

"She never discovered, but it is how I got my name."

"Two Feet. Pítku ásu'." I've been practicing.

"Yes."

"Tell me about her," I say.

"I don't remember very much," he says, quiet.

"What was her name?"

"My father called her Mary. The whites she worked for called her Mary too."

"Son of Mary, walking on the water," I whisper, thinking of Ma's dream.

"Her people called her Dancing Feet. So I suppose I have a . . . part . . . of her name."

"Why Dancing Feet?"

"When she was young, she sat too close to the fire, and the edge of her blanket caught a spark that quickly became a flame. Instead of screaming and letting the blanket go, she stamped the blaze out with her feet."

"Like a dance."

"Yes. That is the way most names come about. Some of the children don't have names until they are half-grown."

"But you did," I say.

"Yes. I did."

"Did she look like you?"

"I don't know. I can't really remember her face." He turns his palms up helplessly. "I don't think so. I look like my father. He never doubted I was his. But . . . I think I might have her mouth. She did not smile much, but when she did, her lips would rise higher on one side. She had a crooked smile."

I want to press for details, needing to see her in my mind so I can create her on paper, but I hold myself back, letting him study the sky in silence, searching his memory.

"Her hair was heavy . . . like a great rope. Or maybe it just seemed that way to me because I was small. I would stand behind her and put my hands in it, like it was the mane of a pony, and I would pretend to ride. Sometimes she would carry me on her back, but most of the time she would sit, her legs crossed, her hands in her lap, her body bowed forward so I could lean into her and hold on to her hair. More than once she fell asleep that way, nodding away as I pretended to ride. Then I would climb into the nest of her lap and go to sleep too."

When I give him a picture of a nodding Indian girl, a little boy at her back with his hands in her hair, a suggestion of a horse transposed over the top of them, he doesn't say anything, but he swallows, his throat working up and down. He rolls it into a scroll and wraps it with the others I've given him in a piece of cloth soaked in linseed oil and dried to make it resistant to water, and when he looks up to find me watching, he gives me one of his mother's crooked smiles.

JOHN

Five hundred miles from where we began, the formations begin to rise up out of the earth, gnarled and notched like ancient parapets washed in a layer of sand and time, abandoned castles that have become part of the landscape. We reach the Ancient Bluffs first, and a group of us scrambles up one of the cliffs after we've made camp. Webb manages to disturb a nest of rattlesnakes concealed in a cleft and comes running, his bare feet hardly touching the ground. I kill a few, skin them, and give Webb their rattles, warning him to keep them away from the animals. Naomi fries the rattlesnakes with a little oil and onions. The May boys all swear it's the best thing they've ever eaten, though I think they're only trying to be brave. We haven't had any fresh meat, though every now and then someone puts up a shout of an elk sighting and there's a great stampede out onto the prairie in pursuit.

We still haven't seen a single buffalo, though we've been told tales of herds so deep and wide that they cover miles at a time and flatten everything in their path. We haven't seen the buffalo, and we haven't seen any Indians, not since Fort Kearny. Wyatt says he never wants to see an Indian again unless it's Charlie, who is talked about in hushed tones of reverence. Webb even thanks the Lord for him when the Mays pray at suppertime. Webb regularly gives thanks for me too, but I'm not sure if he does that just to make me feel welcome when I consent to eat with the family, which isn't all that often.

On the opposite side of the Platte, we can see Courthouse Rock, which recalls gladiators and Roman soldiers in a world completely removed from my own. I will have to tell Jennie when I write another letter. She read me *Julius Caesar*, and I was struck by the duplicity of the senate and the disloyalty among friends, all for power. Jennie just raised her eyes from the book and warned me quietly, "Always watch your back, John Lowry. People haven't changed all that much since then. Almost two thousand years, and our hearts are the same." She turned to Proverbs then and read a scripture, a version of which she made me and my sisters memorize. "These are the things the Lord hates. A proud look, a lying tongue, hands that shed innocent blood, a heart that devises wicked plans. Feet that are swift in running to evil, a false witness who speaks lies, and one who sows discord among brethren."

We pass Chimney Rock the next day, its stovepipe handle shooting up into a cloudless sky, and Scott's Bluff the next, all named by intrepid trappers and explorers who lived to tell about their adventures and make maps for treasure hunters and westward pioneers. One after the other, we trundle past monuments to the distance we've traveled and markers of the miles we have yet to go. I find myself wondering what their other names might be. What do the Sioux and the Pawnee call the landmarks? At the Ancient Bluffs, among the names carved by emigrants, we find figures engraved on the rock as well, figures no white man made.

Naomi has little interest in documenting things as they are. Instead, she draws a towering Chimney Rock with Webb perched on the steeple, Jail Rock with Lawrence Caldwell imprisoned inside—it makes me laugh in spite of myself—and Courthouse Rock, the size of a toadstool, being held in the palm of her mother's hand. I tell her the landscape is making her see things, fanciful things, like a young Indian brave on a vision quest, in search of his destiny.

She seems fascinated by the notion and asks me if I believe in such things. When I don't answer, she tells me about her mother's dreams. She tells me her mother has seen me walking on the water in a feathered headdress, and I put my hand over her lips and shake my head. She falls silent immediately, her mouth warm against my hand.

"Don't imagine I am something I'm not, Naomi."

She nods and I release her, her eyes questioning. It is the only time I have intentionally touched her since she slept at my side when I was sick. The moments we steal when the camp has settled, when she comes to find me, her brother in her arms, are like her pictures. Naomi is a romantic. A dreamer. She sees what others don't, but what she sees, what she draws, is not reality, and our times together have the same otherworldly cast.

I avoid her for several days, jarred by her retelling of her mother's dream. I was raised on the Bible. I know who Jesus is. I don't like the comparison. I also don't like the bird that becomes a man in a headdress. A chief, walking on water. I don't know what it means, and I don't think what it means matters all that much, but it makes me feel like an oddity, something to be examined and exhumed. And that is not what I want to be. Especially not to Naomi.

But my avoidance lasts only as long as I'm not on watch. The moment I'm alone with the herd, the camp quiet, I'm watching for her, and she doesn't disappoint.

I'm cautious when I am with her. I don't get too close. I don't touch her cheeks or her little brown hands. They are so brown from the sun they don't look like they belong to her. I don't try to kiss her. Scaring her away with a kiss didn't work out so well. I didn't end up scaring her at all, but damn if I didn't scare myself. So I keep the space between us, even in the darkness when she walks with Wolfe or makes a nest in the grass.

During the day, we keep our distance, but there is no privacy in the train, and I am too aware of curious stares. Webb is always underfoot, Will too, though I don't mind much. They're good boys, all the Mays. It's like my father said. It's all in the mother; the jack doesn't make much difference. Winifred May is a damn good woman, and William knows it, which is to his credit. The best thing about him is her. I don't care for William much, but I haven't met many men I've especially liked. They're suspicious of me, I'm suspicious of them, and that's the way of it.

Still, I watch Naomi and she watches me, and a train of tired people, gaunt faced and bleary eyed, watches us. I can't help myself. She is too thin. All the women are. The men too, shrunk down to gristle and grit. We don't think about how the food tastes; we just shovel it in, whatever it is. But where others are stooped and skittish, she is slight and straight, shoulders back, eyes steady.

Looking at Naomi makes me feel a little crazy. She matters too much, and I've begun to believe that I might have her, that I might make it all the way to California with my mules and my money and Naomi too. I've begun to hope, and I'm not sure I like the way it feels. It's a little like being thrown from a horse or a green mule and hitting the ground so hard the breath is chased from your chest. For a moment you think you're a goner. Then the air floods back in, and the relief is so strong you just lie there and suck it in.

And you can't suck it in fast enough.

That's what hope feels like: the best air you've ever breathed after the worst fall you've ever taken. It hurts.

Adam Hines pays a few visits to her campfire, along with his mother-in-law, Mrs. Caldwell. His wife has been dead a month, and he's looking for another. I don't think he's a bad man. Just a weak one. Or a typical one. I don't know. The deacon's daughter has let it be known she'll take him on, but she's not as pretty as Naomi. Not as smart or as capable. Not as funny or as fierce. Not by a long shot. So Adam's stopped by to see if Naomi will have him.

I stay away to let her decide, my anger and my painful hope sitting on my shoulders, fighting back and forth. I see how men look at her. Even the married ones. Especially the married ones. Hell, Abbott even looks at her, and he informed me he doesn't have any feeling anymore between his legs.

"Got kicked good and hard by a horse a few years back. Never been the same since," he says. "Can't say I miss it."

I wish I didn't have any feeling between mine. I don't want to be another panting dog, though Naomi doesn't treat me like one. She doesn't give Adam Hines any encouragement. She doesn't give any of the other men her attention or her time. But I will not compete. I will not woo her. And I will not be a spectacle for a train of emigrants who have nothing better to do than watch me watch her. Still, I feel closer to her than I have ever felt to anyone before.

And I've begun to hope.

9

FORT LARAMIE

JOHN

Most evenings, Wyatt or one of the other boys his age—those who do not have wagons to drive—is sent ahead of the train to scout for a place to make camp for the night. He draws the duty again tonight and comes back on Trick half an hour later, racing toward the wagons the way he did when Dog Tooth and fifty Pawnee braves were on his tail. He reports that a band of Indians—men, women, and children, along with their dogs, horses, and tipis—is already camped on the best grass before the slow climb to Fort John, also called Fort Laramie, which we should make on the morrow.

The company is startled by their numbers, and everyone wants to continue on to the fort, afraid to camp nearby in case there is trouble. But the moon is a sliver, and the night will be dark, making travel after sundown difficult. Fort John still lies half a day's journey ahead, and Abbott reassures us that we will have no trouble from the Indians.

"They're Dakotah—Sioux—and they're used to the trains coming through here. They're just as wary of us as we are of them," Abbott says.

They do not appear to be staying long, or maybe, like us, they've just arrived, but they look on in disinterest as we trundle by. They rest from the heat of the day beneath half-erected tipis, the poles they drag behind their packhorses lying about among the skins and supplies.

I've never seen so many fine horses. A sand-colored dun catches my eye, a black dorsal line descending from the top of his head to the tip of his tail, his forelegs wrapped in the same black, like dark-colored stockings that make every step look like he's prancing. He reminds me of Dame in his carriage and coloring, though Dame didn't boast the dun markings.

Webb points to him too, calling out to me from the box seat beside his mother.

"Look at that pretty one, John!" he crows. "Almost as pretty as Dame."

Despite what Abbott says, the Dakotah are not afraid of us at all. We break for the night a half mile from their temporary encampment, a low ridge between us, but a handful of braves and a few war chiefs approach the circle of our wagons an hour later, horses and skins in tow. The Indians are handsome, well nourished, and well appointed, but they demand to be fed. They seem to enjoy the nervous scurrying of the women and the intimidated gazes of the men.

A big Indian, gold bangles streaming from his long hair and wampum layered around his neck, takes an interest in Kettle. I tell him no trade, but he grows more and more adamant, bringing forth one wild pony after another, parading them past, displaying his wealth. I understand little of what he says, though Abbott has appointed me spokesman. The Pawnee and Sioux are not friendly, and my Pawnee tongue is greeted with derision. Otaktay, my knife-wielding half-breed teacher, spoke a mix of Sioux and English that was all his own, and I'm not sure my association with him will help me understand the Dakotah any better.

One of the braves steps forward, claiming he is a Dakotah war chief, an enemy of the Pawnee, but he speaks the language like he once lived among them, maybe as a child, and I wonder if he is a "two-feet" like me. He seems desperate to prove he is not. He says he is the son of the chief, and he will make war on all Pawnee.

He has blackened his face in celebration of taking the scalp off "a Pawnee dog just like me." When I do not react or cower when he dangles the scalp in front of my face, he lunges at me and tries to take my hat. I sidestep his attempt but hand the hat to him. I can get a new one at the fort. Wyatt needs one too; he's been wearing an old straw-brimmed hat that's missing its top. His blond hair has turned white from the sun right at the crown, making him appear to have a bald spot where the hair is bleached. The black-painted brave touches the white spot with the tip of his spear.

"This one is already scalped," he says to me. Wyatt flinches, but he keeps his arms folded, standing at my side like a self-appointed guardian, though I outweigh him by fifty pounds.

Several of the women of the train try to distract the Sioux with food, but though they have demanded to eat, they are not hungry for what we are able to provide. Naomi has brought biscuits and passes them to the Dakotah braves like she is presenting them with a great honor.

They are not impressed, and Black Paint has decided he too wants my Mammoth Jack, though I think he only wants it because I so adamantly refuse. The bangled warrior grows impatient, gathering his ponies as if to leave, but Black Paint stalks back and forth, looking at the cattle and the mules of the cowering emigrants. I don't think he really wants to trade. He is putting on a show of dominance.

Naomi touches her face and then points to his. "Ask him if he has more of his paint, John. Maybe I can give him something he will want more."

I ask, telling him that she wants to honor him with a picture.

Black Paint is made curious by my request; I can see it in the lift of his chin and the dart of his eyes. He turns to his horse and pulls a small pot from his beaded saddlebag. He sets it on the ground and backs away, his arms folded.

"Ask him if I can use his shield."

He hands it over with a deep frown, setting it down beside the paint. The pale skin is strung taut across the willow-branch hoop, and feathers and beads hang from the circlet, but the center is unadorned.

He hisses in protest, and I fear he is going to jerk it back when he sees Naomi's intent; his eyes widen as she sinks down beside the shield, dipping her fingers into the little pot, but his curiosity wins out. Unlike with the pencil, she uses both hands, glancing up at him once or twice, her fingers shading and shaping. Within several seconds his likeness appears, and he grunts in amazement, watching her fingers fly until she straightens, finished. She scoots back from her handiwork and rubs her hands in the stubby buffalo grass to remove the excess paint from her fingers. I pick up the hoop and hand it to Black Paint. He stares at the drawing, flabbergasted, and I know exactly how he feels.

The bangled brave presents his shield next, pointing to the side covered completely in feathers. When Naomi shakes her head, I finger a feather, explaining she can't paint on the feathers. Black Paint tells the bangled brave what I have said, and he turns it over to the other side, which is beaded with a simple *X*. He wants her to paint around it, and she obliges, but when she finishes and he brings her a stack of skins, wanting paintings on all of them, she refuses.

"I want a horse," Naomi says to the bangled one. "I will paint on all these skins for a horse."

"Naomi," I say, shaking my head. I suddenly know what she is trying to do. She has seen the dun—though it is not among the ponies the bangled one has paraded in front of me—and, just like Webb, has noticed the similarities to Dame.

"Tell them," she says.

"No." I am adamant.

Naomi stands up and moves beside me. She points at the bangled brave's horses and then points at herself.

"Naomi," I warn. "You're asking for trouble. Please go back to your wagon."

Black Paint laughs and says something I can't understand to the other Sioux warriors. The bangled brave points at his skins, insistent, but Naomi folds her arms and will not yield.

I tell them we are going to Fort Laramie in the morning, and the painted shields and the food are gifts. I hand him my best blade as well. Then I make the sign for *good*, signifying an end to negotiations, and tell them we don't want to trade, and we do not want a horse. I ask them to take their shields and skins and ponies and leave us.

Amazingly enough, they talk among themselves, and without making any further demands, they mount their horses and withdraw, racing up the ridge and leaving the circle of wagons for their own encampment.

I don't sleep at all, worried that Naomi has made herself a target. Stealing squaws is common among tribes. Recompense is easily made by offering a father something of equal value. Women and horses are the currency. William and Winifred obviously fear the same thing, because William and Warren sit with their backs to their wagon wheels all night, facing the ridge where the Dakotah disappeared.

They are back at dawn, their animals dragging poles bound at either end to support the skins they've piled upon them. But this time it is not a few warriors; it is the whole tribe—their old and their young, their dogs and their ponies, all prepared to follow us to Fort John. Abbott and I walk out to greet them, but Black Paint requests "the woman" and makes the sign for *many* and then *faces*, running his hand over his own features, as he speaks. There is no question that Many Faces is Naomi.

When I tell Abbott, he summons her forward, anxious to keep the peace, but William walks forward with her. His rifle is in his right hand, but he holds it loosely, watching as Black Paint presents Naomi with little pots of paint in red, black, yellow, white, and blue.

Naomi thanks him with a bow of her head. When she tries to retreat again, he raises his voice, indicating he is not finished.

"I will give you a horse," he says to Naomi and points at me, insisting I interpret. He ignores William completely as he continues to speak.

"What is he saying, John?" Naomi asks, her eyes darting between us.

"He wants to give you a horse."

Her eyebrows shoot up, and she smiles. Her smile fades as soon as I tell her the war chief's conditions.

"But he wants something in return. He will give you as many horses as you want, but you have to live with him."

Naomi gasps. She begins shaking her head. I am angry with her for the situation she has put herself in, and Black Paint can tell. He looks at me for a moment and then beckons over his shoulder, calling someone to him. A girl wearing a pale-colored skin, her hair long and unbound, steps forward from the pack. Black Paint summons her closer, impatient. She looks on worriedly, a deep frown on her face, and a young brave lets out a stream of protest, his pony dancing beneath his vehemence. It is all I can do not to groan. The emigrants around us are watching in anxious silence, their oxen yoked, their wagons packed, but no one dares move or draw attention to themselves by pulling out. William and Winifred and all their sons stand a few feet behind me, but Abbott is nowhere in sight.

"She is Pawnee. Like you," Black Paint says to me, pointing at the frightened squaw. "She will not make you angry. I want the woman of many faces. We will trade, and Many Faces can live with me and have many horses."

"She is not my squaw," I say. "I cannot trade her."

I turn to William, but he is already shaking his head, his eyes wide, and I don't have to explain to him what Black Paint is offering.

"He is honored that you want his daughter," I lie, trying my best not to offend. "But she is of great value to her family and these people. Her father will not trade her either. Not for all the horses or all the squaws."

Black Paint frowns but waves the unhappy girl back among the women, and the young brave who has protested on her behalf relaxes.

Black Paint studies us a moment, his eyes swinging back to Naomi several times before he shrugs and fists his hands in his horse's mane like he is preparing to depart.

"It is better for me. White women are not good squaws," he says. He repeats the words in Sioux, and his people laugh.

I don't argue. I say nothing at all. I simply stand still, waiting for his next move. After a moment, he raises his hand, and his people begin to move away, abandoning their negotiations and leaving only the potted paints behind. There is silence in their wake. Men, women, and children huddle in their wagons behind us, peeking out from the little round openings, until the Dakotah have completely departed.

When the band is nothing but a moving line on the horizon, the emigrants erupt in excited chatter, relieved laughter billowing up like campfire smoke. Webb runs to me and hugs my legs, Wyatt hoots, and William claps my back like I have saved the day. Winifred calls me a blessing, Abbott blows his horn to pull out, and all is declared well. But Naomi and I remain frozen in place as the excitement ebbs and the others move away. My anger and my fear have not faded, and I want to chasten her, to make her understand.

"He wanted to trade the girl for you," I tell her.

"I thought so," she murmurs. "What did you say to him?"

"I told him I already have many squaws, and I don't want another." I glare at her and shake my head. It is not what I said to him, and she knows it, but my nerves haven't settled, and my legs are still shaking.

"Would he have really given her away?" she asks, her voice as hollowed out as I feel.

"Yes."

"When you told him no, what did he say?"

"He said white women do not make good squaws."

"Huh," Naomi grunts. "I'm not sure Black Paint would make a very good husband."

I snort despite myself. I am sure Naomi is right.

"Black Paint said he would trade straight across. No horses. Just women. You for her," I scold. She has already begun to relax, as if the event were of no importance. I try to shock her, to take the conversation further than it went in truth. "He was curious about the spots on your nose. He wanted to know if you are spotted all over, like his favorite pony."

"Well, you wouldn't know." She sounds irritated by the fact, and I am immediately hot with outrage and desire. I want to take a switch to her backside. Then I want to hold her tight with no one watching.

"What else did you say?" she asks, impertinent.

"I said your family could not part with you . . . and you were not mine to trade."

She turns her head and looks at me, her eyes leaving the horizon where the Dakotah have disappeared. "I am not yours to trade, John. But I am yours," she says, and I look away, unable to hold her gaze a moment longer. I have no idea what to do with her.

"Will you remember that next time you try to negotiate with a Dakotah war chief?" I plead.

"Nobody was hurt, and you still have your jack, don't you?" She straightens and juts out her chin, defensive.

"Yes. But we are lucky he didn't just decide to take you instead."

∞

The Dakotah move more quickly than we do, even dragging all their worldly goods and herding horses, and we don't see them again until we climb the hill, the fort in the distance. Fort Laramie sits on a rise on the south side of the Platte, and it is enclosed, along with a dozen homes, by a big adobe wall. Just the sight of dwellings not simply hewn from the prairie or erected out of poles and animal skins enlivens the company to spirits not felt in a good while.

Wagon trains dot the country on both sides of the river, and the lodges of French trappers and their Indian wives hug the walls of the fort and line the north and south banks where emigrants cross. The Dakotah pitch their tipis at the tree line, apart from the emigrant trains yet close enough to the fort to conduct commerce.

But reaching the fort from the north side requires crossing the Platte, something even the lure of shelves filled with wonders and a return to civilization cannot entice Abbott's company to do. Most of the men cross without their wives, leaving them to spend the day at the wagons, cooking and doing the wash, while the men head to the fort for supplies. I cross for supplies too, leaving all my animals except Samson and Delilah hobbled with the rest of the stock. I promise Webb and Will a surprise if they keep an extra eye out. I need flour and coffee and dried meat; I didn't set out from St. Joe with enough to cross the country, and though the knife I gave to Black Paint wasn't my only blade, I don't like being shorthanded.

The fort reminds me of St. Joe, though on a much smaller scale. Everyone's doing business, trading, testing, tinkering with their outfits, and restocking their stores. I buy enough flour, food, and grain to fill my packs and a new blade with an elk-horn handle. I purchase a ream of paper for Naomi along with a box of pencils and a whittling knife to sharpen the tips. Her shoes are worn almost bare in the soles, and I purchase a pair of doeskin moccasins so buttery soft she won't even know they are on her feet. A green dress, a few shades darker than her eyes, is piled in a corner with a stack of trousers and shirts that someone has set aside. I grab it and purchase it too, hoping none of the other men from the train will see me doing so.

A bow and a quiver for Webb and Will, a cradleboard for Wolfe so Naomi and Winifred can keep their arms free, and a new felt hat for Wyatt. I don't know what I can buy for Warren. There are no wives on the shelves of Fort Laramie, and Warren misses Abigail. I decide something sweet will do us all good; two pounds of candy wrapped in brown paper is my final purchase. It all costs me more than it should—the trading post is the only place to get goods until Fort Bridger, and they take advantage of the demand.

I return to the camp before most of the rest of the men and approach the May wagons with my packages, wanting to deliver my gifts without William May looking over my shoulder. I have already half convinced myself to just leave Naomi's gifts in her wagon without a word. But Webb and Will see me coming and run toward me, accepting my present with joyful whoops. Each has a piece of candy stuffed in his cheek before I can ask the whereabouts of anyone else.

"Where is Naomi?" I ask Webb, who hops around me with the bow, his little bare feet doing a variation of a war dance while he pretends to shoot at the sun. Will is studying the arrows, his eyes narrowed on the sharp points and the feathered quills, pulling them out of the quiver one at a time like he is drawing a sword.

"She went to visit the Indian ladies. Ma too. But Ma came back ages ago. She's in the wagon with baby Wolfe," Will says. "Do you want me to bring her the papoose?"

I stare at him, stunned. "What Indian ladies?"

Will points to the lodges of the French trappers on the banks of the Platte. Even from a distance, I can see dogs and children and women milling about. The trappers all have Indian wives; at the fort I heard someone refer to the community as the French Indians, though I'm guessing the women don't come from any one tribe.

"Ma says she's painting for them. There's a whole big line," Will adds. He doesn't sound the slightest bit concerned.

I stow my packages, including the gifts for Naomi, in Abbott's wagon and hurry up the hill, trying not to worry. It is not my business. I am not her keeper or her husband or her father. But I'm afraid for her and silently curse her mother for leaving her alone among strangers.

But she is not alone. Wyatt sits beside her outside the biggest lodge, half-breed children skipping around them with dogs nipping at their heels. An Indian woman swats at the dogs and points for the children to go play somewhere else after one trips over the items Wyatt seems to be in charge of collecting. As I watch, a squaw wrapped in a brown blanket sits down in front of Naomi, her legs crossed, her face solemn. Naomi hands her a looking glass, the one I saw hanging from the willow frame inside Warren's wagon when I was laid low. The woman studies her face and smiles, nodding. I wonder with a start if she's ever seen her likeness before.

Naomi sketches quickly—her audience is growing—and hands the piece of paper to the brown-cloaked squaw. The woman compares the picture to her face in the glass and nods and smiles once more. In exchange for the drawing—which Naomi has added a bit of paint to here and there—the woman gives Naomi a blanket, which Wyatt sets on the growing pile. Naomi bows her head slightly and makes the Indian sign for *good*, the way I did with the Dakotah braves, and the next person steps forward. The whole process repeats itself.

Wyatt sees me and waves, like it's all a grand adventure. I tell myself she is fine and I can go. I should go. But I don't. I simply watch, tucked back from the crowd. Naomi draws on her own paper more often than not, though a few hand her pieces of leather or shields like the ones she decorated for the Dakotah warriors; I wonder if word has spread to their encampment. It has definitely spread to the fort. Some of the emigrant women from other trains have straggled in, watching curiously and talking among themselves. A French fur trader, who seems to reside in the lodge Naomi sits in front of, gets a turn as well. He stands, solemn, holding his rifle and wearing a coonskin hat with a fat ringed tail that hangs between his fringed shoulders.

She doesn't take much time with each person. Ten minutes at the most, but the people marvel and clap when she finishes each drawing, and her happy patrons walk away, carrying their prizes in careful hands. An Indian woman, her skirts wet like she's crossed the Platte, brings Naomi a goat.

Naomi blanches for a moment, and the woman rushes to demonstrate the goat's worth, squeezing its teats and squirting a stream of milk into a tin cup. She offers it to Naomi, adamant. Naomi takes it and gives it to Wyatt. He gulps it down without hesitation.

He smiles, wiping his mouth, and the goat's owner claps. Naomi says something else to him, and they both begin to nod. Apparently, they have accepted the goat. The woman puts a picket pin in the goat's lead rope and sinks down in front of Naomi to pose for her portrait.

There is no way there is room in the wagons, packed tight as they are, for all of Naomi's trades. Nor does she need most of what she is being given. But she keeps painting away. Her left cheek is smudged with blue paint, her right cheek with red, and the tip of her nose has a black dot right on the tip, like she leaned too close to her work. Her yellow dress, the dress she was wearing when I first saw her in St. Joe, is splattered; I doubt she will be able to get it clean, no matter how hard the rain falls. Her hair is hanging down her back in a fat braid, long wisps clinging to the paint on her cheeks, but the crowd is looking at her like she's descended from the clouds to walk among them.

Hours pass. I leave briefly to check on my animals and return to an even larger crowd. As far as I know, Naomi has not taken a break or tried to curtail the gathering, and her pile of trades is growing. The trapper's squaw gathers her children and bundles them into the lodge only to come out a few minutes later with water and some kind of meat pie, which Wyatt and Naomi gobble up like they are starving. Naomi hands the woman a blanket from her stack, insisting she take it for the food, and the woman brings her another pie. Naomi points to me, and Wyatt stands, shaking out his cramped limbs, and brings me the pie.

"Naomi says if you're going to wait for us, you are going to eat."

I take the pie, hungry but hesitant, and Wyatt trots back to Naomi's side. I can't guess at what she's trying to accomplish, beyond the obvious: she is painting, people are happy, she's collecting loot. The sun is setting, the train will pull out in the morning, and just as I begin to think I am going to have to interrupt and put an end to the madness, for Naomi's sake, the crowd begins to part and point, and the emigrant onlookers scatter like scared rabbits. Black Paint and the bangled brave approach on horseback. Three Indian women lead a mule pulling an empty travois. Black Paint is leading the dun and a sorrel, his reddish-brown coat the same color as Naomi's hair.

Black Paint says something in Sioux—*Go? Leave?*—and the crowd obeys.

As the people disperse, I make my way to Naomi, standing behind her and Wyatt, who doesn't seem surprised at all by the entrance of the Dakotah war chief. Naomi adds a few strokes to the picture she's drawing for a cavalryman, who's come over from the fort just to have his likeness painted on a bit of burlap. He takes it and scatters like the rest, leaving a pound of bacon in trade.

"Many Faces wants a horse," Black Paint says, addressing me in Pawnee. "I will give her two."

I look at Naomi, attempting to control my expression. She is biting her lip and looking from me to the dun.

"I told you I would get you a horse," she says.

"He wants to give you two."

Her eyebrows shoot up, but she stoops and, directing Wyatt to help her, begins to show the chief what she has collected for him in trade. He directs his squaws to gather it, inspecting every item and leaving what he does not want behind.

"Tell him I'm keeping the goat," Naomi says, looking up at me. "Ma wanted a goat. We haven't been getting any milk from the cows, and Ma is worried Wolfe isn't getting enough. He's hungry all the time."

I do as I'm told, and Black Paint agrees to leave the goat. The women pack Naomi's trades onto the travois, making quick work of the heap. When they are finished, Black Paint inclines his head toward the horses.

"You, Pawnee white man, take. Red pony is calm. Old. She will be a good one for Many Faces to ride so she does not run away from you. You ride the young one, so you catch her." Black Paint's lips twist slightly in mockery, and Wyatt and Naomi look at me for translation. I say nothing. Black Paint tosses me the ropes of the two horses and, with a final look at Naomi, rides away with the bangled brave, the squaws, and the travois trailing behind him.

The dun whinnies, stamps, and tosses his head, but the sorrel mare dips her head in search of something to eat, confirming Black Paint's words.

"How did this happen?" I ask Naomi, grunting at her below my breath.

"She's Black Paint's sister." Naomi points at the woman standing in the doorway of the lodge watching the drama unfold. The woman nods and smiles. "Ma wanted to do some of her own trading and thought maybe, with white husbands, these women would be able to communicate with us."

I stare at Naomi, waiting for the rest of the tale.

"I think she sent word, because not long after we stopped to visit with her and the other women, the Dakotah chief and several others arrived with a stack of skins for me to paint. They left before you got here, but by then, there was a crowd. It was Wyatt's idea to get the looking glass. Her husband, the man in the coonskin cap, told me Black Paint would come back with the horse. I made sure I had plenty to give him in exchange."

I can only shake my head in wonder. "What are you going to do with two horses?"

"Give them to you." She shrugs. "I don't figure they'll be much harder to look after than your mules. I wouldn't mind riding one, now and again, if they're gentle."

"How did he know you wanted the dun?" I ask, stunned. The selection couldn't have been an accident.

"I drew him a picture." She smiles, weary but triumphant, and Wyatt just laughs.

10

INDEPENDENCE ROCK

NAOMI

After Fort Laramie, we stay on the north bank road, though the guide-books we bought for fifty cents in St. Joseph don't follow that route. It's a new road, Mr. Abbott says, and much better than the old. Mr. Abbott says the "old way" means crossing the Platte twice more—at Laramie and Deer Creek—and lining the pockets of the ferrymen who make money off travelers that don't know any better. None of us want to ford the Platte again, especially not twice, so we let Mr. Abbott lead the way into uncharted territory.

The land is changing. Gone are the flats and sandstone castles. Instead we veer north, away from the river, to avoid canyons that can't be crossed and make a slow ascent out of the river bottoms and up into hills thick with cedars and pine. It's a sight looking back. It's a wonder looking ahead. I've never seen mountains. Not like these. Mr. Abbott points out Laramie Peak, a huge dark pyramid with its head in the clouds, a trail of peaks behind it.

"Those are the Black Hills," Abbott says, but they're bigger than any hill I've ever seen. He says we won't cross them but will move along beside them, though when we descend into the valleys, we hardly notice them anymore. The grass is sparse here and abundant there, and John is kept busy herding Kettle and his mules from atop the dun, who hasn't grown accustomed to Dame's saddle. John rides him more each day; he grumbles that it's like bumping down a rocky bluff on his backside after riding Samson, whose tread is as long and smooth as John himself. But the dun's a beauty, and he likes to run. John says the Dakotah must have hunted buffalo with him because he thinks everything is a race. He bolts forward every now and then, taking John for a good ride. He talks to the dun in Pawnee, the hitches and coos no different to me than the speech of the squaws who liked my pictures, and I know he is pleased with the horse.

The sorrel is sweet and doesn't mind a rider, though John seems to have a chip on his shoulder where she's concerned. I don't think he likes that Black Paint gave her to me. I've started calling her Red Paint with great affection just to tease him. I've named our new goat Gert. She's as mild mannered as the sorrel, and the horses and mules do well in her company, even allowing her to ride across the saddle when she can't keep up. Her milk has been a godsend, and Wolfe begins to settle better at night, his belly fuller. I still use him as an excuse to visit John, though we do not stay as long, and I've managed not to fall asleep in the grass again with Wolfe in my arms.

We pass great rounded columns and soaring sugar-covered mounds of gray rock, but instead of the expanse of the prairie, they are encircled by silver streams and pine and cedar green. The air is different. It's thin, and some people get dizzy. Others go a little mad. Maybe it's that gold fever people speak of. Whole wagon trains veer off the trail to start digging when they hear the rumors of rich gold mines at the mouth of a creek on the south side road. A few in our company want to take a day to check it out, maybe do some digging, but leveler heads prevail.

We've passed a few go-backs and two men who are heading back to Fort Laramie with a third man who is trussed and tied on the back of his horse. They tell Abbott that the man went crazy and killed his brother-in-law and his sister, and they're taking him to Fort Laramie to stand trial. Seems the man got tired of them telling him what to do and just shot them dead. Some in the company wanted to hang him and be done with it, but a few folks thought he was justified. The men say he's lucky to get a trial. One man stabbed another in a train three days ahead of ours, leaving his wife a widow and his child fatherless. The company hanged the man from a tree. Most likely we'll pass the site of the hanging in a day or two.

We camp at some springs where the water shoots straight out from the rocks, so clear and cold and sweet we don't want to leave. That is, until Homer Bingham finds a sheet of paper nailed to a tree describing the murder of a man, woman, and child whose bodies were found beneath some wild rosebushes nearby, their throats slit from ear to ear. We can see the fresh, rounded graves covered with rocks so the wolves can't get at them. The burial is marked with a piece of driftwood that simply says, MAN, WOMAN, BOY.

Beware of the Indians, the paper warns, and Mr. Caldwell and others demand to move out immediately, though we've no guidebook to refer to and no idea how far it is to the next good water or grass.

Most nights we don't gather and pray—folks are tired, and most do their own thing, having given up on any sort of schedule when the rigors of the journey set in—but Deacon Clarke gathers us together, and we pray for the dead and pray for protection, from whatever forces out there would harm us.

John doesn't think it was Indians. He says it was more likely an emigrant cutthroat who saw an opportunity to steal an outfit and a team and took it.

"No Indian would try to hide what he'd done. And he wouldn't have taken the wagon. If the bodies were dragged out of sight, you can bet it was someone trying to buy himself some time," he tells the deacon.

With the rumors of troubles and violence among the trains, John's guess is as good as any. He says it's easier to blame the Indians than it is to believe ill of your own, and I'd have to agree with him. Regardless, folks are afraid, the guard is doubled, and no one rests well. Months of little sleep and endless toil, not to mention the roadside graves and daily grief, have us all worn thin. It's a wonder more of us haven't lost our minds.

∞

We leave the Platte for good today, and we all wave good riddance, celebrating the end of our acquaintance with the flat, muddy river that has been an almost constant companion since we reached Fort Kearny. Although we laugh and pretend to be jolly, we suspect the journey ahead will be harder than the one we left behind.

It gets harder real quick.

We travel through a valley thick with mire one day and then push up Prospect Hill, which has no prospects at all that I can see, the next. It's steep and rocky and dry, and we come down the other side only to plod through ten miles of white desert, an alkali plain that coats our feet and clothes in white. No grass, no water, no timber. Just powder, and we spend all day traveling with our eyes to the ground, looking for buffalo chips to burn when we finally camp. It doesn't take us long to realize that even the buffalo don't wander here. Folks ahead of us have discarded a whole new round of possessions in an effort to ease the burden on their lagging teams. Anvils and plows, buckets and barrels, cook stoves and wagon chains lie abandoned wherever we look, even worse than when the journey began. It is a graveyard of oxen, iron, and steel. Amid the strewed belongings are the dead animals that couldn't be coaxed a step farther, no matter how much their loads were lightened.

One of the oxen on Pa's wagon, an ox Webb has named Oddie, collapses midday, and we cannot get him up again. We unyoke him from the team and try to rouse him, sloshing precious water from our barrels onto his black tongue, but he's been listing for days, and the poor thing is done for.

"He's got alkali poisoning," Abbott says, and though he claims there's a remedy, we haven't the supplies to make the brew to revive him. John says he's too far gone anyway. We fear Pa's other ox, Eddie, will give out on us too, and we unyoke him so he can plod along, burden-free, until we reach water. We yoke in two of John's mules to take the place of Eddie and Oddie on the team. We have to leave poor Oddie where he lies. Warren hangs back to put him out of his misery, and when the shot rings out behind us, Webb begins to sob.

"Don't cry, Webb," Will says. "It won't help Oddie, and it won't help you. He's happy now. He's free of the wagon. That's all he wanted."

"Do you think this is what it's like to walk on the moon?" I ask, trying to distract him.

"The moon is cool and dark, I imagine." Webb sniffs. "Nothing like a desert."

"It looks like ash, like we've been through a fire," Will says.

"Well . . . in a way, I suppose we have," Ma says. She collects a bit of the white dust, convinced it will work to leaven our bread.

We don't speak after that. Our tongues are too dry to make words, and opening our mouths to converse just lets the dust in. Eddie allows Webb to ride on his back, and he falls asleep draped over him, his feet and hands flopping with every dusty step.

We stop for dinner, and Will skewers a sage hen with his bow. He is delighted, but I can't cook it because we don't have enough kindling to start a fire. Elsie Bingham offers a few chips she's gathered, Elmeda too, and I manage to boil the little bird until I can pull the meat off the bone. Elsie's belly is beginning to look like Ma's did when we started out, and she, more than anyone else, needs the strength. She eats a few bites and bursts into tears, and her husband looks on helplessly.

We don't camp for the night; we're afraid to stop, and when we finally reach Greasewood Creek, where our animals can drink and rest, Elsie is not the only one who cries in exhaustion and relief.

∽

"They call it Independence Rock," I tell my brothers, imagining all the ways I will sketch the sprawling, creviced monolith in the distance.

"It looks like a whale. See its rounded head and tail?" Will says, and Webb immediately jumps in to disagree.

"It looks like a big gray buffalo chip," he snickers.

"It looks like a turtle," I say. "A giant stone turtle."

"Ícas," John says, and his eyes meet mine.

Halfway.

It is the tenth of July, and we are halfway. Maybe it was the bad, stinking water of the Platte River Valley, or the lack of timber or fuel or rest. Maybe it was the loss of poor Oddie the ox. But it is the sight of the Sweetwater River, not the stone turtle it coils around, that has Ma and Elmeda singing praises.

"I know why they call it Sweetwater," Ma says. "They call it Sweetwater because there's never been a sweeter sight."

To Ma's sentiment there is a chorus of hearty amens. It is not the taste or the quality—though it's cool and clean—but the triumph of our arrival. We camp near its mouth to avoid the wagon city at the base of the big rock, and we splash and wash to our hearts' content, each woman taking a turn in the center of a circle of skirts to scrub all the bits that never feel clean. We wash our hair and launder our clothes, talking and laughing and singing a little too.

Pa takes the boys to the big turtle rock to sign their names. He brings a chisel and a mallet, and they spend the day climbing and combing the monument, making their mark among the rest. John goes too, though he explores on his own, and when he comes back, he is as scrubbed and shiny as the women.

It's a week too late to celebrate the Fourth of July, which is how the rock reportedly got its name, but we celebrate anyway, with a wedding and a day of rest. Adam and Lydia have decided to marry, and every family contributes something to the wedding feast. Lydia's fixed a bit of lace on her coiled braids, and I let her borrow my new green dress. It's a little big on me, and Ma and I haven't had the chance to alter it. It fits Lydia just right, and I hope John won't mind that I'm sharing his gift. He didn't say two words when he gave it to me. He just laid the packages at my feet and walked away. I've been saving it for a special occasion, wearing the blue and pink and splattered yellow, day after day. It is a special occasion, even if it's not mine. I wear my blue dress again tonight but add a matching ribbon to my braid.

Deacon Clarke gives us a heartfelt speech that turns into a sermon. Lydia clears her throat and reminds him she wants to be wed, and her father rambles to a pronouncement, giving Adam permission to kiss the bride. Adam complies, kissing Lydia like a chicken darting down to peck at the dirt. Everyone cheers, raising their tin cups and stampeding for the tables we've constructed out of sideboards.

After we eat, our makeshift tables are emptied and pushed aside for dancing. Homer Bingham has a fiddle, and he knows a few lively songs. I coax Warren to take a spin with me. He's a good dancer, always has been, and before long he's smiling big and breathing hard, a welcome sight to all who have had to watch him suffer. Wyatt cuts between us, showing him up, and I dance a few rounds with him and a dozen others, including the new groom, who thanks me for being so nice to Lydia, before I plead for a drink and a chance to catch my breath. I think I see John standing in the shadows, and I slip away, determined to draw him out. He stands beside the dun, repairing a bit of rope, but he raises his head as I approach.

"That fiddle is out of tune," he says, his tone dry.

I laugh.

"It is. But it doesn't matter. Everyone is singing along."

"A pack of wolves could do better." There's a smile in his voice, but he isn't wrong.

"But a pack of wolves can't dance nearly as well." It feels good to dance. I danced at my wedding. I was the last woman standing. Daniel had to coax me to quit.

"What was his wife's name? Adam's wife," John asks, still braiding his rope.

"Lucy."

He nods, pulling off his hat and setting it aside. "It must be hard for her mother, seeing him marry again so quick."

"Sometimes we do what makes sense. Life is too hard to be alone," I say. "Elmeda said as much herself."

"She would rather it was you, I reckon."

I study him for a moment, and then I grin. "Are you jealous?"

I am pleased at the notion. I haven't caught my breath from the dancing, but I spin a few times anyway, kicking up my heels and swishing my skirts. I can still hear the fiddle and the deacon keeping time with his tin pot and wooden spoon. I grab John's hand and swing his unwilling arm, ducking beneath it, in and out, making him dance with me even though his feet are planted and his left hand hangs at his side.

"You haven't made me jealous," he murmurs. "I like seeing you smile and hearing you laugh. You work so hard, and there is so little joy in your life. But I don't want to dance."

He touches my face, brushing his thumb across my cheekbones and over the bridge of my nose, like he's tracing my freckles. I step into him and rise up on my toes, my body brushing his as I press my mouth to his throat, warmth and salt and smooth skin against my lips. He lowers his chin and returns the caress, moving his lips across my jaw and over my cheek before settling his mouth against mine, inhaling as he does, his lips slightly parted, pulling me in.

He says he doesn't want to dance, but that is what we do. It's just a different kind of dance. His mouth is pressed to mine, seeking and sinking, moving together and apart, all things working toward the same end. Or the same beginning. We are a circle of two.

It is not like the first kiss we shared. That kiss was all clash and confrontation. He wanted me to run, and I wanted to stay and fight. This kiss is not a fight. This kiss is slow and languid like the Platte, hardly moving, while beneath the surface the silt shifts and settles. His arms snake around me, and my palms flatten over his heart, needing and kneading, and heat grows in my belly and in my heart and where our mouths are moving together.

"I need you to marry me, John," I whisper against his lips.

I need it because I know too much. I am not a girl afraid of a man's touch or a man's body. I've lost my maiden dread, and I know the pleasures of the flesh and the marriage bed. Daniel was gentle, and he was quick, doing his business without lights and without baring me or himself more than necessary. I didn't really mind, though I always felt a little resentful that Daniel finished before I could even get started. It only hurt the first time, and I was curious and confident enough to find contentment in the coupling throughout our short marriage.

But even then I knew there was more. I felt it in the liquid expectation in my limbs, in the coiling in my belly, and in the need in my chest. I just never knew how to draw it forth before it was all over.

With John it is an ever-present ache, and he makes me want to find it, whatever it was that Daniel found when he closed his eyes and shuddered like he'd swallowed a piece of heaven. Like he'd found that transcendence Ma talks about.

"Why is that?" John whispers back, and I hear the same need in his voice. It gives me confidence.

"Because I want to do more than kiss you. I want to lie down with you."

For a minute he stays curved over me, his cheek against mine, his big hands circling my waist. And then he speaks, so soft and so slow that his words tickle my ear and the heat grows.

"That isn't going to happen, Naomi. Not here. Not now."

"I know it isn't," I murmur, curling my fingers into his shirt. "But I want to. I want to so bad that I can't wait until we get to California."

"Naomi," he breathes. "I won't live in another man's wagon or marry another man's wife."

"Is that how you see me? Another man's wife?" I gasp.

"That's not what I meant." He shakes his head. "I cannot . . . marry you . . . under these circumstances. Not with your dead husband's family looking on, your family listening—" He stops abruptly, and his embarrassment billows around us. "I have nothing to give you."

"I have nothing to give you either," I whisper. "But all I want is to be beside you."

"That's not your head talking," he says, shaking his head, and his hands fall from my waist, leaving me unsteady. "Thinking takes time. Feeling . . . not so much. Feeling is instant. It's reaction. But thinking? Thinking is hard work. Feeling doesn't take any work at all. I'm not saying it's wrong. Not saying it's right either. It just is. How I feel . . . I can't trust that, not right away, because how I feel today may not be how I feel tomorrow. Most people don't want to think through things. It's a whole lot easier not to. But time in the saddle gives a man lots of time to think."

"What do you think about?" I ask, trying to swallow my disappointment and cool the warmth still coursing through my limbs.

"I think about my place in the world. I think about what will happen when we reach California. What'll happen when you decide you can do a whole lot better than John Lowry." He doesn't sound wistful. He sounds convinced.

"There is no one better than John Lowry."

"And how would you know that?"

"How do you know I'm wrong?" I shoot back.

"Because you don't think, Naomi. You just . . . do."

"That's not true."

"It is. You just throw yourself into the wind . . . into the river—do you remember crossing the Platte? Or demanding a horse from Black Paint? You throw yourself forward and don't consider for a moment that there might be a better way."

"Sometimes when we think too long and too hard, we let fear get a foothold. But I think about you plenty, John Lowry."

"No. You aren't thinking. You're feeling. And I'm glad of it." He clears his throat, pausing. "But I'm afraid of it too."

"Why?" I'm trying not to lose my temper.

"Because eventually, time thinks for us. It cuts through the fog of emotion and delivers a big bowl of reality, and feelings don't stand a chance," John says with bleak finality.

"Then why are you here? Why didn't you turn around at Fort Kearny, if you're so sure about who I am? I thought we had an understanding."

"I'm here because I *have* thought it through. I've thought you through."

"You've thought me through?" I repeat. "What does that mean?"

"It means you're the woman I want. I won't change my mind on it. I won't ever want something different." He pauses and enunciates the next words. "Someone different. I'll always want you."

I stare at him, stunned and stirred, right down to the soles of my aching feet.

"But I'm not going to kiss you again . . . not anytime soon. And I'm not going to pretend you're mine. I'm not going to hold your hand or tell you that I love you. And I'm not going to let that preacher say the words over us."

The joy that coursed through me only minutes before disintegrates like it never was, so completely gone I can't even recall what it felt like.

"You don't know me at all," I whisper.

His eyes search mine, but I cannot tell what he is thinking. "I know you. And I'm sure. But I want you to be sure."

"I've told you how I feel." I swallow back my anger and my disappointment, refusing to cry out my frustration.

He nods. "I know. And I don't question how you feel."

"You just question what I think," I say flatly. "Or *whether* I think. Or if I'm even capable of deep thought."

"Naomi," he says, the word filled with protestation. "I will not ever be an obligation again. My mother did not have a choice of whether she wanted me. Most women don't. My father . . . did his duty. Jennie too. I know that is what life is about. Duty. Responsibility. There is great value in that. But I want you to see all your choices . . . and still want me."

"So all the way to California, huh? No kisses. No promises. No love. Just waiting. Waiting until *you* decide that I've thought us through long and hard. How long do you think that will be, John?" My words wobble with anger, and my heart is so hot with outrage I want to clap my hands over it so it doesn't disintegrate and leave a gaping hole in my chest.

"As long as you need."

"You're a fool, John Lowry. I keep throwing myself at you. I keep telling you exactly what I think. I've never tried to keep it from you. I don't have much. My dresses are worn out. My shoes too. I don't have a husband or a home or even my own pots and pans. I don't have much," I say again, "but I have my pride. And I am not going to beg."

JOHN

I have hurt her. I have known Naomi May—I still can't call her Naomi Caldwell and probably never will—for two months. Two of the hardest months of my life. Two of the worst. Two of the best. I've almost died, and I've never been more alive. I've told her things no one else knows. I've laughed. No one and nothing makes me laugh. But Naomi makes me laugh.

And I have hurt her.

She's been quiet. More than quiet. She's avoided me altogether. I can't blame her. She tells me she wants to lie with me, and I tell her no. She tells me she's ready to be my wife, right now, wagon train and all, and I tell her not yet.

I am a fool, just like she said. I should swoop her up, claim her, bed her, and make sure no one can ever take her away from me. It's what I want. But it isn't what I want for her.

I didn't explain myself very well. I insulted her intelligence and caused affront. Yet thinking back on my words, I don't know how I could have said it any differently. I meant what I said. I just didn't say all the things I could have.

I could have told her I want to lie with her and kiss her more than I want to breathe. That I want to make her smile and talk to her in the darkness. I could have said I want to be with her too. She's the reason I'm here, the only reason I didn't turn back at Fort Kearny and go home. But I didn't tell her those things, and I have hurt her.

California is still so far away.

11

THE SWEETWATER

JOHN

I do not dream in English, and I do not dream in Pawnee. My dreams are like my childhood, garbled with sounds and gestures that belong to both of my worlds—or all of them. My mother worked among whites from the moment I was born. I heard English. I understood it. I heard Pawnee; I understood it. But sometimes what I understood I could not speak. When I went to live with my father, I hardly said anything at all. Not for a long time. Not because I did not understand, but because the words of my mother and the words of my father both danced in my head. Sometimes the words would fade and grow faint in my head. Then I would return to my mother's village and sit at my grandmother's feet, listening until the words were bold again. I started being less afraid when I realized that the Pawnee words always came back. Through the simmering soup of languages in my head, the words would sink like meat into my mouth, heavier than all the others. Then the world of my mother would open back up to me, if only for a while.

As I grew older, there were more sounds and more languages.

A man of the Omaha tribe worked with my father for a while. A Potawatomi village sat a mile from the farm my father sold. A Kaw woman did the wash for Jennie when we moved to St. Joe, and there was Otaktay, the half Sioux who taught me to fight. When Abbott came back from California, he traveled with some trappers from Fort Bridger. One had a young Shoshoni wife who made it all the way to Missouri only to be abandoned in an unknown world when the trapper died suddenly a day out of Independence. Abbott brought her to Jennie, who made her a little room in the cellar and put her to work. The Shoshoni woman reminded me a little of my mother, industrious and unassuming and completely lost. She knew a little sign talk and a few words in English, but Jennie was convinced I would be able to talk to her and dragged me around to interpret, though I'd never heard Shoshoni before.

"You have the gift of tongues, John Lowry," Jennie told me. "You always have. It won't take you long."

There were sounds that were the same and sounds that weren't, patterns that I recognized and those that I didn't. But Jennie was right. It didn't take me long. Abbott called her Ana, though I doubt it was her name. It must have been close enough to the right sound, for she accepted it and referred to herself that way. Ana's voice became part of the soup in my head, and I could speak with her well enough—and understand her even better—by the time she left. She told me her *Newe*, her people, were called Snake by the whites, after the river that ran through their lands.

For three years she lived beneath Jennie's wings, working and watching, until one day she was gone, and Jennie didn't know where. Ana couldn't write, but Jennie found a crude drawing on Ana's cot in the cellar. It was a stick figure depiction of a woman with a pack on her back, the sun above her and pointed triangles of varying sizes in the distance. A curving line ran through them. Mountains. Tipis. A river. I knew what it meant the moment I saw it.

"She went home," I told Jennie.

"All the way?" Jennie gasped. "All by herself?"

"Well . . . she's alone here. She is all by herself . . . here."

I regretted the words as soon as I said them. Jennie looked stricken. "She is not alone," she sputtered.

I just shrugged, letting it go, knowing it would hurt Jennie to insist.

It is impossible to explain to someone who is surrounded by their own language and people just how lonely it is to not understand and to not be understood.

Jennie put the picture Ana left between the pages of her Bible and prayed for her every day. My father said she'd gone with a wagon train. He had it on good authority, and Jennie was slightly reassured. He seemed relieved to have her gone. I think Ana reminded him of my mother too, and he was never comfortable in her presence. My father was never comfortable in *my* presence, and it made me uncomfortable with myself. It made me nervous with others. It made me quiet and cautious. It made me doubt myself.

I'm definitely doubting myself right now. Jennie was right; I am good with languages and good with sounds, but I am not always good at hearing what people don't say. Naomi is not saying anything, and I am stumped. I need her to talk to me in order for me to understand her. She doesn't come find me when I am on watch—she hasn't since I told her I wasn't going to kiss her again—and I'm too proud to seek her out. So I'm miserable. And if her downcast eyes and stiff shoulders are any indication, she's miserable too. Damn, if the days aren't long. It is not easy, once you've been bathed in light and warmth, to be shut out in the cold.

We are forced to cross the Sweetwater again and again as it winds and turns through gorges and canyons where we cannot follow, only to veer back across our path before turning again. One day we ford it three times before making camp and rising again the next, when we don wet boots to walk several miles before doing it again. And like the river, I swing between what I want to do and what I need to do, not really sure which is which.

It is mid-July, yet halfway between Split Rock—a giant stone wall with a vee hacked out at the top—and the Pacific Springs, we walk through canyons where the snow has blown down from the peaks above and collected in shadowed drifts along the roadside. We pick up handfuls and ice the water in our canteens and barrels. A huge snowball hits me right between my shoulders, and Webb hollers like a Sioux brave on the warpath, having hit his target. Naomi pelts him right between the eyes, and a battle is waged for a few frenzied minutes. I'm riding the dun, and he is not amused by the raining clumps of ice. Naomi has no problem lobbing a flurry of snowballs my way, but when the game is over, she reverts to the polite stranger.

We leave the river to skirt an impassable canyon, travel two days without seeing the Sweetwater at all, and swing back down to cross it again. Seven times. Eight? I've lost count, but I don't complain; the river is easier to cross than the hills.

We climb a ridge so steep and rocky we cannot ride our animals for fear of tumbling over and rolling down the graveled slope. We unhitch the teams, walk them to the top, and then one by one, using the teams to help us pull, we push forty wagons—ten fewer than we started with—up the ridge. When the ropes start to unravel on the final haul, the men pushing the Hineses' wagon barely make it out of the way before it crashes to the bottom of the hill, broken, bent, and completely unsalvageable.

Adam Hines and his new bride will be without a wagon at least until we reach Fort Bridger. William offers them the use of Warren's, with the condition that his supplies remain. A few others make room in their wagons for the possessions that won't fit. Lydia walks alongside

Naomi and Winifred, and Adam gladly yokes his oxen to Warren's wagon. My mules and I are freed from duty for the first time since the alkali flats, and I herd them ahead, stripped of an excuse to travel with the Mays, though I hardly needed one before. Samson and Delilah are almost giddy as we ford the river for the ninth and last time, leaving the Sweetwater and the longest week of my life behind.

∞

South Pass is a wide, grassy saddle of land sitting between a range of mountains to the north and another to the south.

"They call this the Continental Divide. The Sweetwater River flows east, and everything to the west flows toward the Pacific," Abbott hollers, pulling his wagon to a halt. "Everything thataway is the Oregon Territory."

"Oregon? Already?" Webb yells, as if the journey has been a buggy ride in the countryside. "Ya hear that, Will? We're almost there!"

Almost there, and still eight hundred miles to go. Webb is riding Trick alongside me, Will behind him. My mules and the horses have picked up the pace, sensing quitting time.

A few trees climb the low bluffs that rise up here and there, but from where I sit, there is nothing but vastness. Vast skies above, vast land below, and nothing to obscure the view in between.

I pitch my tent and see to my animals, keeping myself apart from the rest, still swinging between resolution and regret. I'm carrying buckets from the stream we're camped beside, my hair still dripping from a good wash, when Winifred May finds me and asks for a moment of my time. Wolfe is in her arms, his little legs kicking wildly, freed from the papoose I bought him in Laramie.

"Naomi's gone up the bluff on Red," she says. "She wanted to see the view." Winifred points to the bluff about a half mile off and the lone rider just cresting the rise.

"She shouldn't have gone alone." I sound as irritated as I feel.

"I told her to let Warren or Wyatt go with her, but she's head-strong." Winifred looks at me. "And she's not a child anymore. So I don't treat her like one." Winifred's voice is perfectly mild, her gaze steady, but I don't miss her point. I don't acknowledge it either. "I don't think one needs to climb the bluff to appreciate the view. A body can see so clearly from here. It's all so wide open. Yet it looks nothing like the prairie. We've seen some country, haven't we, John?"

"Yes, ma'am."

"Are you going to follow her?"

"Ma'am?"

"Naomi. Are you going to follow her? I think that's what she wants."

"I'm not sure Naomi knows what she wants, Mrs. May."

Winifred's eyebrows shoot up, but she lets my response drift away on the breeze. She raises her hand to shade her eyes, finding the lone rider ascending the bluff.

"In all her twenty years, I don't think that's ever been true, Mr. Lowry," she says.

We are silent for a moment, standing side by side. Winifred sways back and forth to keep Wolfe content. I've noticed it's something she always does, even when she's not carrying him. It reminds me of the met-ronome Jennie kept on her piano, ticktock, ticktock, and I am suddenly engulfed in a longing for home. It stuns me. Maybe I've just never been away long enough to appreciate it. Maybe that's the way it is with every-thing. Even Naomi. She withdraws, and I miss her so bad I can't breathe.

"Do you love her, John?" Winifred asks softly, her hand still pressed to her brow.

I am taken aback, but Winifred doesn't pause long enough for me to answer anyway.

"Because if you don't, you have my respect. You've told her how it's going to be, and you've stood your ground. But . . . if you do love her . . . the ground beneath you isn't very firm."

"She wants us to marry," I blurt out. "Did she tell you?"

"And you don't want that?"

"I want that." It is a relief to say the words out loud and know them to be true. I want that.

"So what's stopping you?"

My flood of reasons rises like a torrent, a million drops of water inseparable from each other, and I don't know where to start.

"Is it because she's not Pawnee?" Winifred asks.

I shake my head no, though I know that's part of it. There is guilt in choosing one of my feet over the other.

"Then . . . is it because you are?"

I sigh. That too is part of it. "I don't want life to be harder for Naomi because she is my wife," I explain.

"Well, that's something to think about." Winifred sighs, and she studies the girl on the bluff that I'm keeping in my sights; I might lose her altogether if I look away. "But don't think about it too long."

"I've been thinking about it since I met her."

"Then I reckon that's long enough."

"Âka'a," I grumble.

"The hardest thing about life is knowing what matters and what doesn't," Winifred muses. "If nothing matters, then there's no point. If everything matters, there's no purpose. The trick is to find firm ground between the two ways of being."

"I haven't figured out the point or the purpose."

"Just trying to survive makes things pretty clear most days. We have to eat; we need shelter; we have to keep warm. Those things matter."

I nod. Simple enough.

"But none of those things matter at all if you have no one to feed, to shelter, or to keep warm. If you have no one to survive for, why eat? Why sleep? Why care at all? So I guess it's not *what* matters . . . but *who* matters."

From the back of my mind echo Jennie's final words to me before I left St. Joseph.

It's worth it, you know.

What is, Jennie?

The pain. It's worth it. The more you love, the more it hurts. But it's worth it. It's the only thing that is.

"Many people matter," I argue, though it is not a protest as much as a plea. I have very few people who matter to me, and I'm not convinced I matter very much to them.

"Yes. But you have to decide if Naomi matters to you . . . and how much. What would you do to keep her fed, to keep her breathing, to keep her warm?"

"I would do just about anything," I admit.

"And that right there is purpose."

"I cannot give her shelter. Not out here."

"That's what marriage is. It's shelter. It's sustenance. It's warmth. It's finding rest in each other. It's telling someone, *You matter most.* That's what Naomi wants from you. And that's what she wants to give you."

She reaches up and pats my cheek and turns away. She has mouths to feed, and she has said her piece. But she calls over her shoulder after only a few steps. "You'd best be going after her now."

I am in the saddle before Winifred May reaches her wagon.

∞

Naomi descends the bluff before I can reach her, but she sees me coming. She turns the sorrel at the bottom of the hill and veers west around it, making me race to catch up with her. She is a sight, racing across the expanse with her hair streaming out behind her. It's the same color as the horse beneath her, and I can't help but think that damn Dakotah chief knew exactly what he was doing. The sorrel's gait is smooth and long, and Naomi's skirt hangs over on each side, giving the appearance of royal draping. She's a decent rider, as comfortable in the saddle as she is in every other area of her life. And maybe that is the root of my problem. Naomi seems to know exactly who she is, and she gives no indication that she is anything but content with herself. I told her she doesn't think, she just feels, she just does, but maybe it's because she is confident enough to trust her instinct and move ahead.

She slows when she's put the bluff behind her, a barrier between us and the train, and then she comes to a stop, her back to me, waiting for me to draw up beside her.

"I want to be alone, John Lowry." I know she is calling me John Lowry because I've told her not to.

"No. You don't," I counter. "You wanted me to follow you."

She glares at me, her color high and her hair tumbling around her, and for a moment I just drink her in, looking my fill.

"Why are you looking at me like that?" she snaps after I've stared a good minute. "I'm angry with you, and I *do* want to be alone."

I slide off the dun and, trusting that Naomi won't bolt just to spite me, walk to her horse. Without her permission, I put my hands around her waist and lift her down so she is standing in front of me, so close I could bend my head and kiss her tangled hair. Her pulse is drumming in her throat; a cluster of golden freckles dances around it. I brush my fingers across them as she raises her face to me, challenge in her grass-green eyes.

"I thought you weren't going to kiss me again," she whispers.

"I wasn't," I say.

And then I do.

I can tell she wants to punish me; she doesn't respond like she did before. Her hands don't rise to curl against me; her lips don't open in welcome. But I can feel her heart, and it thunders against my ribs, countering the rhythm of my own.

Then she sighs, an almost imperceptible flutter of air, and her hands rise to my face, holding me to her, and I am forgiven.

I kiss her deeply. I kiss her well, taking my time and testing my restraint. The breeze ruffles her skirt and tickles my nape, and I am conscious of the horses grazing a few feet away, unimpressed by my need or the soft sounds of my mouth against hers. We are wrapped in a warm silence—no wagon wheels or bouncing box springs, no toil or climb, no sadness or fear. And I am at peace.

"I don't know what you're trying to tell me," Naomi whispers after a time, and I brush my lips across hers once more before I make myself stop.

"I missed you."

Her eyes search mine. "I didn't go anywhere."

"You haven't even looked at me for the last ninety miles."

"When Ma walked by the graves of the little ones . . . especially in the beginning . . . she wouldn't look at them. She said it hurt, and she didn't want to carry that pain." She swallows and looks at my mouth. "These last days, it's hurt me to look at you too. So I tried not to."

"She's a smart woman, your mother."

"The smartest."

"She and I had a visit. She told me you were out here, and she told me I needed to go after you."

Naomi steps back from me, far enough that I can't extend my arm and pull her back. Her jaw is hard and her eyes are cool, and I realize I've said something wrong.

"I can take care of myself."

"Yeah. I know you can. But she sent me after you anyway."

"Is that why you're here? To make sure I don't do something rash? To make sure I use my head?"

I knew we would circle back to that.

"No. That's not why I'm here."

She takes a deep breath, and it shudders a little as she lets it go.

"You embarrassed me, John."

"I know. That wasn't my intention."

She nods, as if accepting my apology. And I can see her struggling with an apology of her own.

"I guess I got ahead of myself. I know it's not been that long since we met. But every day is a lifetime out here. These days we're living, they're hard. And they're heavy. And it doesn't take long to just start throwing everything that doesn't matter by the roadside . . . and knowing what you can't live without."

"Your ma said something real similar to that."

"She told me to be patient," Naomi whispers. "And I'm going to try."

I nod, stroking the side of my face. I'm nervous, but I know what to do.

"It's another nine, ten days to Fort Bridger," I say.

"It's another eight hundred miles to California." She sounds glum.

"Yeah, well . . . I can't wait that long."

Her eyes search mine, confused. "What?" The word is breathy, like she doesn't dare hope.

"At Fort Bridger we can get you a new dress."

"You already bought me a new dress."

"Lydia Clarke wore it, and I don't want you to have to share your wedding dress."

She starts to smile but bites her lip to hold it back. "I'm done making assumptions. So if you're saying what I think you're saying, I need you to ask me, John. And I need you to be real clear. Otherwise, I won't be able to look at you again for a while, because my heart can't take it."

"Will you be my wife, Naomi?" I say the words slowly, and I hold her gaze.

"When we get to Fort Bridger?" she asks, her eyes gleaming.

"When we get to Fort Bridger," I repeat. "I won't spend my first night with you with everyone listening. And we'll have our own wagon and our own supplies for the rest of the journey. I have some money, and if I have to sell every one of my mules, I will. But we will have our own home. Even if it's on wheels."

"And you can get all of that at Fort Bridger?"

"That . . . and maybe even a room for a night, away from the train."

She swallows, her eyes wide, her mouth unsmiling, and for a long moment, she smooths her skirts like she's soothing herself. I don't know what I expected, but it wasn't hesitation.

"I don't know if I can wait that long," she says under her breath.

"Âka'a," I moan, falling for it.

Then she is throwing herself at me, entwining her arms around my neck and laughing.

I pretend to stagger beneath her weight and fall into the scrubby grass, taking her with me. A rock digs into my back, and our heads knock together as we tumble. But her lips are on my face, her hips are in my hands, and her happiness is in my chest.

"I love you, John Two Feet Lowry."

"I love you too, Naomi Many Faces May," I say, and there is suddenly emotion in my throat, swelling up from her happiness. I have not cried since my mother left me. I didn't think I still knew how. And I have never told anyone I love them.

"Do you believe me?" Naomi asks, her lips at my ear, her body on top of mine.

"I believe you," I whisper, and I close my eyes to gain my control.

She kisses me gently, top lip, bottom lip, lips together, lips apart, and I open my eyes to watch her love me. And love me she does.

We don't emerge from the grass until a good while later, mouths bruised and bodies aching for more. But she'll be my wife before I take anything else.

NAOMI

John insists on talking to Pa. I tell him I can make my own choices, and I'll tell Pa myself, but he just shakes his head.

"I make my own choices too, Naomi. And I'll be speaking to your father."

The conversation isn't long, and knowing Pa, it isn't pleasant, but it isn't John who comes and finds me when it's over.

"They won't look like you," Pa says. "Your children. That's what happens when dark marries light. They won't have your green eyes or your color hair. You need to think about that and what kinda lives they'll have. They'll look like him."

"Well, I guess that's a good thing. The May line is a little homely."

Pa snorts, rubbing at the furrow between his eyes and laughing a little.

"You sure?" he asks, shaking his head.

"I'm sure." Why would I want to stare at my own reflection in my children if I could look at John instead?

"I'm not saying he's a bad choice. He's not. He's strong. Capable. And he seems to want you," Pa says begrudgingly.

"Well, that's good," I say, the sarcasm dripping. My poor pa never was very good with his words. I suppose that is what Ma is for.

"But don't say I didn't warn ya when there's struggles."

"I won't, Pa."

He sighs, a gusty sound that rumbles from his belly. "Does he know what he's gettin' into with you?"

"No. And I'd appreciate it if we just keep it between the two of us."

Pa hoots, shaking his head as the laughter rocks him. "I'm guessin' he knows, girl. The whole company is on to you. And if he's smart, he'll hold on tight. It'll take a good mule man to tame my girl." He's still laughing when he walks away, and I know it's fondness speaking, so I don't get too ruffled.

⚮

We have reached the Parting of the Ways. One road veers right for Oregon, one veers left for California, and for as far as the eye can see, there are two divergent paths, the space between them ever widening. It's a beautiful name for a lonely stretch of goodbyes.

"Ten days to Fort Bridger," Abbott says. "And we've got the better of it. Folks heading that way have a desert to travel through." He points at the ruts we won't be following. "They call that the Sublette Cutoff. I've heard it's pure misery. Used to be that everyone went to Fort Bridger. But folks are always trying to save time. It's funny. Ya take a shortcut tryin' to save time, and ya lose your life. That's what they call irony, John Jr. Irony." He waves his finger at John, nodding his head like an old sage.

Abbott has been cautious. Despite my anger at him for moving on when John's mules were scattered, he has been prudent every step of the way, sometimes more than prudent. The loop to Fort Bridger avoiding the desert called the Little Colorado and the highest ridge on the Overland Trail is easier on both the travelers and the teams, but it adds a good seventy or eighty miles to the distance, and there are some among us who want to brave the cutoff.

The two trails will rejoin for a stretch before they part again, but those who take the north fork at the Parting of the Ways will be—if they make it through the desert and down the steep descents—days ahead. It is agreed that half of us will remain together, taking the Bridger Loop, and the rest will take the pass.

Eighteen wagons in our train peel off, headed by a man named Clare McCray, who they've all elected to be captain. There are tears, knowing the likelihood of ever seeing each other again is slim. We all knew we would part ways eventually, but it doesn't make it any easier for those who have become close in these months of toil.

Then we are moving on, twenty-two wagons and half a herd, our eyes cast southward toward the rest of our journey. But I'm not thinking about California or the miles ahead. I'm not thinking about land or valleys of green or even the day it'll all be over. My thoughts are centered on Fort Bridger.

12

THE GREEN

NAOMI

We travel seven more miles to finish out the day, camping near the Big Sandy River, our circle feeling small and oddly quiet. The water is muddy but swift moving, and Abbott says it's safe to drink, though it tastes unpleasant, especially after the cold, sweet water of the springs we've left behind. We fill our canteens with the water left in the barrels before filling them to the top with the swill from the Big Sandy. We have thirty miles skirting the edge of the desert, and water will be hard to come by, especially in late July.

No trains nip at our heels. The only trains behind us are likely Mormons who will end their journey in the Salt Lake Valley, only another hundred miles west of Fort Bridger.

The distance worries everyone and has Mr. Caldwell and others grumbling in Abbott's ear almost every day. The men sit in council at night, excluding the women, only to go back to their own camps and seek their wives' opinions. Or maybe that's just Pa.

Ma's got a bad cough. She tries to hold it back, but it escapes sometimes and rattles her thin chest. She says she just sounds bad but doesn't feel bad. The dry desert air makes it worse, along with the dust, and she rides with Wolfe in the wagon all day, the canvas pulled tight, but we can still hear her. She says she needs to alter my green dress.

"You can't wear it if it doesn't fit," she says, but it's just an excuse to make us all feel better about her shutting herself away. We feed Wolfe with a spoon, dipping it into a cup of goat's milk and dribbling it into his little mouth, one drop at a time. It's time consuming and tedious, but more and more, Ma's milk just isn't enough.

I haven't told her that John says he's buying me something new. It isn't important. She's happy for me and happy for him, and she's glad we've decided not to wait.

John joins us for meals, sitting beside me on the ground, his back to his saddle, which he carries to and from our fire every night. Just like before, we do not touch unless we are alone, but the word has spread through the camp that a wedding will take place at Fort Bridger. It's most likely Webb who has spilled the beans. He's told anyone who will listen that John is going to be his new brother, and they are going to go into business together when we reach California.

"I been thinkin' on a name, John," he says. "Lowry May Mules. And this can be our brand." He takes a stick and draws a connected *M* and *L* in the dirt.

"There's an idea," John says, nodding. "I like it."

"You can be a partner too, Will," Webb says, not wanting to leave Will out.

"I don't want to breed mules," Will says. "I just want to hunt all day. I want to be a trapper like Daniel Boone." Will doesn't ever set the bow and arrow down. He shoots all day long at everything he sees. Webb wheedles him daily for a "turn," but in truth, Webb is more happy herding mules than doing endless target practice. Webb has a lariat that he swings over his head while he rides. Trick and Tumble have grown accustomed to his constant motion in the saddle, and poor Gert has been noosed several times a day since joining the train.

"Nothin' in the whole world is better than mules, right, John?" Webb asks, dismissing Will's ambitions.

"Oh, I don't know, Webb. There might be a few," John says. He glances at me, and Webb wrinkles his nose.

"I can't think of any." Webb pouts. "Not a single thing."

"What about Ma's songs and blueberry biscuits and Naomi's pictures?" Will says, ever the peacemaker.

"I do like those things," Webb admits. "I wish I had a blueberry biscuit right now. What are your favorite things, John?"

John shifts, not liking the personal nature of the question. "I'd have to think on it," he says. Ma jumps in to save him.

"My favorite things are buttermilk pie, robin's-egg blue, Webb's laughter, Will's prayers, Wyatt's courage, Naomi's sass, Pa's love, Wolfie's snores, and Elmeda's friendship." Ma smiles at Elmeda, including her in the conversation. The Caldwells, the Binghams, and Abbott have joined us around our fire for coffee and a little conversation. We've all been feeling lonelier since the train split in two, and folks have begun to seek each other out at bedtime, almost like we did in the beginning.

"I also love Warren's stories, Elsie's good humor, and John's patience," Ma adds, pinning John with a rueful grin. It's true. John has the patience of Job when it comes to Webb.

"What do you love, Pa?" Webb asks, making a game of it.

Pa rattles off a few things—fresh meat, sleep, clean water, a smooth road. All things we haven't seen much of. Everyone takes a turn until the exercise is exhausted, and we're all feeling a little forlorn and hungry, reminded of apple tarts and feather beds and warm baths in the kitchen. Elsie Bingham has fallen asleep on her side, her head in her husband's lap, her arms resting on her belly.

"Will you sing us a song, Ma?" Webb asks when we all fall silent. We're tired, yet none of us have the energy to ready ourselves for bed.

"I can't sing tonight, Webb. It tickles my throat. I'll sing tomorrow when my cough goes away," Ma says.

"Well, Warren's on watch, so he can't tell us a story." Webb sighs. "Do you know any stories, John?"

A dozen pairs of eyes swing John's way. We've all heard Abbott's stories more times than we care to, and Pa can't tell a story to save his soul.

John sets down his cup and straightens, like he's about to bolt.

"I guess I do," he says, so quiet that everyone bends their heads toward him to better hear. "I don't know if this is a true story. Or an old story, or a new story. It's just something my grandmother told me once, the last time I saw her. It is a story of Hawk, a young Pawnee. Pawnee is what my mother was, what I am too, I suppose—"

"I want to be Pawnee," Webb interrupts. "How do ya get to be one of those?"

"Well . . . this story is about how Hawk became a Comanche—"

"What's a Comanche?" Webb asks.

"Webb!" Wyatt growls. "Would ya listen, please? You're gonna scare John away, and then the rest of us won't get to hear his story."

"A Comanche is another tribe. They were the great enemies of the Pawnee. They loved to make war on the Pawnee, and the Pawnee loved to make war on them and steal their horses. One night, Hawk—Kut-a'wi-kutz—who had many horses and was very good at stealing them from the Comanche, sneaked into a Comanche camp. He saw many beautiful horses outside a big lodge."

"What kind of horses were they?" Webb asks, and Wyatt sighs.

"What do you think?" John asks Webb, not seeming to mind his interruptions.

"One was a dun, one was a roan, and one was a pretty paint," Webb answers, no hesitation.

"I think you are right. Hawk was just about to take all three of them when he saw a shadow inside the lodge. It was a very handsome lodge with feathers and dried buffalo hooves hanging in the doorway and clattering in the wind, making a noise that sounded like his name. Hawk looked around to make sure no one was there, but the clattering hooves and whispering feathers again made the sound of his name. Kut-a'wi-kutz. He thought maybe someone was calling to him from inside. When Hawk peeked into the lodge, he saw a girl brushing her long hair."

"Did she look like Naomi?"

"Naomi's not an Indian," Mr. Caldwell grunts, and there is a collective discomfort around the fire.

"Yes. She looked just like Naomi," John says, raising his eyes to mine in brief appraisal, and I smile at his quiet defiance.

"Hawk forgot about the horses. Instead, he watched the girl all night long. When he finally left, he took two of the horses—"

"The roan and the dun," Webb says.

"All right. But he left the paint, in case it belonged to the girl. He went back home to his people, but every time he saw something pretty, he would think of the Comanche girl, and he would trade one of his horses for the pretty thing, until he had traded almost all his horses.

"His friends said, 'We must go take more horses from our enemies, the Comanche, for your horses are almost gone.' So Hawk agreed, but he took all the pretty things he had collected with him.

"Hawk and his friends went back to the place where the Comanche camp had been, but the camp was gone. They went to another camp, but Hawk couldn't find the lodge of the girl, and he left the camp without stealing any horses. His friends didn't understand. Hawk said, 'Let's go find another camp, and we will steal their horses.' They went to another camp, and another, and Hawk did not steal the horses at any of them; he just looked for the girl.

"At the last Comanche camp, Hawk crept among the lodges, looking for the lodge with the buffalo hooves and the feathers. Then he heard his name, Kut-a'wi-kutz, and knew he had found it. He went into the lodge, and there was the girl, fast asleep. He put all the pretty things he had collected for her at her feet and then lay down beside her, for he was very tired from searching."

Mr. Caldwell scoffs and shakes his head, as if the story has suddenly turned inappropriate.

"What happened then? Did she wake up and scream?" Webb asks, oblivious to any unease.

"She did wake up, but it was dark, and she could not see who was there. She reached out and touched Hawk's hair. The Pawnee warriors shave all their hair except for this piece right here." John reaches out and tugs softly on the hank of Webb's hair between his crown and his forehead.

"Like Dog Tooth," Wyatt contributes soberly. He says he still dreams of being chased by the band of Pawnee.

"Yes." John nods. "The girl was afraid because she knew Hawk was Pawnee. But his skin was cold, and he was sleeping so deeply that she took pity on him and put her blanket over his shoulders before she sneaked out of the lodge and went to find her father, who was the head chief of the Comanche."

"Did Hawk get away?" Webb asks, worried.

"He did not want to get away," John replies slowly.

"He didn't?" Webb squeaks.

"No. He wanted to be close to the girl."

Webb wrinkles his nose, as though he can't imagine it, and something warm begins building in my chest.

"The head chief and all his war chiefs took Hawk and all his pretty things and brought him into the big lodge. They sat around the fire and passed the pipe while they decided how they wanted to kill him."

"Are there lots of different ways to kill a fellow?" Webb asks.

"Yes. Some more painful than others. And the girl's father was very angry with Hawk."

"Because the Pawnee and Comanche are enemies," Webb says.

"That's right. Around and around the circle, the Comanche passed the pipe, and no one could make a decision. But then the old grandfather came into the big lodge, and he saw Hawk wrapped in his granddaughter's blanket, awaiting his fate. He saw the gifts he brought, and he said to Hawk, 'Did you come to take my granddaughter away from her people?'

"Hawk said, 'No. I want only to be near her. If you will let me stay, her people will be my people.'

"The grandfather sat down among the Comanche chiefs, and when the pipe finally reached him, he said to his son, the head chief, and all the braves, 'We will not kill the Pawnee. We will make him one of us. He will bring peace between the Pawnee and the Comanche.'"

"Peace? Isn't there any fighting in this story?" Webb wails.

"No. No fighting." John's lips twitch. "Hawk stayed with the Comanche and married the daughter of the chief. He stayed with her people, the Comanche, until the day she died. Only then did he go back to his own people."

"She died?" Webb squeaks. "How did that happen?"

"My grandmother did not tell me. But that is not the important part of the story."

"What's the important part?" Will asks.

"Peace between people," John answers.

We are quiet for a moment, thinking that over. Even Mr. Caldwell has nothing to say.

"I've heard that tale before," Abbott says. "The legend of Hawk, the Pawnee Comanche chief, has lots of chapters."

"I think I liked the part where he was stealin' horses the best," Webb says, frowning. "I want to know what happened to the dun and the roan and the paint."

"Maybe you can decide, and then tomorrow, you can tell us what happened to them, in your own story, after supper."

"I have early watch," John says, rising suddenly. He's been the center of attention for too long. He says good night, hardly looking at me, and I let him go, my thoughts still on his tale. Abbott and the Caldwells are quick to bid good night as well, taking their dishes and their opinions with them. Homer Bingham rouses Elsie, then helps her to her feet and walks alongside her as she waddles toward their wagon.

Ma sends the boys to bed, letting Pa herd them into the tent and get them settled. For a few moments, Ma and I are alone by the fire, Wolfe sleeping soundly in a basket at her feet. She is wearing her coat of many colors wrapped tightly around her, though the night is temperate and the fire is hot. We have plates and cups to wash and dough to make, but neither of us moves.

"It's your story," Ma says softly. "And John's."

"What is, Ma?"

"The story of Hawk and the Comanche girl. Peace between people."

"Do you think John knows that? I don't want him to give up his people for me."

"I think John knows it best of all. He said much the same thing to your pa when he sought his permission."

"Pa's permission." I sigh. "I don't need Pa's permission."

"Maybe you don't . . . but John did. He told William, 'I will take care of Naomi, but I will also take care of your family. Your family will be my family.'" Ma stares at the fire, her back bent, her arms wrapped around her knees, and I suddenly need to go find John and fall down at his feet.

"Go to bed, Ma. Take Wolfe and go to sleep. I'll clean up here and make the dough and be in beside you soon."

Ma does not argue but rises wearily, hoisting Wolfe like an old crone with her basket of wash. "When you say good night to John, thank him for the story." Her tone is wry, if weary, and I smile at her departing back. She knows me so well. "Tell him I am grateful for him too."

"I will, Ma."

"I love you, Naomi," Ma adds. "I only got one daughter, but God gave me the very best one He had."

"I'm guessing He was glad to get rid of me."

"He won't ever be rid of you. That's not how God works."

"Night, Ma."

"Night. And let John get some sleep, Naomi."

When I hesitate, she laughs, but the laughter turns to wheezing.

JOHN

Other than the sand and the barren stretches of dust and gravel, Abbott was right. The way isn't hard, and we make good time, lifting the pall and easing the worry on furrowed brows. We reach the Green River the following day. Timber lines the banks, and there is plenty of grass, but the river is wide—easily a hundred feet from shore to shore—and swift moving, and when I walk the dun out into the current, he can't touch bottom about a third of the way across, and I turn him back.

"It's too deep to cross here. I'll go upstream a ways. The Mormons have a ferry several miles up, but we might not need to go that far. Water the animals, let them graze, and I'll see if I can find a better place to ford," I tell Abbott, who readily agrees.

I stay on the shore, veering down to check the depth of the water every so often, while keeping an eye open for a break in the trees where the wagons can cut down to the riverbank without too much trouble.

After I've traveled about fifteen minutes, I see a band of more than a hundred Indians—mostly women and children—gathered on the shore, their animals packed to the hilt with lodge poles and skins, an occasional child perched high on the loads. The few men among them begin to urge the animals across as if they are familiar with the river and its low points, and the women don't wait for them to reach the other side but follow without hesitation, children on their backs and baskets in their arms. A few rafts constructed out of branches and braided together are piled with more supplies, and older children cling to the edges, pushing the rafts through the water, keeping a tight hold as the water laps at their chests. The dogs plow into the river alongside them, swimming as fast as they can, fighting against the current and often losing, though they manage to fight their way to the other side eventually. I pull the dun up short, watching the band's progress and gauging the depth of the water, certain that I've found the best place for the wagons to cross.

As I watch, keeping my distance down the shore so the tribe will not feel threatened, I notice a woman near the back of the group. She leads a pack mule with two small children sitting atop a tightly bound pack and carries a papoose on her back, the round face of a black-haired babe peering from the top. Maybe it is the mule that catches my eye. He stops every few feet until she tugs on his rope, and then he bounds for a yard or two before he halts again. The third time he does this, the river bottom evades him, and he panics, dunking himself and the two children on his back and pulling the woman off her feet.

The two children shriek, and the mule drags her along, obviously concluding that crossing is his only option. The woman lurches forward and goes under but recovers almost immediately, never letting go of the rope.

But when she finds her feet, the papoose is empty.

A small bundle whirls in the swift current, rushing away from the chaotic procession, down the river, and the woman starts to scream. She throws herself after the baby but catches a different current and is drawn in the wrong direction. The infant is light, and it offers no resistance as the water propels it forward.

I dig in my heels, urging the dun into the water, and keep my eyes locked on the helpless form whirling down the center of the river. For a moment I think I won't reach the child in time, but the current cuts back, sending it careening toward me, and I let go of my horse, hurling myself toward the baby and scooping him—her—out of the water and up against my chest. The dun begins to swim, but my feet find bottom, and I let the horse go, urging him forward as I fight to stay upright. The baby isn't crying. She is naked—I don't know if she entered the water that way or if the current stole whatever she was swaddled in—and her little limbs are still. She is bigger than Wolfe, older, more substantial, but still so small and slick I'm afraid I will lose her again in the water. I wedge her belly against my shoulder and begin to pat her back with one hand as I cling to her legs and bottom with the other, fighting to maintain my balance the remainder of the way. Several of the men are running toward me; the mother has not yet made it out of the river, though she is almost to the shore. I sink to my knees, setting the baby before me on the sand. I turn her onto her side, still patting her back, and a sudden rush of water erupts from her white-tinged lips. She immediately begins to squall and fight, her arms and legs pumping for air, and I scoop her up, resting her tiny belly against my forearm as I continue to pat her back.

When the first man reaches me, his long hair flying out behind him, his breeches and moccasins wet from the river, I rise and extend my arms to him, holding the angry baby girl out in front of me. He takes her, looking her over before passing her to the old man behind him.

I make the sign for good, and he nods, repeating the hand motion. "*Att*," he says, and I recognize the word. *Good.*

Seconds later, the mother arrives, panting and crying, her sodden, empty papoose still hanging from her back, and clasps her shrieking daughter.

She thanks me as she rocks back and forth, holding the child to her chest, comforting them both. And though she still cries, her words tripping and tumbling out of her weeping mouth, I realize that not only do I understand her, I know her.

"Ana?" I gasp, dumbfounded.

She peers up at me, suddenly seeing beyond her emotion, and freezes midsway, midthanks.

"John Lowry?" she asks, rubbing her eyes as though she cannot trust her vision. "John Lowry?" She says my name in exactly the same way Jennie has always said it, and I laugh as I pull her into my arms, planting a kiss on the top of her head.

The growing crowd around us exclaims at my affection, and the older man who was second to reach my side shoves at my arms. I find out soon enough that he is her father, and he doesn't like the familiarity.

Then she is telling him and the people gathered around us who I am and how we know each other.

"John Lowry, all the way from Missouri," she says. "John Lowry, my white Pawnee brother."

She tells me they are Shoshoni, often called the Snake by trappers and fur traders because of the river that runs through their lands, and though I am out of practice and slow to remember the words to say, I have no trouble understanding her—or them—at all. They call her Hanabi—*Ana* is not so different—and she is the wife of the chief, a man named Washakie, who she says is good and strong and wise. The baby girl is their only child—the two children on the mule are her brother's children—and she wants me to stay with them, an honored guest, so that I might meet him when he and many of the other men return from trading in the valley of the Great Salt Lake.

I tell her I have to go back to the wagon train, that people are waiting for me to help them cross the river, and she confers with her father for a moment before promising to wait for me to return.

"We have just broken camp and have a long journey ahead of us. We will await Washakie in the valley near the forks before we go to the

Gathering of all the People of the Snake. But today we will stay here with you."

I ride back to the place I left the train and lead them upstream to the point where the Shoshoni crossed, warning them not to be afraid of the Indians waiting for us on the opposite bank. Webb wants to know if they're Comanche, and when I explain that they are Shoshoni and one is my friend from years ago, he—and everyone else—is intrigued. Abbott is overjoyed when I tell him who I've found, and he cries when he sees her, mopping at his wind- and sunburned cheeks and saying, "Ana, little Ana. God is good."

True to her word, Ana and the Shoshoni are waiting, their packs already unloaded, their ponies grazing unhobbled in the grassy clearing just beyond the west bank. Before the wagons have even halted, the Shoshoni men and several women have crossed back over and begin the work of helping us cross, piling goods that will be ruined by water atop their rafts and ferrying them to the other side. We try to pay them, but they refuse. Ana says I have saved her daughter's life, and for three years I was family when she had none.

"I will feed your people today," she says.

My "people" are wary and watch with wide eyes and cautious smiles, but twenty wagon beds are unloaded, raised, and reloaded with nonperishables and possessions in less time than it would have taken us to cross two or three. Our passage is much less eventful than the Shoshoni's was, and what would have been a strenuous afternoon crossing the swift-flowing river becomes a day of rest and rejoicing on the other side. We set up camp not too far from the crossing, agreeing to use the day to fortify ourselves and our teams against the next long stretch of dry, grassless trail.

Ana—Hanabi—stays close to my side all day, her daughter slumbering on her back in a new, dry papoose, seemingly unaffected by her near drowning. She asks about Jennie and my sisters and even asks after my father. "He was quiet. Strong. Like my Washakie."

"I know he was not kind to you," I say.

She looks surprised. "He was kind. Always. He helped me come home. He gave me a mule and found a wagon train for me to travel with."

I am stunned by her revelation. He never let on that he had any part in her leaving.

"He did not tell you?" Hanabi asks.

I shake my head.

"I think he was afraid I would take you away."

I frown, not understanding, and she laughs.

"We are not so different in age, John Lowry. But you were not ready for a woman. I was a sister to you."

I introduce Hanabi to Naomi, telling her we will soon be married, and Hanabi insists on giving her a white buffalo robe and a deep-red blanket for our marriage bed. The Shoshoni women cook for us—a dinner of berries and trout and a handful of other things we don't recognize or question. We simply eat our fill, the entire train, and I am tempted to marry Naomi today—right now—and make the feast a wedding celebration, but I hesitate to speak up and create new drama amid the peace. Then we are swept up in the attentions of Hanabi and her tribe, and I resist the impulse.

As we eat, Hanabi tells me of her journey home, about the wagon train and the family who let her travel with them. I translate her tale to the train, growing emotional throughout her account, stopping to search for English words and find my control as she recalls the moment she returned to her tribe. Her mother had died, but her father and her brother still lived. She had left them as a young bride to a fur trader who had befriended her father, who was then the chief of a small Shoshoni tribe. A year later, she was alone, far from home, with no husband, no family, and no people.

"For three years she lived with my white family," I say. "Abbott brought her to us. We have missed her."

"I was afraid to leave. But I was more afraid that I would never see my home or be among my people again."

The emigrants stare at her in hushed awe, and before the night is over, Naomi is drawing again, painting on paper and skins, creating pictures for our new friends until the moon rises high over the camp, and wickiups and wagons alike descend into slumber.

Wolfe is the only one who cannot sleep. He fusses in Winifred's arms as Naomi finishes her last picture by lantern light, a sketch of Hanabi holding her daughter, her loveliness and strength glowing from the page.

Hanabi accepts the gift, marveling at the lines and the likeness. She stands, bidding me good night, grasping my hand and then Naomi's, but she hesitates, her sleeping infant in her arms. For a moment, Hanabi watches Winifred spoon milk into Wolfe's anxious mouth.

Hanabi hands her sleeping daughter to Naomi, who takes her in surprise. Then Hanabi sinks down on the other side of the yoke Winifred is using for a seat and extends her arms toward Wolfe.

"Tell her I will feed him, John Lowry," Hanabi says to me. "I have more milk than my daughter can drink."

Winifred hands her son to Hanabi, her eyes gleaming in the tepid light, and Hanabi, without any self-consciousness, opens her robe and moves the child to her breast, guiding her nipple into his mouth. He latches on without difficulty, becoming almost limp in her arms, his cheeks working, his body still.

Winifred weeps openly, one hand pressed to her mouth and one to her heart, and Naomi cries with her, holding Hanabi's daughter, her eyes on the little boy, who suckles like he's starving, first one breast and then the other, until he falls into a milk-induced slumber, releasing the nipple in his mouth. Hanabi closes her robe and sets the babe against her shoulder, rubbing Wolfe's small back. He burps with a satisfied rumble, and Winifred smiles through her tears as Hanabi lays him back in her arms.

I have completely forgotten myself, struck by the scene and caught up in an intimacy I should have turned away from. I am embarrassed by my own presence, but Hanabi looks up at me without censure or discomfort as she takes her child from Naomi's arms.

"Tell the mother I will feed him again at dawn, before we part. She must eat and rest and let her body make milk for him."

I repeat her words to Winifred, who nods, unable to stem the flow of her tears. She tries to speak, but for a moment she can only cry. Hanabi seems to understand, though she looks to me for reassurance that all is well.

"She is grateful, Hanabi. She has suffered greatly and never complains," I say, battling back my own emotion.

"I saw this . . . in my dreams," Winifred stutters between sobs. "I saw another woman . . . an Indian woman . . . feeding him, and I . . . was afraid. But I am not afraid anymore."

13

FORT BRIDGER

JOHN

We part with Hanabi and the Shoshoni early the next day, restored both in strength and in spirit. We travel a barren fifteen miles and close out the day by crossing the waters of Blacks Fork, which Abbott and the emigrant guide claim we will cross three more times before reaching Fort Bridger.

"It's nothing like the Green. Not at any point. Just a little wadin' is all. Shouldn't need to unload the wagons or worry about being swept away," Abbott reassures us as we make camp on the other side, but I have begun to fret about other things. I am weighed down by the unknown and by my inability to prepare for it. I want to go on ahead. The entire train can't sit at Fort Bridger while I pull together an outfit—wagon, riggings, ropes and chains, spare parts, and two months' worth of supplies—and pause to marry Naomi. I need time, and if I travel the final thirty miles with the train, I won't get it. I talk to Abbott, who is agreeable to the idea, if not optimistic.

"I don't remember there bein' much at Fort Bridger. It ain't like Laramie. It's a good place to stop and catch your breath. Good water and grass and timber to burn, and a much smoother route than the Sublette, but you might be disappointed by what you find."

My uneasiness grows, and I quietly curse him for not speaking out before now. Fort Bridger is a major point on the trail. I'd expected a variation of Fort Laramie where everything a traveler could want was in ready supply, even if it cost extra. Extra I can handle, but I can't work with nothing. When I pull Naomi aside, telling her my plan, she listens without comment, her eyes on mine, her lower lip tucked between her teeth. She needs some convincing.

"Abbott says we're two and a half days' travel out of Fort Bridger if we just go steady. If I take my mules and the dun, I'll make it in one. It'll give me a day to put things in order. Now that we've crossed the Green and the driest stretches, there shouldn't be anything the wagons can't handle."

"I'm not worried about us," she says. "But . . . if you must go . . . will you take Wyatt with you? He won't slow you down, and I'll feel better if you're not alone."

"If your folks don't mind, I'll take Wyatt," I agree. If I take Wyatt with me, he can ride one of my mules and lead a string of three behind him, and I won't have to move my animals in one long line. I don't dare leave them behind with the train. Mr. Caldwell seems to have resigned himself to my presence, but I don't trust him, and I don't want to burden the Mays with their care.

The following morning, before the birds even wake, I kiss Naomi, who insists on seeing us off. I promise her that it'll all work out and I'll see her in two days.

"You aren't going to run out on me, are you?" she asks, a smile in her tired voice. "'Cause I'll come after you. I can be mean when I want something."

"She can too, John. Meaner than a wet hen," Wyatt teases, but he's chipper this morning, excited for the break from the monotony, and he urges Samson forward without looking back. "Let's go, mules, giddyap." He clucks his tongue and digs in his heels, and Budro, Gus, and Delilah move out behind him.

I swing up in my saddle, but Naomi looks so wistful, standing with her lantern in the cool predawn, the red blanket Hanabi gave her wrapped around her shoulders, that I lean down and kiss her again.

"I love you, Two Feet," she says.

"And I love you, Naomi May. Try not to worry. I'll be waiting for you."

The speed at which Wyatt and I travel, my animals loping along like they could run all day, makes me almost giddy. I unstring the dun and race him across the flat, just to feel him go, before swinging back for Wyatt and the mules. It's a relief to move, and we ride at an almost constant clip. The only stops we make are to change mounts and water up before starting again. The relative ease of the journey, with no wagons to slow me down, is a sobering reminder of what I'm getting into. For the next two and a half months, I will be driving a wagon at oxen speed, Naomi beside me on the seat. That thought makes me grin like I've just struck gold, and I let the dun have his head.

We rest for supper at a grassy bend near a cold stream, but we don't camp. We've made good time. The sun sets late this time of year, and we finish the last few miles of our ride several hours before dark.

Fort Bridger—named for Jim Bridger, the mountain man who established it and is purportedly still in residence—is a handful of long cabins made of rough-hewn logs slapped with a bit of mud to keep the wind out of the cracks. The structures are surrounded by a ten-foot wall constructed of the same material. Adjacent to the enclosed square of buildings is a large corral for horses, of which there are many.

But that is all.

I rein in the dun and slow my mules with a soft "Whoa." Then I just sit, my hands resting on my thighs, looking at the sad state of my destination.

A few dozen tents crowd a single wagon in a clearing on the west side; it looks like a small militia of some sort. A cluster of wickiups, not unlike those of the Shoshoni along the Green, can be seen a ways off, with a few more scattered lodges lining the fort walls. A company has just pulled out, ten wobbling wagons moving away with the same dejection with which I approach.

This is not Fort Laramie. Not by any stretch. There will be no private quarters to rent, no dresses to buy, no shelves brimming with supplies.

"I thought it would be bigger," Wyatt says, incredulous. "Are we in the right place?"

A board nailed above two tall posts, creating an unimpressive entrance, declares it so.

"We don't got much, but we got a blacksmith," boasts a thin man with a wispy gray mustache and an even sparser beard when I inquire within the building that serves as the trading post. Every item on the shelf is priced sky high, and there isn't a whole lot there.

"I don't need a blacksmith. I need a wagon," I say, my heart sinking. "I need a whole outfit."

"Well . . . that might be a problem. But I can sell you some flour and bacon, some coffee and beans. Oil. I got oil. Some to cook with and some to grease your wheels."

"I don't have any wheels."

"Yeah. Well. I got plenty of cornmeal left and a cookstove. A kettle. A pot. I got two tin cups, two plates, and one spoon too. Some lemon syrup. Odds and ends."

"And what about the other buildings?"

"The blacksmith. He can sell you some riggings too. A harness. A saddle. There are some bunks in one and a mighty fine stove. That's not for sale, though. You need a bunk?"

Again the welling despair. I need more than a bunk.

"Vasquez and his missus live there. That last one. Bridger has a room in the bunkhouse too. When he's here. He ain't. Don't know that he'll be back either. We got the Mormons here makin' a fuss. Say Bridger's been sellin' firewater and gunpowder to the Indians. That is a violation of federal law, they say. Mostly, they just want to buy the place. I got a hundred of 'em camped out there, waiting for Bridger to show up so they can arrest him. Scarin' all the traders off."

That explains the small tent city, but it doesn't help my situation.

"I got a supply wagon coming in the next day or two," he says. "I'll have more to sell then. If I was you, I'd get what you need right now before that next train comes in. There will likely be a few more before the season ends. Most of 'em are going to the Salt Lake Valley. Don't know how many of the others we'll see."

"You'll have one rolling in tomorrow," I say, grim. I turn away from the shelves and the old trader, looking out into the yard, where Wyatt is watering the animals. A few folks mill about—Indians, Mexicans, and whites alike—but the fort is quiet in the wake of the last train, and I don't know what I'm going to do. I've got money, but not money to throw away. The prices of the goods on the shelves are ten times what they sell for in St. Joseph. The sad part is desperate folks will pay. I've got mules, but I think I'd rather starve than trade one for trail rations. But it's not going to be just me.

The man behind the bar walks out to stand beside me, wholly unconcerned with the lack on his shelves and my obvious displeasure. "Hey . . . you wantin' to sell that jack? That is some kind of animal. I got a few mares I wouldn't mind gettin' a couple good mules out of. Those big mules bring big money round here. Fur traders and mountain men like the mules."

"I won't sell him . . . but if you'll give me what I need for a fair price—and when I say fair, I mean about a quarter of what you're selling it for now—I'll take a look at your mares. If one of them is agreeable to it, I'll give you stud services for free."

The man tugs on his beard, his eyes narrowed. Then he shrugs.

"I don't know that I'll see another jack like that come through here. I'll set whatever you want aside. How's that? Your jack does his thing, we'll come to an agreement on price. That way it won't get sold, and it'll still be there if'n the animals don't cooperate. I got a chest I can give ya. We can load it up. Got a fellow who follows the trains and just picks up what they toss out. Like pickin' fruit off a tree. I got a room full of his finds."

I tell him what I want—the utensils and dishes, the skillet, hard-tack, flour, and everything else I think I can afford if all goes well. I try not to think about the fact that I still don't have a wagon to put it in, and there's no obvious way to get one. The man keeps a running tally on a strip of paper, and my tension grows as I calculate the number. I help drag the chest from the other room, and we load everything into it, pushing it behind the counter and bolting it closed when we're finished.

"Teddy Bowles," the man says, extending his hand.

"John Lowry."

"John, there's something happening out front," Wyatt says, sticking his head through the doorway, his eyes shifting from me to Teddy Bowles. "Indians on one side and white folks on the other, and it don't look good."

"Damnation!" Teddy wails, running for the door. "I better get Vasquez."

NAOMI

The number of times we cross Blacks Fork reminds me of the winding Sweetwater River and John's rejection. I was sure I was going to spend the rest of my days pining after a man who wouldn't settle. He tied me in knots and walked away, all because he thinks too hard. I've never known a man who thinks so hard. I just hope he finds what he's certain we need, because if he doesn't, there won't be a wedding. When I told him we could just share Warren's wagon with Adam and Lydia, he looked at me like I had three eyes and a pair of horns.

When Daniel and I married, we had two bowls, two spoons, one trencher, a plate, and a new skillet with which to set up house. Ma and I made a quilt, and Daniel built me a chest as a wedding gift, but we spent our first night beneath his father's roof, as well as our second night and our third and our forty-fifth. A month before Daniel died, we'd moved into a one-room cabin a few miles from his folks. It had a fireplace and a window, and it was just big enough to accommodate a bed, a cupboard, Daniel's chest, a small table, and one chair. At supper, I would sit on the bed and give Daniel the seat at the table. When Daniel died, I couldn't sit in that chair. It felt wrong. And I couldn't sleep in the bed. In fact, I never slept in it again. I was afraid of being swallowed in sadness and loss. I slept on a pallet on Ma and Pa's kitchen floor instead, and they never made me go back.

When we left Illinois, I sold everything in the cabin for a few dollars and closed the door on my life as a wife. There was no room in the wagon for my belongings, scant as they were, and that suited me fine. I have never had a room of my own or even a bed of my own. Most folks don't. The only space I've ever had to myself is the quiet of my own thoughts and the blank page in front of me, so I don't know why John is so insistent that we have a wagon of our own. I can spend two months in a tent. I can spend a year in a tent. But I can see it in the set of his mouth and the stiffness in his spine. He isn't going to yield on it, and it'll do me no good to try to convince him otherwise. John is proud, and he is private, and I suppose if I'd spent my life feeling like a stranger in my home, I would be more driven to have a place I could call my own.

John is driven . . . and I'm going to let him drive, wherever he needs to go and whatever he needs to do, just as long as he lets me ride beside him. Just as long as he'll let Ma and Pa and my brothers tag along. They've all become quite attached.

When we stop to noon at yet another branch of Blacks Fork, Ma brings out the old family Bible. In the front is written a long line of names and dates, marriages, and births from generations past, meticulously recorded. Ma never reads from it; she has another Bible for reading. She keeps it wrapped in a cloth inside a wooden box, and it's been stowed beneath the main bed since we began.

"I've let this go for too long. It's been on my mind," she says as she adds Wolfe's name and his birth date to the long list of her children and records the day Abigail died.

To the right of my name she adds a connecting line and writes *John Lowry, m. July 1853*. A line to the left of my name says *Daniel Lawrence Caldwell, b. Oct 1830, m. Oct 1851, d. Jan 1852*. The *b* stands for *born*. The *m* stands for *married*. The *d* stands for *died*.

I don't want to blot Daniel out, but I don't like the way it looks, my name centered between the two men. I can't imagine John will like it either and am glad Ma's chosen to bring the Bible out while he's away.

"Don't you think you better wait until we're married?" I ask.

"No. When was John born?" she answers serenely, her quill lifted, awaiting my response. She's feeling better today. Hanabi's generosity restored her.

"He doesn't know. Winter of 1827 or '28."

"Winter?"

"His mother told him there were tracks in the snow, so it must have been winter."

"What kind of tracks?" Ma stills, and a great black drop of ink splatters onto the page.

"Footprints. Like a man wearing two different shoes," I answer, but Ma is distracted by the blot.

"Oh no. Look what I've done," Ma mourns, staring at the spot. It has completely obscured her name.

JOHN

A standoff is taking place. The men from the tent city have taken a position about twenty yards in front of the fort, barring the way to a mounted band of Indians, who are weighted down with meat and furs and have no doubt come to trade.

"We're looking for Jim Bridger," I hear someone shout. "Nobody's getting in this fort until we find him."

"We got in the fort," Wyatt says, frowning. We're stringing Kettle, the dun, and the mules behind us, and they're not happy to be heading out again. I'm not happy to be heading out again. I have business to conduct and very little time to do it. We hug the outer walls just east of the entrance, keeping back from the fray.

Teddy Bowles and a man I assume is Vasquez stride out of the fort moments later. Vasquez looks about my father's age, though his hair has not yet lost its color. It's slicked back, and he's clean shaven, an oddity among mountain men. He's wearing a cloth shirt rolled at the elbows and a leather vest with a gold watch chain dripping from his pocket. He looks like a banker, but he has a rifle in his hands and a furrow on his well-tanned brow.

A woman emerges through the gate behind him, wearing a deep-blue dress striped in white and adorned with a little white collar. Her hair is perfectly coiled, her back is perfectly straight, and when Vasquez barks for her to go back inside, she ignores him completely. She reminds me of Naomi.

Vasquez and Bowles push through the Mormon militia to stand in front of the mounted braves, and the woman observes it all, only ten feet away from me and Wyatt.

"You are out of line, Captain Kelly," Vasquez shouts, pushing his way toward the front. He speaks English with a slight French accent, and I'm confused by his name. *Vasquez.*

Suddenly, I know who he is.

"Louis Vasquez. Well, I'll be damned," I breathe.

A Missouri boy, born and raised, and the son of a Spanish father and a French-Canadian mother, Louis Vasquez is a fur trader who's been back and forth across the plains and traipsed through the mountains enough to make a name for himself back home, where tales of the West have been on every tongue and part of the American consciousness for the last two decades. My father, who never talks about anything, sold him a mule once and was impressed enough to bring the story home. "Louis Vasquez purchased a Lowry mule today. Imagine that." You'd have thought he'd seen George Washington—a renowned mule breeder himself.

"The Indians who shot and scalped two of our men were Shoshoni. I don't want trouble. But I don't want it to happen again, and Jim Bridger selling powder and spirits is only making things worse. Until I get some answers, I'm not budging," the Mormon captain shouts.

"Isn't your friend Hanabi a Shoshoni?" Wyatt asks. "You could probably talk to him, couldn't you, John?"

Wyatt doesn't wait for me to answer but calls to the woman, drawing attention to us both. "Mr. Lowry speaks Shoshoni, ma'am. Maybe he could help."

The woman rewards us with a blinding smile. "I believe he could. Louis," the woman calls, projecting her voice above the tense assembly. "We have someone here who can speak to Chief Washakie for Captain Kelly."

Washakie. I have no doubt this is Hanabi's chief.

When all heads swivel toward us, the woman smiles and inclines her head like she's a queen greeting her subjects. She looks at me and extends her hand toward the conflict, indicating that I proceed.

"Mr. Lowry?" she prods.

"Stay here, Wyatt," I say under my breath. "And next time, let me speak for myself."

The Mormons part judiciously, clearing a path to their captain and Vasquez. The Shoshoni leader sits straight in the saddle, and he does not seem unnerved by the reception he is receiving, but he doesn't like it either. He meets my gaze as I approach, and without thinking, I remove my hat. To leave it on my head would feel like an insult, though no one else has removed theirs. His buffalo robe is bunched at his waist, and a few feathers stream from his long hair. He is broad chested and fine looking, but I cannot tell how old he is. No gray streaks his hair, and his face is unlined, but he is old enough to be chief, which is not a young man's position.

Teddy Bowles claps me on the back like we are old friends, but Captain Kelly eyes me suspiciously.

"You speak Shoshoni?" Vasquez asks.

"I do. Well enough."

"We want to ask him what he knows about the attack. It is believed that the Indians were Shoshoni. Can you ask him about that?" Captain Kelly asks.

I try, stumbling a bit over my words.

The chief looks me over, his eyes lingering on my face before he dismisses me. He is angry, his shoulders tight, his gaze flat. He is insulted by the confrontation.

"I want to trade. Now," he says.

"You've traded with this man before?" I ask Vasquez, uncomfortable in the corner I've been shoved into.

"Many times. Bridger considers him a friend," Vasquez says.

"Every year," Captain Kelly agrees. "He is highly regarded."

"Then what's the problem?" I protest.

"The problem is two men are dead and Bridger's been breaking laws. Ask him again," Kelly insists.

"Do you know who killed the patrol and took the horses?" I ask Washakie, careful not to accuse.

"I know they probably deserved to die," Washakie says. I don't tell Captain Kelly what he's said but wait for him to continue. He changes the subject instead.

"Are you a white man?" Washakie asks.

"My father is a white man."

"Where is your tribe?"

"I have no tribe."

"You are not Pawnee?"

He has caught me off guard. I wonder if he can hear the Pawnee in my speech.

"My mother was Pawnee," I say.

"Not you?"

I am silent for a minute, considering. I don't know how to answer. In the end, I just introduce myself. "I'm John Lowry."

"John Lowry," he repeats. "I know that name."

"Hanabi lived with my family." I say her name with trepidation. I don't know if it is ever wise to claim familiarity with another man's wife.

He shows no expression when I mention Hanabi, but after a weighty pause he answers my question, and his voice has lost all hostility.

"It wasn't my people who killed the soldiers. We don't kill white men. We kill the Crow. Sometimes we kill each other. But we don't kill white men," the chief says.

"Why?" I am genuinely curious.

"They keep coming. It won't do any good." He shrugs.

I tell Captain Kelly and Vasquez what he has said, and the chief waits until I look at him again.

"It was probably Pocatello," he concedes.

"Shoshoni?" I ask.

He nods once. "He doesn't like white men. He likes scalps. He has white scalps of every color and size."

"Are you his chief?"

"No. He leads his own people. He would like my scalp most of all. I am not his chief, but he worries his people will follow me." Washakie shrugs again as if it makes no difference to him.

I repeat what Washakie has told me, filtering out the details that might ignite tensions.

"Ask him if Bridger's been selling him any firewater," Captain Kelly demands.

Washakie understands the word, and he sneers at the captain. He turns and barks an order to his men, who have been guarding their wares. A flurry of motion ensues, an indication that they are leaving.

Vasquez protests, obviously wanting what Washakie has brought to trade.

"Stay, Washakie. Please," Vasquez begs, his hands upraised in supplication. "Tell him I will give him whatever he wants," he says, turning to me. "No more questions."

Captain Kelly sighs, but he doesn't object, and I tell Washakie that Vasquez wants to trade now.

Washakie folds his arms and rattles off a list of demands—sugar, paint, guns, beads. He wants more because he has been made to wait and treated poorly. Vasquez is quick to fill the order, sending Teddy Bowles scrambling, and Vasquez and a handful of other traders, who have emerged from the fort now that the trouble seems to have passed, commence with trading. I marvel at Washakie's carriage and demeanor. He is not intimidated or even accommodating, but he is also not overtly aggressive, which reassures the people around him. His warriors reflect his confidence. They are a handsome people, arrayed in a manner that demands respect.

Kelly's men relax, and some disperse, though just as many step forward to engage in some trading of their own. A few ask me to interpret for them, and I do, easing the negotiations back and forth. I motion for Wyatt to bring me my packs, but when I try to conduct an exchange for myself, Washakie shakes his head. He points at the furs and the buffalo meat I have set aside. The meat is enough to feed the May boys for a month.

"For Hanabi," Washakie says. "No trade, John Lowry. Gift." And he will not even look at what I try to give him in return.

When he rides away, his ponies and packs laden with new provisions, Vasquez is still beside me, though Captain Kelly has withdrawn with his men.

"Louis Vasquez," he says, sticking out his hand, since we have not been formally introduced.

"So I heard," I say. "You are a bit of a legend where I come from." He laughs, but he's enough of a dandy that he is pleased.

"My father sold you a mule a decade ago. He never let me forget it," I add. "And my father isn't impressed by much."

"John Lowry," he says, nodding. "I remember it well. I thought there might be a connection when I heard your name. I still have that mule your father sold me. Ten years now. Never given me a moment's grief, never quit on me."

"When I write home, I'll tell him. He'll be happy to hear it."

"This is my wife, Narcissa," Vasquez says, introducing the woman in the deep-blue dress who has just joined us. She ducks under Vasquez's arm, confident in her place. She's small and well made and at least two decades younger than he is, but when she smiles, I see how she managed to convince a man like Vasquez to stay put—if he had to be convinced.

"Hello, Mr. Lowry," she says, setting her hand in mine. "You have saved the day. Where in the world did you come from?"

"Uh . . . well," I stammer, not knowing quite how to respond. "I'm with a wagon train. They're still a day out. I came ahead to do some business."

"Those your animals?" Vasquez asks, eyeing the animals Wyatt is still guarding nearby.

"Yes, sir."

He moves toward them, Narcissa beside him, and he shakes Wyatt's hand over Samson's long back.

"You sellin'?" Vasquez asks me.

"No, sir. Not if I can help it. I have to get to California, and I'm going to need them to pull my wagon."

"Too bad. I'm interested in buying if you're interested in selling. I owe you one, Lowry. You calmed that whole situation, and I'm indebted to you. I don't speak Shoshoni—not like that—and Captain Kelly even less so."

"The fort isn't . . . what I expected," I say, shifting the subject to my immediate concern.

"It was not what I expected either, Mr. Lowry," Narcissa says, darting a good-natured look at her husband.

Vasquez rubs his face and sighs. "Bridger and I can't stay put long enough to make it prosper. Fur trade is changing—we've got more emigrants coming through here than trappers anymore, though most of them are heading to the Salt Lake Valley. And the Mormons don't like how we run things."

"I can see that."

"Prices too high and the pickings are too small."

"I can see that too," I say, my voice as neutral as I can make it. I don't think it's right to gouge desperate folks, and he sighs again, hearing what I don't say.

"It's expensive getting goods out here. But the grass is plentiful, and the water is mountain fresh and cold. And we don't charge for any of that," he says. "Still . . . I'm thinking of just letting the Mormons have it." Vasquez sighs, and Narcissa gives him a look that speaks of long, private conversations.

"Has there been trouble?" I ask.

"Between Bridger and the Mormons? Yeah. And they're right. The US government looks down on selling spirits to the locals. God knows the whiskey trade has destroyed the tribes in the East. The Sioux won't touch it."

"Smart, the Sioux," Narcissa interjects.

"Still . . . you try telling a band of Utes or Blackfeet you won't trade with them." Vasquez snorts. "If they want whiskey and they have the robes and the pelts—we trade. Jim says he's not interested in being a wet nurse to the local tribes."

"The Utes and the Blackfeet?"

"They aren't all like Washakie. He gets along. You can't push him around, but he gets along. He trades with us, trades with the Mormons too. That's why it's surprising they gave him any trouble. The Utes and the Blackfeet—the Blackfeet around Fort Hall are nothing but trouble—don't have much use for any of us."

"And the attack on the patrol the captain was talking about?" I ask.

"I don't know anything about it. That kind of thing is rare, and more often than not, the settlers get scared and shoot first."

"More often than not," Narcissa agrees.

"Captain Kelly isn't a bad man, and he's got no quarrel with Washakie, despite what it may have looked like," Vasquez says. "His quarrel is with Bridger, and I'm tired of the whole business. I'm thinking I should sell out. Get my money and go. Maybe start a store in the valley—maybe go back to Missouri."

"And now you have all the sordid details," Narcissa Vasquez says, smiling at me and looping her hand through her husband's arm as if to buoy him up. "But what can we help you with, Mr. Lowry? To show our thanks."

"We're in need of a wagon, ma'am," Wyatt blurts, inserting himself into the conversation.

Vasquez whistles, low and soft. "We get wagons through here. But all of them are full of settlers. They're abandoned along the way, but if they roll in *here*, they roll out."

"Jefferson might be able to help," Narcissa says. "But why a wagon now, gentlemen, when you are this far along in your journey?"

Wyatt looks at me, expectant.

"There's a . . . woman . . . I'd like to marry in the company coming in. She's got family ties and responsibilities, and that means staying with the train."

"Ah. I see," Narcissa says, nodding with understanding.

"I told her we'd marry when we reached Fort Bridger."

"And you thought you would find something akin to Fort Laramie, where some comfort and privacy might be enjoyed. Louis and I were married at Fort Laramie by Father de Smet. It was very exciting. Have you heard of him? He is quite famous in church circles."

"No, ma'am."

"Narcissa, I doubt the man's Catholic," Vasquez grumbles.

"No, sir," I say.

"Do you have someone who can perform the marriage?" Narcissa asks.

"I do."

"Then you must marry in our home. In the parlor. I insist. And you will have my room for the evening. I cannot help you with a wagon, but I can help you with this."

Vasquez seems surprised, but his wife continues without pause.

"Louis is leaving in the morning for the Great Salt Lake Valley with Captain Kelly. I think we've convinced him Mr. Bridger isn't returning anytime soon, if at all. I will sleep with the children. I often do when Louis is gone."

I glance back at Wyatt, whose face has gone crimson with all the discussion of weddings and rooms. I don't know what to say. My pride and my need are warring in my chest.

"That's kind of you, ma'am," Wyatt says, saving me. "But there's quite a few of us. The whole train will want to attend. It might be better if we do it outside. But my sister deserves something good, something fine. I'm sure she would appreciate the room."

God bless you, Wyatt.

"Very well, young man," Narcissa says, smiling. "There's a small clearing just behind the fort. I have a garden there, though we have a while before harvest time. There's some yarrow that grows wild all around it. It'll be prettier than any church. Tomorrow, at sunset. It's the perfect time of day. And Mr. Lowry, when your bride arrives, you will bring her to me."

14

THE CUTOFF

JOHN

I spend the next morning trying to earn a wagonload of discounted supplies out of Teddy Bowles. He does indeed have a few mares, and after looking them over, I inform him that one is probably already pregnant, despite his efforts to keep them away from the other horses, but one is in heat. The breeding season for mares extends from early spring to the end of summer, with cycles of fertility throughout. I tell him this as I explain my process, but he just wants to get started.

"Let's get him in here," he says, clapping his hands.

"She won't be interested in the jack," I warn. "She's a mare, and she wants a stallion."

Bowles frowns, not understanding. "But I want a mule outa that jack."

Wyatt is trying not to laugh.

"I understand," I say. "But I'm going to need a stallion to make her cooperate."

I rattle off a few other things I'll need and agree to meet him near the fence that divides the interior corral in an hour.

I don't think he's convinced, but he sends a stable hand named Javi, a Mexican boy a year or so younger than Wyatt, to secure the stallion while he gathers the other things I've requested, and Wyatt and I head to the enclosure with Kettle.

"Why do you need a stallion?" Wyatt asks.

"We're going to have to tease the mare, get her ready, and give Kettle a chance to do his business."

"How long do you think that'll take?" Wyatt asks.

"Jacks are slow. And they prefer jennies. Mounting a mare doesn't come naturally, as natural as all this is."

"Huh," Wyatt grunts, impressed.

I scratch Kettle between his ears. "You gotta coax him. You gotta convince him. Tell him, 'You like her, Kettle. You do.'"

Wyatt grins and removes his hat, swiping at the dusty strands of blond hair that stick to his forehead. "Can you usually convince him?"

"I usually can if I don't get pushy."

Bowles delivers what I've asked of him, and within a half hour, I've cleared out all the other horses to the back paddock and created my stalls. Each stall consists of parallel boards jutting out from the fence that divides the corral in two. When the mare and the stallion are in their stalls, they will face each other but be separated by the fence.

"Lead the mare into the stall, Wyatt, and stand there with her, holding her rope, but leave it nice and loose." The makeshift stall is just wide enough for the mare to stand within it but narrow enough to keep her from turning.

I point to Bowles. "Bring the stallion in on the other side to face her. That's right. At home we call the stallions the dandies. He just has to look good and kiss her a little."

Bowles tells Javi to do as I ask and then climbs up on the dividing fence so he can get a better view.

The mare tosses her head, and the stallion nips at her neck, baring his teeth. I let this continue for a minute, allowing the age-old ritual to unfold, before I lead Kettle up behind the mare. I let him sniff at her and nuzzle her, butting her hindquarters with his nose, before allowing him to retreat to think on it. She's distracted by the stallion and doesn't even realize he's there.

I've attracted an assortment of observers, including Vasquez and a small boy I assume is his son, some men from the Mormon encampment, and a ragtag assortment of trappers, Indians, and Mexicans who have emerged from places unknown.

Kettle rises up on his hind legs against the mare's flanks, testing the waters, before coming back down and backing off. My crowd sighs, and the mare quivers, tossing her head at the stallion and lowering her hips.

"Do you think he's gonna be able to do his business with everyone watchin' like this?" Wyatt mutters, still holding the mare's lead rope in his hands.

Bowles hoots, and I just shake my head.

"Patience," I say.

It takes an hour for Kettle to get good and ready. He mounts and backs off. Mounts and backs off. And I let him take his time. My crowd gets tired, and Bowles begins to look doubtful, but I ignore them.

Finally, after several false starts, the mare lowers her hips with her tail raised and her flanks wet, the object of her interest posturing before her, and Kettle mounts, connects, gyrates, and within thirty seconds has withdrawn again. Task complete. He receives a smattering of applause from those who waited it out, and Bowles throws his hat in celebration. He tells Javi to take the stallion and "give that poor fellow an extra cup of grain."

Slipping the lead rope from the mare's head, I back her out of the stall with a flat hand and a firm push on her chest, and she willingly goes. Bowles leads her away, already wondering out loud about the color of her offspring. Wyatt and I remove the boards on both sides of the fence, hammering the nails loose.

"When can your jack go again?" Vasquez asks, slinging his arms over the top rail of the fence. "I've never been in the breeding business. I realize there's a lot I don't know." His son is no longer with him, but a man with a huge wagging mustache and hair that touches his shoulders stands beside him.

"Tomorrow. Maybe. I'm a little surprised he cooperated. He's come almost a thousand miles, and he's tired."

"That right there is not work for a jack," the mustached man says. "That's play."

I don't argue with him. It's work if it's done right and cruel if it's done wrong. I've always enjoyed the challenge of redirecting nature, but I've never pretended I can control it.

"John Lowry, this is Jefferson Jones. He's the blacksmith here at the fort. He thinks he can help you with that wagon."

I set the boards aside and shake his hand in greeting.

"There's a ridge on the Mormon Trail, about ten miles west of here. Steep as all get-out. There's a half dozen wagons at the bottom of that hill," Jefferson says.

"A half a dozen wagons in pieces," Vasquez interjects.

"Yep. But that's how all wagons start. I got an outfit we can haul the parts in. It'll take us a half a day to go after it, another half a day to bring it back, but the bones are all there. If an axle is bent, that's easy enough to fix if I can get it back here."

"I'm a mule man, not a wheelwright or a wagon builder. How long is it gonna take to put it all back together?" I ask.

"Another day. I worked on the Erie Canal when I was about his age." The man points at Wyatt. "All I did was fix the wagons. I could build one in my sleep."

"Two days?"

"A day to go get it. A day to assemble. And you're on your way," he says.

I shift my gaze to Vasquez, not sure whether I can trust his blacksmith. He shrugs. "You aren't going to find a better option," Vasquez says.

"And what do you get in exchange?" I ask, looking back at Jefferson.

"I want the jack."

Wyatt curses beneath his breath.

"No."

"You must not want that wagon very bad." Jefferson chuckles. I don't laugh with him. I want the wagon, and I don't know what in the hell I'm going to do. But I would carry Naomi on my back all the way to California with Mr. Caldwell prodding me with a stick before I'd trade Kettle. I've already given one jack away to make this journey; I can't afford to lose another.

"I think your price is too high. Make me another offer," I say.

He sighs like I'm being unreasonable and folds his arms over his barrel chest. "All right. No jack? Then I want a mule. I want that big black one." He points to where my animals are cordoned, but I don't need to look. He wants Samson.

I can tell Wyatt wants to protest. He's biting his lip and blinking rapidly, but he doesn't say a word. The hardest thing about the mule business is trading the mules.

I nod slowly. Considering I will be leaving Fort Bridger with a wagon, supplies, and a wife, the loss of one mule isn't that bad a bargain.

"Do we have a deal?" Jefferson presses.

"We have a deal. When I get my wagon, you'll get a mule."

NAOMI

You don't realize how dirty you are and how worn until you stand in a stranger's parlor. From the outside, the structure didn't look like much, a two-story log house tacked onto the end of the trading post, but inside is a different story. A carpet covers the floor, velvet drapes frame the window, and patterned paper covers the walls. A tinkling chandelier hangs above our heads, two rows of fresh candles waiting to be lit.

"Isn't that something?" Narcissa Vasquez crows, following my gaze. A bright smile colors her voice and creases her pink cheeks. "A train came through last year. And a gentleman traded it for two bottles of whiskey. I think he would have given me two bottles of whiskey just to take it off his hands. His wife passed on not long after they made Pacific Springs. He'd fought with her the whole way about that chandelier. But she wanted it and wouldn't let it go." She exhales. "We women want to make the world brighter, don't we? Even if we have to fight our men every step of the way."

"Thank you for inviting us into your home," Ma says, her voice thin. I know she is trying not to cough, and her breaths wheeze in her chest. Neither of us dares move for fear we'll soil something. When I take a step, dust billows from my skirts.

The moment we rolled in, circling our wagons about a half mile from the rough-hewn walls of the fort, I braced myself for bad news. We made camp and set the animals loose to graze, and all the while I watched for John, preparing myself for a postponement of our plans. But when he finally arrived, Wyatt beside him, his mules strung out behind them, he surprised me again. He confirmed with Deacon Clarke that he would conduct the service and told everyone in the train they were invited to attend.

"Sundown. Behind the fort. Mrs. Vasquez said we'll even have cake," Wyatt exclaimed.

Then John told me to come with him and bring my green dress. He said he couldn't buy me a new one, but everything else was arranged. He told me to bring Ma too. And now we're standing in Narcissa Vasquez's pretty parlor, as out of place as two tumbleweeds in a tropical paradise.

"Yes . . . thank you for inviting us into your home," I repeat, parroting my mother. I have a huge throbbing lump in my throat. I want to marry John. I want that more than anything, but I'm filthy, I'm tired, and for the first time in my life, I'm acutely aware of what I lack.

"It is my pleasure and privilege. I get lonely here," Narcissa confesses. She is lovely in every way—her dress, her hair, her figure, her smile—and I can only stare, baffled. She presses her hands together and beams at us as though she has a great surprise.

"Now. Come with me. We've heated water for a bath. The men can wash in the creek, but a bride must have something special. Her mother too."

Ma starts to shake her head; she has nothing better to don, and Wolfe is asleep in her arms. "Oh no. No, we couldn't possibly."

"Yes. You can," Narcissa insists. "I will hold the little one. I have a pile of dresses you can choose from. I'm a bit of a runt, but without a hoop beneath the skirt, they will be plenty long. There's one in particular that I think will do nicely. I wore it when I was expecting my youngest. It has a little more room in it."

Ma gapes.

"And Naomi. That green dress will be lovely with your eyes. You are so tall and slim. I have a bit of lace you can wear at your throat, if you wish, or you can wear one of mine as well. There might be something there that you love."

We trail obediently behind her, careful not to brush up against anything as she leads us into a kitchen manned by a Mexican woman who is pouring steaming water into a big cast-iron tub. She swishes her hand in the water, mixing hot and cold, and nods in approval. There are trays of little cakes on the table, iced in white and begging to be tasted. My stomach growls, and Narcissa winks at me.

"The cakes are for the party. But Maria's set some bread and butter out. There are dried apples and apricots too. And cheese. Please help yourselves."

"But . . . ," Ma protests. I know she is worrying about the boys and what they'll eat while we stuff ourselves on bread and cheese and apricots.

"We will go so you can bathe. Give me the baby," Narcissa says, extending her arms for Wolfe.

Ma wilts beneath her vehemence and settles him in Narcissa's arms. She gives us another radiant smile and swooshes out of the kitchen with Maria trailing behind her.

For a moment after the two women leave, Ma and I stand in stunned silence. Then we begin to laugh. We laugh until we are doubled over, we laugh through Ma's coughing, and we laugh until we cry. And then we cry some more. For the second time in less than a week, we have been embraced by the grace of strangers.

"You bathe first, Naomi. So the water's clean," Ma insists, and I cry again because of her sweetness. She pulls up a chair like she did when I was a girl bathing in the washtub on Saturday nights. I always went first then too, before my brothers took their turns and made the water murky with their little-boy dirt.

Ma pours water over my head, rinsing out the soap. It smells like roses, and I'm overcome once more. When it's Ma's turn, I do the same for her, turning the tin cup over her sudsy hair until nothing remains but little silver streaks amid the glistening brown.

"Someday my hair will look just like yours," I murmur, following the stream of water with my palm.

"Yes. But you have a life to live before then. And today is a new beginning."

Maria reappears before we are finished and whisks our dirty clothes away, leaving crisp cotton bloomers and chemises behind, and we begin to laugh in amazement all over again.

∞

There is no place to sit, so everyone stands, making a crowded half circle in the clearing cloaked in flowers and guarded by the trees. Webb isn't wearing any shoes. He hasn't worn them since we crossed the Big Blue.

His feet are as tough as horse hooves, the dirt ground in deep, but Pa has made him comb his hair, and his cheeks are still pink from the cold water of the creek. Ma keeps mending the holes in his clothes, but he's starting to look like a patchwork quilt. They all are. Wyatt and Warren and Will and Pa. They've made an effort, it's easy to see, but nothing has been left untouched by our travels.

The families of our company are all here too, wearing dusty clothes but freshly scrubbed faces. Abbott, Jeb, Lydia and Adam, Elsie and Homer, all smiling like I belong to them. Even Mr. Caldwell is here, his white hair neatly parted above his sunburned brow, and Elmeda is already weeping. Grief and joy are complicated. Love and loss too, and I know tears aren't always what they seem. I smile at her as I approach on Ma's arm, and she smiles back through trembling lips.

Narcissa has made us wait until very last to make our entrance, directing the service like she's directed everything else today. Pa is crying too, but he's not looking at me. He's looking at Ma in Narcissa's lavender dress; it's a little short in the sleeves and tight across the shoulders, but she looks like a girl again. We drew her hair back in soft waves from her face and coiled it at her nape, and Narcissa gave us both a handful of little white blossoms to carry. She called it yarrow, and it surrounds the clearing on every side.

I keep my gaze averted from John. I know he is here, waiting for me. From the corner of my eye I can see him standing next to Deacon Clarke across from all our guests. I'm afraid if I look at him, I won't be able to keep my mind right. I'm feeling too much, and I don't want to share my emotion with anyone but him. I suddenly understand why he is so private, why he keeps things locked down tight. It's because the moment you let go, those feelings aren't just yours anymore. And I've been crying all day. I've been lost all day.

I decided against the green dress. It's a day of new beginnings, as Ma said, and when I saw Narcissa's yellow dress, it made me smile. Yellow, for the first time we met. It isn't fancy, but it's the nicest dress I've ever worn. The full skirt is a tad short, but the round-necked bodice fits me just right, and the elbow-length sleeves are forgiving, hemmed as they are with a skirting of lace. I've saved the doeskin moccasins John bought me at Fort Laramie, and I wear those too.

Deacon Clarke is wearing a black necktie and a fine black coat with his tattered trousers, but I stare at John's boots. He's shined them so they gleam like his glossy black hair. It's grown considerably, and he's brushed it straight back so it touches the collar of his new shirt, which is stiff and clean like his trousers. His sleeves are rolled, and his forearms are strong and brown like the column of his neck, the line of his jaw, and the blade of his nose. I look everywhere but his eyes, and then I look there too.

He is not smiling. He isn't even breathing. But then his chest rises and falls, a deep breath, once and again, and his eyes shine down into mine. The lost feeling flees, and I am me again. Confident. Sure. Ready. I smile at him the way I did that first day, sitting in the middle of the street on a barrel in St. Joe. I think I knew even then.

"Therefore shall a man leave his father and his mother and shall cleave unto his wife. And they shall be one flesh," Deacon Clarke says, and I feel his words to the bottom of my soul. He takes us through our promises, and we repeat his words.

"I take you, John."

"I take you, Naomi."

"To have and to hold, from this day forward. For better, for worse, for richer, for poorer, in sickness and in health. To love and to cherish, till death do us part."

JOHN

She is sitting at the little writing desk in the corner of the Vasquezes' room, a candle flickering at her side, and she is wearing my shirt. The sleeves are rolled to free her hands, and the hem falls several inches above her knees, baring her pale legs. It is not a comfortable shirt. It is new and scratchy, and I couldn't wait to take it off, but I like the way it looks on her. Her long, tangled hair tumbles down her back, and in the flickering light she is a collection of lovely shadows. I watch her between half-closed lids.

"You are beautiful," I whisper.

"You only say that when you are dying or half-asleep," she answers, not raising her gaze from her pencil, but her lips curve.

"But I always think it."

"I didn't mean to wake you. I'm sorry." She sighs. But I'm not sorry. I can sleep later.

"What are you doing?" I ask.

"I am drawing a picture for Mrs. Vasquez. To thank her. A portrait. She has a lovely smile."

"You are wearing my shirt."

"It was easier to pull on than my dress."

"It is easier to pull off too."

"Yes." Again the curve of her lips.

"Did you sleep at all, Naomi?"

"I was too happy. I didn't want to waste it in sleep. If I stay awake, the night will last longer." Finally she looks at me, and the same turbulence that glowed in her eyes at our wedding is there again.

"Come here," I say.

She makes a stroke here and there on the page in front of her and then rises, the obedient wife, the candle in one hand, a sheet of paper in the other. She climbs into the bed beside me, burrowing her cold toes between my calves.

"I drew this too," she whispers. "A wedding gift for my husband."

The lines are clean and dark, our bodies intertwined, my head bowed over hers, the length of her naked spine and the curve of her hips visible beneath the circle of my arms.

"I don't know if that is how we appear, or if it is only the way you make me feel. I don't ever want to forget this day," she says.

I take the candle from her and the picture too and, pulling my shirt over her head, vow to help us both remember. I kiss her, and she returns my fervor, but when she pulls back for a ragged breath, she cradles my face in her hands, and her thumbs stroke my lips. Love wells in my chest, so fierce and so foreign that I have to look away. I turn my face into her palm, pressing a kiss to its center.

"I don't want to leave you behind tomorrow," she whispers. I have told her my plans to build a wagon, and we've agreed that the rest of the train will leave in the morning without me and Wyatt.

"You know what I'm going to say, don't you?" I murmur.

"Yes. You're going to say it's only a few days." She pauses a moment. "And what do you think I'm going to say?"

"You're going to say we don't need a wagon. You're going to say we can just continue on the way we have been."

"Exactly." Her voice is soft, and she rests her head against my arm, her eyes pleading, her lips rosy and well used.

"But if we continue on the way we have been, I won't be able to do this." I kiss the tip of one breast. "Or this," I say and kiss the other. "If we go back to the way we were, I will have to keep my distance, and you will have to keep yours."

"I can't," she moans.

"I know." I laugh. "So now what are you going to say?"

"We need a wagon of our own," she says, making me laugh again.

"We need a wagon of our own," I repeat, pressing my face into the crook of her neck, nuzzling, tasting, my mouth opened against the sweetness of her. Her pulse quickens, and the hand that cradled my face is now at my heart . . . and at my hip . . . and at the small of my back, urging me to her. She is ready again.

Then her lips are beneath my lips, and her body is beneath my body, flesh and bone and beautiful indentations, and we both forget all the things we didn't say.

꩜

I post a letter with Teddy Bowles the next morning, worried that I will forget in the days ahead. He promises someone will be going east before long. He's got two canvas satchels packed to the brim with emigrant letters. I do not write two this time. I don't have the patience or the paper. I scrawl out a few lines letting Jennie and my father know I am well, the mules are fine, and by the way, I just got hitched. There is no way to break the news more artfully in a very small space, so I don't even try. I sound stiff and cold, maybe a little simple too, and I wince at the inadequate lines. But my gift for language does not extend to the written word, and I finish with this:

> Her name is Naomi May. You met her once, Father. Her family is traveling with the train, and we will remain with them until the journey is through. Jennie will be happy to know we were married by a deacon and scripture was read and a hymn sung. Naomi is a fine woman, and I love her. I found Ana. She is the wife of a Shoshoni chief and has a beautiful baby girl. She is grateful for you both. As am I. I will write again when I reach California.

> Your son,
> John Lowry

15

SHEEP ROCK

JOHN

More than one wagon lies at the bottom of the hill, all in various states of decay and destruction: missing wheels, tattered canvas tops, rotted tongues, and bent axles. I can only stare, my hands on my hips, feeling the same wash of despair I felt when I saw the fort.

"Don't worry, Lowry. I don't get my mule if you don't get your wagon. We take the best and leave the rest," Jefferson says, starting down the incline, his boot heels digging into the shale-covered climb.

I have never built a wagon, and I don't know if I'll recognize what's good and what's not, but I slide to the bottom of the ravine with a willingness to learn. Jefferson begins to dig through the tired remains, grunting and discarding before he declares one wagon a "gold mine."

"The box is intact, and there's no rot. Looks like everything's here underneath too: pins and plates . . . the hound is in good shape. Looks to me like the brake beam snapped. I can fix that, put on some new brake shoes." He has crawled underneath the wagon to survey its underpinnings. "We need bows for the top and a new piece of canvas—Teddy can help us with that."

I search the wreckage and find a dozen bows to support the cover, and before long Jefferson has selected two wheels from other wagons that aren't warped or cracked.

"They've seen wear, but we'll grease 'em good. Maybe replace some of those spokes. The hubs are here, axles too, and this one even has one of them tickers that records the miles. Never used one myself, but it might be handy to have."

Jefferson enjoys the hunt, and he picks around at the bottom of the ravine for another hour, muttering about tar buckets and feed boxes, before he calls it good. With my mules and a set of chains, we drag the wagon up the hill, Wyatt at the top, Jefferson and me scrambling up beside it. Halfway up, the chain slips, and Jefferson's gold mine slides back down the hill, snapping off another wheel.

"No problem at all," Jefferson bellows. "I can fix that."

An hour later, we manage to pull the wagon all the way to the top, but Jefferson decides it'll be easier to repair the wheels and reinforce the snapped brake line right here rather than taking it apart to haul it back to the fort.

"If I do that, it'll save us some time."

He gets started before realizing he doesn't have all the tools he needs, and we end up pulling it apart after all, unscrewing wheels, removing the wagon box from the undercarriage, and loading everything into Jefferson's wagon.

It takes all day. We roll into Fort Bridger an hour after sunset, a full fifteen hours after Abbott and the train pulled out. Jefferson said it would take a day to retrieve it, so we're not behind schedule, but my confidence in him is shaken. I expect I'll have snakes in my belly until I'm with Naomi again. I'm becoming used to the sensation, but the snakes are heavier and rattle harder when I'm at the mercy of someone else, and I am at the mercy of Jefferson Jones.

"We will work all day tomorrow. Don't worry," Wyatt says when we roll out our beds for a few hours of sleep. "We'll be able to move a lot faster than the train with your mules. If we're three days back, we'll still catch up before they reach the turnoff. You heard Abbott. Northwest to Soda Springs, then left at Sheep Rock to the cutoff, and the road is tolerable all the way. We'll catch up to 'em by then."

NAOMI

When we reach Smiths Fork, two days out of Fort Bridger, we're able to cross a bridge completed only the year before by some industrious travelers. It is a good deal easier than unloading the wagons and wading through hip-deep water, but Trick and Tumble don't like it at all and have to be coaxed, along with every other mule in the company. Webb has learned a thing or two from John and shows them how it's done, his little arms spread wide, trekking back and forth until he can convince them to follow. The grass is green and plentiful at the fork, but the mosquitoes are so thick the animals can't eat. None of us can, and Abbott presses us to move on.

"There's only one road he can take, Miss Naomi. He'll catch us before long. But we do ourselves no good to camp here. No one will rest," Abbott explains, and the consensus is to move on.

I rip a long strip off the bottom of my tattered, stained yellow dress and wrap it around a tree near the heaviest ruts and leave a message nailed beneath it.

> John and Wyatt,
> We've gone on. We are all well. Mosquitoes bad.
> Heading to Soda Springs.
> Love,
> Naomi

We forge on, walking much of the night by the light of the moon, and reach Thomas Fork the next day, eager for sleep and grass and water without mosquitoes floating on the top. We're moving north along the Bear River, and the valley is lush and green, but the bugs plague us continually. A swarm of grasshoppers descends on us just past Thomas Fork, and we walk with blankets slung over our heads, shrieking and striking at our clothes as they land. The mules like the grasshoppers even less than they liked the bridge, and they kick and shimmy, trying to be free of the horde. The oxen just bow their heads and plod on, their tails swishing like the pendulum on a clock.

Elsie Hines is afraid to ride in the wagon. Her baby could come any day, and she doesn't want her waters to break. She's been riding Tumble, who has the smoothest gait, but with the grasshoppers making the mules skittish, she waddles along, even more miserable than the rest of us.

Six days have passed since we left the fort. Six days of praying and looking over my shoulder. We reach Soda Springs, where the water gurgles and spouts like it's boiling even though it's cold. In one place, the water shoots straight up into the air with a great rumbling and whistle, and we can hear it and see it from a good ways off. A few of the men experiment a little, setting items of varying weight and size over the opening to see whether the pressure is enough to propel them into the air. Jeb Caldwell puts his saddle over the opening, thinking he'll ride the stream, and gets flipped like a coin. He doesn't get hurt, but Elmeda isn't amused. The water tastes odd but not entirely unpleasant. It bites and bubbles, and Abbott says we can drink it.

"It's the minerals in the water that makes it taste funny. Some folks like it. They say it soothes the stomach."

Four miles beyond the soda springs, the range of mountains directly before us ends in an abrupt and jagged point, and the Bear River we've been following for miles makes a sharp curve around it and heads back in the direction from whence it came. We've made Sheep Rock, where the trail splits again, another parting of ways. North to Fort Hall and the Oregon Trail, straight west to the old California road.

"It's only noon, but let's stop and make camp," Abbott says. "We have a hundred thirty-two miles of dry, hard travel ahead of us, so we'll take the rest of today to rest the teams and gird up. Plan on pulling out first thing in the morning."

"We told Wyatt and John we would wait at Sheep Rock," I protest, trying to maintain my composure.

"I told John we'd take the cutoff at Sheep Rock," he says, his voice gentle. "But he knows we can't wait."

"What if we wait and he doesn't come?" Mr. Caldwell chimes in. "Then we've waited for nothing."

"He'll come," Abbott reassures me, patting my shoulders. "I have no doubt. You watch—he'll pull in here before tomorrow morning, you mark my words."

I mark his words, but John doesn't come, and the train pulls out a few hours after dawn, our teams watered and fed, our barrels filled, and our path set. I leave a note and another strip of my yellow dress tied around a tree. I try not to doubt, but even Ma's grown pensive.

"They'll take care of each other," she says, "just like they did before," and I nod and try to breathe, doing my best to hold back the tears. We don't discuss it; we don't voice our fears or wonder out loud what's holding them up, but I know Ma's thoughts are churning too, and she's saying her prayers, just like I am.

It doesn't help that my menses have started, soaking my bloomers, chafing my legs, and making it hard to keep clean. I tell myself it's good that John is gone. Maybe when he returns, my time will have passed, and I won't have to worry about being close to him the way I want to.

We make ten miles over sage and lava rocks before Abbott blows his horn and veers away from the road, searching for a spring he's certain isn't far. We've just begun making our circle around a pathetic patch of green a couple of miles off the road when Pa's wagon hits a rock and busts a wheel, and Elsie Bingham, sitting on the back of Tumble, tells us she's through.

"I can't go no farther," she moans. "I gotta get down." Her pains have started, and she's afraid she'll tumble from the mule. Ma and I help her slide from the saddle and support her as she steadies herself.

"It could be a while yet, Elsie," Ma says. "It's your first one, and you know all the stories. The best thing you can do is rest now, while the wagons are stopped and the pains are still far apart."

"All right," Elsie says, nodding. "But . . . if it doesn't come tonight . . . will you stay with me in the morning? I know we gotta keep moving, but I don't know if I can."

"It's gettin' dark, and our wheel is broken," Ma says, smiling a little. "So we're not going anywhere."

"Well, thank the Lord for broken wheels," Elsie breathes.

"Ma and I will stay with you as long as you need," I agree.

I just hope John and Wyatt don't pass us by back on the road. They won't know where we are.

JOHN

When the mules begin to prick their ears and lift their noses, I straighten on the torturous wooden seat and scan the horizon like I've been doing all day. We are heading west now, and the sun is high and the dust is thick, making the way before us hard to see. We should catch up to the train today, and the mules' sudden interest has my heart quickening in anticipation. We passed Sheep Rock this morning, and I found Naomi's yellow streamer and the note she nailed to a tree. She put a date at the top and the time they pulled out—yesterday morning—so they can't be far now.

"You see something, John?" Wyatt asks, grimacing against the sun and gritting his teeth against the dust. He's taken a position beside me on the seat, rifle in hand like we're driving the stage.

"No." I shake my head. "I don't see anything. But I'm guessing the mules know Trick and Tumble are out there."

"I thought we'd have caught up to them by now," Wyatt says. "They got farther than I thought they would."

We're late. Days late. Jefferson Jones came through, but not before I almost killed him. He spent a day tinkering in his shop and another assembling the wagon, only to realize he was missing a part. We went back to the ravine, and he puttered around until he found what he wanted, losing half of another day. At the end of the fourth day, I told him I was leaving in the morning and taking my mules—all of them—with or without the wagon. He got angry, but then he got serious, and the wagon was ready to go at dawn, provisions loaded. I didn't give him Samson. I gave him Gus, and he didn't argue. I harnessed up the other six to share the load and tied Kettle to one side and the dun to the other.

We've been riding hard and fast, resting for the darkest hours of the night and rising well before dawn. The mules are holding up. The wagon is holding up, and Wyatt is downright cheerful. I am not holding up, and I am not remotely cheerful, and were it not for the notes and the strips of yellow in the trees telling me all is well, I would be a damn sight worse.

"They might still be a ways ahead," I say. "Mules are sensitive. They usually know what's coming a while before anyone else does. We're getting close, running over miles where the train traveled not too long ago. That might be all it is." But I let the mules lead, letting them set the pace. Their hooves begin to eat up the ground, their eager pursuit tightening my hands on the reins. When they start to slow of their own accord, chests heaving, a cloud of dust rising around us, and then come to a stop altogether, I let the dust settle and stay put. My eyes sweep the distance, scanning the brush and surveying the rocky outcroppings, looking for a line of white tops against the muted greens and browns of August. Heat and silence and a long stretch of no one greet my gaze.

"It's hard to tell with all the dust, but doesn't that look like smoke?" Wyatt asks, pointing at a grayish funnel rising off to our right. It's far enough away that I can't make out what's on fire. "I think it is." He sniffs at the air. "Smell that?"

I do. But that is not what has caught my eye. Directly in front of the column of smoke are two small figures, no bigger than the freckles on Naomi's nose. I watch, not certain what I'm seeing. The sparse trees of the West have fooled more than one man into thinking he's got company.

The mules have begun to stomp and shimmy, but the dun is perfectly still, his head high, his nose turned in the direction of my gaze.

"Whoa, mules. Whoa," I reassure them. They have their ears pinned back like they're sensing a watering hole being guarded by a wolf and aren't sure whether they want to risk an approach.

"Giddyap," I urge, giving the reins a shake.

They begin to move, veering away from the road to pick their way around the rocks and sage to another set of ruts. These tracks aren't nearly as deep and distinct as those on the main, but they head toward the tiny shapes that quiver in the distance.

Wyatt is quiet beside me, and I'm grateful for his silence. I have questions and no answers. I only know as long as the mules are walking and not balking, we're not in any immediate danger. They pick up speed, chuffing and bearing down on the reins, and I hold them back, mindful of the wheels beneath me and repairs I don't want to make. Within minutes the figures reveal themselves.

"John, I think . . . I think that's Will and Webb."

I forget about the wagon and the unforgiving seat beneath me and let the mules go. Wyatt clings to the seat with one hand and to his rifle with the other.

"Where's the rest of the train?" he shouts over the squeal of the wheels. "Where the hell are the wagons?"

The two boys have begun to run, their arms and legs pumping, their shaggy hair bouncing around them. They see us too. Neither of them is wearing hats or shoes—not that Webb ever does—and they are very much alone.

The distance between us is a thousand miles, and I am gripped with dread. For a moment, everything slows and fades, and all I hear is the sound of my heart drowning out everything else. Then I am reining in the mules and jumping down from the seat with my gun and my canteen, running across the uneven ground toward the news I don't want to hear. Will collapses at my feet, and Webb clings to my legs. I pull Webb up into my arms, and Wyatt tries to help Will stand, but Will's legs give out again, and Wyatt kneels beside him.

"Will?" Wyatt says, putting his arm around his brother. "Will, what happened? Where is the train?"

"I d-don't know. They w-w-went on," Will stammers. "Pa broke a wheel, and Mrs. Bingham was having her b-b-baby." He's begun to shake so hard he's bouncing.

I make him drink a little water, Webb too, though he's crying and struggles to swallow. And then they tell us the rest.

"Indians," Will says. "I k-killed one. I didn't mean to. And then they killed Pa and W-Warren. They killed Mr. B-B-Bingham. And they b-b-burned the w-wagons. The wagons are gone. Ma's g-g-gone too."

"We hid in the rocks," Webb cries, interrupting him. "We hid in the rocks for a long time, and the wagons burned. Will wouldn't let me up. He laid on top of me and covered my mouth. I woulda killed 'em. I woulda saved Naomi."

Each breath burns my throat and scalds my chest, but I ask the question.

"Where is she? What happened to Naomi?"

Wyatt is shaking his head, adamant, denying everything he's heard, but tears are streaming from his eyes. Will is crying now too, and it is Webb who answers me.

"They took Naomi," Webb cries, lifting his shattered eyes to mine. "They took her away."

∾

About a mile down the rutted path, I halt the wagon again and make the boys wait for me inside. One wagon is a pile of smoking embers. One wagon is only partially burned, the cover hanging in ashy shreds, like the fire never caught hold.

"Maybe they're not dead," Webb insists. And his face carries the hope and dread of every question not yet answered, but Will knows.

"They're dead, Webb," he whispers, and he covers his face.

Wyatt wants to come with me, but I threaten to tie him down if he sets foot outside the wagon. "You stay here with Webb and Will. And you don't come out, none of you, until I come back for you." Wyatt's holding his rifle, and his face is striped with dust and tears, but his jaw is set like he's ready to fight.

"Stay here," I repeat, holding his gaze. He nods once, his hands flexing on his gun, and I turn away and cock my own. I won't need it, but I bring it anyway.

I study the scene as I approach. Two wagons, one partially burned and the other a pile of smoking rubble. The oxen weren't taken. They're bunched together around a watering hole, none the worse for wear. They lift their heads as I near and watch as I discover the bodies beyond them.

The top of William May's head is a raw, bubbled wound. Blood discolors the ground between him and Warren, who is facedown, his splayed feet at his father's head. Homer Bingham is turned away, his back to the others, but his arms are flung forward, reaching for something, clawing at the dirt as though he attempted to crawl to his wife but made it a mere foot before succumbing to the destroyer who took the top of his head.

The indignity of the death stuns me. Not just the death itself. I have seen death, but not like this, and a deep, inexplicable shame wells up in my chest. This is death I don't understand. I can do nothing for them but give them some dignity and shield them from the eyes of the boys waiting in my wagon. Using a bit of water and my handkerchief, I do my best to clean off the worst of the blood from their faces and pull their hats over the clotted mess on the tops of their heads. And then I brace myself for what is next.

The May wagon fared better than the other wagon, though the cover is gone and the box is black. I know it's William's because it's missing a wheel. Inside the May wagon are blackened provisions and sooty blankets, but that is all. The straps that kept the feed box and the water barrel attached to the side have melted and snapped, releasing their cargo. The barrel has rolled to a stop near the smoldering remains of the other wagon.

Nothing is left of the Bingham wagon but the charred skeleton and a single willow branch jutting up from the remains. An iron dutch oven, none the worse for wear, sits amid a rounded pile of debris I can't distinguish. It radiates heat and an acrid stench, and I make myself approach it.

There is very little left of them, no hair, no shape, no flesh at all. I cannot tell who is who or the details of their suffering. What is left is just a charred suggestion of two bodies clothed in ash, lying side by side, and obscured by a four-foot section of the wagon box that has collapsed against them. My throat aches, my heart thrums, and I can't feel my hands. I turn away and steady my breaths.

I don't know what to do.

Winifred. William. Warren. The Binghams. The boys. Naomi.

"Âka'a," I moan. "Naomi."

I don't know where she is. I don't know how to find her, and I can't leave the Mays. Not the boys, and not their dead. Our dead. They are mine too. They are Naomi's. And I promised William I would take care of them.

I look around me, helpless, desperate for direction. William's tools are scattered around the wheel he was working on, and suddenly I know what to do. I've just spent a week building a wagon, and I grab what I need and slide beneath the Mays' wagon and find the bolts that secure the box to the underpinnings. When I've removed the bolts, I drag the box off the frame, letting it crash to the side, spilling the blackened provisions and contents onto the ground. I roll it, end over end, over to the remains of the other wagon. I need something to bury them in. Something to bury them *all* in. The ground is hard, and I don't have much time. One by one, I drag the three men beside the remains of their women, and I cover them all with the upended wagon box. It looks like a table, sitting there among the rocks and the brush, but the death is hidden, the worst of the horror concealed. I go and get the boys.

I have to confirm what Will already knows. Webb knows it too, though I think Will shielded him from the worst parts. I don't know how long Will kept them hidden, cowering among the rocks, waiting to feel safe enough to run for help, but it was a good while if the Binghams' wagon had time to burn.

"I don't know how long," Will says when I ask him. "But when it happened, it wasn't much past noon."

It's nearing four o'clock now.

"We gotta find Naomi and baby Wolfe, John," Webb whimpers.

"I know. And I will. But I need your help now."

We pile rocks onto the overturned wagon box to weigh it down and then line the sides with the same, creating a monument of stones to mark the spot. From pieces of the undercarriage, I create a cross and bury it deep so it stands upright.

"We need to say something or sing a song," Wyatt says. His jaw is tight, and he wears the calm stupor of disbelief. I am grateful he won't ever have to see what his brothers saw.

"We need Ma to sing," Webb says, and his face crumples.

"I can do it," Will says, his lips trembling but his shoulders squared.

He sings a song I know, a song Jennie used to sing about grace and the sweet sound it makes. Will's voice is clear and true like Winifred's, but he starts to cry when he begins the third verse, and Wyatt and Webb have to help him finish. I can't sing, but I say the words with them.

The Lord hath promised good to me;
His word my hope secures.
He will my shield and portion be
As long as life endures.

When we are through, I unharness my mules and change the rigging on my wagon to accommodate William's oxen, and then I gather them so I can yoke them in. Not far from the watering hole, I find some blood and a loose page from Naomi's book. She was here when they surprised her. A cluster of tracks—unshod ponies—lead away from the area. At least I have somewhere to start.

"Why are you yoking the oxen?" Wyatt asks. "The mules will be faster. If we're going after Naomi, we want to go fast, don't we?" He and his brothers have culled through the Mays' provisions and pulled out the things they can save, and they're piling them in the back of my wagon.

"I can't follow those tracks in a wagon, Wyatt," I say.

"We're leaving it here?"

"No. I'm going after Naomi and Wolfe, and you're going to take this wagon and your brothers, and you're going to follow the ruts until you catch up with Abbott and the train."

"No, no, no. We're going with you," he says, shaking his head emphatically.

"Wyatt."

Wyatt shakes his head again, and his mouth trembles. He's close to breaking down, and I need him to hold on.

"You can do this, Wyatt. You have to. You remember what your ma said to you when we made it back to camp after my animals were scattered?"

"No. I don't remember," he chokes.

"She said you were a man now. She got to see that. And you are, Wyatt."

"It's easy to be tough when I'm with you, John. But I don't think I can do this by myself."

"I have to go find Naomi, Wyatt. And I can't take Will and Webb. You know that."

He groans, fisting his hands in his hair.

"You've got money in the wagon. You know where I put it. You've got oxen. You've got supplies to get you through, and you've got people in that train who care about you. You keep on that westbound route until you find them. They're only a day ahead. Then you stick with Abbott. He'll get you all the way to California, and when I find Naomi, I'll come find you and your brothers."

"Do you promise?" He's crying now, and I want to cry too. But I'm too afraid to cry.

"I promise you I will. I don't know how long it'll take me, but I promise I will."

"Okay," Wyatt whispers.

I've watered my animals. They're ready to go. I might need the dun, and I'll need a few mules, but I leave Kettle and a mule for each of the boys, securing them to the sides. They might need them. I help Webb and Will into the back of the wagon, and I tell them what I've told Wyatt.

"I can't go with you. You gotta take care of each other so I can take care of Naomi and Wolfe," I say. "Listen to Wyatt. Mind him. Webb, you take care of Kettle and the mules. They're May mules now. Will, you keep looking after Webb."

Webb throws himself into my arms, and I reach out for Will, who is pale and quiet. His tears have dried and his eyes are hollow, but he lets me take his hand.

"All of this is my fault, John," Will says. "I killed one, and that's why they attacked us."

"You can't take the blame for what other men do. I don't know what happened. I don't know the why of it. But I know this—you saved your brother, and you kept your head. I'm proud of you."

"I hate them. I hate Indians," Webb cries, his voice muffled by my shoulder.

"Do you hate me?" I ask quietly. "I'm an Indian."

"No. I love you."

"And I love you too. There's good and bad in all kinds of people. Indians and emigrants alike. Do you remember when Mr. Caldwell set my animals loose?"

"Yeah. I hate Mr. Caldwell too," Webb sobs.

"Do you remember my friend Hanabi? And Charlie? They helped us. Without Charlie . . . Wyatt and I wouldn't have made it back to you and the others," I remind him. "So you be real careful about who you hate."

Webb is quiet, and I ease him back from my arms.

"It's time to go now," I say.

"I'm scared, John," Will says.

"I know. I'm scared too. But we all have jobs to do. And we're going to do them."

I watch as my wagon pulls out, lurching from side to side, Wyatt prodding the oxen along with his father's staff, Webb and Will staring back at me, framed by the oval opening in the wagon cover.

16

NOWHERE

NAOMI

Wolfe sleeps, and I stagger. For miles and miles, I stagger. I am accustomed to walking, but I am not accustomed to being dragged, and the pace we've kept is mild for the horses but bruising for a woman with a child in her arms. My skin is slick and my dress damp with sweat. The cut beneath my eye stings, and my head throbs in time with my steps, but like everything else, the sensation is distant; I recognize it, the way I recognize that the sun has moved in the sky and there is a pebble wedged into the hole in my shoe. I keep my eyes forward, on the trail of black feathers one Indian wears in his hair. They extend all the way down his back to the top of his leather leggings. I have not looked behind me. No one follows, and I am afraid that if I turn my head, I will fall and will not find my feet again, or worse, Wolfe will be taken from my arms.

Ma says the things we fear most tend to find us. Just like Job from the Bible. People think the Lord was testing him—and Ma said He was—but she said that wasn't the only thing to be learned from Job. *For the thing which I greatly feared is come upon me, and that which I was afraid of is come unto me.*

"Some trouble can't be avoided. Some you must face. Job was the best of men. Yet trouble still came."

We reach a river and cross it, and the men let the animals drink. They don't remove the rope at my neck but drop it, shooing me toward the water. I shuffle down the banks and collapse beside Gert. I am trembling, and I pull too hard on her teat, making her bleat and spraying Wolfe in the face, but I manage to work a stream of milk into his mouth for several minutes before I am pulled up again, away from the river. I did not get a chance to drink. We veer northwest, away from the river. I am thirsty, and Wolfe has started to wail. I beg the men to stop, but they ride on unconcerned until Wolfe's cries become ragged sighs, and he sleeps again.

The sun is sinking, and we are nearing a camp. A cry goes up, and I know we've been seen. The fear that floated above me all day is perched on my shoulders now, and my back is fiery with the strain of staying upright. Dogs bark and rush my legs, and I trip over one. Wolfie's bunting is soaked through, and the smell of urine is strong. The warriors celebrate with yipping and spears and shields lifted high. The scalps dance, and I sway. The man on the painted pony slides to the ground and with no warning yanks Wolfe from me. My arms are cramped and will not straighten, and I cannot even reach for him. The painted brave hands Wolfe to a woman, who stares at my brother with disdain. She sets him on the ground and turns away. The man calls after her, and he is angry. He picks Wolfe up again and follows her. I am encircled by women and children who tug at my clothes and pull at my hair. One woman slaps my face, and the cut beneath my eye begins to flow once more. I cover my head with my unbending arms, and I push through the crowd toward Wolfe. I hear him crying, but the sound recedes as he is carried away. I scream for him, and the Indian children throw back their little heads and howl too. I realize they are copying me, and his name is like the call of the wolves.

Then the women are moaning and crying too as the dead man is pulled from his horse, the grieving of the village rising like a sudden storm, the kind that sent the waters rushing down the Platte without warning. One of the men slides from his horse, then moves into the circle of women and children and buries his hand in my hair, yanking my head back. He turns my head this way and that, talking all the while. With the hand not gripping my hair, he parts my lips with a dirty finger, and I taste horse and blood. He cracks a knuckle against my teeth and snaps his own, as though my teeth please him. The finger that is in my mouth moves to my left eye, and he peels back my eyelid. I cry out, trying to twist away, but he seems entranced by the color of my eyes. He is showing everyone, wrenching my head, keeping my eye pinned open. A woman spits, and I am blinded by the glob of saliva. The man releases my face but not my hair, and I am dragged, stumbling, behind him, trying to keep my feet beneath me, my hands wrapped around his wrist to prevent my hair from being torn out by the roots. I can't imagine being scalped would hurt much more.

I don't know if anyone will come looking for me or baby Wolfe. I don't know. John. John will come looking. I shudder, and my stomach roils again. Pa and Warren are dead. Ma. Ma is dead too. My mind goes black. Blank. I can't think of them. I hope John doesn't come after me. They'll kill him. They'll kill me too. I just hope they do it quickly.

JOHN

Naomi is wearing her moccasins. I can tell by her print. Her foot is small, and her tread is short, like she's stumbling along. There are no footprints besides hers. The rest are horses and two mules. Trick and

Tumble. A set of smaller, cloven-hoofed prints makes me think they took Gert too. I've lost the trail a few times and have had to circle back. I've lost it again and am sure I'm going the wrong way.

A flutter of white tumbles over the dry ground, and I race toward it, chasing it for half a mile before it finally presses up against the sagebrush, momentarily caught. I am screaming in frustration by the time I reach it, and my voice, raspy and raw, frightens my animals. They shimmy and sidestep, and I slide from Samson's back, pulling the animals forward so I can snag the page I've chased for half an hour.

It is a sketch I've seen, one I admired. *Bones in Boxes* is written across the bottom in Naomi's curling scrawl. I have a vision of her blood-soaked body lying somewhere in the rocks, her book lying open beside her, her pictures scattered in the wind. Then I remember the way she left a trail of pictures for me and Wyatt when we'd gone after my mules, and calm quiets my anguish. Naomi is leaving pages for me again.

NAOMI

I do not open my eyes when I hear the camp stirring, and for a moment I am still with the train, wondering if I am the last to wake. Then I remember where I am. I remember why, and I am flooded with grief so heavy I cannot take a breath. I start to wheeze, gagging and gasping, and the dog I spent the night beside begins to nuzzle the juncture of my thighs, where the blood of my menses has seeped through my dress. I kick him away, giving up my pretense of sleep, and roll to my side, tucking my legs to my chest. Another nudge in my side. Thinking it is the dog, I swat at it and touch someone's leg instead.

She looms above me, the old woman, her face so worn and brown she looks like she is made of tree bark. She peers at me, deep-set eyes black and shining, and beckons me to follow. I duck out of the lodge and flinch against the rising sun. They are breaking camp. Children are running, the men are gathering the horses, and women are packing. The other shelters have all been brought down, and the fires have been doused. They are leaving in a rush, and many stare, but no one stops me. It was much the same the night before. The man who dragged me by the hair took me into his lodge. He shoved me in a corner with a mangy dog and growled something I couldn't understand. The old woman brought me water and a blanket. I drank, and then I slept.

Now she urges me down toward the stream. She is small, a full head shorter than I am, but her grip on my arm is firm, and I don't know what else to do but obey. And I am thirsty. I move downstream, the old woman watching me from the banks. I set my satchel with my book of pictures, still hanging around my neck, on a rock and remove my stockings and my moccasins and sit, fully clothed, in the creek. The water engulfs me to my chin. I scrub at the soiled fabric between my legs and pull the rags free from the pockets in my dress, rinsing them too. The water is cold and the morning young, and I shiver and quake as I try to wash as best I can. I consider escape, floating away with the current. I look at the old woman; she stares back at me. A wisp of her gray hair waves goodbye, and I wonder if she knows my thoughts. Then a child cries, and I am ashamed. I cannot leave without Wolfe. I rise, water sluicing from my dress, and hobble back to shore, my tender feet curling around the slick stones.

I cannot ask her where Wolfe is. Instead, I mime a baby in my arms. The old woman doesn't react, and I try harder, tapping my chest and cradling an invisible infant. She says something I don't understand, says it again louder, then breaks the circle of my arms, forcing them to my sides, shaking her head. I fear she is trying to tell me what I already know. Wolfe is no longer mine.

I try to tell her my name. "Nay-oh-mee," I say slowly, patting my chest. "Naomi."

She grunts, and I say it again, desperate. "Naomi."

"Nayohmee," she repeats, running all the sounds together.

"Yes," I say and nod. "Yes. Naomi Lowry." Naomi May Lowry. I blink back sudden tears.

She pats her own chest and says something I can't even decipher enough to repeat. I shake my head, helpless. I can't even make out the first sound. Softer than a *p*, harder than a *b*.

She says her name again.

"Beeya?" I attempt, but my voice trails off, unsure of the rest.

"Beeya," she repeats, satisfied. "Nayohmee," she says and touches my chest. She bends and picks up my leather satchel and looks inside. She pulls the book out, and a few loose drawings tumble free. The leather string I keep wrapped around the pages is undone. I am lucky the book is even inside. I must have shoved it into my satchel without tying it when I stooped down next to Gert to feed Wyatt. Not at the river . . . but before. Before.

Beeya wants to see what's inside. Shivering and afraid she will take it, I open it. Wyatt grins up at me, fully fleshed in a thousand lines.

I shut the book again. I am too wet to tuck it away, and Beeya reaches for it, not understanding my agony. I crouch and begin to put on my moccasins, my fingers stiff and uncooperative, my stockings so filthy I consider abandoning them. Beeya is sifting through my pages, hissing and moaning, and I pray she will not destroy my book.

She hands it back abruptly, thumping it against my breasts. I try to take it, but she simply uses it to underscore her words.

"Nay-oh-mee."

I nod.

She points at the book, adamant. "Beeya." Her desire is clear. She wants me to draw her face, to add it to my book.

JOHN

I find another picture caught in the grass about a mile from the river. It is Webb asleep on Eddie the ox, his arms and legs loose and dangling.

I remember that day. Oddie gave out, and we had to leave him behind. I cannot follow Naomi's trail in the darkness, and I hunker down to wait for daylight not far from the water. I have traveled north, moving from the flat, dry expanse of baked earth and burned rocks to long yellow grass that gives little clue—beyond bent stalks—if I am on the right track.

I doubt Naomi is studying the pictures and sending a message with each one that falls, but the image is disturbing; the desperation and despair of that day echo in me now. For all I know, the wind picked up the page and sent it miles from her course, and I am wandering aimlessly. My mules are thirsty and tired and settle quickly. I sleep in fits and starts, dreaming of Naomi stretched over Oddie's back, both of them dead and powdered in white. I awake, shaking and sick, and fall back to sleep sometime later only to dream of the white desert again, with a slight variation. It is not Oddie but Naomi who has given up, and I can't make her move.

I do not know the river's name or where it will take me, but when the morning comes and I cross to the other side, I can find no sign of a continuing trail. I search the banks up and down, going upstream for half a mile before turning around and going the other direction, scanning the soft soil near the banks. I return to the other side, convinced that Naomi's captors didn't cross after all, and search some more, but I cannot find a single print of an obvious path in the grass leading away from the river. I know horses. I know mules. And I know Indians don't shoe their horses, and mules don't need to be shod, but I'm no tracker, and I don't know where to go.

I scan the distance for a flutter of white but see only empty swells and distant mountains and a river that winds away to my right and away to my left. There are no trees to speak of, and no wagon trains. No white men or brown men or horses or herds. No Naomi. I cross to the other side once more; it was where the trail led last night, but I continue to follow the river. The land is dry and the days are hot, and I can't imagine such a small band would be too far from home. Villages, both permanent and temporary, are erected near the water. Within a few miles, my instinct is rewarded. The river bends, straightens, and turns back, creating a stretch of land with water on three sides.

An Indian village is tucked into the shallow peninsula.

I dismount and lead my mules to the water, keeping my distance. The wickiups look Shoshoni, and I experience a flash of relief followed by a stab of dread. Washakie said Pocatello is Shoshoni. I'm not familiar with the land or the local tribes. Webb and Will could not describe an identifiable trait on the Indians who attacked the train; when I pressed them for details they blanched and cried, and I left it alone.

I have a spyglass in my pack, and I hobble my mules near the water's edge and find a high spot where I can study the camp without getting too close. From a distance the village is quiet, almost sleepy, as though the whole camp is resting. Horses mill about, and people move in and out of the wickiups, but there is no industry or urgency in the camp, and I am convinced it is a temporary rest stop, a day or two spent beside the river before moving on to somewhere new.

I watch the wickiups for more than an hour, keeping an eye on my mules while I scan every animal in and around the camp, looking for Trick and Tumble, the red horse, or Homer Bingham's mare. There is no sign of any of them or the goat. I see nothing at all to make me think Naomi and Wolfe are here, but I see another horse that is familiar. He is a deep brown with white forelegs and a dark mane, the white triangle on his forehead pointing down to his nose. Washakie rode a similar horse at Fort Bridger.

Then a woman steps from the doorway of a large wickiup covered in elk skin and heads toward the river. She has a baby in her arms, and her hair is in a long single braid down her back. It is Hanabi. I am sure of it. Children play at the river's edge, and through the spyglass I can make out the children of Hanabi's brother. Hanabi appears to be scolding them as a dog bounds up from the banks and races to greet her. He gives a violent shake, and she scurries back toward the wickiup to escape his wet affection.

The children see me coming and run, pointing and yelling. People begin to stream out of the lodges. Some look frightened, and a few men shout, running toward their horses, but I keep my hands raised and ride slowly, greeting them in their own tongue. Most of the men were absent when we camped with the tribe on the Green, and I expected this response. Moments later, Hanabi and Washakie rush from their wickiup. Hanabi is no longer holding her daughter, and she throws her arms wide in excitement like she is welcoming me home.

"You are here, John Lowry!"

Her joy in my presence is both a balm and a blade to my heart, and I slide from my saddle and grasp her hand, my eyes on Washakie, who stands at her side. He is not so joyous or welcoming, but he greets me softly.

"John Lowry."

"Chief Washakie."

"Where did you come from?" he asks, his eyes raised to the distance behind me.

"Yes! Where did you come from? And where is your woman?" Hanabi asks, looking beyond me. "Your family? Have you come alone?"

For a moment I can't speak. My words are stuck in my tangled thoughts, and I lack the emotional endurance to unravel them. I have not grieved or broken down. I have not let myself feel much at all. Telling the story, saying the words out loud, might break my control.

"John Lowry?" Hanabi asks, her brow creasing in concern. Washakie shares the same expression.

"My wife . . . is . . ." I don't remember the Shoshoni word for *taken*. I try again. "Naomi is . . . lost."

I tell Hanabi and Washakie all that I know, from the moment Wyatt saw the smoke to the moment I set off in pursuit of the men who took Naomi. I have to stop many times. Hanabi brings me food. Water. Washakie hands me a bottle of whiskey. I don't care for it. Never have, but I slosh a little into my cup and drink it down.

It doesn't steady me or ease the vise in my chest, but the burning distracts me, and I am able to choke out what Webb and Will told me about the Indian with Will's arrow in his belly. Washakie asks me how many there were and what they looked like, and I cannot tell him. Only that there were enough to make quick work of three men and two women. From the number of hoofprints, difficult though they were for me to distinguish, I would guess nine or ten.

"Why didn't they kill your woman too?" Washakie asks.

I have asked myself that question, and I don't know.

Hanabi has grown still, but there is grief in her eyes and the turn of her mouth.

"I am sorry, John Lowry," she whispers. "This is a great sadness."

"There were no others in the train?" Washakie asks. "They were alone?"

I describe why they were there and why they were alone and how far they'd traveled from the Bear River and Sheep Rock. He knows the places by different names but nods as I explain, describing the spring and the jutting black rocks and the distance to the river where we now sit.

When I have finished, he sits still, his hands on his thighs, his back straight. He doesn't speak for several minutes, and I don't press him. I sit in numb exhaustion. Hanabi's daughter is awake, and Hanabi rises from the robes to go retrieve her and returns with the baby in her arms.

"Pocatello," Hanabi says, looking at her husband, and her mouth is flat and hard. Pocatello. The chief of the Shoshoni thought responsible for the trouble with the soldiers. I remain silent, as does Washakie.

"Pocatello," Hanabi insists when he doesn't respond.

Washakie grunts, but he seems to be wrestling with a decision. Finally he raises his eyes back to mine.

"We go to the Gathering Place every three winters."

Like the Pawnee, most tribes measure time in seasons, not years, when it is measured at all.

"All Shoshoni. North, east, and west," he adds.

I remember Hanabi telling me this when we camped at the Green.

"You are going there now?"

"Yes." He sighs heavily. "Pocatello will be there."

"I do not know if it was Pocatello's band," I say.

"It was," Washakie says simply. "These are his lands. He will take the animals he stole to the Great Gathering. He will trade them. He will trade your woman too . . . or kill her. And the white men will never know who is to blame." He shrugs. "But word of the attack will spread among the whites, and it will cause trouble for all tribes. For all Shoshoni. For all the people."

He is so certain, and he speaks of Naomi's fate so emotionlessly.

"Will you take me there?" I choke, trying to control my rage.

"He will not give her back to you. You will be alone in a sea of Shoshoni."

"He will not be alone," Hanabi says, folding her arms and gazing at her husband fiercely. "He will have you," she snaps. "He will have our people."

Washakie doesn't argue with her. He simply studies me.

"You want to kill Pocatello? You want to kill his men?" he asks.

William's bubbling scalp and Warren's face rise in my mind. Elsie Bingham with her cheerful smile and her adoration for her homely husband. Winifred. Winifred, who I loved. Wyatt and Webb and poor Will, who carries the weight of it all on his twelve-year-old shoulders.

"Yes. I want to kill him. I want to kill his men. And if my wife is dead when I find her, I will kill him, and I will take his scalp back to her brothers so they know I have not looked away from what was done," I vow.

"And if she is not dead?" he asks. "If I can get her back for you?"

I do not know what he wants from me, and I wait, my jaw clenched over my fury and fear.

"I will take you to him," Washakie says. "I will take you to the Gathering. But you must promise me that if your woman is alive, you will take her and the *tua*, the child, and go. No killing. No revenge."

"And if she is not alive?" I have to whisper the words.

"If she is not alive, I will help you kill Pocatello."

Hanabi bows her head, and I sit in stunned silence.

"But only him. Then you will go, and you will leave the white man out of it. You will not go to the white army and send them here. You will not show them the graves and point your finger."

Hanabi raises her worried eyes to mine, waiting for my response.

"You understand?" Washakie asks, and now his voice is almost gentle.

"It won't be just Pocatello and his men who suffer," I say, understanding more than I'm willing to admit.

He nods. "Newe." *The people.* "They will all pay."

I cover my eyes with my hands, the way Will did, trying to erase the horrors he'd seen.

"Is your woman strong?" Washakie asks, still gentle.

"Yes," I whisper. "She is very strong."

"Then we will go and get her."

NAOMI

The man who took Wolfe from my arms and gave her to his wife is named Biagwi. He is the only one who did not kill, but I wish he had. I wish he had killed me. I think the one who dragged me into his lodge by my hair is Beeya's son. His name is Magwich. And he killed Pa.

That's how I identify them: the one who took me and Wolfe. The one who killed Pa. The one who killed Warren. The one who stabbed Homer Bingham, and the one who took his scalp. I didn't see Ma die. I didn't see Elsie die, but I know who carries their scalps too. I know who burned the wagons. One of the men is their chief, but I do not know his name.

We walk all day. We go where wagons would never go, moving north. The morning of the second day we walk within a mile of high white adobe walls surrounded by circled wagons and clustered lodges, and I realize with a start that it must be Fort Hall. I wonder what they would do if I started to run toward the wagons. Would Magwich chase me on his horse? Would their chief put an arrow in my back? That would not be so bad, and maybe I would get away. But I cannot leave Wolfe, and I keep walking. We are too far for anyone to notice a white woman in the tribe, and I am dressed like an Indian.

Beeya took my yellow dress and brushed my hair with a block of wood bristled like a pine cone before braiding it down my back. My dress was in filthy tatters, but I was very angry with her when I discovered it was gone. The pale doeskin dress and leggings she gave me to wear are too warm for August, and the sun beats down on my face.

We are moving toward something. We are going somewhere. We have not made a permanent camp for days, and we don't seem to be following a herd. Beeya has loaded me down like a pack mule, and she is always at my side. Beeya isn't her name. It is the word for mother. Pia? Beeya? I can't hear the difference. She is mother to Magwich, and now she considers herself mother to me. I understand when she points to Biagwi's wife, who carries Wolfe upon her back, his white face and pale hair in stark contrast to the dark papoose.

"Weda beeya," Beeya says, pointing, insisting. "Beeya." She is telling me the woman, whose name is Weda, is now Wolfe's mother.

I think she is trying to reassure me, to tell me he is being taken care of, but I cannot be grateful. I shake my head. "No. No Beeya," I say.

Beeya wants me to draw for her, and I do, but I feel no joy in it. I have pulled every one of my old drawings from my book, every beloved face, and put them in my satchel. I leave only the blank sheets behind. I'm afraid Beeya will take it to show the other women or her sons, and I can't lose the pictures. I'm afraid Magwich will toss it in the fire when I displease him. He is afraid of the color of my eyes and slaps me when I watch him. So I don't watch him. I track him from the corner of my eye. He does not have a woman. Maybe he did. I only know that Beeya lives in his wickiup and takes care of him, and as long as I don't look at him, he leaves me alone.

One night, while the men sit in the chief's lodge, Beeya sits me among the women with my book and my pencil. She is very proud. Very excited. I don't understand anything that is said, and no one understands me. It's been five days, and it feels like five minutes. It feels like five years. Like five hours, like five decades. A part of me is waiting, and a part of me is dead.

I embrace the lifeless girl, the one who does not yearn for John or talk to Ma, the one who does not worry about my brothers. The lifeless girl walks and works and draws faces that I do not remember moments after I finish. Lifeless girl watches Weda feed Wolfe from her breasts and doesn't flinch; I only wonder where Weda's real baby has gone. Maybe he is with Ma.

17

DEER LODGE VALLEY

JOHN

Washakie tells me the river is called the Tobitapa. We leave it in the morning. The Shoshoni travel with the skins and poles for tipis, but when they reach the Gathering Place, they will build their wickiups, the dome-shaped shelters covered in skins and sometimes brush for the longer stay. The Gathering lasts weeks at a time. When it is done, they will hunt buffalo one more time before they go to the winter range. It takes us days to reach the Snake River—the Shoshoni call it the Piupa—and I help the women make rafts from the bulrushes to get everything across. Some of the men ask if all Pawnee work like women.

"Only the good ones," I say. Hanabi says I work as much as two squaws, which only makes them laugh harder.

Washakie sat in council with his war chiefs the night I arrived. I don't know what was said when I left. I told my story sitting among them, and then they asked me to leave them alone to talk. I did not point fingers of blame or mention Pocatello, the Gathering, or the promise I made Chief Washakie and the promise he made me. I left that up to him. Hanabi tells me that even though the family group they travel with is small—250 people and seventy wickiups—Washakie is head chief over many bands of Shoshoni, and they will listen to him.

Every day Washakie asks me if my woman is strong.

Every day I answer that she is.

I wish he wouldn't ask. It makes me wonder exactly how strong she will have to be. He does not ask like he needs to know. He asks like he is trying to remind me, to make me say the words out loud. He asks me many things, and the conversations distract me from the snakes, hissing and writhing, so big and loud now that there is no room for anything else. I lie awake in my tent at night, among the tipis, convinced I will keep the families awake with the rattling. I rest because I must, but even in sleep my stomach is not free from the coils.

Washakie wants to know about my white father and my Pawnee mother. So I tell him. I talk and he listens, and then he presses for more. He is hungry to know, and I answer every question forthrightly, restricted only by my limited Shoshoni vocabulary.

"You were not raised by your people?" he asks, and I know he means the Pawnee.

"They did not like me. I was a two-feet. Pitku ásu'."

He waits for more explanation.

"My mother brought me to my father. I never thought he liked me either, but maybe I was wrong. I don't know anymore."

"He was a good father?"

I am reminded of the time I asked Charlie if Dog Tooth was a good chief and his response: "What is a good chief?" What is a good father? I'm not sure I know.

"He never . . . shunned . . ." I'm not sure I am using the right word, but Washakie nods like he understands. "He never shunned me. He worked hard. Made sure I knew how to fight. And I am . . . loved." It is an admission I have never made before, but I have come to believe it is true.

"My father was not one of the people," Washakie says after a moment of silence. "I am a two-feet like you."

"He was not Shoshoni?" I ask, surprised.

"He was Flathead. He died when I was a young boy. When he died, my mother returned to her people, the Lemhi Shoshoni, and I was raised Shoshoni." He points to a woman riding an old horse. "That is my mother. Her name is Lost Woman. I am the only family she has left."

I have noticed her before. She was with Hanabi by the Green River. But she keeps herself apart, and Washakie has made no move to introduce us. Hanabi rides beside her now, and the contrast between them is marked. Hanabi is young and straight, her hair heavy and dark. The woman beside her is bent, her hair is white, and she shares a weary long-suffering with the horse she rides.

"Why is she called Lost Woman?" I ask, my heart aching for her.

"It is what she has always been called." He shrugs. "And that is what she is. A lost woman. She is lost in grief. A husband, a daughter, two sons. All gone. My brothers died not long ago. They were hunting in the snow along the hillside. The snow began to slide and fall, and they were buried in it. My mother went looking for them. She knew they had been buried. She dug all over the hill with her hands. She would not listen to reason when I begged her to stop. We found them when the snow melted."

∞

We move far more quickly than the wagons would have, but each day is torture. I am plagued with worry and strain, and the distance we must travel is not insignificant. We move steadily north, and though

Washakie's people seem eager for the Gathering, there is no sense of haste or hurry to arrive. We see some buffalo a ways off, but when the men yelp and want to hunt, Washakie shakes his head. It will take too much time to dry the meat and treat the hides, and we continue on. If there are a few resentful looks cast my way, I do not see them, and I am grateful. It is all I can do not to gallop ahead, to seek Naomi by myself, but I know how foolish that would be, how futile. And I endure the snakes.

"Someday we will all look like you," Washakie says to me one day, almost a week since we left the Tobitapa. He has been morose and has not spoken to me all morning, though he insists I ride at his side. His sudden comment startles me.

"What do I look like?" I ask, not understanding his meaning.

"Like an Indian dressed as a white man."

After a moment he continues. "The blood of the Indian and the blood of the white people will flow together. One people. I have seen it." He does not sound happy about it. He sounds resigned, and I don't know what to say.

I tell him about the turtle, about living on both the land and the water, like Naomi told me to do. He smiles, but he shakes his head.

"We will have to become entirely new creatures. Then we will all be lost people . . . like my mother."

NAOMI

Beeya is excited. All the women are. We've quickened our step, and everyone is smiling and chattering. The men move ahead, scanning the wide valley and pointing as they argue. The chief—Beeya calls him Pocatello—has the final word, and the people spill down behind him as he chooses a spot where the ground is flat and the creek runs through it. This is not a temporary encampment; we have arrived.

The day is spent erecting wickiups and staking out territory. We are the first, but we are not the only. Another band comes in from the north midday. Another from the west not long after. Each stakes out a position in the valley, and by the end of the day there are easily a thousand lodges and twice that many horses and dogs. And they keep coming.

At nightfall, the celebrations begin. It is like the shrieking from the night I carried Wolfe into camp, but this is not mourning, and it goes on for hours. The leaders of each band make up the inner ring around their scalps, which are strung from small poles. The warriors dance around the leaders, and the women and children take the outside. Around and around, dancing and singing songs I have never heard and hope to never hear again. Beeya does not dance, but she enjoys herself, swaying and yelping softly, sitting at my side in the grass beyond the wide circle where all the activities take place.

There are far more horses than people, and when the morning comes, the races begin. The men race all day long, betting on the outcomes and bartering when they lose. Beeya and I watch as Magwich loses five of his horses and wins five more from someone else, only to lose them again. His mood is black, and Beeya keeps me away from the wickiup much of the day. She has dressed me like a doll. Feathers hang from my braids, and beads hang from my ears. When Beeya came to me with a rock, a fishhook, and a chunk of wood the size of a cork, tugging at my ears, I let her have her way. I have no fight in me. The pain was sharp, but it didn't last. I almost missed it when it fled.

The women move among the camps and congregate around the clearing, visiting and displaying their wares: beaded clothes and moccasins, painted pots and feathered headpieces, armbands, belts, and cuffs. Some women cluster and string beads onto long strands of what appears to be hair from a horse's mane, keeping their hands busy as they chatter. No language barrier exists among them; they are the same nation, if not the same tribe.

Some of the women wear cloth instead of skins, simple tunics and long skirts sashed at the waists and decorated in the style of their people, but I do not blend in. I am stared at with wide eyes and open mouths, but Beeya likes the attention. She tugs at my arm and makes me sit, spreading a skin in front of me along with little pots of paint. She pats the skin and says my name, "Nayohmee," and pats it again. Then she pulls a woman forward through the crowd, pointing from the woman's face to the skin in front of me.

The woman is someone of importance or esteem, because the other women part immediately. The woman stares down at me, hostile but curious, and Beeya motions for me to begin. I paint obediently, long black hair parted down the center, scowling eyes, bangled ears, simple lines. I have made her more beautiful than she is. I am not a fool. When I am finished, the women watching murmur and shift, and the haughty woman stoops to study it closer.

"Att," she says to Beeya, ignoring me. The woman takes off several strands of beads from around her neck and puts them over Beeya's head before she picks up her portrait, holding it gingerly to protect the wet paint. The women murmur again, and Beeya beams.

I am a novelty, and I draw for hours, making pictures on hides with the paints Beeya brings me. My fingers are stained from knuckle to tip, but I do not mind. It is easier to draw than to drown, and I am drowning. I paint one skin, one face, and then another. Beeya collects her pay and basks in the warmth of attention. After a while, the haughty woman comes back with a man. A thick scar runs from his forehead to his ear, but it only enhances his face. He wears a neck plate of bones, and his long hair is drawn back from his face. Red and yellow tassels hang from each temple and brush his prominent cheekbones.

I paint his image on a white skin that his wife lays down before me. I accentuate his scar and the harsh lines of his face, creating a portrait both startling and severe, and he is pleased. He says something to Beeya, something about Magwich, and Beeya doesn't like what he says.

She shakes her head, adamant, and begins gathering the paints and her prizes in a rush, shoving them into my arms to help her carry them. She is suddenly ready to leave, though others still await their turns around us and complain loudly. I follow her obediently, relieved to be done, but the man calls after her, insistent. She doesn't answer this time but hurries away. We return to Magwich's wickiup and dump Beeya's treasures by the door. She pushes me down on the buffalo robes and barks a command—*stay?*—before she rushes out again.

I am stunned by the silence, by my sudden, unexpected freedom. And I do not stay. I have not been left alone once since I was taken, not even to relieve myself, and I don't hesitate. I know where Weda and Biagwi's wickiup is, and I stride toward it, not looking right or left. I do not care what happens to me; I only want to see Wolfe again.

No one stops me. No one seems to see me at all. I duck into the wickiup, heart pounding and stomach clenched. It is shadowed within, like Magwich's was, and for a moment I stand, chest heaving, eyes adjusting to the different light.

He is here, asleep on a pile of skins, his small arms stretched over his head, his little legs tucked like a frog's. His lips move up and down as though he suckles in his dreams. He has grown. In two weeks he has grown, and I sink down beside him. I do not touch him; I'm afraid if I do he will wake and I will be discovered. There is a quaking deep within me, beneath the denial in my chest and the ice in my belly, and I moan in dread, pressing my hands to my lips, trying to contain it.

The skin over the door shifts, and light spills into the wickiup as someone enters. A heartbeat, a gasp, and Weda begins to scream in bloodcurdling alarm. "Biagwi, Biagwi, Biaaaaagwiiiii," she yells, staggering back, the skin hanging over the doorway still clutched in her hand.

"No, no, please," I beg, but she can't understand me. I step away from Wolfe, my hands held aloft, but her screams have awakened him. His lower lip protrudes and trembles, and he releases a long, sad wail.

Then Biagwi is there, Magwich too, pushing into the wickiup, and Beeya stumbles behind.

Magwich grabs my hair as Weda scoops Wolfe into her arms. Biagwi is shouting at Magwich, and Magwich shouts back, dragging me from the enclosure. Beeya pounds her fists on his back, and for a moment he releases me to push her away. She steps past him and runs her hands along my braids and fingers my earrings before patting my breasts and my hips, her tone full of desperate cajoling, and I know what she is trying to do.

She is trying to convince him that I am pretty. That I am desirable. That he wants me, like John does with his jacks. I heard Wyatt telling Warren all about it, his mouth full of cake, after John and I said our vows.

"You gotta convince the jack he wants the mare, while distracting the mare with what she wants most."

John scolded Wyatt, but I made him explain when we were alone. He did so in a very delicate way, whispering into my ear and nipping at my neck, his hands splayed on my hips, and I did not need any convincing.

I shove at Beeya's hands. She scolds me, shaking her head like she is trying to help me. Magwich grunts and grabs my hair again, snapping my head to the side and hissing when Beeya tries to get in his way, but he does not slow. I wrap my hands around his wrist, trying to relieve the pressure on my braids, and stagger along at his side. I don't know where we are going. We do not stop at his wickiup or at the edge of the camp. Minutes later, we enter the clearing where the men are gathered to race and the women display their wares. People gape at Magwich and me, but Beeya has disappeared.

The warrior with the big scar is standing with a group of men. He has Magwich's horses, and he is waiting for us.

"Oh, no, no, no," I moan. The lifeless girl is gone. In her place is the girl who has been waiting to wake up, waiting for rescue, waiting for hope, waiting to forget. This is not rescue or hope, and I begin to beg, clinging to Magwich's arm. If he gives me away, I will never see Wolfe again. I will not be able to watch over him, even from afar. As bad as life is, the knowledge that it can be far worse crashes over me.

Beeya is back. She has my satchel. My pictures. My precious faces. She runs between me and Magwich and the scarred chief, waving my loose pages and babbling, babbling. Magwich roars, and the chief frowns, but he takes the pages from her. His men crowd around him.

The scarred man studies them, one by one, raising his eyes to me every once in a while. He hands them to his men, and they do the same. Magwich has grown quiet beside me, but he hasn't released my hair.

The scarred warrior hands my drawings to Beeya.

"Those are mine. That is mine!" I hiss at her, hanging from Magwich's arm. But the scarred man shakes his head and points to me. He wants me, not the pictures. He speaks, and Magwich answers. Back and forth they negotiate, and Beeya clutches my satchel to her chest, her eyes swinging between the men. The scarred one signals for two more horses, and Magwich releases my hair. He folds his arms and walks along the animals, thinking. Then he shakes his head, takes the satchel from Beeya, and hands it to the scarred warrior, a note of finality in his voice.

My vision swims. I expect to be taken, dragged away by a new set of hands, but the scarred warrior turns, my satchel in his arms, and his men lead the horses away.

Magwich pushes me toward our camp, but my legs are limp, and I almost fall. He barks at me and takes my arm, but his grip is firm, not bruising, and he urges me forward. Beeya is smiling and cooing, hurrying along behind us. I don't know what happened. The warrior improved his offer, but Magwich changed his mind.

∞

Beeya brushes my hair and sings a song that has no tune. We do not leave the wickiup again, though I can hear the swell and the fervor of the scalp dance beginning. She is happy Magwich has not traded me, but I am shaken. I don't understand anything, and my pictures are gone. I have nothing left.

When Beeya lies down to sleep, I do the same, staring up through the hole in the wickiup at the gray-black heavens. The sky is even bigger here, and I am much, much smaller here.

Put your energy into rising above the things you can't change, Naomi. Keep your mind right.

I hear Wolfe cry; it is distinct and unmistakable, like every child's cry, and I sit up, straining to hear him. I am in the grass again, waking up to find him missing, but it is not John who holds him; it is a stranger. It doesn't last long, a few angry bellows, and he quiets. I lie back down, but I don't stop listening. The sky is bigger here, and I am much, much smaller here, but this is where Wolfe is.

Magwich returns while I am still awake. I don't expect him, and I jerk upright when he enters the wickiup, drawing his eye. He walks toward me, his hands on his hips, and stops beside the buffalo robes. I avert my eyes so he won't get angry, but he stoops down and grips my chin so he can study my face. His breath is sharp with spirits, and I lean away. He puts his hand on my chest and pushes me back so I am lying down again. Then he bunches his hands in my dress and flips me over onto my stomach.

I cry out, but I don't dare fight. If I fight him, I will lose. If I fight him, he will give me away. My heart has fled my chest, and it pounds in my head, pulsing against the backs of my eyes. I can't breathe, but his breath rasps in my ears. He grips my hips and hikes me up to my knees, shoving my dress up around my waist. I have nothing underneath. I removed the leggings before I lay down to sleep. Beeya rolls over, muttering in her dreams, but if she were awake, she would not help me. She would be glad. Magwich has decided he wants me.

It hurts, but I do not fight.

I do not fight. I do not scream. I cry silently, and I endure.

I distract myself with what I want most.

He is not gentle, but he is quick, and he finishes with a grunt and a shiver and pushes himself away from me, staggering to his feet before falling onto his own pile of robes on the other side of the wickiup with a long, belching sigh. He is snoring almost immediately.

I walk out into the night and into the creek, lifting my skirt as I sink into the water to wash him away. I sit for a long time, waiting for the cold to make me numb. A dog barks, but there are so many dogs that no one listens. Distant singing. Distant fires. The sky is bigger here. I am much, much smaller here, but this is where Wolfe is.

"I gotta get my mind right," I whisper. "Gotta find transcendence." But I've already begun to float away.

JOHN

The valley is teeming with tapered tipis and domed wickiups on the morning we arrive. Camp after camp, thousands of people, thousands of horses, and a billion dogs. It is worse than the hills of St. Joe during the jump-off season. Washakie and his chiefs move up into the lead as we slowly proceed through the Gathering. A slice of the valley has been left open for him, one that extends up from the surrounding creek to an enormous circle in the center, where the people seem to congregate. I cannot help but scan the faces, searching desperately for sight of Naomi, but the numbers are too vast, and though we wind our way through the camps, Washakie and some of his men greeting other leaders of other bands, I do not see her. Washakie says that we are the last to arrive, but he does not prolong my agony.

"I will not go to Pocatello's camp, but Hanabi and some of the other women will visit. There is good feeling among the Newe, even if their chiefs do not see eye to eye. They will look among the women for your wife and her brother. If they are here, I will call a council. We will not cause panic or raise an alarm. That would not be good for your woman or the tua."

Washakie and some of the men go to watch the horses race and mingle among the warriors of other tribes. I see to my mules and help Lost Woman set up Washakie's big wickiup and start a fire for cooking. The women seem to carry the brunt of the labor in the tribe. It is no different among the Pawnee. The men kill the meat, but the women skin it, quarter it, pack it, and drag it home. Then they cut it into strips, dry it, pound it, dry it some more, and pack it up again. They gather the wood and prepare the skins and herd the children and feed the tribe, and the work never relents.

Lost Woman works quietly, efficiently, and she stays close to me. I haven't spoken more than a few words to her since I arrived, but she sleeps in Washakie's wickiup, she knows my story, and she senses my snakes.

"You are scared," she says.

"I am. If she is not here . . ." I can't finish. If Naomi isn't here, I don't know what I'll do.

"She will not be lost forever," Lost Woman reassures me quietly, and I pray forever ends today. We wait for hours. I don't know the customs or the traditions that occur in a visit between tribes, and I even crawl into my tent and try to sleep, exhausted by not knowing. Lost Woman promises to wake me, but I know the moment the women return, and I have scrambled out of my tent before she has time to alert me. Washakie and his men have returned as well.

Washakie's face has no expression, but Hanabi runs to me.

"She is here. The babe too," she says, slightly breathless.

I am overcome with relief and cannot stand. When I sink to my knees, Hanabi crouches beside me and takes my hand.

"The boy has fattened since I saw him. He is well." She is smiling, but there is something else. I can see it in Washakie's face. Hanabi is trying to buoy me up, but there is something wrong. His people are watching, and Washakie extends his hand, helping me to my feet.

"Come," he says, and I follow him to his wickiup, Hanabi and Lost Woman at my heels.

"Tell him everything," Washakie says to Hanabi.

"They have given the boy to a woman who lost her baby only days before the attack. Her husband, Biagwi, spared the Wolfe boy because of this. It was Biagwi's brother the arrow killed," Hanabi says.

"They talk of the attack?" Somehow I imagined they would try to conceal what was done.

"They call it a battle. Weda, Biagwi's woman, is very proud. She did not hide the Wolfe boy," Hanabi says.

"A battle?" I gasp.

"One of their own was lost," Hanabi reminds me, and her gentle voice is a lash against my skin.

"It was not a fair fight," I hiss.

"To them, it was. And it was a battle they did not start."

"And Naomi?"

"We saw her, but she was taken away as soon as we arrived," Hanabi says.

"The men are talking about her. She is Magwich's woman now," Washakie says softly. "She lives in his wickiup. They say she paints faces—*waipo*—on the skins. She is valuable to him, and he will not trade her."

"She is called Face Woman," Hanabi says. "It is good, brother. If she is valued, she will be safe."

"She is valuable to him," I whisper. My mind is reeling, and I'm going to be sick. I will kill this Magwich, and I will kill anyone who tries to stop me. If I die, it could not be a worse hell than this.

Washakie touches my shoulder, and his eyes are bleak. He sees what is in my heart, and he's troubled by it.

"I have sent word to the leader of every band. We will meet in council at nightfall. You will come. You will tell them what has been done. You will ask for the woman and the child to be returned. And I will speak for you."

NAOMI

I saw Hanabi. I thought she saw me too, but I'm not sure. Her baby was strapped to her back, just like before. Beeya is skittish, and we haven't left the wickiup since Hanabi and the women came to visit. John said Hanabi's husband's name was Washakie. He met him at Fort Bridger and was greatly impressed.

I've heard the name Washakie many times since we arrived in the valley. He is admired among the Shoshoni. They are *all* Shoshoni. The same people who killed my family fed my family. The woman who nursed my mother's child sits with the woman who stole my mother's child. And I am lost.

I lie down on the buffalo robes and close my eyes. I don't think I am unwell. My skin isn't hot and my throat isn't sore, but something is loose inside my chest. I can feel it sliding and slipping when I move.

Beeya pokes at me and tries to get me to paint, but I can't, and she lets me sleep. Magwich comes in hours later. He is angry that I am sleeping. He argues with Beeya and prods me with his foot. Beeya brushes my hair and braids it down my back. She hands me a long skirt and a cloth blouse, something a woman gave her for one of my paintings. I put it on with shaking hands. There are beads at the neckline and beads at the cuffs, and a thick beaded belt wraps around my waist. It is beautiful, and Beeya is pleased.

She is taking me somewhere, and I'm too weary to be afraid. I should be. The moment I think I am saved is the moment I open another window to hell.

18

THE GATHERING

JOHN

Word has spread, and the clearing is teeming with warriors. There are too many leaders to fit inside a wickiup, so the council is being held outside. A fire has been built in a hole so the men can sit around it and still see each other, and Washakie says it's a rare occasion that the people can observe, even if they can't hear all that is spoken.

Hanabi thinks I should dress like I belong to the people. "He is not so white," she says. "We can claim he is one of us."

But Washakie shakes his head in disagreement. "He is here to claim his white wife and her white brother. He must be a white man too. That is how he must be seen."

Washakie sits on the east side, the northern bands to his right, the southern bands to his left, the western bands across the flame. I sit behind him with his war chiefs. He tells me that when it is my turn to speak, I will stand. There are old chiefs and young chiefs, but most, like Washakie, are caught somewhere in between, though Washakie stands out from the rest. He is respected and lauded, and I am reassured by his position among the leaders. Pocatello sits among the chiefs of the Northern Shoshoni. He is feathered and proud, but his lower jaw juts out too far, competing with the beak of his nose, and his eyes are mean and small. Beyond the circle of leaders, the field is dense with their men. The women make a circle around the edges, standing so that they can see. Hanabi is among them, Lost Woman too, but I do not see Naomi.

They begin with the pipe, passing it from one leader to the next. Each speaks of the prosperity and prowess of his tribe. Pocatello speaks the longest, describing his battles against the Crow and the Blackfeet and the white enemy that invades the land of the Shoshoni. He shakes his scalps, suspended from a pole that he lifts into the sky, and the people murmur and nod in approval. He does not speak of Naomi or Wolfe. He does not know why the council has been gathered.

Some of the older chiefs speak slowly, their voices muffled, and the crowd gets restless; the leaders grow sleepy. Finally it is Washakie's turn. He says that it is good to defeat our enemies and protect the lands, and it is good to make peace to protect the people.

"We made an agreement at Horse Creek to let the white men pass in their wagons. When we break our agreement, we give the white chiefs reason to break theirs."

"They do not keep their agreements," Pocatello yells out, interrupting. "They want to deceive us."

Washakie nods, acknowledging this, but he turns to me and asks me to stand. Curiosity ripples through the crowd, and the chiefs straighten. My presence, which has obviously been noticed, is being explained.

"This is John Lowry. Two Feet. He is a friend to my people and a brother to my woman. He saved my daughter from drowning." He pauses, letting the people look at me, letting his words settle. "His white woman and her brother were taken by Pocatello. He has come in peace, asking for their return. We will listen to him."

Pocatello shakes his scalps, and there is an audible shifting among his men, but the other leaders stare at me, waiting.

I am nervous, and I begin speaking Pawnee without realizing what I have done. When the people grumble and hiss, I stop, find my words, and try again. I have been preparing, but the weight of the moment, of Naomi's fate and my own, tangles my tongue.

I do not have an orator's skill, and the language does not flow from my lips, but I tell the story as well as I can. The burned wagons, the boys who hid in the rocks, the dead women and men. I tell the story of the bow and the child who wielded it, accidentally killing Biagwi's brother. I speak of Naomi, my wife, the woman who paints faces wherever she goes, and her infant brother. I tell them she is here—many of them have seen her—and I ask that they give her back to me, along with her brother.

When I am finished, there is a moment of silence, but then a young brave stands, his face twisted in anger and grief, and he shakes his fist at me and the leaders sitting around the fire.

"My brother is dead. I claim the child in his place. A brother for a brother." This is clearly Biagwi, whose wife has adopted Wolfe. The people murmur and nod, and another man comes to his feet beside him. He is burly and bare chested, and black feathers hang down his back, fluttering when he turns his head to address the people around him.

"The woman is mine. I will not give her to this *Pani daipo*," he shouts. The people snicker at the name—*Pawnee white man*—and the snakes in my stomach coil and hiss, their venom rising in my throat. And this is Magwich.

"You have taken something that is not yours," Washakie says, addressing Magwich. "You stole a man's wife, and you have no claim." He turns to Pocatello, and his voice is cold and hard. "You will call death and vengeance down upon your people, upon all the Shoshoni people, with your white scalps."

Pocatello is angry at the admonishment, and he stands from the council. "You are afraid of the white man. You bow to his demands. We did not attack first. They did."

The crowd rumbles. It is not going well.

"Bring the woman and the child here," an old chief says, and the leaders around the fire nod in agreement. "And we will decide what is to be done."

Biagwi protests and Magwich sputters, but Pocatello barks a sharp order, and the men leave to do his bidding. Washakie does not sit again but remains standing at my side. Pocatello remains standing as well, his arms folded, his expression black. And we wait for the men to return.

Biagwi's woman carries Wolfe in her arms, his blond head clutched to her breast. She is afraid. Biagwi is afraid. He has one hand at the woman's back and one hand on his spear. He is tense, grim, and I see in him the same violent strain that hums beneath my skin.

Then I see Naomi. She is dressed like the Shoshoni women, beads at her throat and her ears, her ruddy-brown hair pulled back in a braid and swinging at her waist. Her green eyes are huge in her thin face, and her hands are stained with paint. When she sees me, she stumbles, and Magwich drags her to her feet. An old woman follows behind them, moaning and wailing like someone has died.

"John?" Naomi cries. "John?" And her legs give out again.

I want to go to her, but Washakie extends his arm across my chest. "No, brother."

The old chief raises his hands for silence. He has taken on the role of mediator, and the people quiet. He looks at me. "You will tell the woman we have questions for her. You will tell us what she says."

I nod and look at Naomi. She is only ten feet away, but Magwich has not released her arm. I tell him to step away, and he tightens his grip.

"Let go," I shout, and the old chief shoos him off. Magwich releases her and takes a single step to the side, bracing his feet and gripping his blade.

"Naomi, they want you to answer their questions," I say in Shoshoni and then in English, doing my best to ignore him.

She nods, her eyes clinging to my face.

"Who is this man?" the old chief says to Naomi, pointing at me. I translate.

"John Lowry. He is my husband." Her voice breaks, and she says it again, louder.

"Who is the child?" the chief asks, pointing at Wolfe.

"He is my brother," Naomi responds.

"She cannot feed him," Biagwi shouts. "She is not his mother and has no milk in her breasts."

The chief begs silence again, and we continue on, the old chief asking questions while I interpret, and Naomi responding. Washakie steps in when the old chief asks where the wagons were. He knows the area and the Shoshoni names; he knows the path the emigrants take. There is sympathy in the audience. I can feel it, and I feel the moment it slips again.

"Who killed first?" the old chief asks Naomi, and she hesitates, her chest rising and falling in distress.

"We didn't see them. We didn't know they were there. It was an accident," Naomi pleads, and when I translate, Pocatello begins to yell.

"They attacked us! They chose to fight."

The old chief raises his hands again, pleading for order.

"Let him take his woman. That is just. But the child stays," Biagwi cries out, his voice ringing above the din, the firelight dancing on his skin. Magwich spits, but everyone else falls silent.

Naomi is frantic, her eyes shifting wildly from one face to the next, trying to understand what has happened.

"Release them both. Biagwi's brother was avenged," Washakie says, his voice booming, but the leaders around the fire shake their heads.

"We will vote," the old chief says. And the pipe is passed once more. One by one, the leaders state their opinions. Washakie says release them both. Pocatello says keep them both. The rest agree with Biagwi. A brother for a brother. The woman holding Wolfe is weeping, and Biagwi shakes his spear at the sky. Naomi stands amid the crush, her face bright with terrible hope, Magwich beside her, the old woman wailing and holding on to her arm. The old chief stands and points from Naomi to me.

"Go," he says to her in English and again in Shoshoni. The old woman releases Naomi like she's taken an arrow in the chest, screaming and falling to the ground, and Magwich turns away, giving his back to the council. Naomi runs toward me, her mouth trembling and tears streaming, her stained hands fisted in her skirts. And then she is in my arms, her face buried in my chest.

"Take the woman and go in peace," the old chief says to me.

"What about the boy?" I shout, desperate, my arms braced around Naomi. But the leaders are standing; the council is finished. The decision is made.

"He will be raised as a son, like you were. A two-feet," Washakie says. "Biagwi is a man of honor. The boy will not be harmed." He has not moved from my side, but his eyes are on the woman in my arms, who does not yet understand.

"John . . . what about Wolfe?" Naomi starts to pull back, searching my face, searching for Wolfe. And Washakie turns away.

I can't tell her. I can't say the words. And she sees the terrible truth. She begins to fight against me, thrashing and crying, but I do not let her go.

"I can't leave him, John. I can't leave him!" she begs, crazed.

"And I cannot leave you," I shout into her hair, shaking her, the weight of the last two weeks crashing down on me. "I will not leave you!" I pull back enough for her to see my face, my own wild desperation, and something dawns in her eyes, like she is coming awake. I see my own horror and fear and suffering mirrored back at me, and she folds into herself, her sobs raw and heartrending. I swing her up in my arms and carry her into the darkness, leaving the clearing as the scalp dance begins.

NAOMI

He walks and walks, his arms tight around me, his tears dripping down his chin and onto my cheeks. Or maybe they are my tears. I don't know anymore. When he finally stops, there are no fires and no camps. No voices raised in strange celebration. There is only the sky riddled with stars above us and the grass beneath us. He is panting. He has carried me a long way, but he doesn't put me down. He just sits, folding his legs beneath us, keeping me in his lap with his arms wrapped around me. His tears come harder, streaming silently down his face. He cries like it's the first time he's ever cried, like all the pain of all his twenty-odd years is rising up at once, and I can only lie in his arms, spent and useless, unable to comfort him.

I have nothing to give him. Nothing left. I try to quiet my own sobs to ease his pain, but the thing that was loose inside my chest is now broken completely, and the pain is like nothing I've ever felt before.

"Âka'a, Naomi. Âka'a," he whispers again and again, stroking my hair, and after a while my sobs slowly abate, leaving a gaping hole behind, one I'm afraid will never heal. As if he knows—or maybe he has the same pain in his chest—John presses his palm against my heart, his hand heavy and warm, and the tears seep from beneath my lids again. I press my hands over his, and he curls into me, pressing his cheek to my hair.

I can't speak. I can't tell him everything. I don't know if I can tell him anything. There is too much to say, and some things . . . some pain . . . can't be spoken.

I've been alone with my words since Pa said "Praise the Lord" and the Lord struck him down. Those words are crowding my throat and swarming in my head, and they shudder in my chest beneath John's hand, but I don't know how to let them out.

I don't know how he found me. I want to ask. I want to hear it all. I want him to tell me why they let me go and what will happen to Wolfe. I need him to explain how I'm supposed to go on. But I cannot speak.

Beeya brought me to the clearing to sit among the women who gathered along the edges, too far from the center to hear what was being said or done. I didn't know what was happening, didn't understand the chatter or the excitement. Beeya wanted me to paint, and she set up torches all around me so I could see and be seen, and I did what was expected of me. Then Magwich came, striding through the crowd to retrieve me, his face hard and his grip harder, and I thought the bartering had begun again. Instead, he brought me to the center of the clearing, where twenty chiefs sat around the fire and another fifty sat behind them. A sea of faces gazing up at me. Then I saw John, so close and so impossible, standing beside a tall, imposing Indian chief in full headdress that hung to his knees, like something from a dream. None of it felt real. Not John, not the questions, not the words that were spoken, not Biagwi and Weda and Wolfe. And then it was over, and I was in John's arms.

But Wolfe is not in mine.

And it is all real.

A sound rises behind us, the chuff of a horse and a soft tread. John pulls a gun from his boot, his arm tightening around me, but a reedy voice calls out from the darkness, saying his name, and he wilts. For a minute I think it is Beeya, come to drag me back, but the woman is older than Beeya, her hair so white it glows in the moonlight. She slides from her dappled pony and walks to us with hesitant steps. Her arms are filled with blankets, a waterskin, and a sack of dried berries, meat, and seeds. She sets her offering down and crouches beside us, her short legs tight against her chest, her white hair billowing. Her eyes are filled with compassion, and she brushes my cheek with a trembling hand. Then she rises and touches John's head, speaking to him softly before she turns back to her pony and rides away, melding with the night.

"They call her Lost Woman," John says. "She is Washakie's mother. She followed us to make sure . . ." His voice breaks, and he doesn't finish, but I think I know what he was going to say. She followed us to make sure we weren't lost.

"But we are," I say, my voice raw. Three words. I said three words. Maybe there will be more.

We are quiet after that. He pulls a blanket over me and makes me drink a little, but my stomach revolts after a few sips, and I push it away.

"I promised Wyatt and Webb and Will that I would find you," he says.

Webb and Will. Their names make the hole swell and contract. Webb and Will. I had feared they were dead . . . and I had feared that they weren't. *Oh God. Oh, dear God, my poor brothers.*

John lifts his head to look down at me, but I cannot meet his gaze and I close my eyes and turn my face into his shoulder.

"I found them, Naomi. And I put them in my goddamn wagon, with Wyatt leading the way, and I sent them ahead to find the train." John thinks it is his fault. I can hear it in his voice. The agony, the guilt. But if he had been with us, he and Wyatt would most likely be dead too. John's absence saved him. Saved Wyatt. And probably saved Will and Webb too. That much I know.

"We buried your ma and your pa and Warren. We buried Homer and Elsie. And Will sang a song. We looked after them, the best we could." He says nothing about Elsie's baby, and I cannot ask. I cannot speak of the cries and the screams and the burning wagon. I cannot.

"I promised those boys I would bring you back. And I promised them I would find them again, no matter what. They need you, Naomi. I need you. But I will do whatever you want me to do. For as long as it takes. I will stay with you until you're ready to go. Until we find a way to get Wolfe back."

JOHN

I want to pack my mules and go. I want to put Naomi on Samson's back and leave, to get as far away from Pocatello and his band as I can, but when the morning comes, the eastern sky changing from black to smudges of gray and gold, I gather the blankets, the waterskin, and the food that Naomi wouldn't eat, and we walk back to the city of strangers, to the boy she won't leave. I have no plan. No course of action. But we return.

She is so quiet. She walks by herself, her arms wrapped around her stomach, her eyes forward, but when we reach the creek, she scans the clustered camps until she finds what she is seeking. Her shoulders relax a little, like she feared Pocatello and his people had fled in the night. When we reach Washakie's camp, the women are already stirring. Hanabi and Lost Woman sit in front of Washakie's lodge. Hanabi is braiding her hair. Lost Woman is stoking the fire. They see us coming and do not pause, but their eyes search our faces. My tent still squats like a small white flag among the skin-covered wickiups. My mules—two, four, six of them—still mill close by, grazing among the sea of ponies.

"Brother, Naomi . . . come. Sit," Hanabi urges, pushing her braid over her shoulder as she rises, hands beckoning. "We will cook for you."

Lost Woman takes the blankets from my arms, and I reach for Naomi. She flinches when my hand circles her arm, and I release her immediately.

"They want us to sit with them," I say.

"Not now," Naomi whispers. "Is that yours?" She points toward my tent. When I nod, she hurries toward it and crawls inside.

"Come, brother," Hanabi says softly, her hand light on my shoulder, and I comply, sinking down beside the fire. My limbs ache with fatigue. I did not sleep. I held Naomi all night, yet she flinches when I take her arm.

"I thought you would be gone before I woke," Hanabi says. "I am glad you are not."

"She can't leave him," I confess, hoarse. Raw. Hopeless. "And I can't make her go. If I do . . ."

"She will be lost forever," Lost Woman says.

"She will be lost forever," I whisper.

"Then you will stay," Hanabi says. "You will stay with us."

"But . . . I have nothing," I say. It is a million times more complex than that, but she has taken me by surprise.

Hanabi frowns. "What is nothing? You have mules. You have your woman. We will build a wickiup. You will hunt. You have all things."

"You will stay," Lost Woman agrees, nodding.

19

THE RACE

JOHN

I sleep beside Naomi for a few hours in my tent, but I am restless and troubled, and I rise without waking her. She is huddled on her side, her arms tucked and her head bowed like a bird in a storm. I wash myself in the creek and tend to my animals, who have little need of me now. They greet me and let me rub their necks and scratch their noses but resume their grazing as soon as I stop. I slide a rope over the dun's neck, a pang in my chest, but he comes along without resistance, clopping along behind me. He thinks we are going to run. But I can't run, not away, not now, and despite what Hanabi said, there are things we need.

Naomi has nothing but the garb she is dressed in. She doesn't have her book or her satchel. When I asked her where it was, she said Magwich gave it away.

"The scarred warrior liked my pictures," she said, as though every word took effort. When I pressed her, she just shook her head and whispered, "They're gone, John."

I don't know how I will be received; I am a stranger, a Pani daipo, but when I enter the clearing, I am regarded with suspicion but no fear. I have the last of my tobacco, a bit of ribbon, and a pouch of beads and buttons I can trade. And I have three mules and the dun. The money in my bags won't get me anywhere. Not here.

I search the men on horses and those making bets for the warrior with an obvious scar. It doesn't take me long. The man is seasoned but not old, an obvious leader, but not a chief. A thick, ridged scar cuts across the left side of his forehead, over the bridge of his nose, and down his right cheek, ending just below his ear, dividing his face in two. He is a collection of hard lines—his hair, his limbs, his back, his scar—and he sits astride a gray roan who shimmies and dances, wanting to run. While I watch, the race begins, a gun blast that makes the ponies bolt, fifty riders running at full speed down the length of the clearing. A woman and her papoose narrowly miss getting trampled, and one pony bucks and writhes down the course, sending his rider soaring. When he slowly rises, his arm is bent the wrong way, but the race—and his horse—continues past a break in the encampments, over the creek, and back again. It ends in the clearing where it all began, the yipping and yelping like coyotes in a frenzy.

The scarred warrior wins easily, a victory that seems to have been expected, though the anger and upset among the racers and the watchers is evident. Magwich is among those who have lost a horse in the contest. He demands a new race, but he is roundly ignored as his horse is led away by one of the scarred one's tribesmen. A new round of betting has begun, and I make my way toward the triumphant winner. He sees me coming and cocks his head, the conversation around him waning. They are surprised at my presence; I should be long gone. Everyone stares.

I did not want this; I thought I might be able to negotiate quietly, but I continue forward, leading the dun and keeping my eyes straight ahead on the warrior.

"You want to race, Pani daipo?" the man asks as I near. He knows who I am. I'm guessing they all do. If these men didn't see for themselves what happened in the council, they heard about it.

"No," I say, stopping in front of him.

He frowns. "No?"

"I want the—" I realize I don't know the word for *picture* in Shoshoni. "I want the paper faces Magwich gave you." There is a murmur at his name, like my words are being repeated, and I know I am courting trouble.

"You have the Face Woman," the scarred warrior says. "You do not need her drawings."

"They are the faces of her people. Her people are gone."

He is silent, considering. He turns away, holding up his hand for me to wait, and returns seconds later with Naomi's satchel. He opens the latch and pulls out a stack of loose pages. Winifred May looks up at me, and I am flooded with sudden grief.

"I do not want to give them to you," he says. His tone is not belligerent, and no one laughs; he simply speaks the truth: he does not want to part with them.

"There are many," I rasp, trying to speak around my emotion. "I do not need them all."

He nods, acknowledging this. I pull a pouch of tobacco from my saddlebag and point at the picture of Winifred. "I need that one."

He frowns, considering this for a second. Then he nods, and I hand him the tobacco. He gives me the picture on top, revealing a drawing of Warren, his face pensive and tired, his hair sticking up from his brow, staring off into a distance he'll never reach.

"I need that one too," I say, digging for my beads. The scarred warrior purses his lips, studying the picture, but then hands it over too, taking my trade. I exchange the ribbon for a sketch of William, the kerchief for a picture of a laughing Webb, and then I have nothing more to trade. A stack of precious images remains in the warrior's hands. He puts them back in the satchel and closes the top.

"I will give you the dun for all of them," I say. I'm no good at this. I want them too much, and he knows it. He looks at the dun, appreciative, but he shakes his head.

"It is a good horse, but I don't need another horse. I have won many horses. Fifty horses. Wahatehwe always wins!" He yells these last words, goading the men around him, and some whoop and some hiss.

"I will beat you, Wahatehwe!" someone yells back. It is Magwich, and he is astride another horse.

"I have beat you ten times, Magwich. You will have no horses left. Who else will race me?"

He waits, his arms extended in challenge, but no one answers. He laughs, shrugging it off. "No one wants to race me now. Wahatehwe always wins."

"I will race you," I say. The men around us crow in excitement. "And if I win, I get Face Woman's pictures."

"I will race you both!" Magwich yells. "And if I win, I will take the woman and my horses."

"I will not race for the woman, and I will not race Magwich," I say, my eyes on Wahatehwe. "Only you. For the pictures." I do not yell or even raise my voice, but the men around us spread the word.

"If I win? What do I get?" Wahatehwe says, but I can tell he wants to accept, regardless.

"You do not need another horse," I remind him. He laughs, teeth flashing. His big scar makes his smile droop on one side, and I like him more for it.

"If I win, Face Woman will paint another skin for me," he says, but I hesitate again.

"Face Woman is not well," I say. Naomi is not well, and I need her pictures. Wahatehwe frowns and looks at Magwich. He grunts and looks back at me, his gaze hard. I don't think he likes Magwich, and my esteem for him rises again.

"We will race. If you win, I will give you the pictures. If I win . . . I will keep them. That is all," he says.

"Let's race!" Magwich shouts.

Wahatehwe looks at me, his eyes speculative. "Magwich is angry. I said I would give him all the horses he lost in exchange for the Face Woman. Five horses. He decided the woman was more valuable. Now he has no horses and no woman. And he continues to lose."

Magwich is going to lose his life if I remain in his presence, but I say nothing.

Wahatehwe looks away and raises his voice, addressing the gamblers.

"Wahatehwe and the Pani daipo will race. Not Magwich."

"You are afraid of Magwich!" Magwich yells from atop his horse. Wahatehwe ignores him. I ignore him. A cry goes up, and bets are placed, and I send a boy from Washakie's band back for my saddle. It's outside my tent, the only tent in a valley of wickiups and tipis; he won't have any trouble finding it. Washakie has arrived. He sits at the edge of the clearing astride his dark horse with the white star and stays clear of the gambling. If he has raced at all, I don't know, but I doubt he would risk that horse. Pocatello and his men are at the starting line, placing their bets; Magwich is complaining to whomever will listen.

The boy returns with my saddle, his face alight with anticipation, and I hand him a coin from my bags. He flips it, smiles, and scampers away. I saddle the dun and swing up onto his back. He dances and tosses his head, eager to go, and I hear a few of the bets change. I don't know how their system works and have no wish to find out. If I win, I get the pictures, and that's all I care about.

I let the dun scamper a bit, warming up his limbs, but no one is patient enough for me to test the course. I move toward the line, but

Wahatehwe is not the only one waiting there. Magwich insists on racing, and no one dares deny him.

"If I win, I get the woman," Magwich insists.

"No. If you win, you win. You get nothing from me," I say. I don't even look at him. Wahatehwe is between us at the line, and I move the dun beside his paint, refusing to be goaded by the loathsome Magwich.

"If I win, I will take my horses," Magwich warns Wahatehwe. The crowd goes silent, awaiting Wahatehwe's response.

"If you win, I will give you the five horses I won from you," Wahatehwe relents, letting his voice carry.

Magwich bellows, raising his hands like he's already won, and the bets are cast yet again.

"But if the Pani wins," Wahatehwe shouts, his eyes gleaming with mischief, "I will give the five horses to him."

Magwich is stunned into silence, and the men around us whoop, but there is no time for argument.

"We race!" Wahatehwe yells. "Cross the creek and come back, Pani."

Then the gun fires, making the dun jump, and Magwich and Wahatehwe are off, kicking their horses' flanks, their hair flying out behind them, the dust billowing. I don't even have to spur the dun. He sees the others leaving him behind and gives chase, almost unseating me. I mold myself to his back and bury my hands in his black mane, letting him go. He pounds down the clearing and past the camps, in pursuit all the way. Wahatehwe leads Magwich, and neither is paying any attention to the dun closing in. I cross the creek as they are turning around, and the dun hits the far bank and is back in the water without me taking the reins at all. It's a race, and he is losing, and the dun doesn't like to lose.

By the time we reach the edge of the clearing, the dun is stride for stride with Wahatehwe's paint. Magwich is behind us, and I don't look back to see how far. The dun flies, running with all the joy he's been denied since leaving the Dakotah at Fort Laramie, and when we reach the finish, we are a full length ahead. The dun doesn't want to stop, and I draw hard on his mane and bear down in the stirrups to bring him around.

Wahatehwe is laughing, his head and his arms thrown back, and those who shifted their bets at the end, gambling on the long shot, are yipping and dancing with the same zeal. For a brief, sweet moment, my heart is light and the snakes are quiet. I trot my horse back toward the finish, shaking my head in disbelief.

"Didn't know you had that in ya, Dakotah," I say to the dun, laughing. It's about time I gave him a name. He's earned it.

"I want that horse, John," Wahatehwe yells, his teeth still flashing behind his lopsided lips. It seems I've earned a name as well. Washakie is approaching on his horse, his war chiefs beside him, and all are grinning. It was a good race.

I slide from the dun, reaching up to take the satchel from Wahatehwe's outstretched hand. He is still astride the paint, incredulous and laughing, and then he isn't. His eyes flare, and Washakie shouts out in warning. "Brother!"

I whirl, stepping to the side, and a knife sinks to the hilt in the dun's right flank. The horse shrieks and bolts, and Shoshoni scatter like a drop of oil in a too-hot skillet, spitting in every direction.

Magwich runs at me, another blade flashing, his teeth bared, and I spin, narrowly avoid being split from my navel to my neck. He slashes again as I feint left, but he nicks my face and takes off a piece of my hair. I stagger back, reaching for the blade in my boot, and he dives again as I scramble and spin. His blade catches my shirt, and the tip of his knife scores my stomach in a long, shallow slice. The welling blood behind the gaping cloth makes him smile. The area around us is wide and empty. No one interferes. No one calls out. They watch.

"I will take your scalp and take your woman . . . again," Magwich spits out. "I will put the Newe in her belly. Again." Magwich is panting with his confidence, his knife wet with my blood, but Otaktay, the half-breed Sioux, taught me how to kick and bite and gut a man a dozen ugly ways before I was thirteen years old, when my rage had nowhere to go. My rage is bigger now.

Magwich thrusts again, his stance wide, his powerful thighs braced to run me through, and I drop, kicking out like a mule and connecting with his knee. When he falls forward, I drive my elbow into the side of his head as hard as I can, making him stumble and reach for the ground to catch himself. He drops his knife, and I step back, letting him pick it up again, waiting to see if he wants to die. I want to kill him, but I don't want to die. I made a promise to three boys and a dead man that I would take care of Naomi. I can't do that if I kill this man and have to face two thousand more. I am not one of them. He is.

"I don't want to kill you," I lie. "Take your knife and Wahatehwe's horses and go. I don't want them."

He laughs. I am bleeding, and he is not. Some in the circle around us jeer, and others jostle to see. Magwich picks up his knife and begins to circle, his stance low and his feathers dancing. He is favoring his knee. He lunges, and I kick out again, connecting with his injured leg, but the dirt is thick and loose from the pounding of hooves and the near-constant racing. I slip, and he pounces, bringing his knife down in a wide arc. It glances off the ground above my head, but my knife is already in his belly. He stiffens, his big body flexing in surprise. He tries to roll away, to escape the blade that is already embedded, but I wrap both hands around the hilt and yank upward, splitting him open before shrugging him off.

He gasps and grabs at his belly, but he is dead before I jerk my knife free. Then I rise to my feet, bloodied and tattered, my blade up and ready for whatever is next.

I expect a rush of knife-wielding Shoshoni, but I am greeted by a brief silence followed by whoops and wails and nothing more. Wahatehwe raises his arms and howls, and Washakie does the same. Some of Pocatello's men come forward out of the circle, their eyes cautious. One asks if I will take the scalp. My stomach rebels, and I shake my head, refusing the rite. They lift Magwich onto their shoulders, his blood spilling down their backs and onto the ground, but no one rushes me with a spear or a blade. No one confronts me at all. Someone shrieks in mourning, and many voices join in as the body leaves the clearing, but like the final decision at the council, the matter is decided. It is done. Magwich challenged, and Magwich lost. I pick up the satchel, covered with dust and splattered with blood, and go in search of my horse.

NAOMI

I awake to distant wolves wailing, and I am alone in John's tent. It is midafternoon, and I have slept for hours; I could sleep for hours more, but the sound rising up beyond the encampment has me crawling out of the tent to see what new hell has arrived. No one in the camp seems especially concerned by the noise, though many are gathered near Hanabi's wickiup. The chief, Washakie, is speaking, and both men and women are listening intently, their eyes wide, mouths agape, like he is relaying a tale. Occasionally another brave cuts in, providing added emphasis or explanation—I can't tell which—and then Washakie continues. But I hear John's name.

Then I see John.

He is leading the dun toward the camp, and both he and the horse are caked in dust and blood. Everyone in Washakie's camp exclaims, and a few run toward him, but he lifts his hand the way he does with his animals, reassuring them, quieting them. I want to run to him too, but I stay rooted to the spot. There is too much blood—his clothes are soaked in it—and my legs have gone numb. John scans beyond the heads of those huddled around him and sees me. He moves through the people, and they part for him. I think one asks to take the horse, but he shakes his head and leads the dun toward me. Hanabi claps her hands, snapping something, and the people disperse, leaving us in relative solitude.

"Are you hurt?" I choke, trying not to look at him, willing the bile in my belly to settle. I pin my eyes to the western sky beyond his shoulder. For months I've been looking at the western sky, walking toward it, but now I'm standing still.

"No. The blood isn't mine," he says, calm. Quiet.

"Okay," I say. Nodding.

"You need to sit," he says. "You're white as a ghost."

"I'm fine." He reaches out a hand to steady me, and I step back. I don't mean to. I just do, and he drops his hand.

"I'm sorry," he says. "I'll go to the creek to wash."

"I'll get you a fresh shirt," I whisper. "And your soap and towel." He protests, but I turn away—I run away—and he lets me go. I search his packs just inside the tent with shaking hands and sip some water from the canteen John left beside me while I was sleeping.

When I reach the creek, he's already stripped off everything but his pants and submerged himself in the water, washing most of the blood from his skin and hair. He seems more concerned with the dun and is using a tin cup to pour water over his back and his legs, cleaning away the gore and the grime. The horse has a cut on his flank about an inch wide, but it oozes like it's deep. I hand John the soap and then sink down into the grass with his shirt and towel, not trusting myself to stand.

Some of the blood is John's. He wasn't completely honest about that. A long, shallow slice crisscrosses his stomach, and there's a small gash on his cheekbone.

"Your satchel is there." He points with his chin, indicating the grass beside me. "I think if I wipe it with a cloth and oil it up some, it'll be as good as new. You might want to check the pictures inside. There are a few more in that saddlebag." Another lift of his chin. "I had to roll them to make them fit, but they're there."

I stare at the battered satchel and touch the clasp, stunned. It's dusty and spattered, but it's here. I open the cover and check the contents, the thick white pages filled with the faces I can't look at right now. I close it again, overwhelmed with dumbfounded gratitude.

"How?" I whisper. "How did you find them?"

"The scarred warrior—Wahatehwe—gave them back."

"He gave them back?" I gasp, but John isn't listening anymore. He's dunked himself in the creek again and is scrubbing his hair and skin with the soap like he can't bear to look at me either.

Someone calls out behind me in Shoshoni, and I turn to see the same scarred warrior walking toward the creek, leading five horses. The same five horses he offered Magwich in trade for me. My chest grows tight, and my stomach twists, but John stands, the water sluicing off his hair and his body, and greets the man. John introduces him—his name, Wahatehwe, is beautiful on John's tongue—but I don't look up. I ignore them both. The scarred warrior and I have already met, and I would rather forget him.

They converse for a moment, and I feel Wahatehwe's eyes touching on me before he turns away, but he leaves the horses behind. They bow their heads beside the creek and drink, unconcerned with his departure.

"They are ours now," John says quietly. "We'll need some skins for a wickiup and some buffalo robes to sleep on if we're going to winter here. We can trade the horses for whatever we need."

My head is spinning. *Winter here? A wickiup? And why are the horses ours?* "I don't want anything that belonged to Magwich," I stammer.

"That's what I told Wahatehwe, but he said it's not a horse's fault who his master is. Who his master . . . was."

"Who his master was?" I ask, still reeling.

John doesn't answer. He busies himself with Magwich's horses, pretending not to hear. But I know him too well. "Why did . . . Wahatehwe . . . give you the horses, John?"

"I won them . . . in a race. Dakotah won them."

"Dakotah?"

"The dun. That's his name."

"Since when?"

"Since he won your satchel and five horses from Wahatehwe," John says quietly.

"And who put a slash across your belly and a gash on your cheek and a knife in . . . Dakotah?"

"Magwich." John says the name like it tastes bad.

"And what did you do to Magwich?" I whisper. The hole in my chest fills with something black.

He is silent for a heartbeat, and then he raises his eyes to mine, solemn and dark. "I killed him, Naomi."

I am caught in a deluge of relief and loathing, and I grit my teeth, close my eyes, and sink my hands into the grass so I'm not washed away.

"Naomi?" John murmurs.

"Yes?"

"I need you to look at me."

"I will. I will, John. I just can't . . . quite yet," I say, keeping my eyes shut tight. I hear him walk toward me and crouch down beside me, but he doesn't touch me. I can feel the cold coming off his skin and the warmth of his familiar breath.

"I need you to look at me now," he says gently. "Please."

I open my eyes and lift my head. And I steel myself to hold his gaze. So many words. So many. And I feel like a liar when I look at him.

"I promised Washakie I wouldn't seek revenge if he helped me find you. And I kept that promise. But Magwich thought he could kill me, and today he tried. I killed him instead."

My words are rising and spilling from my eyes, and I want to look away.

"He deserved to die, and I'm not sorry. I'm not ashamed to admit it. I got nothing to be ashamed of. And neither do you. Nothing. You hear me?" John's voice is fierce, but his lips are trembling, and I reach up and touch his mouth, comforting him even as I break down. He grips my wrist and kisses my palm, and for a moment we struggle together, fighting the grief and the guilt and the words that we don't say.

20

WIND RIVER

JOHN

Washakie's band was the last to arrive at the Gathering, and we are the last to go, but two days after I killed Magwich, Pocatello and his people are gone before the sun rises. Naomi is inconsolable. I hold her as close as she will let me, and when she finally sleeps, Lost Woman sits with her awhile, letting me escape to my mules and my horses. Washakie finds me there, tending to Dakotah's wound.

"Pocatello is gone," he says.

I nod once, brittle and beaten. "I know."

"Nay-oh-mee cannot go home." He uses her name, and I am grateful. She is not Many Faces or Face Woman. She is Naomi, and she needs to remember that.

"No, Naomi can't go home . . . though I'm not sure where home is. Home is a wagon that I turned into a grave."

"His people are not far," Washakie says.

I grunt. "How far do you have to be to be gone?"

He doesn't answer, but he appears to be thinking on it. He looks the horses over, running his hands across their backs and down their legs.

"I know where they winter. We will winter there too. So Naomi is close to her brother," he says abruptly, rising to his feet, finished with his inspection.

I freeze, my eyes meeting his over the back of the spotted gray.

I don't know what to say. I try to speak and end up shaking my head.

"We cannot live in the next valley forever. But for now . . . for now we can. Until Naomi is ready to go home," he says. Then he nods like it is decided and turns away, leaving me to weep among the horses. When I tell Naomi we will follow Pocatello, she reacts much like I did, with awed gratitude and tears. It doesn't solve the problem, but it eases the immediate agony.

I trade three of the horses for skins, robes, and clothes, along with tall moccasins lined in sheep's wool for the cold. I build a wickiup with Hanabi and Lost Woman's help, and I am pleased with the result. It's a good sight warmer and more comfortable than a wagon, and there are no wheels to fix or axles to straighten. The thought shames me.

The Mays are never far from my mind. All of them, but especially Wyatt, Will, and Webb. In my head, I'm calculating distances, trying to figure out where they might be, looking at my maps and my guidebook, filled with all the things one might see on the journey west and none of the toil that accompanies it. By the end of August, when I found Naomi, they should have traveled over two hundred miles. Four hundred miles to go. Now it's September, and they will need to cross the Sierra Nevada before the snow falls. Naomi and I would have needed to cross the Sierra Nevada before the snow falls too, but we don't. We stay, sealing our fate, at least until spring.

We don't talk about what comes next. She holds my hand when we sleep, and we've started to talk about small things—Shoshoni words and Shoshoni ways and how Hanabi and Lost Woman are teaching her how to prepare skins and dry meat and sew beads onto our clothes. She doesn't talk about her family, and she doesn't kiss me. I don't press on either count. Her fire isn't gone, and neither is her love. I can still feel it when I'm near her, the same heat that had her asking me to marry her because she needed to lie with me. But the fire is banked, and I don't try to stoke it.

We travel east out of the valley instead of retracing our steps south. Washakie wants to hunt the buffalo before the herds move south and the cold sets in. We are moving into Crow territory, and Washakie sends out scouts as we hug the mountains and wind down between thick forests to the west and a wide plain to the east. A party of Washakie's men scouts a Crow village several miles away, and when we've broken camp and headed out, they go back to the village to steal horses under the cover of darkness. Washakie says the same band stole fifty head from his people the winter before, and they've been waiting for an opportunity to recoup their losses. He says the men will not return with the stolen horses if they are successful but make a wide arc around us to keep the Crow from our trail. Then they will drive the horses to the Shoshoni lands and wait for us there.

The men who do not go on the raid are wistful and spend the next few days wondering aloud how many horses their brothers will steal and if the Crow will give chase. It inspires stories from past raids, to and from the Crow, and I am convinced the tribes steal from each other mostly for sport, though someone always seems to get wounded or killed in the process.

We come across a huge herd of antelope, and spirits are enlivened, including those of my horse. Dakotah gets to run again, and like in the race at the Gathering, he knows exactly what to do. We cut off a section of the herd and take turns running the poor beasts in circles until they are so spent they lie down in the grass and wait to be slain. There is no gluttony in the kill, and nothing is wasted. We take only what we can eat or pack and move on.

Three weeks after we leave the valley of the Great Gathering, we make camp at the edge of the Wind River Valley, the wide expanse of low plateaus, rolling grass, and blue sky before us, the peaks of the Wind River Range at our backs, looming but distant, unconcerned with the lives beneath their shadow. I know where we are. South Pass, the wide saddle of land that divides the continent, lies at the bottom of the range. We've come back to the Parting of the Ways. Little did we know where the path we took would lead.

Washakie says this is the place he loves most, the place where he spent most of his boyhood days. "My father is buried here. I will be buried here. It is my home," he says simply. "We will stay here until the leaves are in full color. Then we will go east. We will winter where the springs run hot, even when the snow falls. Pocatello will not be far."

The raiding party is already there, flush with victory and thirty of the Crow's best horses. We tuck ourselves back against the spruce and fir, where the water winds through the valley and cuts away again, and the camp is protected from the open range. I spend one morning with Washakie and a handful of braves, scouting the herds and planning the hunts, and return at midday to find the women circled together, plucking pine nuts from their cones, their fingers fast but their conversation easy. Hanabi knows a few English words from her years with my family. She is rusty, and Naomi must speak slowly, but Hanabi tries.

"I was once Naomi, brother," she says. "I understand her."

She seems to, and I am grateful. Lost Woman is infinitely patient with her and doesn't even try to speak. She just demonstrates, loves, and looks after. There is a stillness about them both, an unspoken communion, and Naomi is drawn to her. But Naomi is not among the women seeding pine cones, and she is not in the wickiup or among the horses. Lost Woman points to the stream, where it disappears into the forest, and tells me Naomi wanted to be alone.

"She is alone long enough. You should go," Lost Woman says, shooing me toward the trees. I find Naomi in a dense copse of trees near the creek. She has removed her leggings, and her doeskin dress is hiked up around her thighs. She is washing blood from her pale legs.

"Naomi?" I've startled her, and she jerks upright, slipping on the rocks and landing on her bottom in the creek. She stays down, her dress bunched around her, her hands in her lap and her legs splayed.

"Naomi?" I don't want to laugh, and I'm not sure she's okay.

She looks up at me and tries to smile. A smile, eye contact. We've come that far at least. "I didn't hear you. I tried to go a ways from camp so . . . so I could wash."

I walk toward her, halting at the water's edge.

"You're bleeding."

"Yes." She nods. Her eyes are bright, but she's not crying. "I'm bleeding. Finally. I was afraid."

I don't understand.

And then . . . I do. The realization weakens my legs and steals my breath.

"I was bleeding when we reached Sheep Rock. I haven't bled since."

"And we haven't been together since." My voice is as hollow as I feel.

"No. We haven't," she whispers. "I've been . . . waiting. I needed to know. To be sure."

"Âka'a," I whisper, sickened. Angry. I sit down beside her in the water, not caring that it is cold or wet or that I am fully clothed.

"But I'm bleeding now," Naomi says, falsely chipper. "And that is good."

I'm afraid to speak, so I nod, looping my arms around my bent knees, trying to control the rage that has nowhere to go.

We sit that way for a while, side by side, numbing ourselves in the shadowed creek. I don't know how to fix what has been broken or ease a pain beyond my understanding.

"I didn't fight, John," she blurts, releasing the words in a rushed confession.

I wait, not breathing.

"I didn't fight," she says again, stronger. Louder, like she's making herself face them. "I was afraid Magwich would trade me to another tribe, and I would never see my brother again. So I didn't fight."

I don't touch her. Not for comfort or support. She's not done.

"I didn't fight." Her voice shakes, and her eyes have filled and flooded over, but I hear anger, and I'm glad. "It hurt. And I wanted to scream. I wanted to run and keep on running. But I didn't. I took it." She takes a ragged breath. "I didn't want it. I didn't ask for it, and I'm not lesser for it. I know that." She nods, reaffirming her words. "But I didn't . . . fight, and that's what I can't get over."

"You fought," I say.

"No. I didn't." She shakes her head, adamant, and swipes at her angry tears with the back of her hand.

"There are many ways to fight, Naomi Lowry."

My use of her name lifts her chin, and she looks at me, really looks at me, and she is listening.

"You were fighting for your brother. You were fighting for Wolfe. For your life. It would have been easier to scratch and kick and bite. Believe me, I know. I spent the first fifteen years of my life fighting everything and everyone. But . . . endurance . . . is a whole different kind of battle. It's a hell of a lot harder. Don't ever say you didn't fight, because that's never been true. Not one day of your whole life. You fought, Naomi. You're still fighting."

There are tears on her cheeks and tears on her lips, but she leans forward and presses them to mine. I taste salt and sadness, but I also taste hope. It is a kiss of gratitude, brief and sweet, and then she pulls away again.

"That is not the way I want to be kissed," I say, hoping I'm not overplaying my hand.

She laughs, throwing her head back, and for a moment I see her, my Naomi, the one who barters with Black Paint and does her laundry in a deluge and tells me point-blank how she likes to be kissed.

"No?" she says, not missing a beat. "How do you want to be kissed?"

"Like you've been thinking about it from the moment we met."

She laughs again, but there are tears in her throat, and it sounds more like a sob. She touches my lips with the tips of her fingers, her hand cold and wet from the water, but she does not kiss me again.

"I love you, Two Feet," she says.

"And I love you, Naomi May Lowry."

NAOMI

They spotted buffalo this morning, and the fervor in the camp was manic. The fire was stoked high, and the medicine man and the old warriors danced around it for hours, sweating and pleading with something—or someone—to bless the hunt to feed them through the winter. The women didn't dance or pray. They kept vigil around the edges, keeping the fire burning and the men moving.

Two worlds exist in a Shoshoni tribe. A world of women and a world of men. The two worlds overlap, creating a slice of coexistence, a place of shared toil and trouble and dependence on one another, but there are still two worlds. Maybe it's the same among all tribes, all Indians. All people. I don't think the Dakotah near Fort Laramie were any different. I don't think my own world is that dissimilar. Maybe with Ma and Pa, that overlap was just greater. Ma had her duties and Pa had his, but those things were on the edges, and they lived and loved in the middle.

The middle is narrow here.

The men eat first. Always. The women prepare the food, present the food, and then wait for the men to be done with the food before they gather and eat what's left, sitting among the children, just enough apart from their men that the distance between the two worlds feels like an ocean to me. John always finds a space between—he too lives in the middle—talking with the men but waiting for the women. Hanabi clucks her tongue, and Lost Woman shows me how to serve him, but he will not eat until we do.

"Jennie," Hanabi says to me, as if that one word is enough explanation of John's peculiarities. I suppose it is. I know exactly what she means. John was not raised by a Shoshoni woman, and he will never be completely comfortable as a Shoshoni man.

In other ways, this life suits John. His hair has grown, and his skin has soaked up the sun, making him almost as brown as Washakie. He speaks with an ease and fluency that amazes me. He is well liked, and he likes in return, and I can't help but wonder what his life would have been like had his mother not died, had he not been dropped into a white world and forced to adapt. I watch him the way I've always watched him, fascinated by him, awed by him, trying to find my way back to him.

He is excited for the hunt and lies beside me in the wickiup, a bundle of nervous energy, eager for the morning. He reminds me of Webb or Will, a little boy, unable to hold still or rest because something special is coming. He tries to damp down his enthusiasm for my sake, but I can feel it pouring from him, and it makes me glad.

He feels guilt when he is happy. We both do. We don't talk about my brothers—any of them—but they, even more than Ma and Pa, are always with us, waiting. Watching. Disturbing the peace between us. In the quiet darkness of the wickiup, we have all the privacy we once longed for, but I feel the weight of a dozen May eyes, and I cannot turn to him, even though I want to. Even though I need to. Even though he needs me.

I don't know where Wolfe is or if he's well, and it haunts me. But I'm comforted by one truth: Weda can do what I cannot. She can feed Wolfe. She can keep him alive, for now. Washakie has promised John that when the hunt is over, the meat dried, and the skins readied, we will go to the valley where Pocatello winters, and we will stay until the snows melt. After that, I don't know.

∞

I watch from the plateau, sitting with the women and looking down on the matted, humped backs of the buffalo below, our horses grazing behind us. They are saddled with the empty packs and the tethered poles we will use to pack the meat when the hunt is over, but for now, we just watch.

We are only twenty feet above the meadow; the jutting cliff face provides a place to observe without getting in the way or trampled by the herd if they swing too close, and judging from the excitement among the women, I don't think our view is typical. Hanabi keeps saying, "Naomi! See? See?" and clapping her hands. I do see, and my heart is pounding with dread and anticipation. John says Dakotah and Washakie will do the hard part, but knowing John, I am not convinced.

The men have made a wide circle around the herd and carry long spears, and as we watch, they begin closing in, working in teams, isolating a bull or a cow and running it down. John is with Washakie and another brave named Pampi, and he races along behind them as Washakie and Pampi engage in the dance of bringing down a two-thousand-pound bull.

It is a bloody art, and I stare transfixed as Washakie, hanging from his horse at a dead run, slashes the bull's hind legs with his spear, severing its hamstring so it collapses midstride. The bull careens, his momentum sending him end over end as Pampi, running toward the buffalo at full speed, raises his bow and shoots, putting an arrow in the bull's neck.

Washakie whoops, and they are off again, but this time it is Pampi who chases the buffalo down with his spear and Washakie who comes in on the angle, John on his heels. Pampi dangles, slashing at the bull's legs, and Washakie shouts and veers to the side, leaving John to take the shot. He raises his rifle, bearing down into the path of the animal at full speed, and shoots without hesitation, right above the bull's eyes. The bull slides, coming dangerously close to the dancing legs of the dun. I scream, but the horse doesn't balk or bolt. Lost Woman pats my leg, Hanabi crows, and across the meadow, Washakie whoops in victory. John does the same, shaking his rifle in the air, his white teeth flashing, his chest heaving. Then they are off again, selecting a bull, turning him, and chasing him down.

When the hunt is over, the harried herd pounding away to safer pastures, fifty buffalo lie dead in the yellow grass: two buffalo for every family, one for me and John, and one for the feast that will feed the whole camp for days.

John returns to the buffalo-strewed field, shirtless and smiling, joyful even. With Lost Woman demonstrating, he helps me split the buffalo from its head to its tail, peeling back the hide to remove the meat from its back before tying two ropes to its front and hind legs and using the horses to flip it over. We repeat the action on the other side, slicing the buffalo from chin to tail to remove the meat on the front. It is heavy, messy work, and neither of us has ever quartered a buffalo before. Lost Woman and Hanabi have two cows skinned and packed in the same time it takes us to do one, but we are both breathless and proud—and covered in blood—when we return to camp.

We slice the meat into thin strips and hang it up to dry. Hanabi says tomorrow we will pound it with rocks and let it dry some more. The hides will take days to treat, but for now, those will wait. We are hungry, and preparations for the feast begin.

Fires dot the growing darkness as the buffalo is fried over the flames in strips and steaks. Lost Woman is turning a roast as big as my head on an iron spit, and the smell hangs in the air, even at the creek, where John and I retreat to wash, scrubbing our clothes before we pull them off and wash ourselves. We keep our backs to each other, shivering in the cold water, before stepping onto the banks and pulling on the homespun clothes John managed to acquire at the Gathering.

John has not come down from the hunt. His smile is easy and his countenance is light, and when he twines his hand in my wet hair to keep it off my dry blouse, his eyes are soft on my face. I breathe in his joy, letting it sit in my lungs and warm my limbs, my lips parted, my hands curled at my sides. His eyes are full of asking, and I step closer, chasing his mouth. He groans and sinks in, wrapping an arm around my waist, leaving the other buried in my hair. He is careful and the kiss is quiet, though my heart is loud and my soul is needy.

I taste him, just a touch of my tongue to his top lip, and he stills, letting me find my way, letting me tell the story of a woman coming home again. He welcomes me there, opening his mouth and letting me linger by the door.

I slide my hands along the rough of his jaw, holding him to me while I tiptoe through the room we shared, back when I was unafraid. I want to lie on the bed and watch him sleep; I want to touch him like I did before. But I hesitate too long, my mouth on his, lost in the memory of then, and he thinks I've fled.

His body is thrumming, his breath hot, but he steps back, softly closing the door behind me, letting me go. He takes my hand, and without a word, we walk back toward the wickiups.

JOHN

The fat drips from the meat in our hands and slides down our arms, but we cock our elbows, trying to keep our clothes clean, and keep on eating. We eat too much and then eat some more. I don't know if Naomi's been full in a long while, and she eats like she's starving. She probably is.

The swaying and pleading of the buffalo dance last night have faded into lazy feasting and contented conversation. It's been a long day, but I've never had a better one. I've had better moments. Better hours. A better night in a borrowed room at Fort Bridger. But never a better day, and I bask in it, setting aside the worry and the wear, the grief and the guilt, for a few more hours.

Drowsy children, nodding off in their mothers' laps, are herded to bed. Then a bottle is passed, and the stories begin. I sit not in the circle of men but just outside it, against my saddle, my legs stretched out, with Naomi at my side. Lost Woman folds herself beside us, and when the bottle comes, she takes a deep pull and passes it to Naomi with a look that says, *Drink.*

Naomi obeys, chokes, but then tips her head back and gulps it down.

"Easy, woman," I say, and she hands the bottle to me, wiping her mouth with the back of her hand. I take a sip and pass it on, the burn reminding me of the last time Washakie gave me whiskey, when I told him Naomi had been taken. I push the thought away. Not tonight. I found Naomi, and tonight, that's all there is.

An old warrior tells a story of a white buffalo who never dies, and I whisper every word to Naomi as she gets sleepy at my side. When I urge her to go to bed, she resists, and I pull her head down in my lap and let her doze. Her hair has dried in waves around her. She's left it loose, and I love it that way.

Lost Woman leans over her, patting her cheek. "She is coming back," she murmurs.

"Yes," I whisper, moved. "I think she is."

"Spirits help," she says. She smiles, but her eyes are knowing, and I'm not sure which spirits she's talking about.

"They make you brave and keep you warm," she adds, clarifying. I nod.

"They watch over us. I see their prints in the snow sometimes."

I look at her, brow furrowed, but she is rising, moving toward her wickiup with a hunched back and small steps. She has worked hard today, and her body is sore.

Around the fire, the stories have changed to the hunts of the past and the never-ending battles with the Crow. As I listen, I wonder how old the tales are and how much longer they'll be told. The world has remained unchanged in the Wind River Valley for a thousand years. Maybe more. But the millennium is coming to an end, and Washakie knows it. He knows, and he is silent by the fire, listening to the old men talk and the young men laugh. His eyes meet mine across the way, and I am suddenly weary.

I rouse Naomi, who sits up with bleary eyes and stumbles to the wickiup in search of water and a softer place to lay her rumpled head. Washakie calls out to me, his voice low and warm.

"You are a buffalo hunter now, brother. You will see them in your sleep. Don't shoot."

His men laugh and Washakie smiles, and I bid them all good night.

∞

I don't dream of buffalo. I dream of oxen pulling wagons. I dream of Oddie the ox being left behind and Naomi sitting beside him, drawing pictures of people we'll never see again. I come awake with a start, breathing hard, not certain where I am. Then Naomi reaches for my hand, reminding me.

"You had a bad dream," she whispers.

"Not bad," I whisper back. "Just strange and . . . lonely."

She sits up, crawls to the canteen, and brings it back to me, as if water cures loneliness. I drink even though I'm not thirsty, and she does too.

She lies back down, but we are both wide awake, and she whispers after a long silence, "Do you want to tell me about the dream?"

"Sometimes I dream about Oddie." I don't tell her the rest, and she doesn't ask me to, but after a moment, she shoves the buffalo robes aside and crawls up on my chest, spreading herself over me, her cheek against my heart. I shed my shirt before I slept, and her breath is warm on my skin.

"Poor Oddie. He was tired of carrying all of us," she says softly. I close my eyes, savoring the feel of her against me, solid and close. I reach up to stroke her hair, following its length to the base of her spine.

"I worry sometimes that you will get tired of carrying all of us, John."

"I would carry you to the ends of the earth."

She raises her head and looks down at me; her walls are down, and her gaze is tender. She braces her hands on either side of my head and kisses me—lips, chin, cheeks, brow—softly, sweetly, and then does it all over again. When she returns to my mouth for the third time, her breath is shallow, her heart thrumming, and the kiss is not nearly so soft or sweet. Her lips cling to mine, hungry and hopeful, and I respond in kind, my hands still but my mouth eager, molding her lips and chasing her tongue.

She wears a ragged homespun shift when she sleeps, something Hanabi gave her. It's thin beneath my hands as I draw it up over her hips and pull it over her head. Her eyes don't leave mine, and her mouth returns, wet and welcoming, and I can't be still any longer. Her arms curl around me, and her legs twine with mine when I roll, changing our positions. When she stiffens, I immediately stop, lifting myself up onto my arms and taking my weight from her body. But she grips my hips and guides me home, insistent. We moan as one and move together, slow, slow, slow. Our eyes are locked and our bodies are joined, but tears begin to seep from the corners of her eyes and trickle into the pool of her hair.

"Naomi?" I whisper, kissing them away. I hesitate, but she tightens her arms and legs around me, holding me close.

"No, don't stop. Don't go. It's not . . . I'm just . . . happy. And it hurts to feel good."

"Why?" I whisper. Naomi let me know, right from the beginning, that she wanted me, and I never doubted her. I doubted fate and my good fortune, I feared and fled her advances, but Naomi never played games, and she isn't playing now. My own pleasure is the swollen Platte, surging from a far-off place, but I hold it back, waiting for her, feeling the answering quake in her limbs. She is on the brink, but her heart is breaking.

"It hurts to be happy," she says.

"Why?" I ask, gentle. Careful.

"Because they can't feel anything."

"Who, Naomi?" I know the answer, but it doesn't matter. She needs to tell me.

"Ma and Pa and Warren. Elsie Bingham and her baby. Her husband. They're dead. And I'm not, and it doesn't feel right."

Everything about us feels right. The cradle of her hips, the silk of her skin, her breasts against my chest, her lips against my face. I don't move, though my body screams to do just that, but I don't pull away either.

"I am here, with you, loving you and being loved, and they are in the ground," she says, almost pleading for me to understand.

"I know."

"So it hurts . . . to feel good."

"Yeah. It does." There is no denying it, and admitting it eases the ache in my chest and the strain in her face.

She wipes her tears, and I kiss her forehead, resting my lips there. We breathe together, feeling the pain and holding each other close.

Then we begin to move again.

21

FALL

JOHN

The nights are colder, and the light has changed. It doesn't beat down from overhead but slants across the land and curls around the peaks, leaving the shadows alone. It's more golden and faded, and soon it will be gone. We leave the Wind River Valley in mid-October—I'm not sure of the exact date anymore. I lost track after Fort Bridger. I think it's the tenth, but I could be wrong. The boys should have crossed the mountains by now. The trail was going to end at Sutter's Mill, and I pray that Abbott will find them shelter somewhere to wait out the winter ahead. I trust the Caldwells and the Clarkes will look out for them too; Elmeda loved Winifred, and I think she loves Naomi. I hope she'll love the boys until we find our way to them.

Naomi's cheeks have some color beneath her freckles, and her face is not as thin. She rides on Samson's back, her hair braided to keep it from whipping in the wind. She is eating serviceberries from a small sack, and her lips are stained red from their juice. We found the bushes where we camped last night. The season is late, and many had ripened and fallen to the ground, but we filled our bellies and saved what was left. Naomi said she's never tasted anything better. We've lived on meat and the occasional roots and seeds, so the fruit is a treat, but there's something to the Shoshoni diet. The people age slowly, and everyone has their teeth.

Naomi catches me looking at her and smiles a little, sending a bolt of heat from my chest to my toes. The space between us is gone, the tentative touches, the careful words. We've built a raft in my wickiup, an ark like Noah's, where only the two of us live. And when it's dark, we float together, shutting out the flood, the fear, and the uncertainty of a world that won't be the same when the waters recede. Some nights Naomi is fierce, all speed and heat and frantic coupling, like she's afraid the storm's about to sink us. Other times she lies in my arms for hours, loving me slowly, like I am dry land.

We round the north end of the Wind River Range and go west toward the peaks Washakie calls Teewinot, which loom like a row of pendulous teats jutting out from Mother Earth. We cut through ridges and valleys heavy with trees for almost a week until we drop down into a bowl between the mountains, where the grass is long and green and the animals gorge while we rest for a day. Washakie doesn't let us tarry longer, and we exit the valley at its south end, following the Piupa through a chasm where rivers converge and warm springs bubble in pale-blue pools, attracting the children and Naomi, who begs for a bath. Washakie promises there will be more in the valley on the other side of the mountain.

When we come out of the canyon two days later, the valley stretches in front of us, green and flat, with mountains behind us and rivers beside us, one running west, another south. As promised, a hot spring bubbles up among the rocks near the base of the hills, and Washakie says the animals will gather around it in the cold, making hunting and trapping easy when the cold makes it difficult. We make camp just below the tree line, east of the junction where the two rivers meet. Timber will be plentiful for fires, and the animals can forage beneath the trees when the snow covers the grass. Wild chickens and grouse abound, and the rivers are filled with fish. A huge elk herd is sighted just to the north, and a prettier spot I've never seen. The soil is rich with the minerals that bubble in the hot springs, the water plentiful, and I can't imagine the farmland isn't prime.

I ask Washakie why his people don't grow corn and harvest the land, why they don't claim this spot and stay year-round. He doesn't like my suggestion.

"The problem with the white man is they want to tell the Indian how to live. They say, build your fence. Grow your food. Build a house that has no legs. A house like that is like a grave. Do you want me to tell you how to live?"

"I wish someone would."

He frowns at me for a moment, surprised, maybe even a little offended, but then a smile breaks across his face, and he laughs, a sound rough and choked, like he has a fly caught in his throat.

"You are like a man whose feet are stretched across the banks, trying to live in two lands at once, Indian and white," he says, and his ire is gone.

"That's why they call me Two Feet." I shrug. It has always been this way for me, but I'm more at peace with it than I've ever been.

"Maybe we are all stretched across the banks," he says, thoughtful. "Living in the land of yesterday and the land of tomorrow."

Like many of my conversations with Washakie, this one leaves me pensive and sad. The banks seem to be crumbling, and soon the land of yesterday will disappear.

He comes back to me a few days later and asks me about planting. He's been thinking about it.

"I don't know much," I say. "I am not a farmer. My father's not a farmer. My mother's people raised corn, but their crop was constantly getting burned by the Sioux. Her whole village was burned out and gone the last time I returned."

"Your father was a mule man," Washakie says, remembering. We've talked about it before.

I nod. "He bred and sold and broke mules. He didn't want to farm. He wasn't any good at it."

"I don't want to farm either," Washakie says, his mouth hard. "But when the herds are gone, my people will be hungry."

In a place like this, it's hard to imagine the herds being gone or the food being scarce. The trees are radiant with color and the valley thick with abundance, but I know why he worries. Washakie has his own pit of snakes. I promised to look after the Mays—not that I've done an especially good job of it—but Washakie feels the responsibility of a people.

"You are a mule man too," Washakie says, abandoning talk of farming and pointing at my little herd of three—Samson, Budro, and Delilah—grazing among the horses. I started my journey with twelve.

"Can a mule man tame horses?" Washakie asks. Several of the horses stolen from the Crow haven't ever been ridden, and the men have been taking turns getting thrown. I've had other things to do. I've made it my job to make a woodpile, saving the women from traipsing into the timber for hours on end when the snows come. I overheard a few of the men grumbling to Washakie that I am making them look bad, doing women's work the way I do. The next thing I knew, Washakie was beside me with an ax, chopping away. We have enough firewood now to keep the village warm for six months. Lost Woman just watched us, dumbfounded.

I am at it again, chopping, chopping. It clears my head. Washakie does not help me this time; he made his point to his men. But he has an air of mischief about him.

"I've broke more green mules than I can count," I say, my thoughts returning to the question at hand. "It isn't much different."

"Horses kick higher and run faster than mules," he says, a gleam in his eyes. He gestures to a gray stallion with a black mane and a blacker temper. "If you can ride that one, you can have him. Then the men will see you can do women's work and their work too."

I put down my ax and swipe at my brow, turning toward the horses. Washakie laughs and follows me, calling out to his men and drawing their skeptical attention. Naomi is helping Hanabi somewhere; I hope she doesn't make an appearance. She won't like this at all. I won't like it, but I'm going to do it.

This isn't going to be leading the mules across the Big Blue or convincing Kettle he likes the mare. The stallion won't want me on his back, so I'm going to get there as quick as I can. Once I'm there, I just have to outlast him.

A few of the braves goad me, telling me not to get too close, but the stallion isn't all that skittish; he just doesn't want a man on his back. He doesn't react as I draw close, especially when I offer him a handful of dried berries from my pocket. His big lips curl around my flat palm, letting me stand at his side, one arm outstretched, the other resting lightly on his rump, willing it to stay down. When he lifts his nose from my hand, I move, using his mane to swing myself up onto his back in one smooth motion. And that's where smooth and motion part ways.

The stallion bolts like I took a hot poker to his rump, and I hear Naomi cry out my name. I don't look back or sideways or down. I hardly look at all. I just hold on and let the stallion go.

And he goes and goes.

He doesn't buck and doesn't rear up, and I count myself lucky, keeping my belly to his back, my hands in his mane, and my knees pressed tight to his sides. When he finally slows, several miles from where we started, he is spent and subdued. I can't feel my fingers or my thighs.

"Damn *bungu*," I moan. *Bungu* is the Shoshoni word for horse, and it fits him. When this is over, I'll have a new black-maned bungu and some new black bruises.

I don't dare unclamp my hands or my legs, afraid he'll bolt when I'm not holding on and shake me off at last. We're both sweat slicked and panting. The river isn't far, and he can smell it. We've run along the flat, the land rising away from the river, which now sits below us down a steep bank. I can see the tops of the trees that crowd the shores, but I don't slide off Bungu's back. I'm not walking. He picks his way down to the water; I'm sure it's the same river that runs south from our camp. When we make it to the bottom and step out from the trees, I discover we're not alone.

A dozen Indian children play about a hundred yards upstream in a little cove, stabbing at the water with pointy sticks like they're hunting fish. They'll never catch anything; they're too loud. They don't notice me or Bungu, and I let the horse drink, keeping my eyes peeled for trouble. A group of women descends from the ridge to the water on a path more sloped than the one Bungu took, and I realize that if he'd gone any farther, we would have run right into their camp. Two of the women carry papooses, and I will Bungu to finish so I can ease away without being seen. My throat is dry and my hands are cramped, but I don't dare leave his back, especially now. They are far enough away that I can't see small details, but when one woman turns to assist an old woman behind her, I see the papoose on her back. Pale hair curls around the baby's pink face; the child's identity is unmistakable.

Washakie was right. Pocatello's people are in the very next valley.

NAOMI

He is gone so long, and I am angry and scared. Washakie laughed for a long time when John jumped on the back of the gray horse, but he isn't laughing anymore. Lost Woman is wringing her hands, and from the tone of her voice, Hanabi is scolding Washakie. He acts as though he isn't concerned, his arms folded and his face serene, but he hasn't stopped watching the distance where John disappeared. He returns, finally, a dark speck that becomes a plodding horse and a single rider, and I swallow the relief and swipe at the angry tears that are brimming in my eyes. When he's close enough that I can see he's uninjured—no blood, no broken limbs, and a straight back—I turn and stomp into our wickiup. He can come find me.

He doesn't do so immediately, and by the time he enters, my tears have dried, but my temper is hot, and I'm waiting cross-legged on our bed of buffalo robes.

"That was a fool thing to do, John Lowry," I snap, not even waiting for the skin over the door to fall back into place.

He walks to our bed and sinks down on his haunches so his eyes are almost level with mine.

"Lost Woman was terrified," I add.

"Her daughter was dragged from a horse. That's how she died. I already got an earful." He sounds sad for Lost Woman but not especially penitent.

"What took you so long?" I rage. I want to wrap my hands in his hair and shake him.

"Bungu ran until he was done. That took a while."

"Bungu? You named your horse Horse?" I am so angry that I'm being mean.

He smiles at me like he's proud. "You know that word."

"I do. I know that word and a few others, like *kutise*. Crazy. That was crazy what you did, John."

"Oh, Naomi." He places his big hands on my hips and pulls me toward him. I flop back against the robes to get away and realize my miscalculation when he climbs on top of me, his elbows braced on either side of my head. I'm well and truly pinned, and I'm not done being mad. He smells like horse, leather, and pine sap. He smells like

John, and I love that smell. I love him, and I don't want to lose him. I try a different argument.

"What would happen to me if something happened to you, John?" I ask.

"I've been breaking mules since I was twelve years old, Naomi. That's kinda what I do. And now I got us one more horse. Washakie said he'd give him to me if I rode him."

I close my eyes, despairing. He isn't sorry at all.

He kisses my closed lids and runs his mouth along my jaw. When he tugs my lower lip into his mouth, I relent and kiss him back, biting his tongue to show he's not forgiven. He bites me back on the side of my neck, but when I think he's bent on making me forgive him without even saying he's sorry, he raises his head and takes a deep breath.

"I saw him, Naomi. I saw Wolfe."

Pain knifes through my belly, and I hiss at the sharp yet familiar agony.

"They're here. Just like Washakie said they would be. They're close too. Bungu almost ran right through their village."

"You saw W-Wolfe?" I stammer.

"He looks just fine. Just fine," he whispers, reassuring me. He recounts going to the river to water the horse and seeing the children and the women upstream.

"I don't think they saw me. No one ran or got scared, and no one followed me back here."

"I want to see him," I demand. "I want to go, right now."

He nods slowly, as if he expected that, but he keeps me pinned beneath him. "I told Washakie. He's going to go and bring Hanabi and Lost Woman and some of the chiefs with him for a visit. He doesn't think you or I should go. He wants to let them know we're here so they don't get scared and run . . . or attack. It will be a visit of peace and goodwill."

"Goodwill?" My chest is tight, and I push up against John, needing to breathe. He rolls to the side but stays propped up, looking down at me. "Goodwill, John? I don't especially feel goodwill toward Pocatello and his people."

John sits up, wrapping his arms around his legs, his head bowed, but he doesn't respond. I don't understand his silence.

"My family was massacred. I heard my mother's screams. I saw my father and my brother lying in a pool of blood," I whisper.

"I know you did," he says softly. "I saw most of it too."

"He's not like Washakie, John. Pocatello is a bad man. Bad men hurt people. All kinds of people. He'll keep hurting people. There is no place in this world for men like him, but no one seems to want to stop him." My voice rings with accusation, and I wince. I don't blame John. How could I? I don't blame Washakie either. He has been a true friend. But I do blame Pocatello, and he and his men haven't been held to account.

"There is no place in this world for any of these people," John says, looking back at me, his eyes troubled. "Washakie's war chiefs sit around the fire and talk of defending their lands and their way of life, but Washakie knows it's just a matter of time."

"What way of life is that? Scalps? Burned wagons? Selling and raping women?" I don't understand him, and my chest is hot with indignation and suppressed emotion. John is silent beside me, and when he finally turns his head again, I see . . . disappointment. He looks hurt and disappointed. In me.

"Washakie told me a cow wandered away from an emigrant train into a Blackfoot village near Fort Hall. The Blackfeet killed it and ate it. They didn't steal it, and they didn't know who it belonged to. It was in their camp, so it belonged to them. Someone complained, the cavalry was sent out to ask questions, and half the village was wiped out in the confusion. There's plenty of ugly on every side, Naomi. It isn't fair to make a statement like that."

I press my hands to my chest, trying to hold back my outrage, the injustice of his disapproval, but find that I can't. I rise to my feet and stumble out of the wickiup, out into the pink-and-purple remains of the day. The sun is almost gone, and the mountains beyond us are black. I take a few deep breaths to ease the fire in my heart and stagger on. John doesn't follow, and I am glad.

I climb up through the trees to the pool of hot water that reminds me of the springs where Adam Hines was bucked clean off his feet by the force of the water. That was just a few days before my whole family was taken from me. John's worrying about preserving a way of life when my whole life is already gone. *Oh, dear God, I need my mother.* I need her to tell me what to do and how to feel. I gotta get my mind right.

"Ma?" I say, and her name is an audible cry. "Ma, if you can hear me, I need to talk. I need to say a few things, and no one here understands a word I say. Not even John. I need you so bad, Ma. I will never see you again. And I'm angry about that. I'm angry that you're gone, and I'm angry about the way you were taken. It's not right! It's not right, Ma. And it's never going to be right."

"Naomi?"

I jerk, embarrassed, but I don't look over my shoulder. I know who it is, but I'm embarrassed. I am babbling at the water like I've lost my mind. I keep my back turned and try to slow the tears that never seem to let up.

Lost Woman comes closer and stops at my side. She says something to me that I don't understand, and the longing for my mother wells even deeper.

"I need my mother," I tell her, and my voice breaks on a sob. "I don't know what to do, and I need Ma. *Sua beeya,*" I beg. I don't know if I'm using the right word for *need.* John has tried to teach me.

I can't see her face; my eyes are too blurred with tears. I am foolish, and I groan in frustration.

"Naomi?" Lost Woman says.

I rub at my eyes, trying to control myself, trying to meet her gaze.

"Talk . . . Lost Woman," she says softly.

She takes my hand and pulls me along beside her, but when we are down from the hill, she releases me, and we stroll through the darkness together, not touching, the wickiups at our backs, the fires leaching the orange from the night sky.

"*Daigwa*," she says. *Speak.*

So I do. I talk to her like I would talk to Ma, and she listens, her hands clutched behind her back, her eyes on the steps we take. We pace in front of the wickiups, close enough to not get lost, far enough to be alone. I tell her how angry I am. I tell her how hurt and scared and *angry* I am. I give her all my words. Every ugly, terrifying one. I tell her I am trapped where the lost wander, and I don't see any way out. I will never be able to leave. Not without Wolfe. And he is not mine anymore. He is not ours—mine and Ma's. He is theirs. And I am so angry. I tell her I wish I were dead . . . and yet . . . I'm so happy I'm alive. I tell her I love her and I hate her. And that makes me cry, because I love her far more than I hate her. I say I hate John too because I need him so much.

I hate and I love. I hate that I hate, and I tell her everything. When I am done and there are no more words in my chest, I stop. Then I breathe. Lost Woman stops too and looks up at me as if she understood every word.

"Att," she says, nodding. *Good.* And I laugh. She smiles too, her white hair billowing around her, and the sky doesn't feel nearly as big, and I don't feel nearly so small. She points toward the edge of the darkness where John stands, waiting for me, and we walk together toward him.

He speaks to her, words I don't understand, and she answers softly, touching my cheek. Then she leaves us alone.

We lie in the dark, not touching. I don't have any words left right now, but when I turn my back to go to sleep, he pulls me into his body and buries his face in my hair.

"What did you say to her?" I ask. He doesn't ask who.

"I thanked her for bringing you home."

"And what did she say?" I whisper.

"She reminded me . . . gently . . . that this is not your home. And she told me you miss your mother."

I swallow the lump in my throat and close my eyes, spent. I am drifting off when he begins speaking again, so softly that I'm not sure he's talking to me at all.

"I miss my mother too," he murmurs. "I am all that remains of her. My skin. My hair. My eyes. My language. This is not my home either, Naomi. But I remember her here. I feel close to her here. When these people are gone . . . when their world is gone . . . she will be gone too."

I lie in silence for a long time, my heart aching but my eyes open.

"Forgive me, John," I whisper, but he is already asleep.

I feel close to her here.

For a little while, walking and talking with Lost Woman, I felt close to Ma too, like she walked beside us, listening.

"Ma?" I whisper. "I don't know what to do. Help me find my way home, wherever home is."

22

WINTER

NAOMI

It snows while Washakie is away, and a two-day goodwill visit to Pocatello's village becomes five days. When the small party returns, John and I go to Chief Washakie's wickiup to eat and hear the news. Hanabi tells me that Wolfe is fat, and she puffs out her cheeks and hugs me tight. She is happy for me. Relieved. Her own daughter has grown since we first met at the Green, and she toddles around the wickiup, entertaining us while the men talk. Chief Washakie seems relieved too, even lighthearted, and he keeps us there for a long time.

When John and I are back in our wickiup, John tells me Washakie is confident there will be no trouble between the two bands during the winter.

"He says Biagwi and Weda might even bring Wolf Boy—*isa tuineppe*—for a visit so you can see him," John says, hesitant, searching my face for my reaction. His eyes are dark with strain.

"They call him Wolf Boy?" I ask, stunned.

"That is what Washakie said."

"Isa tuineppe," I say. The sounds comfort me. "He is still Wolfe."

"Yes. He is still Wolfe."

It is good news, and I am grateful in spite of everything. I try to thank Washakie, stumbling over the Shoshoni words John has helped me practice.

He listens and grunts, nodding his head. "Naomi *gahni*," he says. "John *gahni*."

John says he is telling me that we have a home with him, for as long as we need. I wonder if that's my answer. I begged Ma to help me find my way. Maybe home is with Washakie . . . forever.

The winter days are dark and long. John sets snares and takes long walks in the snow, unable to stay cooped up inside for any length of time. Sometimes at night he studies his emigrant map, tracing our journey from St. Joe.

"I hope Abbott will write to Jennie and my father," he says. "Jennie says my father suffers when I go. I didn't believe her. But I understand better now, and I don't want him to suffer, wondering where I am. I don't want your brothers to suffer either. When the spring comes . . . we . . . have to go find them. You know that, don't you?"

I know that. And I don't know how I will ever be able to ride away.

"We can come back. We can make a home with the tribe and watch over Wolfe . . ." His voice fades away, helpless. "Or maybe we should wait until Wolfe is old enough to make the journey . . . and take him."

"By force?" I whisper. I can't imagine the two of us riding into Pocatello's camp, guns blazing. I picture John covered in blood the way he was after he killed Magwich. He has killed for me before. I am sickened at the thought, shaken, and we stop talking about it.

I've begun drawing again, painting faces on skins. I've drawn whole families on the walls of their wickiups. I don't have any paper. My book never made it back into my satchel, and the pages inside it are full. Hanabi doesn't want faces. She wants trees and animals, and I paint a pattern around the door and the floor, wolves and deer and horses and birds. Her daughter gets her hand in the paint, and I use her print to decorate too, including it in the pattern. Washakie watches me, and one day he asks John to translate for him so I can paint his dream. He brings me a huge elk skin and sits in our wickiup, his legs crossed, his eyes sober.

"He doesn't want to upset his mother or Hanabi. Or his people. So you will paint"—John waits for Washakie to finish—"but it is only for him."

I nod, and John reassures him, but Washakie seems torn, and after a short pause he speaks again.

"He doesn't understand the vision. Not all of it. It is strange to him. He can't describe some things that he saw," John says.

"My mother had dreams," I say, and John tells Washakie. "I don't think she understood them all. She dreamed about John before she ever met him. And she dreamed about another woman—an Indian woman—feeding Wolfe. My mother knew about this." I raise my hands, indicating my surroundings. My journey. "She knew something was coming . . . something . . . hard."

Washakie is listening to John, but he is watching me speak.

"She did not run from it," Washakie says.

I shake my head slowly. "No. She always . . . kept her mind right. Always found . . . transcendence."

John is struggling to translate. Transcendence is hard to explain. He and Washakie talk for several minutes, a flurry of discussion that I don't understand.

"Washakie wants to know how she did that," John says, turning to me.

Are you angry with the bird because he can fly, or angry with the horse for her beauty, or angry with the bear because he has fearsome teeth and claws? Because he's bigger than you are? Stronger too? Destroying all the things you hate won't change any of that. You still won't be a bear or a bird or a horse. Hating men won't make you a man. Hating your womb or your breasts or your own weakness won't make those things go away. Hating never fixed anything.

It's like Ma is right here, reciting all her simple wisdom in my head, and I tell Washakie what she told me.

"Ma said transcendence is when we rise above the things we can't change," I add.

"How do we know what we can't change?" Washakie asks John, and John asks me.

I shake my head. I don't know the answer to that.

"We can't change what is. Or what was," John says slowly. "Only what could be."

Transcendence is a world, a place, beyond this one. It's what could be.

Washakie mulls that over, and then he touches the elk skin and looks at me. He's ready for me to paint.

"He had this dream—this vision—a few years ago. He was worried about the lands of the Shoshoni being overrun by other tribes who were pushed out by the white tide. He went away by himself and fasted and . . . prayed . . . for three days. These are the things he saw," John says.

Washakie is quiet for a moment, his eyes closed and body still, like he's trying to remember. When he begins to speak again, I don't think. I just paint, using my fingers and a few horsehair brushes that John made me for finer details.

He talks of carriages that pull themselves and horses made of iron. He describes people flying on giant birds that aren't birds, going to places he never knew existed. He says the world will be small and the land will be different, and the Indians will be gone. Red blood and blue blood will flow together, becoming one blood. One people. John's voice cracks with emotion as he interprets, and tears drip down my nose, but I keep painting, listening, and Washakie keeps talking.

"I saw my life. My birth, my death, and the days between. The feathers on my head and a weapon in one hand, a pipe in the other. In the dream . . . I was told not to fight," he says. "To choose the pipe. To choose peace with the white man whenever I can. So that is what I will do."

JOHN

Washakie does not take his painting when he leaves. Naomi isn't finished. She's been at it for hours, hardly conscious of me at all. I keep the wick of my lantern burning, the coals hot, and she works, paint up to her wrists and dotting her doeskin dress. She doesn't have any clothes that don't have some paint somewhere. Her hair was tidy when the process began, but her braid has come undone, and she swipes at the loose strands absently, making a black streak across her face. I gather her hair in my hands and knot it up again with a bit of rope, gazing down over her bowed head at the dreamscape she's created. She looks up at me, almost startled, and touches her hair.

"I have paint in it, don't I?"

I crouch down beside her. "Yeah. You do. And everywhere else. But it was worth it."

She sits back on her knees and studies the painting. "I've never done anything like this before. But . . . I'm finished." The details of the vision are in clusters of action that focus, then fade, following the path of Washakie's narrative. It's blurred but not dreamy. It's harsh but not hopeless, and she has captured Washakie's despair and desire in the swirling lines and discordant scenes. Color, confrontation, and connection merge in Washakie's image.

"I can see his face," I exclaim, stunned. "It's not obvious the first time you look at it, but now I can't see anything else."

"It emerged as I went. His face—more than anything else—tells the story. It's his vision."

"Naomi and her many faces," I say. "It's—" I pause, trying to find the right word. "It's . . . transcendent."

She smiles at me, her eyes wet, her lips soft. "Do you think he'll . . . like it?" she whispers.

"It's not that kind of a picture, honey."

She smiles at my endearment and pats my cheek. "No. I guess it isn't."

"But maybe it'll give him comfort . . . or courage . . . or a place to lift his eyes when he starts feeling lost."

"You're a good man, John Lowry." She leans into me, her hands on my jaw, holding me to her as she kisses my mouth. "You're a good man . . . and now you have paint all over your face," she says, giggling. "I'm sorry."

"So do you." I laugh. "But I know where we can fix that." It's late, no one is wandering about, and I've been dreaming about that hot spring since we walked into the valley.

We strip off our clothes and wrap ourselves in buffalo robes and tiptoe out of the sleeping camp up to the pool secluded in the trees. We scare an owl and something bigger away but slip into the heat with a gasp and a moan. I brought a lump of soap, and we remove all the paint from our faces and Naomi's hair, but her hands are too stained to fix with soap and water.

"My hands are hopeless," she says, holding her palms up to the lantern light.

"I love the stains. I noticed the stains on your fingers that very first day. Remember?"

"I do. I saw you staring. You didn't know what to think."

"I still don't," I whisper, teasing. "But you wouldn't be Naomi without the stains."

"I have so many," she says, quiet. And I know she isn't talking about paint. She plops her hands back down in the water and sinks beneath the surface, a baptism of sorts. When she comes back up, she's focused on me.

She wouldn't be Naomi without the stains, and she wouldn't be Naomi if she didn't make good use of the hot springs. We descend the slope an hour later, overheated and freezing, the ends of Naomi's wet hair already stuck to her robe. We hurry along, our feet crunching on the snow. We have extinguished the lantern to save the oil. We don't need it. The moon is high and huge, and it reflects off the snow, making the night soft and gray.

When dark shapes loom to the south, rising up over the pristine expanse, I freeze, pulling Naomi behind me. Two figures, bundled against the cold, ride toward the wickiups. They aren't Crow come to steal the horses; there is no stealth in their approach, only haste, and two men would not carry out any kind of attack. It's late, nigh on midnight, and I can't conjure a reason for their presence, but they ride straight into the village.

"Washakie!" a voice calls out before the horses even stop. "Washakie!" the man shouts again, urgency ringing through the camp. "Washakie! I need Face Woman. It is Biagwi. I have Wolf Boy. He is sick."

∞

Naomi and I change into our clothes in rushed silence. Washakie has ushered Weda and Biagwi into his wickiup, but we do not wait to be summoned.

When we arrive, Weda and Biagwi are standing just inside, still wrapped in the buffalo robes of their journey. Hanabi has stoked the fire, Lost Woman is making a poultice, and Washakie has gone to rouse the medicine man. Biagwi looks wary. And scared. Weda's arms are wrapped around her chest, sheltering the boy within her robes.

"Please?" Naomi asks, extending her arms toward the woman. "Can I see him?"

The woman looks at Biagwi, who jerks his head, giving his approval. With great hesitance, she unwraps the baby from her robes and hands him to Naomi.

He has grown a great deal; his little legs are dimpled, and his wrists and thighs are ringed with fat. Blond hair curls wildly about his round face, but his cheeks are flushed, and he is very still.

Weda moans in distress and asks Naomi if she can make the wolf boy well. She touches her chest and breathes with a rasp, demonstrating what ails the child. But Wolfe is not coughing or wheezing now. He lies feverish, hardly breathing, and Naomi gathers him close, her lips trembling.

"He's been sick for three days, but he would still feed, and he would smile. He did not cry. But now he will not wake," Biagwi says, his face tight.

Hanabi urges Biagwi and Weda to sit by the fire and take off their robes, but they are anxious and weary, and though they shrug off their robes, they remain standing, Biagwi with his arms folded in defiance, Weda rocking back and forth as though she still holds the babe. It reminds me of Winifred. Winifred used to sway like that.

Washakie returns, the medicine man in tow. He takes his time, clearing the air with sage and repeating a string of sounds that I don't understand. He puts something on Wolfe's temples and on his chest and shakes his rattles over him to drive out the sickness in his body, then moans and meanders around the wickiup before circling back again to shake the rattle above Wolfe some more. Naomi's eyes never leave Wolfe's face, but Biagwi is angry with the old ways and tells Washakie that the medicine man in Pocatello's camp did much the same for three days, and the boy has only grown worse.

"He wants all the *daipo* to die. He wants the tua to die. He does not use his real medicine," Biagwi growls.

Naomi looks up at me for translation. "Biagwi says the medicine men do not like the whites. He doesn't think they are trying to heal him," I murmur.

Washakie tells the medicine man to leave, waving him away with a weary shake of his head. The medicine man is insulted, but in the face of disbelief and Biagwi's rage, he gathers his things and goes. Hanabi leaves too, her daughter in her arms, afraid of the illness that plagues Wolfe. She urges us to stay, saying she will be near in her father's wickiup.

Lost Woman leads Naomi to the fire and urges her to sit. She doesn't make her release the boy or lay him down, and I am grateful. Naomi needs to hold Wolfe. Lost Woman presses a thick, pungent poultice onto the boy's chest, promising it will help him breathe and make his body release the fever. The vapors are strong, and Naomi's face begins to bead with sweat. Weda sinks down beside her, her back bent and her head bowed. I doubt she's slept in days. Biagwi paces like a caged mountain lion, and Washakie stands at my side.

At one point, Wolfe emits a little cry, and Naomi lifts him to her shoulder, rubbing his back, trying to clear his throat. No one breathes, hopeful, but he doesn't cry again, and we all sink back into our vigil.

Weda tries to make him nurse, clutching him to her breast, her chest wet with perspiration, her damp hair clinging to her face, but Wolfe does not latch, and he does not wake. Weda does not give the boy back, and Naomi doesn't insist. They sit side by side, their eyes heavy, and watch him hour after hour. Lost Woman changes the poultice and makes us all drink. The heat is stifling, and Biagwi stumbles for the door, unable to bear a moment more.

Wolfe opens his eyes near dawn, and Weda exclaims, jumping to her feet and calling for Biagwi, who comes running. We all gather around, staring down at the small boy, hopeful that the dawn will bring new life. Lost Woman holds back, watching.

"Let her say goodbye," she says to Weda. "Let Face Woman hold her brother so she can say goodbye."

Naomi does not understand what's been said, and she does not lift her gaze from Wolfe's staring eyes. Weda argues, tightening her arms and scolding Lost Woman in weary protest. She has new hope, the babe is revived, and she doesn't want to relinquish him, but Biagwi takes the boy from her arms and hands him to Naomi. She takes him, her eyes shining with gratitude, and looks down into her brother's face.

"Hello, Wolfe," she whispers. "Hello, sweet boy. I have missed you."

Wolfe's eyes fix on her face, and his rosebud lips turn up in a hint of a smile. Then his lids close, his breath rattles, and he softly slips away.

NAOMI

The scarlet fades from his cheeks, and the warmth leaves his limbs, and I know that he is gone. Weda screams, and Biagwi moans in shock, and Wolfe is snatched from my arms. Weda falls to the ground, wailing in denial and despair, Wolfe clutched to her chest. I feel her anguish echo in my belly and kneel beside her, but she scrambles away, screaming at me, at Lost Woman, at Biagwi and John. At Washakie, who watches her with silent compassion.

She stands near the door, her eyes wild and streaming, staring as though we've all betrayed her. Then, with one last look at Wolfe, she sets him gently on the ground the way she did when Biagwi first laid him in her arms, a son to replace the one she'd lost. And she walks out into the snow.

JOHN

The air is cold and clean, and when I pull it into my nose, it eases the ache in my chest and the grief in my throat. I stand silently, my eyes raised upward, and I ask my mother and Winifred May to look down on me. I talk to them in Pawnee, though I know Winifred won't understand. It is the language of my mother, and I need my mother.

The dusting of snow has left the morning new and untouched. Tracks lead from Washakie's door to the cluster of hoofprints where Biagwi and Weda hobbled their horses. Weda ran away without her robes, riding in dazed exhaustion back toward her village. Biagwi followed, her robes slung across his horse, his back bent beneath his burdens.

Their grief is a comfort. It's like Jennie said. It isn't love unless it hurts, and their pain tells me Wolfe was cherished, he was loved, and he is mourned, and at the end of life, no matter how short, that is all there is.

They left Wolfe's body behind. It is a gift, a mercy to Naomi, and she is with him now. She washed him and wrapped him in a small wool blanket with a stripe of every color. Washakie gave it to her, and Naomi said it reminded her of her mother's coat, the coat of many colors, like Joseph sold into Egypt. I gave her a moment—gave myself a moment—to mourn alone. She is composed. Serene even. But the grief will come. We will bury him here, and the grief will come.

"There are tracks in the snow," Lost Woman says behind me.

I nod, but Lost Woman isn't looking at the trail left by Biagwi and Weda. She pulls at my arm, bidding me follow. The snow is deep, almost up to our knees, and we sink as we go, stepping and falling, stepping and falling, kicking up the new powder.

"See?" Lost Woman points down at the tracks leading from the rear of Washakie's wickiup in a long straight line into nowhere. No other tracks mar the new snow.

I hunch down to see them better, and Lost Woman crouches beside me.

Footprints, too small to be a man's, too large to be a child's, sit on the surface of the snow. Beside the footprints, the toes clearly delineated, is a small set of paw prints, scampering away toward the trees.

A woman and a wolf. I follow them, bemused, until they suddenly disappear.

"The mother came for her son," Lost Woman says.

I stare, not understanding, and Lost Woman explains.

"Sometimes the spirits leave tracks in the snow. The tracks can guide us. Sometimes they comfort us. Other times, they lead us home. I saw tracks after my sons died and again the morning after my grand-daughter was born. Different tracks . . . but always . . . the same."

The tracks of a woman . . . and a little Wolfe.

"The mother came for her son," I whisper, stunned. Overcome.

"Yes. And now Naomi can go home."

1858

EPILOGUE

NAOMI

John says Wolfe freed me. I couldn't save him, and I couldn't keep him. I couldn't take him, and I couldn't leave him. So he had to leave me. John says Ma came and got him, but when he took me to see the footprints Lost Woman showed him in the snow, there was nothing left but drifts and depressions. I believed him, though, and to this day I think about Ma's prints in the snow and what it all means. Maybe there is a place called transcendence where all the blood runs together and we're one people, just like in Washakie's dream.

We left the valley in early May, when the snow was gone and the grass had begun to cover the ground. Washakie's people went one way, and John and I went another, riding Dakotah and Bungu and stringing the three mules and Magwich's two horses behind us. We didn't have enough possessions to fill John's packs, but Washakie made sure we had enough dried meat to see us through to our journey's end.

I realize now that life is just a continual parting of the ways, some more painful than others. We refused to say goodbye to the Shoshoni;

we just kissed Lost Woman and embraced Hanabi, and John promised Washakie he would see him again. When I looked back through tear-filled eyes, the tribe remained where we left them, their belongings on their backs and piled on their horses, a watercolor painting I've since tried and failed to recreate.

John wouldn't look back. It hurt too much, and I was reminded of Ma keeping her eyes from the graves of the little ones because she couldn't carry that pain. John carried it anyway. He carried that pain all the way to the gold fields at the base of the Sierra Nevada and for a long time after that. He will always be Two Feet, straddling two worlds, and there is nothing I can do but give him something—someone—to hold on to. To belong to. Worlds pass away. People do too, but he left a part of himself among the Shoshoni, wandering in the hills and along the streams beside Washakie. I'm sure one day, when ages have passed, his spirit will return there, and mine will have to follow.

A week after we left the winter range, we reached the spot where John and my brothers had buried the wagon. The cross was still standing, though it had teetered some. We straightened it and piled more stones on top of the wagon box, but this time when we left, I didn't look back. I couldn't feel my loved ones there, and I was glad to leave that desert behind.

It was July 1854 when we reached Coloma, a mining town that had sprouted up in 1848 when a man at Sutter's Mill had found gold. John and I shed our skins and wore the only homespun clothing we had left, which wasn't in the best of conditions. John's hair was so long he was afraid someone would shoot and ask questions later, so I rode in front, shielding my eyes from the setting sun, stunned by the shelters and the ramshackle cabins dotting the landscape in every direction. I didn't know how we would ever find my brothers.

But they saw us coming.

Abbott had a claim from '49 with a one-room cabin that wasn't much more than a shack, but he kept the boys together. They hunkered down, waited out the winter, and eked out the spring working at the sawmill and panning for gold. Webb still had no shoes, Will had grown a foot, and Wyatt had no boy left in him, though he cried in my arms like a baby.

There are no words for joy like that. Our legs wouldn't hold us, and we fell on each other in a quivering pile, laughing and crying and embracing. We tried to speak and finally gave up, weeping until we were all dried out.

"John promised us. He promised, and he kept his word," Webb said, and what was dry became wet all over again.

❧

John has a way of making things work. He managed to trade a little of this and exchange some of that, and before we knew it, we had a place to call home, a storefront, and a round corral, big enough to start a mule business with Kettle and a few mares. Wyatt got work, and Abbott got married, much to all our surprise, considering his purported lack of feeling from the waist down. We sent letters to Missouri, and Jennie and John Sr. always wrote back. They even sent a little money and presents for the boys. It wasn't a bad life, not at all, but John still carried that pain.

In 1856 we took the boys and the budding mule business to the Great Salt Lake Valley so John could keep another promise. Through the long summer, John watched the travelers and the tribes coming in and out of the market, knowing that one day, Washakie would come to trade.

You can imagine the joy on the day he did; John brought him home, and he and his men spent two days camped in our paddock, telling stories and reminiscing. Washakie is well thought of here, and no one gave them any trouble. Webb, Will, and Wyatt sat among them, listening and laughing, though they couldn't understand a word anyone said.

Washakie didn't ask about our babies and why there weren't any, but before he left, he told John he would have a son. John said he already had three May boys to father, but Washakie said there would be a whole line of John Lowrys, and John's descendants would tell his story and honor his name.

He's like Ma that way, Washakie, with his dreams and premonitions. When we saw him again the following year, I was rounded with child, and the night I delivered, there were tracks in the snow.

AUTHOR'S NOTE

There really was a John Lowry, born in Missouri to a Pawnee woman and a white father, who came west and ended up in Utah in the 1850s. He was my husband's five-times great-grandfather. Some disputes in the family exist over whether his father (also named John Lowry) was really his father or just the white man his Pawnee mother married after her Cheyenne husband (Eagle Feather) and newborn daughter died. That is something we won't ever know for sure. John Lowry was the name he passed on to his son, also named John Lowry, and to the generations after that, but I sincerely hope there is an afterlife so I can hear the real story from him. I don't know if our John Lowry ever knew Chief Washakie, but after writing this book, I feel like I know them both.

As a boy, my husband spent summers traipsing the Wind River Range with his father, and he keeps a picture of Chief Washakie tucked into an old harness that hangs in our room. He grew up with a reverence for Chief Washakie that I didn't understand until I started forming the idea for this story. Washakie predicted people would write about him in their books, and I'm just one person making that prediction a reality. Washakie made many predictions that came true. The vision mentioned in this book happened in 1850, though Naomi's part was fictional. I wanted to include it in the story because it was such a formative part of Washakie's life and leadership. A painting of the vision was made in 1932 by Charlie Washakie, one of Chief Washakie's sons. I made

Naomi's depiction nothing like the real thing, so as not to confuse the reader. *Washakie's Vision*, painted on elk skin, can be seen in an exhibit at USU Eastern.

Chief Washakie was born around the turn of the century and died around the turn of the next. He was thought to be at least one hundred years old when he died. He is one of the only Native leaders to retain the lands of his choosing in negotiations with the US government. The Wind River Range and the lands of Washakie's boyhood still belong to the Shoshoni (and the Arapahoe) people.

Washakie's mother, Lost Woman, was as true to life as I could make her. I read an autobiography called *The White Indian Boy* about Elijah Nicholas Wilson (1842–1915), who lived with the Shoshoni for two years in the mid-1850s and knew and loved Washakie's mother well. He never called her Lost Woman, only his Indian mother, so it came as a great surprise to me when I did more research and found her name, Lost Woman. For me, Lost Woman captures the spirit of this book, the struggles of all women, all mothers, in the landscape of 1850s America. Hanabi too was real, though she never lived with the Lowry family. Not much is known about her. She was Washakie's second or third wife and died young. Washakie and Hanabi had one daughter, who grew up and had children of her own. The year of my story is 1853, but it's most likely that the death of Lost Woman's sons in the avalanche happened a year or two after that, as well as the birth of Hanabi's daughter.

Chief Pocatello was a real person too. He and Washakie had a fractious relationship, most likely born of their different ways of addressing the concerns and hardships of their people. Pocatello was a hero to some, a villain to others. I hope only that I didn't portray him too harshly but represented the conditions and circumstances of the time in a factual and even compassionate light.

Naomi's family, the Mays, was named after my own pioneer ancestors, who came to Utah in those early years of the westward migration. I am also eternally grateful for another of my husband's five-times great-grandfathers, Milo Appleton Harmon, who kept a journal when he crossed the plains, which he did multiple times. He left a legacy on paper for his children to read, and I have been richly blessed by his diary. What a humble, hardworking, amazing man he was.

Louis Vasquez, trapper and fur trader and co-owner of Fort Bridger, was a real person. It seems he did sell his half of the business to the Mormon leaders, which led to continued strife between Jim Bridger and the Saints. The Mormons burned the fort in 1857 so it wouldn't be taken over by Johnston's army, which is a whole other story. Narcissa Vasquez, Louis's wife, was also real. I had to take some liberties with her description and personality, but those who knew her said she was small and vivacious with a lovely smile. By all accounts, she was a fascinating woman with a great story—another person I would love to talk to—which you get a glimpse of in *Where the Lost Wander*.

As with any work of historical fiction, fact and imagination must be woven together because so many of the facts are in dispute or simply don't tell the whole story. One thing that is not in dispute: life was hard for the emigrants who crossed the plains. I read countless pioneer journals and compilations. The people suffered, they had very little, and most of them just wanted a better life and went west to find it. There was good and bad, ugly and beautiful, shameful and hopeful, and it's all wrapped into one very rich heritage. In order to accurately reflect the times, I had to use terms and words and talk about things that I am not comfortable with and you might not be comfortable with either. I hope the reader will experience the story in the spirit it was written, recognizing that who *we are* is not who *they were*, and judging historical people by today's standards prevents us from learning from them, from their mistakes and their triumphs. These people helped build the framework that we now stand on. We should be careful about burning it down.

A final disclosure: As with many indigenous languages, Pawnee and Shoshoni have different dialects and spellings, and regional usage varies. In old accounts, many of the Native words are spelled phonetically, the way people heard them, and there is wide variance even among native speakers. I did my utmost to get it right and used the languages sparingly for color and context, and I ask for forgiveness if there are mistakes. I love the Native heritage of my country and want only to shine a light on some of the forgotten people that new stories can bring back to life.

Amy Harmon

ABOUT THE AUTHOR

Amy Harmon is a *Wall Street Journal*, *USA Today*, and *New York Times* bestselling author. Her books have been published in eighteen languages—truly a dream come true for a little country girl from Utah.

Harmon has written fifteen novels, including the *Wall Street Journal* and *Washington Post* bestseller *What the Wind Knows*, the *USA Today* bestsellers *The Smallest Part*, *Making Faces*, and *Running Barefoot*, as well as the #1 Amazon bestselling historical novel *From Sand and Ash*, which won a Whitney Award for book of the year in 2016. Her novel *A Different Blue* is a *New York Times* bestseller. Her *USA Today* best-selling fantasy *The Bird and the Sword* was a Goodreads Best Book of 2016 finalist. For updates on upcoming book releases, author posts, and more, go to www.authoramyharmon.com.